center
stage

center stage

Magnolia Steele Mystery #1

DENISE
GROVER SWANK

Other Books By Denise Grover Swank

Magnolia Steele Mystery
Center Stage
Act Two
Call Back
Curtain Call
Let Sleeping Dogs Lie

Harper Adams Mystery
Probable Cause (short story)
Little Girl Vanished
Long Gone
Luck of the Devil

Maddie Baker Mystery
Take the Wheel
Gone Without a Trace
Echoes of Her

Rose Gardner Mystery

Rose Gardner Investigations and Neely Kate Mystery

Carly Moore Mystery

Darling Investigations

chapter one

I stepped onto my mother's front porch for the first time in ten years. Typical of my moth er, not much had changed. Same red brick with white trim. Same black, steel-reinforced front door. Same silver knocker, the word STEELE etched into it in bold capital letters.

"Get it?" my dad used to ask when I was a little girl. "The door is made of steel, and our last name is Steele."

I worshiped my father, so I always laughed even though I *didn't* get it. I would have done anything to please him.

Until he disappeared.

My mother put a lot of stock into the safety of that front door. When I was younger, she would tell me it kept the boogeyman away. A month after my father left—when I was fourteen—I heard my mother whispering with her best friend Tilly as they lay sprawled out on the patio chairs on the deck, drinking their third—or was it fourth?—white wine sangria.

"If only he'd been home that night," my mother drawled with

a slur. She may have spent most of her adult life in Franklin, Tennessee, but you couldn't remove her Sweet Briar, Alabama roots.

"Lila," Tilly groaned. "Not that again. The Good Lord has his mysterious ways."

My mother had bolted upright and pointed her finger at her best friend, swaying in her seat. "The Good Lord had nothin' to do with it, Tilly Bartok. It was that good for nothin'—"

She looked up at me and her face went blank. "Magnolia. How long have you been standin' there?"

"Not long. I just finished my homework."

"Then go on upstairs and tell your brother to wash up for dinner." She gestured toward the house.

I turned around to do as I was told, wondering if the Good Lord wasn't to blame for my father's absence, who actually *was*? But I knew better than to ask. Besides, I'd heard the whispered rumors.

"Magnolia!" she called after me. "Did you lock the front door?"

"Yes, Momma."

"Good. You can never be too careful."

A lesson learned too late. Perhaps if I'd been more careful after my high school graduation, the big bad thing wouldn't have happened.

But now I stood before her front door again, prepared to eat a heaping slice of humble pie, wearing the wrinkled clothes I'd worn to the theatre yesterday afternoon. Maybe the disheveled look would make my groveling more convincing.

While I had grown accustomed to the anxiety that slammed into me whenever I thought about coming home, I wasn't prepared for the wave of fear that almost brought me to my knees. I was nervous about my mother's reaction, yes, but this was pure terror.

I started to turn around, but the door swung open before my

fist made contact with the wood. My mother stood in the threshold, looking noticeably older. I counted backward to the last time we'd seen each other. Had three years really passed since that Christmas in New York City?

She gaped at me in shock, her face turning pale. She looked like she was staring at a ghost. I hadn't haunted her house in ten years, so I could hardly blame her. It wasn't as if I'd issued a warning.

The sight of her quieted my fear. "Hello, Momma."

"Magnolia." She blinked, taking in the sight of my two large suitcases. "You've come for a visit?"

I shifted my weight, fighting every instinct to flee. "I've come home to stay."

"For how long?"

"Maybe for a while." Although I sure as hell hoped I was wrong about that.

"But . . . what . . ."

My mother was speechless, but I was too nervous to truly bask in the moment. Maybe hell was freezing over.

She finally regained her senses, wrapping her arms across her chest and squeezing tight. "I thought you were making your big Broadway debut this week."

I grimaced. "I did." Last night, actually.

"Then what are you doing here?"

Rather than answer her, I glanced over her shoulder into the entryway. Like the exterior of the house, it appeared as unchanged as if it had emerged from a time capsule. But one thing was different: me. I was no longer the sheltered naïve girl my mother had raised. I was cynical and jaded, and it had nothing to do with the ten years I'd spent in the Big Apple, even if all the scraping by and trying to make a living in the theatre world had sharpened my edges.

"Oh," she finally said. "I see." She took a breath, still blocking the entrance, a true sign that I had thrown her off her game. She would never dream of keeping a guest standing on the front porch. Even me. "Do you have a job?"

"What?" I asked, surprised by her question. "No." Two days ago I'd been the lead in *Fireflies at Dawn*, the hottest new musical to hit New York in several years. Now I was jobless, penniless, and homeless.

Oh, how the mighty had fallen.

That seemed to jar her out of her stupor. "Then you can help me out tonight." She stepped through the doorway, grabbed one of my suitcases, and rolled it over the threshold. "I know you're into theatre music, but have you heard of Luke Powell?"

"Luke Powell?" I asked in disbelief. You had to be living off the grid—and for the past five years at that—to have never heard of the hottest country music star. "Yeah, I've heard of him."

"We're catering a big event at Luke Powell's to celebrate the release of his new album. It starts in two hours, and I'm short one member of the wait staff. It has to go over perfectly. I only have inexperienced fools to take her spot, so you can fill in."

"*What?*" My mother's catering business must have exploded if she was working the hottest country music star's album release. But she wanted me to work as a waitress? Had she lost her mind?

She sensed my reluctance. "You used to wait tables up until three years ago, right?"

Two, not that I was about to admit it. "Well, yeah. I have food service experience, but I was on Broadway, Momma. I can't be wait staff."

"If you're so high and mighty on Broadway—" she said the name as though it were a curse word, "—then what are you doing here?"

I couldn't tell her. At least not yet.

She pursed her lips. "That's what I thought. If you're moving back home, you'll need to pay rent. And since you're unemployed, you'll need work. I can apply your salary to your balance."

"Rent?"

She put a hand on her hip. "It wouldn't be fair to your brother if you didn't. Roy lived here for two years after he graduated from the University of Tennessee, and he paid rent the entire time."

I pushed out a sigh. "I'm not living here forever, Momma. Just until I figure some things out."

She put her hand on her hip, looking down her nose at me even though we both stood five foot seven. "And Roy didn't live here forever either. But if you plan on doing nothing but fussin' and thinkin', you've got plenty of time to fill in for Patty at this party. She's going to be off for another two weeks with a sprained ankle."

"Momma, I just got here. I've had the worst two days of my life, and I just want to hide out in my room."

Fire filled her eyes. "Magnolia Steele, I raised you better than that. We don't hide from our problems. We take 'em *head on*." She curled her hands into fists and shook them.

I'd done the exact opposite after my high school graduation. I'd run as fast and as far as I could. But of course my mother didn't understand why I'd packed a single suitcase and left town without warning. No one understood.

Not even me.

Hazy dreams had haunted my sleep for those first two years in New York City. Each night, I would cry myself to sleep from fright and loneliness, trying not to wake my cranky roommate. But the very thought of going home was enough to give me a panic attack, so I never did. No matter how much it hurt my mother.

Something had happened the night of my high school graduation party. Something I couldn't entirely remember. The nightmares had faded over time—terrifying dreams I couldn't remember when I woke—but the horror was still a part of me. But I was sure I knew someone who did know what happened. . . or was maybe even responsible.

Of course Momma didn't know any of that either. Sometimes my acting skills had a practical purpose. "You're made of steel, Magnolia Mae, so no whining. Now carry your suitcases up to your room, and I'll bring you a uniform to change into."

I stayed on the porch for a moment, trying to decide if it was worth crossing the threshold. If I walked over that line, it would mean going back into her world, her rules. I would be reopening the very Pandora's box that I'd shut the moment I stepped onto that plane on a warm May afternoon ten years ago. But if I stayed on this side, I had nowhere else to go. I'd burned too many bridges.

I took a deep breath, and walked inside.

If I'd known then what I know now, I would have turned around and run.

I wasn't just crossing the threshold to my mother's house. I was walking through the gate to hell.

chapter two

My room was exactly how I'd left it, which was simultaneously comforting and frightening. Same full-size bed with the white wood headboard. Same pale pink bedspread with the OPI Big Apple Red nail polish stain in the middle, a relic of my friend Maddie's clumsiness our junior year. I opened the top drawer and found my old underwear and bras. Buried underneath the plain white panties were two of the three sets of Victoria's Secret bras and panties I'd hidden from my mother. I'd bought all three the April before graduation, preparing for my *first time* with Tanner McKee. I'd only needed one, but since I couldn't decide which color would be best, Maddie—always the wiser member of our duo—told me to get all three. The red and black set were still pushed back into the corner of the drawer. The white set were God knew where . . . I'd worn them under my dress to graduation. Momma had never offered to bring the rest of my things to me, and out of pride, I'd never asked.

I shut the drawer and moved on to the closet. All my clothes still hung on the plastic hangers Momma had bought in an attempt to make me organize my closet. For some odd reason she'd thought the matching hangers would inspire a sudden desire to clean. Luckily for me, Maddie loved to organize as much as I hated it. She'd spent a Saturday afternoon cleaning out my closet while I wrote her English paper.

Definitely a good trade, especially since she got an A minus.

A cardboard box sat on the floor in the back corner with the words *Photos—Keep Out, Roy!* scrawled in black marker on the side. Eleven years of memories with Maddie Hoffman were stuffed into that box. Maybe I'd look at it later. It hurt too much right now.

I sat down on the bed, nearly moaning with happiness when the duvet cover and mattress topper sank underneath me. Then I flopped backward, spreading my arms wide as I stared up at the ceiling. I hadn't realized how much I'd missed this bed. This room. My mother.

But an undercurrent of fear hummed behind all the warm and fuzzy feelings.

I shouldn't have come back.

Too late for that now.

"No time for a nap, Magnolia," my mother said as she bustled into the room, then laid a set of clothes on the bed. "We need to go over the protocol for the night as well as the menu."

I squeezed my eyes shut. "Momma, isn't there anyone else you can get to fill in? I don't feel well."

"That's a fat load of bullcrap. You don't think I can see through your excuses? I'd hoped you would grow out of the drama, but then you've spent the last ten years trying to get paid for being dramatic, haven't you?" she said in a theatrical tone. My mother was chock full of drama. Where did she think I'd acquired it from?

"That's not entirely true," I said, sitting up. Fighting my mother was like wrestling with a bull. While it was possible, it wasn't always worth the effort. "I didn't start acting until I'd been in New York for two years."

She was silent for a moment, her blue eyes holding my own. "Then why *did* you leave, Magnolia?"

She'd asked me in the beginning, of course, but I'd refused to tell her so many times she'd stopped asking. My unannounced appearance must have knocked the question loose.

I leaned over and picked up the uniform. A white button-down shirt, black pants, and a black tie and vest. "No skirt?"

"The men and women match this way. Everyone's more uniform." She paused. "You change the subject every time I ask you why you left. Even now, after all these years." Her voice was quiet, and she sounded more vulnerable than I'd ever heard her.

I studied the shirt in my lap, fingering a button. "It had nothing to do with you. I promise you that." That was more than I'd ever given her.

"You just left, Magnolia. And you never came back. Not even for holidays. *Never*. And now you're back out of nowhere when this was supposed to be your big break."

I looked up at her with tears in my eyes. "I'm here because I literally had nowhere else to go."

"Is that supposed to make me feel better?"

"No, but just know that when I decided to leave New York, *you* were the person I turned to for help."

"But I don't even know what I'm helping you with."

"It doesn't matter. All that matters is that you let me come back home. After everything."

She bit her bottom lip, then rolled back her shoulders and lifted her chin. The take-charge woman who had raised me was returning. I knew better than to expect declarations of love from Lila Steele. She took her acquired last name to heart. "Well, get dressed and come downstairs. We need to get to the store to make sure things are ready to go."

"The store?" Momma used to prepare for her events in her

own kitchen. Apparently that had changed. I could smell something delicious floating through the house, but Lila Steele's kitchen always smelled like fresh baking, whether she was preparing for an event or not.

She put her hand on her hip and narrowed her eyes. "You'll figure it out soon enough. Now hurry up and get dressed. I'm running late as it is. It's a good thing Tilly has everything under control."

It was only after she shut the door behind her that it occurred to me what a disaster this might be. Theatre and country music people don't exactly share the same circles, but with the advent of social media, those circles had begun to overlap. I'd spent most of the last eight years in chorus roles and off-Broadway parts. But I'd gotten a lot of attention after landing the lead role of Scarlett in *Fireflies*, and the previews had gone really well. The fact that the songs had been written by a country music crossover artist made it likely that there might be people at Luke Powell's party who would know me.

I wasn't sure I could handle the embarrassment.

But no more running. I had decided that the moment I stepped off the plane at the Nashville airport. Of course it could be argued that I'd run away from New York, but that was a moot point.

I could face those country music industry professionals and hold my head high. What had happened on the stage on opening night wasn't my fault—not really—no matter how many people thought differently. Besides, I owed my mother for all the grief I'd put her through. What was one night of serving at a party? And who would expect to see Magnolia Steele holding a tray of appetizers at a country music artist's release celebration?

I pushed out a huge breath. I could do this.

I quickly changed, touched up my makeup, then put my long brunette hair into a French twist and studied my reflection in my dresser mirror. My concealer had covered most of the dark circles under my eyes, the aftereffects of two sleepless nights and weeks of stress. My blue eyes were wide, my dark lashes long and thick. I'd dusted my high cheekbones with a hint of blush and applied pale gloss to my full lips. A director had once told me that I had a face for movies—something he'd meant as a compliment—but I had no desire to have my face in the public eye any more than it already was. When I'd started acting eight years ago, most people couldn't have named a Broadway star if their life depended on it. I'd taken a chance by accepting the role of Scarlett in *Fireflies at Dawn*, but the risk had seemed low. That would teach me.

"Magnolia!" my mother shouted up from downstairs.

"Coming!" I grabbed my jacket off the bed and slipped it on as I headed down the staircase. I stopped halfway down to look at the photos on the wall. They were still the same ones that had hung there ten years ago. A family photo of Momma, Daddy, me, and Roy, taken back when we were happy and complete. School photos of my brother and I that spanned all the way from kindergarten to senior year. But there was a new photo I hadn't seen before—one of Roy and a woman in a white dress. A photo from the wedding he hadn't invited me to attend.

My stomach cramped at the reminder that I didn't belong here and hadn't for a long time. My family had moved on without me.

"Magnolia!"

I met Momma at the foot of the stairs. She was wearing the same monochromatic outfit I had on, minus the tie.

"Let me look at you." She grabbed my shoulders and looked me up and down before her gaze rested at the base of my throat. "You put your tie on by yourself. And it's straight."

"I worked at a restaurant where a tie was part of the uniform. I got tired of asking the waiters to knot it for me."

Thinly veiled annoyance covered her face. "You could always get the boys to do whatever you wanted."

DENISE GROVER SWANK

I rolled my eyes and headed out the front door. "I couldn't help that, Momma."

"You can't rely on men to solve all your problems, Magnolia," she said, following behind me.

"The very fact that I'm here with you now is proof enough that I know that." Anger simmered in my chest. Her statement was also proof that she didn't know me. Not anymore. I'd spent two lonely years in a city of eight million people, living with a roommate who didn't give a shit about me other than if I paid the rent on time. I'd lost track of how many nights I'd cried myself to sleep that first year, wishing I'd never seen Ashley Pincher giving Maddie's boyfriend Blake a blowjob. Wishing I hadn't run into the woods to get away from him. Wishing I could remember what had happened after that, but also wishing that I could forget anything *had* happened.

But wishing never got you shit.

We both got into her car and she backed out of the driveway, then took off down the street.

"There's no need to get snippy with me." Her mouth pursed as she gripped the steering wheel, staring at the road like she thought it would get up and walk away. "I'm only pointing out the obvious."

I held my tongue.

"What happened with your debut?"

"Do you want to know so you can gloat?"

"Was it that bad?"

"Worse."

"Want to talk about it?"

Not really, but she was bound to find out, and I wanted her to hear my version first. "There was an . . . *incident* on stage. On opening night."

"What happened?"

How much did I tell her? That I'd been living with the director for the past three months? That rumor had it I'd only

12

gotten the part because I was screwing him? The thing that stung the most was that I'd really believed in the asshole. Griff had claimed to love me, and I'd hoped that I could learn to love him in return. That we could build something together. Griff, me, and the play. I had wanted that so much that I'd given him pretty much every penny I had for the sake of *Fireflies at Dawn*. Then, minutes before our opening performance, I'd caught him screwing my understudy.

"I tripped on stage," I said, opting to give my mother as little fodder for gloating as possible.

"You lost your job because of a little trip?" she asked in disbelief.

"It was more than just a little trip." I'd knocked down part of the set when my understudy—who also filled the role of *Girl on Train #3* in the sixth scene of Act One—had started taunting me on stage. I'd lost it and tackled her, knocking over a good bit of the backdrop. Of course my mic had picked up my expletive-laden rant. If my mother found out about that part, there was a good chance she would disown me.

"Did you embarrass yourself?"

"You could say that." Scarlett's costume was a short, tight, strapless dress, and the understudy had grabbed the front and ripped it down the middle. While topless scenes weren't unheard of on Broadway, there definitely wasn't one in the *Fireflies at Dawn* script. There were more photos and videos of me on the Internet than I could count.

"Are you going to tell me *anything*, Magnolia?"

I looked out the window, taking in the rolling green hills. It was springtime in middle Tennessee, and I'd forgotten how beautiful it was here. "I got fired, Momma. Is that what you wanted to hear? But I'm pretty sure I was going to get fired anyway. My director was about to replace me with his newest conquest." He always used his muse, and apparently I no longer fit that role.

"And who was his previous conquest? You?"

My silence was answer enough.

"Then I'm glad you didn't go down without a fight," she said with a hard edge in her voice.

I whipped my head around in surprise.

"Don't look so shocked, Magnolia. It sounds like that man used you, then tossed you aside for another pretty bauble. I taught you to stand up for yourself. Good for you."

Had she known all of the details of the fight—*Man on Train #2* and the *Conductor* in scene six had dragged us apart, but not before *Man on Train #2* rounded to second base right in front of the one thousand two hundred six people in the audience—she probably wouldn't have sounded so proud.

She'd find out soon enough. Of *that* I was sure.

"Have you catered a party since you left?" she asked.

"No."

"You're to remain in the background, Magnolia. No looking for the spotlight. You're not center stage at this event."

"Momma," I sighed. "Trust me. That last thing I want to do is draw attention to myself."

"You can't help yourself, darlin'. It's in your blood . . . your father's influence."

I rolled my eyes. "Not that again."

"Which part?" she demanded, narrowing her eyes. "That you can't help yourself or that your father always demanded to be the center of attention? Both are true, but for the moment, let's focus on *your* need for attention."

I turned in my seat, my irritation growing. "Need for attention? I told you that I wanted to hide in my room. Does that sound like someone who wants attention?"

"Like I said, you can't help yourself, Magnolia." She waved her hand in my direction. "It just oozes out of you. Like sap from a tree. Or oil from a sausage on the grill."

"I could do without the mental image." I cringed. "Besides, you've barely seen me in the past ten years."

"And whose fault is that? You refused to even come home for a visit. I have a business to run. I can't just traipse off to New York whenever I feel like it." She wrinkled her nose. "All that's beside the point. Your need for attention is innate and you know it. It's like breathing to you."

One thing I'd learned very early in life was that once my mother made up her mind, no amount of talking would change her opinion. Yet fool that I was, I wasn't about to let it go. "You name one instance of me seeking attention."

"One?" Her eyebrows shot up so high they touched her bangs. "I've got more than I can count. How about Roy's eighth-grade graduation party? Or my Bunco night."

"Which Bunco night?"

"*All* of them." She shook her head as she turned on a street headed downtown. "When you were a cheerleader, you were in the middle—"

"What?" I protested. "My cheer coach put me there!"

"You were still front and center."

"This is ridiculous." I shook my head. "I'm not having this conversation."

"Because you know I'm right."

"Because there's no talking sense to you when you've made up your mind about something." She pulled up behind a building on Main Street, and I sat up straighter in my seat. "Your kitchen is *downtown*?"

"Yep. Has been for about seven years."

I knew she'd kept a lot of her life from me as punishment for running away, but it had never occurred to me she'd keep something this big secret. "Isn't the rent expensive?"

A grin lit up her face. "We can afford it."

Franklin, Tennessee, had a picturesque downtown. Brick buildings and trees lining the sidewalk. A roundabout with the statue of a Civil War soldier in the middle. Franklin was home to several Civil War battle sites, and the history added to the charm. Downtown was a huge draw for local residents and tourists alike. I could only imagine that the rent was pricey. The smile on my mother's face confirmed it.

She pulled into a parking space behind a row of buildings, next to a white van with the words Southern Belles Catering painted on the side.

"You have a van too?" I asked in surprise.

"Two vans."

"Wow." We walked inside the back door, past two women who were loading foil-covered pans into the back of the van.

"Hey, Lila," one of the women said.

"Y'all ready for our big night?" my mother asked cheerfully.

"Yes, ma'am."

I followed my mother into a small kitchen prep room, my chest tightening when I saw the woman placing appetizers onto a pan. It was my mother's best friend and business partner, Tilly Bartok.

"Lila, everything's ready on my end," she said, concentrating on her task. "Did you find a replacement for Patty?"

"I did." But Momma's voice sounded off, even to me.

Tilly's head shot up and her mouth dropped open when she saw me. "Maggie? Is it really you?"

I nodded, unable to push words past the lump in my throat.

Tilly rounded the stainless steel prep table and reached for me, pulling me into a tight hug. "I thought I'd never see you again, girl."

Tears stung my eyes as I rested my cheek on the shoulder of the woman who had been like a second mother to me. While my mother fit her surname to a T, Tilly was her soft and comforting counterpart. She was the one I'd always turned to when I needed sympathy—especially after my father took off. My mother was the one I turned to when I needed action.

Tilly leaned back and grabbed my cheeks in her hands, searching my face. "You haven't changed, sweet girl. You're still as pretty as the day you left."

"And you haven't aged a day," I said with a soft smile. Her jet-black hair was pulled back into a bun, but it was still sleek and shiny with no hint of gray. Other than a few crow's feet around her eyes, her face was free of wrinkles. The only noticeable change was the additional twenty pounds around her middle.

She looked me up and down, her eyes widening as she took in my uniform. "What are you doin' wearing that?" Her gaze jerked up to my mother. "She's not filling in for Patty, is she?"

"She sure is."

"She can't be wait staff! She's a Broadway star!"

"Not anymore she's not."

Tilly looked like she could have been knocked over by a feather.

"It's okay, Tilly. I want to help." My mother released a soft scoff, but I ignored her. "Looks like you and Momma are doing well for yourselves. A downtown storefront. Two catering vans. I remember when you started, cooking in our kitchen and using your minivan."

Pride filled her eyes. "We sure have come a long way."

"We don't have time for this trip down memory lane," Momma interrupted. "We've got a party to cater. This event could take us to the next level. We can't afford a screwup, so let's go. You both can cry over each other later."

Tilly gave me a squeeze. "You can ride with me in the van and tell me all about your New York adventures on the way."

"Good luck with that," Momma muttered as she headed out the back door. "She's got more secrets than a CIA agent."

chapter
three

L uke Powell lived in a sprawling home on multiple acres that backed up to the Harpeth River. He'd only been successful for six or seven years, but in that time he'd amassed millions and achieved mega-stardom. Like a lot of people who had acquired a fortune after being born into nothing, he wanted everyone to know he'd done well. His house was a white, southern-plantation-style, two-story house with a center entrance and a wrap-around porch on both floors. There was a gated entrance, and the long driveway U-turned on a circle drive in front of the house.

But that entrance was for guests. We were staff, of course, which meant Tilly pulled the van up to the side of the house so we could enter through the catering kitchen. Like many sprawling estates, Luke's house had a special kitchen just for servicing parties. It chafed that I'd fallen back to staff level in less than twenty-four hours, especially since I'd been the darling of several *Fireflies at Dawn* parties. Just last week I'd attended a party thrown by Sarah Jessica Parker and Matthew Broderick.

I helped Tilly and several of the staff members carry trays

into the kitchen. As we slid the trays into the warming drawers, Momma stood to the side talking to Luke's personal assistant.

"Luke is feeling a little on edge tonight," the twenty-something woman said, keeping her gaze on her smart phone screen as she furiously typed. "His release sales aren't what he hoped for, and now I'm worried the seafood theme will upset him."

"You picked the seafood theme weeks ago, Amy," Momma said, her Alabama drawl thickening. I knew from experience that meant her patience was wearing thin. "It ties in with the beach theme of the album."

"His agent now thinks it was a mistake to record a country album with a Jamaican tone."

"Be that as it may, we still have seafood appetizers."

The assistant gave my mother a pouty look. That had never worked for me in the eighteen years I'd lived with the woman. Bless her heart for trying, but it wasn't going to work for her either. "Are you *sure* you can't change it?"

My mother's jaw set, and I saw the tic in her eyelid.

"Uh-oh," Tilly mumbled.

Do not get involved. Yet I found myself walking over to them anyway. I dusted off the sweet southern accent I pulled out whenever I wanted to get away with something in New York. It often worked with men, but it was fifty-fifty with women. "So let me ask you this," I said. "The problem is that the seafood will remind him of his album?"

My mother shot me a glare that said, *Stay out of it, Magnolia.*

The assistant looked me up and down, then rolled her eyes in dismissal. "I thought that part was obvious."

Her attitude didn't dissuade me. I was used to fighting tooth and nail to get what I wanted. "But his second album—*Freefall*—had several songs about the Gulf of Mexico, right? Like 'Beach Baby.'" I started to sing the chorus. "*I want to play all day in the sand, beach baby.*"

The assistant suddenly looked interested. I couldn't help

thinking it was partially because I could actually sing, but then again, we *were* in the country music capital of the world. Almost everyone could sing here. "Yeah."

"So if he'd like to take the focus off his new album, why don't you treat the party as a celebration of his career? Concentrate on his successes and call this his experimental album. Play it like he's so successful he can afford to take risks and be a little fringe with some projects."

Her eyes lit up. "That might work. Are you a publicist filling in for the caterer?"

"Nope. Just a dried up has-been Broadway actress."

She acted like she met a couple of those every other day. "Stick around after the party. I suspect Luke will want to talk to you." Then she spun around and left the room.

My mother was furious. "What in the Sam Hill are you doin', Magnolia?"

"Helping you, in case you hadn't noticed. I got her off your back."

"You were busy trying to find yourself a new career."

"As a *publicist*?" I asked in disbelief. "I'd rather be forced to sing the national anthem on live TV at five in the morning in a North Dakota blizzard. I just had an idea for how you could satisfy his ego without making a last-minute change to the menu."

My mother was not appeased. "You had no *right* buttin' in *my* business."

"What are you talking about, Lila?" Tilly asked in disbelief. "She smoothed that over."

Momma's eyes narrowed. "It wasn't her place."

Several of the catering staff had stopped to stare at us, their mouths gaping like catfish as they took in our showdown.

Tilly crossed her arms under her breasts. "The problem is that the both of you are mule-headed—too stubborn to admit when you're wrong. She saved us a potential beef with the client, and we do *not* want to piss off Luke Powell's assistant. We need the referrals this job's gonna get us."

But my mother's frown only deepened. "You may have helped this time," she said, pointing a finger at me, "but you have no idea how we run our business."

"Maybe not, but I do know how temperamental A-listers can be. I understand how they think. I've defused situations liked this as both a waitress and an actor."

"Because you're just as self-centered as they are," Momma spat out, her eyes alight with fury. "You ran off without a backward glance, and now you think you can just waltz in and try to insert yourself into my business. You have another think coming, missy."

"Lila!" Tilly said in horror, grabbing her arm and tugging her to the side. "Your prodigal girl has finally returned. Why can't you just be happy about that?"

Momma watched me for several long seconds, then turned away. "We need to unpack the crystal."

Tilly sighed and patted my arm as my mother walked away. "She'll come around."

I wasn't so sure about that. Which meant I needed to get my shit together fast. Especially if I was paying her rent. I hadn't even bothered to ask how much she was charging.

Luke's assistant returned twenty minutes later to inform us that the party theme had indeed been changed and new banners were being rush printed. Thank goodness we didn't have to deal with anything but the food and booze. The theme shift would be someone else's headache.

We had forty-five minutes until the party was scheduled to start. The bartending crew had arrived, and they'd checked in with Momma and Tilly before splitting off to set up four stations. One of the men walked past me as I placed the last shrimp in an elaborate display.

Tilly grabbed his arm, and he shifted the box in his arms. "Colt, wait up. Take Magnolia up to help you."

I sucked in a breath when he turned to face me. He was movie-star handsome, and his bright blue eyes would rival Zac Efron's. His dark blond hair was cut close on the sides but swept up and gelled on top. He had a light hint of stubble.

A slow, country boy grin spread across his face, and his voice was pure silk and honey when he said, "Magnolia? As in Mrs. Steele's daughter?"

He had to be a wannabe country singer. He was too smooth to be a Christian artist. Too pretty to be just a song writer. Nashville and Franklin were teeming with all three. You could practically trip over them when you walked out your front door.

"One and the same," Tilly said, dropping her hold on him and pushing me toward him. "We're in a bind tonight with Patty being off, so she'll be filling in. She used to work for us when she was in high school, so it's been over a dec—"

"A few years," I interrupted, giving him an innocent smile. No actress ever wanted to volunteer her age, and while I took offense to my mother's supposition that I always liked to be center stage, I wouldn't deny a little vanity. "I think Tilly's sayin' I'm a little rusty and could use a refresher course." The words were spoken in a slight drawl, unintentional this time. I'd been in Tennessee for less than four hours, and I was already reverting to my roots.

Colt gave Tilly a mega-watt smile. "Of course. I'd be happy to. Come on, Magnolia, you can help me stock the bar."

I grabbed a box and followed him through an elaborate dining room with a table that looked like it could easily seat twenty, then into a large round foyer with a gray and white marble floor and a massive chandelier. Large, sweeping spiral staircases flanked each side, leading up to a large landing.

There had to be twenty or more people bustling around,

covering high-top tables in crisp white cloths and centerpieces filled with candles and seashells. Bartenders were stocking two bar stations downstairs, and a few of Momma's staff were setting up the obligatory chocolate fountain.

Colt led me upstairs, shifting the box in his arms, and I struggled to keep up with him.

"Magnolia Steele, huh? I'm surprised you're working this event. Aren't you some big Broadway star?"

"No," I said, trying to keep my tone breezy. "I've spent the past eight years auditioning and working my way up the ladder. You know, chorus and secondary roles."

"But you got the lead in some new play. Lila couldn't stop talking about it."

"She did?" I asked before I could stop myself. My mother always seemed so disinterested in my acting aspirations. "I mean . . . yes, but it didn't work out. I'm taking a little break."

"But you haven't been home in years. Why now?"

I forced a smile. "It's always good to return to your roots, don't you think? Where are you from, Colt?" If my time with the Broadway crew had taught me anything, it was that people liked to talk about themselves. What better way to deflect his question than to make him the subject of our conversation? "Your accent sounds Georgian, but not Atlanta. Further south."

His eyes widened in appreciation. "Very good," he said, coming to a stop beside a bar station on the top level of the party. He hefted the box down next to a couple of others already waiting by the bar. "I'm from a place you've probably never heard of—Waycross. How'd you know I was from southern Georgia?"

"You're right," I laughed. "Never heard of it. And it's part of my job to know accents, although I confess I'm a bit obsessed about the differences between southern ones, mostly because a lot of actors try to pull out an Alabama accent for the role of a Texan." I stopped talking, realizing I'd inadvertently shifted the conversation back to me. "So let me guess why you're here in Nashville—you're a country singer. Colt what?"

"Colt Austin. And not just a country singer. A song writer too." I heard the defensiveness in his voice. "I know what you're thinkin'."

"If it's that you're here for the same reason every other male in his twenties who wasn't born in the Nashville area is here, then yeah, but you have the right look, which isn't true of all of them. The *real* question is if you can sing."

"Oh . . . I sing. And play the guitar." He flashed his grin, and this time I noticed the dimples on his cheeks. Sexiness exuded from him like the delicious aroma from cookies fresh out of the oven. I suspected he couldn't help himself. "I'll play for you, Magnolia Steele. After we finish tonight."

Holy seven circles of hell, I didn't usually fall for his type, but I was feeling a slight tug in my ovaries. I suspected most women probably fell at his feet, and even I was a bit affected by his charm. I put my hands on my hips. "It's my first night back in town, Colt Austin. What makes you think I want to spend it with you?"

"The fact that you're working Luke Powell's party and talkin' to me now."

I pulled out my best sassy attitude. "I'm working this party because my momma was in a bind. You'd do the same for your momma, wouldn't you, Colt?" Any self-respecting southern boy would practically lay gold pavers in a path for his mother if she asked him to. "And as for standing here, talking to you now, Tilly asked me to help you. And since she's like a second mother to me, I'd do anything *she* asked. Don't read anything more into it."

He clasped his hands over his heart. "That was a mortal blow."

"And yet, somehow you'll survive. Now tell me what to do."

When he gave me a devilish grin, I added, "To help set up the bar."

We unpacked the boxes, setting out the various bottles, and Colt flashed me a grin as he arranged his tip jar. It was undoubtedly an open bar party, but I was sure Colt would get plenty of tips from the female guests and a few of the male ones too.

"I better head back to the kitchen. My own job calls."

"I'll be watching you, Magnolia Steele."

I lifted an eyebrow. "I think you'd do better to pay attention to your own job."

A trickle of guests arrived soon after, and I fell back into serving like a duck took to water. I had so many years of waitressing under my belt that it was practically second nature at this point. The party was in full swing within an hour, but there was still no sign of the host. I was glad Tilly had assigned me to the relatively sedate downstairs living room area. Most of the guests were milling around the upstairs landing, the large entry foyer, or the public area of the pool. I caught Colt watching me from upstairs a few times, but I did my best to ignore him and do my job. The last thing I needed was a man in my life. For the most part, I blended into the background. I caught the attention of a few men, but I was sure none of them recognized me.

Then my luck ran out. I was walking around with a tray of bacon-wrapped shrimp and mini sliders when I heard a voice that sent chills down my back.

"Maggie?"

I froze and turned around in slow motion.

"Tanner." I hadn't seen Tanner McKee since the night of our graduation. The night I'd lost my virginity to him. The night my whole life had changed.

His mouth dropped open in shock. "It's really you."

"Hey." I gestured to him with the tray of sliders, the buns scooting dangerously close to the edge. "You look good." And he did. He was dressed in a gray suit paired with an ice-blue tie. His light brown hair was shorter, but his brown eyes were the same milk chocolate color I remembered. "What are you doing here?"

He swallowed. "*Me?* What are *you* doing here? And working as one of the wait staff . . ." He looked around, definitely confused. "Why aren't you in New York?"

"Uh . . . research," I said, coming up with the idea off the top of my head. "I'm researching a part."

"Well, you look good too. Just like when we were in school and you worked your mom's parties."

I glanced down at my uniform, then back up into his face. "How are you?"

His eyes clouded. "It took me a long time to get over you, Magnolia."

I truthfully couldn't say the same—the fight we'd had that night had revealed our utter incompatibility—but seeing him was a reminder of everything I'd left behind. Of all the people I'd hurt, him included.

My eyes started to burn, so I widened them slightly. I couldn't afford to break down in public. Or in private, for that manner. I needed to live up to my last name.

He cleared his throat. "I'm sorry for what I said that night. For what I accused you of . . ."

I turned back to him and forced a smile. "That's all water under the bridge."

"Why didn't you answer any of my phone calls? It wasn't our first fight. We should have at least talked it over."

I didn't feel like going for a stroll down memory lane, and besides, I'd long ago decided that walking away from Tanner was the best thing that had come out of me leaving Franklin. If I'd stayed, I probably would have married him and been miserable. I needed to end this conversation and end it soon. "It had nothing to do with you, Tanner."

I tried to walk around him, but he blocked my path.

"How could you say that, Magnolia?" His voice was thick with anger. "You slept with me, and then you ran away and never came back. You didn't answer my texts or calls or even my emails. It's like you fell off the face of the earth."

"I'm sorry if I hurt you . . ."

"That's not enough, Maggie. Your apology is ten years too late. Why? Why did you leave?"

"Apology?" I spat out in a whisper as I glared up at him. "You're the one who owed *me* an apology!"

"And I would have given you one if you hadn't run away like a spoiled little brat."

People had turned their heads to listen to our conversation, and I wished the floor would open and swallow me whole. So much for staying under the radar. "The reason I left had *nothing* to do with you."

"You said that already," he said, his voice hard. "But that's not an answer. You owe me an answer."

Maybe that was true. But how could I give him an answer I didn't have? How could I tell him that something terrible had happened, something that had shaped my life despite the fact that I remembered it in feelings instead of words? And besides, if I owed him anything, it wasn't a fraction of what I owed my momma and Roy. What I owed Maddie.

"I—" I didn't have the faintest idea what I was going to say, so perhaps it was a blessing that we were interrupted.

"Tanner." A tall blonde in a tight red dress sidled up to him. "You're talking to one of the *wait staff?*" She was nearly his height, which meant she had to be five foot nine without the heels. She looped a possessive hand around his arm.

He blinked. "Oh. Chelsea. This isn't one of the wait staff. It's Magnolia."

Her face froze and her gaze turned icy. "Magnolia? Magnolia *Steele?*"

"One and the same," I grumbled, wishing I could hide in the kitchen.

"Uh . . ." Tanner stammered. "Magnolia, this is my fiancée, Chelsea Coleman."

My blood turned to sludge. Tanner was engaged. The regret caught me off guard, but it wasn't the kind of regret that comes of jealousy. It was regret for myself—for eighteen-year-old Magnolia Steele who'd had simple dreams and a clear path. Here was another reminder that the girl I'd been was lost to me. On top of my disaster on stage the night before, it was too much. "Congratulations to you both."

Her eyes narrowed, and her grip on his arm tightened. "I thought you were in New York?"

I wasn't so sure it was a good thing she knew so many details about me. I tried to step around them. "I need to get back to the kitchen."

Tanner let me go this time, but I heard Chelsea say behind my back, "Her boobs are so obviously fake."

I stopped in my tracks. *Let it go, Magnolia. Just let it go.* I'd let my temper get the best of me the night before, and look where it landed me. Nevertheless, I found myself spinning around to face her. "My boobs are not fake."

The surprise in her eyes told me that while she'd intended for me to hear her, she hadn't expected me to confront her on it. She gave a little shudder, as if settling her icy exterior back in place. "Then they must be the only thing about you that's real."

I put one hand on my hip, balancing the catering tray with the other. The food sloshed around like the wave pool at Nashville Shores. "You don't know the first thing about me."

Sadistic glee filled her eyes. "Oh, I know plenty about you, including how you broke poor Tanner's heart."

What had Tanner told her about me, and what else did she think she knew?

But she must have decided she was done. She jerked on Tanner's arm like he was a stubborn puppy. "Let's go."

He followed her, but he cast a glance back at me, looking like there was more he wanted to say.

Tears burned my eyes. I had never expected to see him here. In fact I'd never given much thought to seeing him at all. Momma had told me he'd moved to Memphis years ago, and the Facebook stalking I'd done a few years ago had confirmed it. Did my mother know he'd returned?

I found her in the kitchen, barking orders at a server.

"He's back," I said, placing my tray on the island.

My mother swung to face me. "Who's back? Luke Powell? Last I heard he hadn't even deigned to make an appearance yet."

"No. Tanner," I said, feeling lightheaded. "Tanner McKee. You told me he'd moved to Memphis."

There was a flicker of sympathy in her eyes, but it was gone so quickly I would have missed it by blinking. "Last I heard he was still there. I saw his mother a few months ago, and she was braggin' that he was engaged."

"Well, he's back." I pointed to the swinging door. "And he's *here*. With his fiancée."

My mother looked exasperated. "Magnolia, you moved away. He moved on. Literally. Why do you care if he's engaged?"

"I don't know." And I didn't. It was just that everything at home was so different. A secret little part of me had hoped my old life would be waiting for me if I ever chose to come back.

"You have a job to do, Magnolia. Now get out there and serve."

I grabbed a new tray and exited through the swinging door, taking a deep breath to compose myself. Coming home had been a mistake, but I still had nowhere else to go.

For better or worse, I was in Franklin to stay.

chapter four

T anner and Chelsea had left the living room, and I spent the next half hour looking for them in my peripheral vision. I still hadn't figured out if I actually wanted to see him or not. At least there wasn't too much time to think—the party had picked up, and it was plenty busy. Tilly had moved me out to the large marble entryway, which was a grand hall in and of itself. I was offering a crab puff to a country music power couple when I heard my name again, but this time I knew it wasn't Tanner.

"Magnolia Steele. My, my, my. How quickly things change."

I sucked in a breath and slowly turned to face Max Goodwin, agent and mega sleazeball. We'd met at a rehearsal, after which he'd invited me to dinner. Over tiny pieces of prosciutto-and-Muenster-cheese-stuffed quail breasts, he'd offered me representation. He said he had big plans for me—a country music album, fame, and movie stardom—and it would all be mine if I went back to his hotel room with him.

I'd lifted my black camelback shoe to his crotch and started to gently roll the ball of my foot over his important parts.

"You want my undivided attention?" I asked with a sexy smile.

His eyelids lowered, his jaw tensed, and his breathing sped up. A knowing smile spread across his face. "You make my dreams come true, and I'll work on yours."

"That's such a generous offer, Mr. Goodwin," I cooed as I increased the pressure.

He gripped the table, his diamond-studded ring flashing in the candlelight. "I can be a very generous man."

"And if I don't feel like going to your room . . . ?"

He gave me a sly grin. "There are plenty of others who will."

"Well . . . When you put it that way, I know exactly what to do."

He leaned back, giving me better access to his crotch. "I knew you'd see it my way."

My smile fell. "Oh, I see it your way all too clearly."

I slid my foot higher and pressed my four-inch stiletto heel over his favorite body part. "That's why I'm willing to give you this." Then I jabbed, admittedly harder than I'd intended.

Max had to be taken to the hospital by ambulance to receive some kind of hush-hush emergency medical treatment. I was lucky he hadn't pressed charges, but what man wanted to admit that his penis had been shish-kebabbed by a woman's heel?

But now he stood in a room full of close to hundred people —along with probably fifty more on the upstairs landing—and judging from the look on his face, he still held a serious grudge. He was going to fry me alive.

I started to walk away, but he grabbed my arm and spun me around to face him, sending crab puffs flying off the tray.

"Let go of me, Max," I growled in a low tone.

"Aren't you supposed to be on a Broadway stage right about now? The curtain went up about an hour ago."

I jerked out of his hold and took a step back. "What I do is none of your business, Max Goodwin."

"You're no talent wannabe, Magnolia Steele. You got that role because you were sleeping with the director. And once he realized you were only good at one thing, and it wasn't acting, he knew he had to fire you. That was quite a temper tantrum you threw on stage. You'll never get another theatre role again after that performance."

I jabbed my finger into his chest. "My reviews were amazing. *The New York Times* called my performance in previews fresh and inspiring."

An ugly grin spread across his face. "Who'd you sleep with to get that review?"

"You of all people know I don't sleep around to get ahead in this business. And even if I did, James Marlow wouldn't be interested in what I have to offer seeing as how he's gay."

"If you're so amazing, what are you doing here serving crab puffs?" He glanced at the appetizers on the floor. "You can't even handle *that* job. You're a loser, Magnolia Steele. If you're here in Nashville to try to make it in the country music world, I'll make damn sure you never see a single second in a single recording studio."

Gritting my teeth, I decided to dust off the excuse I'd used with Tanner. "I'm working this party as research for a part."

"What part? A play? A movie?"

"Nothing you know about."

He laughed. "There is no part, Magnolia. You're a washed-up has-been at thirty-three."

"*Thirty-three?*" I screeched. "I'm not a day over twenty-five." I was twenty-eight, but he didn't need to know that.

He shook his head. "More lies. You really are a sad little person."

"Why? Because I didn't sleep with you to get some made-up role?" I asked, narrowing my eyes. "Just so you know, I haven't lost my taste for stilettos. Next time my heel might end up stabbing your non-existent heart."

The people around him began to laugh . . . which was when I realized we'd attracted quite an audience, my mother included. She must have heard about our confrontation and come out of the kitchen to investigate.

Well, shit on a stick.

My mother's eyes locked with mine, and I knew I had three seconds to vacate the room before she physically dragged me out. I headed toward the kitchen, but Max called out after me. "Magnolia, you need to clean the trash off the floor. Isn't that part of your job now? Poor white trash serving sub-par appetizers."

My mother stopped in her tracks, her eyes narrowing. "Did he just call our appetizers sub-par?"

Tilly slid through the back of the crowd, holding a tray of mini cheesecakes. I didn't miss the little push she gave my mother, but most of the people in the room probably didn't notice—they didn't know Tilly and my momma as well as I did. There was a big, fake smile plastered on Tilly's face. "Luke Powell knows how to put on a party. Food *and* entertainment."

She was followed by Colt and a pretty blonde who was part of the catering staff. Both of them were holding trays of mini cheesecakes, but they started to belt out a rendition of a duet Luke had recorded several years before with a flavor-of-the-month female pop star. Colt and his singing partner were both good-looking, and the girl actually had the vocals to pull off what the pop star could only achieve via auto-tune.

I hoped Luke Powell couldn't hear them; Colt sounded better singing his song than he did. By the time my mother and I left the room, Colt and his partner had the audience eating out of their hands. My confrontation with Max had been forgotten.

As soon as we reached the sanctuary of the kitchen, I expected my mother to launch into me—and possibly kick me out of the party—but she focused on another source of irritation first.

"Can you believe the audacity of that man?" she said, putting her hands on her hips. "He called our food sub-par."

The only insult that would have been worse was if he'd accused my mother of using ground worms in her sliders. "He didn't even have any of the food, Momma. He was only trying to get back at me."

Her eyes narrowed, and she pulled me into a corner. "What were you thinking, Magnolia Mae?"

And there it was. My tongue felt like a ten-pound weight at the bottom of my mouth, but her accusing stare finally jarred it loose. "I'm sorry."

"I'm sorry too. I'm sorry you didn't have a heel to stab him with." The hand gesture she made mimicking the act only added to the surreal moment.

My mouth dropped open.

"Don't look so shocked. You're my daughter. I can insult you all I want, but the minute someone else does it, you can bet your ass I'm going to be like a barracuda on a bloody stump. Nobody messes with my kids."

I had the urge to tell her the details of how I'd handled Max in New York, but Colt and his cohort entered the kitchen with empty trays.

"We had them eating out of the palms of our hands. Almost literally. Disaster averted."

My mother lifted her chin and nodded, then turned back to plating desserts.

Colt shot me a grin and a wink before heading out the door, but the waitress hung back, probably waiting for my mother to offer her words of gratitude. She obviously hadn't been working at Southern Belles Catering very long if she thought Lila Steele handed out compliments and thank yous like they handed out samples at Costco on Saturday afternoons.

"Why are you standin' around?" my mother demanded,

34

pointing to the door. "You waiting for an engraved invitation to get back to work?"

She ran off, sniffling a little.

"You could have been nicer," I admonished as the door swung shut behind her. I walked over to help my mother plate more mini cakes.

"She has a job that pays damn good money. What more could she expect?"

"She and Colt helped you out of a difficult situation."

"Me?" she demanded. "From where I was standing, it was all you."

"What difference does it make? One of your staff members was involved in a heated verbal exchange. She and Colt defused the situation beautifully."

She glared up at me. "How did it come to happen at all?"

"I know Max Goodwin from New York." I paused. "It didn't go well."

She harrumphed. "Hell, I'm not blind and deaf, Magnolia. I figured that part out myself."

Tilly came through the swinging door, looking far more stressed than when she'd made her sweeping entrance into the living room. "Oh, Mylanta," she exclaimed, leaning her butt against the counter and resting the back of her hand against her forehead. "I need a drink."

"Not yet, you don't," Momma grumbled. "We've got to get through this night first. Then you can get shit-faced six ways to Sunday." She shot a scowl at her best friend of thirty-plus years. "Good thinking with Colt."

Tilly preened for a moment, basking in the glow of the rare compliment.

Momma shoved the tray at me, her scowl deepening. "Now get back out there, Magnolia."

Tilly blocked the doorway. "You really think that's a good idea, Lila? After what just happened?"

My mother assumed her favorite fighting stance, her right hand on her hip. "Hell no, I don't think it's a good idea, but I had Trey do a head count. There are far more people than the two hundred Amy told us to expect. We need every person out there."

"Oh, stop blowing smoke up my ass," Tilly muttered, looking halfway amused. "We knew there'd be more than two hundred. We planned for three. And we sure as hell aren't sending her back out there. She's like a keg of powder just waiting for a match."

I was pretty sure that wasn't a compliment, but I didn't have time to decide whether I was offended.

"You never should have insisted she work the party in the first place, Lila," Tilly added. "What were you thinking? You had to know people would recognize her."

The flash of guilt in my mother's eyes only confirmed it. She'd sent me out there with the intention of humiliating me. I crossed my arms, weighing my options—should I leave? But I realized I had only one option, and at the moment it didn't sit very well.

When my mother didn't respond after a beat of silence, Tilly rolled her eyes and said, "Maggie stays back here for the rest of the night. I'll work her section."

"You?" my mother exclaimed.

Tilly shrugged. "Sure. Why not? I can play a little undercover boss."

My mother released a little shudder. "For heaven's sake, woman. What are you thinking? Besides that gambit with Colt and the girl, you haven't worked as part of the serving staff for years."

Tilly grabbed hold of the tray in my hand and jerked it from me. "If you and I can't step into every position in this little outfit, we're not worth a hill of beans. I can handle this."

"You have your own job to do, Tilly!" my mother shouted as

her friend made her way to the door. "Who's going to prep the rest of the food?"

"Magnolia can do it," Tilly said with a mischievous grin. "She's done it before. It's like falling off a bike."

"Uh . . ." I said, nibbling on my bottom lip. "I think that's riding a bike."

She winked. "That too." Then, like the smart woman she was, she ran.

I spun around to face my irate mother.

"Don't just stand there! Get started," Momma barked. Then she continued to yell at me for the next half hour.

Tilly was right. I'd worked plenty of parties for my mother in the past, and it all came back quickly. The only difference was that this one was a lot bigger than all the others.

I was preparing a platter of fruit for the chocolate fountain when Luke's assistant bustled into the room, looking frazzled.

She scanned the room until her eyes landed on me. "Magnolia, right?"

My heart stuttered, and I cast a quick glance at my mother before I answered. "Yes?" She must have heard about my encounter with Max Goodwin. Was she here to kick me out? Humiliate me?

"Luke would like to meet you. If you'll come with me." She gestured toward the door.

I looked at my mother again, but she waved her hand in a casual dismissal. My stomach twisted into knots as I followed Amy, who set a quick pace through the dining room, the clicking of her heels drowned out by the party crowd. We stopped at a door leading to a private pool deck separated from the public area by a billowing white curtain. Two stereotypical security men stood at the door to the deck, but they let Amy and me pass with a nod.

Twinkle lights hung from the ten-foot ceiling, making the curtains glow. The sun had set, but the gas heater burning behind him diminished the chill of the night air. Luke sat on a stool at a high-top table in the back corner, surrounded by a group of people, including several women who seemed to be hanging on his every word. I could see why he was out here, despite the fact that he'd missed the majority of his own party. It was quieter and less chaotic than it was inside. Besides, it was a power move for a country star to miss his own ten-thousand-dollar party.

"Luke," Amy said, walking right up to him and interrupting the group. "This is the woman I told you about."

His eyes lit up as he turned his attention to me. "Luke Powell, pleased to meet you," he said, extending his hand. "Amy says you're Magnolia. Magnolia what?"

I straightened my shoulders and shook his hand. "Magnolia Steele."

A knowing grin spread across his face. "You don't say."

I offered my best *I don't give a shit what you think about me* smile.

One of his cohorts laughed and leaned closer. "You've got a nice rack. Why are you hiding it behind that schoolgirl shirt? We've all seen the videos."

I turned a steely gaze on him.

Luke backhanded him in the chest. "Magnolia's a guest, Rocky." He cocked his head. "Is Magnolia your real name or your stage name?"

"You mean stripper name," another guy said with a smirk.

"Hey, Steele! I think she was in that Grey movie," a bearded guy added.

This was an incredibly bad idea.

I shook my head in disgust. "The *character's* name was Steele, you imbecile." If I had a dollar for every Anastasia Steele joke that had been pointed at me since the book catapulted into popularity, I would be a very rich woman. And I wouldn't be back in Franklin, Tennessee. I'd own a private island somewhere.

But unfortunately I was stuck here.

"If that's all you need . . ." I said in an icy tone, turning on the balls of my feet to head back inside.

But Luke was up in an instant, blocking my escape, and I found myself looking up into the hazel eyes of country music's favorite poster boy. Up close and personal like this, I could see why women dropped at his feet. He was stunning. But I'd met plenty of pretty boys in New York. I was immune to their charm, even when they had massive bank accounts and flew around in private jets.

"I realize I'm in your home, Mr. Powell, but I'm here as a temporary member of the staff for Southern Belles Catering. So if you'll excuse me . . ."

"Amy told me you saved my party."

I gave him my best haughty gaze. "Had I known how ill-mannered you and your friends were, I would have kept my mouth shut."

To my surprise, he burst out laughing.

I tried to walk around him, but he stepped in the same direction, holding up his hands. "You're right. I'm sorry."

His friends continued to snicker behind him, but one glance from him shut them right up.

"Look, Magnolia—do people call you that?"

I cocked my head and gave him a tight smile. "My friends call me Maggie, but you can keep on calling me Magnolia."

He broke into laughter again, but it didn't stop him from blocking my next attempt to bypass him. "I like you, Magnolia."

"Which is why you're holding me hostage?"

"What?" he asked in genuine surprise. "No. I'm just trying to talk to you."

"You mean *ridicule* me."

"No! You just caught me by surprise is all. I had no idea I had a celebrity working as kitchen staff. What are you doing back there anyway?"

I sure as hell wasn't about to spill my family connection. "Is there a point to this, Mr. Powell?"

"It's Luke. I asked to see you because I wanted to know if you were a publicist, but now I'm not sure what to make of you."

"Then I'll get back to the kitchen so you can figure it out."

"You're researching a part, aren't you? Are you one of those method actors?"

I crossed my arms and stared at him, deciding to wait him out.

He grinned and leaned closer. "I get it. It's a hush-hush part. You signed an NDA."

"Mr. Powell . . ."

"I told you, it's Luke. And you might not be a publicist, but you have good instincts. I'd still like to get your opinion about something." He paused. "Besides, I suspect you could use some good publicity of your own. Maybe we could be seen together in public. That could help your . . . *situation*." He waggled his eyebrows.

He was probably on to something. If I were seen in public with someone as high-profile as Luke Powell, it would take away some of the sting of my debacle. "I'm listening."

"Tim McGraw is having a big party next week. Come with me. The press will see you and take photos. I'll have my people call in an insider tip to TMZ."

I heard gasps and cries of dismay from his groupies behind me. One of them had obviously hoped to go with him.

It was tempting. But considering the way I'd left, I didn't want to seek attention here in Franklin, and being seen with Luke Powell was not the best recipe for blending in. On the other hand, if I managed to get some good publicity, I could possibly get another job on Broadway.

Luke misinterpreted my hesitation. "Let me wrap things up with my friends. We can discuss this in my study."

I rolled my eyes. "I'm not that gullible. I'm not some teenager fresh off the bus from Nowhere, Texas." But that wasn't entirely true. I'd let Griff Templeton make a fool out of me many times over. I just wasn't that gullible *anymore*.

My answer amused him. "Calm down, Maggie. If I wanted to see you half naked, all I'd have to do was go on YouTube. I'll meet you in my study in fifteen minutes. Second floor. Left wing. Fifth door on the right. Tell the security guard 'Dauphin Island.' He'll let you pass."

"'Dauphin Island'? As in the song from your *Freefall* album?"

"You know my music." He grinned. "Fits the theme, wouldn't you say?"

"Yeah . . ." I was truly unaffected by this guy. He was just a good-looking bastard who could carry a tune and had the backing and money of a country label. A freaking trained monkey could do it. But *he* thought I was playing hard to get. *Great*. "Am I free to go now?"

He winked. "See you in fifteen minutes, Maggie." Then he stepped aside and let me pass.

His buddies laughed uproariously when he returned to the table, and as I stalked back to the kitchen, all I could think about was how crazy it would be to actually show up in his study. So why was I considering it?

Momma just sniffed and gave me a dirty look when I got back to the kitchen, so I kept what had happened to myself. After ten minutes and an epic internal battle—in which my dignity lost by a landslide—I strode out of the kitchen with my head held high. "I'll be back in a few minutes."

"Where are you goin'?"

I didn't answer, but she was already barking orders to a server.

I headed for the stairs and climbed the staircase, my feet

feeling like I was snowshoeing in cast iron skillets. When I got to the top, I caught a glimpse of Colt from the corner of my eye. He had a line of women waiting for drinks, but he waved me over. Since I was beginning to have second thoughts about the meeting, I decided it wouldn't be the worst thing to stall for a minute.

"What are you doing up here, Maggie Mae?" he asked with a wink. "Couldn't stay away from me?"

His nickname caught me by surprise. "Nobody calls me Maggie Mae. Not anymore."

Not since my father left.

He looked like a deer in the headlights for a moment. "Don't tell me your middle name really is Mae." When I didn't answer, a cocky grin lit up his face. "Well, that's a lucky coincidence. Good guess on my part." He shook his metal tumbler, then poured its contents into a glass and handed it to a younger woman. Leaning toward her, he crooned, "That's my own special secret recipe, darlin'. I made it just for you."

Her face flushed as she stuck several bills in his overflowing jar.

"Oh, my God," I groaned. "You're a piece of work."

He leaned into my ear, his breath making the hair tickle on the back of my neck. "I'd be happy to demonstrate why women love me."

I jerked backward. "What the hell is it with you cocky country bastards? You think you can say some pretty words and women will just fall at your feet."

He flashed me a smile before turning to the next woman in line. "What can I get for you, beautiful?"

She gave him her order, and he shot me a glance as he started to make her drink. "So you never answered my question. What are you doing up here?"

I eyed the dark hallway branching off the end of the room. Sure enough, there was a guard standing sentry. All I had to do was hear Luke out. He'd implied his offer wasn't salacious, but if that was a lie, I could always turn around and leave. I'd be a fool not to at least listen.

"I'm here to try and salvage my career," I said as I turned to leave.

He called after me, but I kept right on walking until I reached the guard. He looked down at me—both literally and figuratively—and said, "No one goes back there, miss."

"Luke Powell invited me."

"You and every other woman trying to find his bedroom."

"Uh . . . *no*. I'm supposed to meet him in his study. He told me to tell you 'Dauphin Island.'"

He stepped to one side and tilted his head. "The hall forks off back there. If you're going to his study, keep to the left. If you're going to his bedroom, go to the right," he said with a smirk.

"I'll keep to the left," I said in disgust as I headed down the carpeted hallway. The overhead lights were out, but the wood-paneled walls were lined with paintings, and the picture lights emitted a soft glow. After I passed two doors on either side, the hall forked. I stayed left. This hallway was darker, the picture lights dimmer. I stopped at the fifth door on the left, the third door after the turn, and rapped lightly on the closed door. When no one answered, I pushed it open and stepped into the dimly lit room, letting my eyes adjust.

A large mahogany desk sat directly in front of me, and framed albums lined the walls. To my left, there was a long leather sofa and three windows that looked out onto the backyard and the river.

But something else caught my attention. Or rather, *someone* else.

There, on the floor by the sofa, was Max Goodwin. His pants were pooled around his ankles, and a letter opener was sticking out of his chest.

The glassy look in his eyes confirmed that he was dead.

43

Well, shit.

chapter five

I 'd be the first to admit that I didn't handle it well. I stared at him for a good ten seconds, trying to figure out what to do. Seeing him lying there like that, surrounded by a puddle of red, triggered a deep-seated terror that left me paralyzed with fear. Images flooded my head. A rainy night. Screams. Blood. Lots of blood. They were *familiar*—even if I didn't remember why.

My head turned fuzzy and my knees started to buckle as my body forgot to breathe. But then some rational part of my brain took over. Those visions had nothing to do with the man in front of me, and I had to deal with this situation first.

Do something, Magnolia.

Blood was dripping from the letter opener. If Max were still bleeding, he might not be dead yet. Feeling like I was going to throw up, I forced myself to move closer and dropped to my knees beside him, my eyes locking on to the huge bloodstain on the rug. Panic bubbled in my chest.

Don't look at it.

I closed my eyes and pressed my fingertips to his neck,

searching for a pulse. When I didn't find anything, I opened my eyes to make sure I was in the right spot. My gaze drifted down south. Looking at his semi-erect penis was better than the spreading bloodstain, although not by much. I dug my fingertips harder into his neck, still feeling nothing. That was when I noticed it—a puckered circular scar on his penis. I had given him that scar two years ago.

It was at that exact moment that Luke Powell appeared in the doorway. His mouth dropped open in shock.

I straightened upright and lifted my hand from Max's neck, horrified to realize that I'd not only touched Max Goodwin, but I'd touched a very *dead* Max Goodwin.

"What happened?"

"He's dead."

His eyes went wide as they bounced from me to Max and back. "You killed him?"

"What? No!" I scrambled to my feet and took several steps backward, bumping into his desk. "I came here looking for you. But he was lying on the floor."

"I need to get my security team up here right away. If word about this gets out . . ." He pulled his phone out of his pocket and spoke in a low tone. ". . . dead body . . . police . . . big trouble . . ."

Luke was staring at me in shock the whole time he talked, and when he hung up, the words spilled out of me. "I didn't do this, Luke!"

"Then why were you kneeling next to him? Checking out his dick?"

Oh, God. This was an utter nightmare. "I walked in and found him lying there. I froze up for a half minute, but then I realized he might be alive. So I knelt by him to check his pulse."

"And the other?" He looked completely wigged out.

"See that dimpled scar?" I asked, pointing to Max's crotch. "I did that." I cringed. "I wanted to see it. I'm not proud of it, but I was curious."

His face paled. "You stabbed his dick too?"

"No! Oh, my God! Will you just listen to me? I didn't stab any part of him!"

"You just said you gave him that scar."

"Two years ago. When he came on to me. But it was an accident. And I didn't stab him. At least not technically. It was from my shoe."

He took several steps backward toward the doorway, then shut the door. With me on the inside with a dead body.

A tidal wave of hysteria washed over me. I ran to the door and tried to open it, but he must have been holding it shut. "Luke! Let me out of here *right now!*"

"I can't do that, Magnolia," he said, his voice muffled by the door. "I found you leaning over his body. What if you run off before the police get here?"

The blood rushed from my head, and a feeling of overwhelming terror stole over me. Max's body was freaking me out, but most of my panic came from a different source—well-hidden deep within me.

But I needed to focus on the present. Would the police really think I was responsible? If I were a suspect, it would make the news, and I really couldn't handle more bad publicity. Feeling lightheaded, I decided it would be a good idea to sit, but the sofa was out since Max was sprawled out in front of it. I stumbled over to the desk and sat on the edge, gripping the sides to help me balance.

Deep breaths. Slow deep breaths. I tried to calm down, but Max's body was right there, growing colder by the second. Sitting wasn't helping. If anything, I was getting more freaked out. I had to get out of here.

I got up and beat on the door with both fists, close to sobbing. "Let me out of here right now!"

The door swung open, making me trip backward.

The security guard from the hallway filled the space, taking everything in.

"I walked in and found her next to him," Luke told him.

"And I told you I was trying to find out if he was still alive! We need to call 911!"

But no one listened to me as more security guards showed up, followed by a shaken-looking Amy, who glanced from me to Max and then back.

"Someone needs to call 911," I repeated to Amy, hoping she would listen.

She turned to me, her eyes glazed with shock. "But he's already dead."

"You don't know that!" I said. My gut told me she was right, but it seemed so wrong for us to stand around without even trying to save him. While I detested Max Goodwin, I didn't want him dead.

"Luke!" I shouted, trying to break through the barricade of muscled men wearing security uniforms. "We have to call an ambulance!"

"It's been taken care of," one of them told me. From the steely-eyed look he gave me, it was obvious he didn't much believe in innocent until proven guilty.

Several minutes later, two uniformed policemen walked into the room, followed by a middle-aged man with pasty skin. His dark brown pants and tan blazer looked over a decade old. He eyed me up and down before turning his attention to the body. "No one leaves this house until we've interviewed people."

One of the officers leaned in close to the man in the blazer. "There are over two hundred people here."

"Then you better barricade the exits and start interviewing," the man in the sport coat barked. "We're going to need more men here." As one of the officers left to do his bidding, the plainclothes man added, "But don't give the people you interview any details." His gaze shot to Luke's security. "Anyone have a name for the body?"

I cringed at his callous tone.

"Max Goodwin," Luke said, stepping forward. "A talent agent."

My eyes drifted to Max's body. It was all too much, and I suddenly felt a little woozy.

The guy in charge shot me a glance. "Get those two out of here!" He flicked a finger toward me and then at Amy, whose greenish pallor could be seen from across the room. "They look like they're about to barf on my crime scene."

I looked up in surprise as the remaining uniformed policeman grabbed my arm and ushered Amy and me to a bedroom across the hall.

Not trusting my legs, I sank onto the fluffy white comforter that draped the canopied bed, but Amy paced the room, holding her face between her hands.

I closed my eyes, sucked in slow even breaths, and imagined I was lying on a warm beach. I was no stranger to anxiety attacks. My first few years in New York had been riddled with them. I'd learned to shut them down as a survival tactic—it didn't matter how good you were at waiting tables if you periodically disappeared into the bathroom to fight off freak-outs.

As soon as I felt like I could reengage with the world without fainting or screaming, I opened my eyes to evaluate my surroundings. Amy was seated in a wingback chair now, her eyes glassy, her shaky hands gripping the armrests.

"Did you do it?" she asked, but it lacked the conviction to suggest she considered it a legitimate possibility. More like it was an obligatory question.

"No. I couldn't stand him, but I never would have killed him."

She nodded and then looked out an open window to the

concrete drive below, staring at the police cars' flashing strobe lights.

She'd turned on a lamp that cast a warm glow, but I still found myself shivering.

"Was he alive when you found him?" she asked so quietly I barely heard her.

It took a second to register her question. "No." My voice croaked, so I started over. "No, I think he was already dead."

"Have you ever seen anyone die?" she asked.

"Yes," I whispered. "Once."

But I'd never even seen a dead person before, so where had that come from? A new wave of panic bubbled up, and while I did my best to stomp it down, it still simmered below the surface.

"I saw someone die once," she said, her voice flat. "In an accident. There was lots of blood. Like with Max."

All this talk about death and dying and blood was sending my anxiety skyrocketing. But while Amy was acting creepy as shit, at least this new prison wasn't shared with a corpse.

I needed help, but who should I turn to?

I pulled out my cell phone, ignoring all the recent missed calls and texts from friends in New York. None of them could help me. Of course the only person I could really call was my mother, but she was going to go ballistic. I hadn't even spent my first night back in my childhood bed, and I was already a murder suspect.

I knew how bad this looked. But the plain and simple truth was that I was innocent of any wrongdoing. Max had been stabbed with a letter opener, and I'd never touched it. Surely the fact that my fingerprints weren't on the murder weapon would prove my innocence.

Amy was now twisting her hair so tightly around her index finger she was either going to pull out a chunk of her blonde strands or amputate her finger.

"Did you know him?" I asked. She was acting guilty as hell. But what exactly was she feeling guilty about?

She stopped twisting and turned to stare at me. "Yes."

"Through Luke?"

She hesitated. "Yeah."

The door swung open, revealing the pasty guy who'd issued orders in the other room. He stood in the threshold, eyeing Amy and me as if he couldn't figure out which one of us to torment. I gave him a good once-over. Unfortunate comb-over, check. Smarmy smirk, check. Over the years, I'd become a pro at reading people, and my instincts told me this guy had a massive ego complex.

"Magnolia Steele?"

I was pretty sure it wasn't a good thing he knew my name.

"Yes," I answered in a croak. My mouth was dry. The only way to get through this was to play a part. That was how I'd learned to survive those first few years on my own. The question was what role?

"I need to ask you a few questions."

I stalled. "Can I get a bottle of water first?"

"Sure. Of course," he said, his tone all fake sympathy. He glanced over his shoulder. "Officer Ryan, could you get Ms. Steele a bottle of water?"

"Yes, sir."

"What about me?" Amy asked. "I need to go. I have a million things to do."

He narrowed his eyes. "We need to question you as well."

"Why?" she asked defensively. "*I* didn't find him."

He gave her a long look. "We're questioning everyone . . . Ms.?"

"Danvers," she said, her face turning a pasty gray. "Amy Danvers. I'm Luke Powell's assistant, and he needs me to handle the press . . . along with a host of other things. I really need to go."

"Well, Ms. Danvers, if you'll head out into the hall, my partner will be happy to get your statement." He turned back to me, but he didn't speak until she left the room. "Ms. Steele," he finally said. "I'm Detective Timothy Holden, and my partner Detective Ray Murphy is out in the hall. I'm the lead detective on the case, and I've been told you found the body."

Showtime. I pretended to be brave and strong, a favorite role from a decade ago.

I nodded, pressing my hand to my chest. "Yeah. I did."

"Can you walk me through that?"

I recounted the event, leaving out the part about looking at Max's scar. I knew that wouldn't be in my favor.

A uniformed officer appeared in the doorway, holding a bottle of water. The detective took it from him and handed it over to me.

"I hear you had a previous incident with Mr. Goodwin," he said, still sounding sympathetic.

I stared at him as I uncapped the bottle. My mind automatically went to Max's penile deformity, but then it struck me that he was referring to our encounter downstairs.

"Oh," I said, sounding nonchalant enough to deserve an Oscar. I'd threatened to stab Max Goodwin in the heart with my shoe, and it had happened less than an hour later, albeit with a letter opener. "What exactly did you hear?"

"I'd rather hear it from you." He sounded light and breezy, my definitive clue that he was trying to snow me.

I had two choices, and neither was good. My courage was slipping. "I'd like to speak with my lawyer."

Surprise flickered in his eyes, then shifted to thinly veiled hostility. "Do you have something to hide, Ms. Steele?"

I was scared, but I was also pissed. I was innocent; I didn't deserve this kind of scrutiny. "I'm not stupid. I've seen all those shows where the police twist things around and use them against you."

"You got something we can use against you?"

I crossed my arms, trying to appear calm and cool even though my pulse was pounding in my temple. My mind was scrambling, trying to figure out who in the hell I'd call. I hadn't exactly kept in touch with my circle in Franklin, and I certainly didn't know any criminal attorneys. And then there was the little matter of payment.

Detective Holden shifted his weight. "Come on, Magnolia. Why don't you save us both some time and tell me your story? I know there was a disagreement between you and the victim downstairs about an hour ago. I've got plenty of witnesses to back up that claim."

I reminded myself of my role. I was brave, even if I didn't feel it. "If you already know what happened, then you don't need my statement at all."

"Don't get flippant with me, Ms. Steele."

"I'm only stating the facts."

"So you're really not going to tell me?"

"No."

He stared at me for several long seconds. "Don't leave this house. And don't tell anyone that Mr. Goodwin was killed. If word gets out and I trace it back to you, I'll have you arrested for interfering with an investigation."

That sent a shiver down my spine.

"I'll let you know when you're free to go."

If I were free to go was probably more like it. There was a very real chance he was going to haul me to the police station and make me give a statement or—even worse—arrest me. I needed to find an attorney fast.

He left the room, and I didn't waste a second before bolting out of it. There was no sign of Amy or the other detective, but the hall was filled with multiple policemen, all of whom watched me like I was a sideshow attraction as I ducked under the crime scene tape blocking off the hall at the fork. I continued down the hall, unsure of where to go. The logical place was the kitchen, but I wasn't sure I was ready to face my mother.

Unbelievably, people were still partying. Then again, the police probably wanted their witness pool to stick around. Colt still had a line of hotties waiting for drinks, but he abandoned his post and made a beeline for me.

"Magnolia."

I stopped and spun around.

"What happened? Rumor has it that someone got killed."

I fought to keep from crying. Crying wouldn't do me any good at this point. I took a deep breath and tried to center myself. I knew I wasn't supposed to tell him, but I couldn't keep the words in. "Max Goodwin. But you can't tell anyone."

His eyes bugged out. "What? But I just saw him about half an hour ago."

"You know Max Goodwin?"

"Everybody in the business knows Max Goodwin. How do you know it's him? I can't get a word out of anyone."

"I was the one who found him."

He ran a hand over his head. "Shit." He pushed out a breath, then looked back at the crowd surrounding his bar station. "Are you okay?"

"Yeah." I was dangerously close to losing it. I needed to go hide alone somewhere. "You go on back to work. I need to find a lawyer."

His mouth dropped open, and he grabbed my wrist and pulled me aside. "Why do you need a lawyer?"

"Think about it, Colt. Max and I had that huge fight. Then I was the one who found him. The fact that his pants were around his ankles probably doesn't help, especially since I just accused him of sexual harassment in front of about two hundred witnesses."

"What?" He shook his head. "So you were the one to call 911?"

"No." I pressed my knuckles to my bottom lip. "Luke Powell found me kneeling next to the body."

A new glint of suspicion shone in his eyes. "Why were you kneeling next to Max?"

"Not for the reason you're thinking. I found him bleeding out on the rug, and I figured I'd better check his pulse. But I couldn't find one. Then Luke found me next to him . . . I need to find my mother. I really need to find an attorney." I still wasn't looking forward to talking to Momma, but I wasn't sure I had a choice.

He pulled out his phone. "What's your phone number?"

I rolled my eyes in disgust. "Now is not the time to try to pick me up, Colt."

He shook his head, but a smirk ghosted across his face. "I never said I was trying to pick you up, Maggie Mae. I'm offering to be your friend if you need one. So what's your number?"

I rattled it off, feeling like a jerk. "Sorry. I'm just a bit shaken."

He grinned. "Why? Because you thought I was trying to pick you up? That was at the top of my agenda until you talked to me like I was a naughty schoolboy. Now it's been moved to second place."

I shook my head as I headed down the stairs to find my mother.

She was muttering under her breath in the kitchen. Two staff members were in there getting new trays, but they hurried out the moment they saw me. My mother's gaze lifted to mine, and I was surprised to see the worry there before it morphed into anger.

"Where on earth have you been, Magnolia? The police are here investigating something, and everyone keeps saying there was a murder."

"I know," I said with a sigh, looking around to make sure we were really alone. "I was the one to find the body."

Her eyes narrowed. "What? Who was it?"

"Max Goodwin." Her blank look told me the name meant a lot less to her than it had to Colt, so I added, "The guy I had that huge fight with."

She sagged against the stainless steel prep table. "Oh, Magnolia."

I sucked in a breath. "I know. They've already questioned me."

"Do they think you did it?"

"Honestly? Yes. But I doubt they can do much. Yet. I need to find a lawyer."

Tilly burst through the swinging door. "I still can't find her anywhere, Lila," she said, sounding close to tears. When she saw me standing there, she collapsed on top of the island, her elbow landing in a platter half-filled with cheesecakes. "We thought you were dead, Maggie."

"Dead?" I blurted out. "Why would you think I was dead?"

"We couldn't find you anywhere, and we heard someone was murdered. It was the logical conclusion."

"Well, of course it was," I said in a snide tone. They had been worried about me, though, and I couldn't begrudge them that. I shook my head. "Sorry. I'm a little stressed."

"They think she did it," my mother said.

"What? Who was killed?" Tilly asked, standing up.

"That asshole she had an argument with earlier tonight."

Tilly covered her chest with her open hand. "Oh, dear."

"It gets worse," Momma said. "She was the one who found the body."

"Oh, no." Tilly started to weave in place, and if her pale face was any indication, she was about to faint.

I rushed forward and led her over to the closest chair. I

pushed her head toward her knees, and Momma got a clean wet rag and plopped it on the back of her neck.

"Get yourself together, Tilly Bartok. Now is not the time to fall apart."

Tilly twisted her head to look up at her, and the movement sent the rag tumbling into her lap. "Of course. You're right."

"We need to find her an attorney."

Tilly sat up, nodding her head, slowly coming to her senses. "Got anyone in mind?"

"A lot of someones. The problem is they'll either cost a fortune or they're idiots."

I was in a world of crap. "I don't have any money."

My mother put her hands on her hips and gave me a look that told me she thought tadpoles were more intelligent than I was. "No shit, Magnolia. Why else would you show up on my doorstep after a decade? We know you're desperate and destitute."

Her tone was harsh, but I saw the pain in her eyes. She was a casualty in the mess I'd stumbled into. Collateral damage. I wanted to tell her I was sorry. I was sorry for so many things, but if I tried to apologize, I'd fall to pieces. Now more than ever, I needed to keep it together.

"What about Mitch Chidsey?" Tilly suggested. "He's a great defense attorney."

Momma crossed her arms and shook her head. "He's pissed at me after I wouldn't budge on our proposal for his Christmas party two years ago."

"What about Percy Talbot?"

"He's an idiot. He lost that trespassing case with Tina's boy. Even a gorilla in a suit could have won that one."

They were silent for a moment, and I started to give serious consideration to bleaching my hair and going into hiding. I'd heard the weather was nice in Mexico. Or South America.

"Emily Johnson," my mother said under her breath. When she looked up at me, her eyes were full of determination. "She's perfect."

"Wait." I sucked in a breath. "You mean Emily Johnson from high school?" When she didn't answer, I shook my head. "No. No way. How can *she* be perfect?"

"She's having a big party in another month. I'll barter for it."

I turned my head. "Let me get this straight. You're going to barter catering for legal fees with my worst enemy from high school?"

My mother rolled her eyes. "Don't be so dramatic, Magnolia."

"She hates my guts, Momma! She'll probably lose the case just to get me back for all the atrocities she's convinced I committed against her."

"Oh, my word, Magnolia Steele. Isn't it time you outgrew your stupid grudge against that girl?"

"She did have a reason, Lila," Tilly said, getting to her feet. "Emily sabotaged her in the girls' locker room."

"Oh, for heaven's sake!" my mother shouted. "She thought Magnolia stole her boyfriend." She gave me a haughty look that told me she firmly believed Emily was in the right.

"Emily and Tanner weren't even dating, Momma. If I had tried to lay claim to all the boys I liked in high school, I would have been enemies with half the school." I shook my head. "Why are we even discussing some stupid fight from high school? I'm about to be charged with murder!"

My mother pointed her finger in my face. "Well, you better kiss and make up, Magnolia Mae, because that girl is about to save your life." She pulled out her phone, opened an app, and pressed the phone to her ear.

"Oh, my God!" I exclaimed. "You have Emily Johnson's name on speed dial?"

My mother shrugged. "We have coffee sometimes."

"Wait." Tilly put a finger to her chin. "Last I heard, Emily was getting ready to retake the bar. Did she pass this time?"

South America was looking pretty good. Antarctica was looking better.

chapter
six

My mother's call to Emily was short and sweet, and my name was never once mentioned. She simply explained she had an emergency she needed help with at the Luke Powell estate. Emily agreed to come right away.

"Just how close are you two?"

My mother gave a half shrug and harrumphed.

Cringing a little, which only roused my suspicions, Tilly clasped her hands together. "I'll get some of the staff to start packing things up."

I would have given anything to follow her out of the kitchen. Instead I started stacking trays and hauling them out to the vans. I was rearranging some serving dishes in the back of one of the vehicles when a figure streaked past me into the kitchen. All I saw was a glimpse of long black hair against a tan jacket, paired with jeans and tall brown boots.

I hopped out and followed her, entering the kitchen in time to see the woman wrapping my mother in an embrace.

My mother was *hugging* someone?

"Lila, is everything all right? I came as fast as I could." I hadn't heard that voice in years, but I would have recognized it anywhere.

Momma broke loose and patted Emily's arm. "I'm fine. I didn't call about me." She looked over Emily's shoulder at me, giving me a warning look I recognized all too well from childhood.

Emily turned as if in slow motion. Her first reaction was shock, followed fast by anger. Dammit, she was still just as pretty as she had been in high school, actually more so. Her black hair was still long, but the cut was more sleek and sophisticated. She looked slightly older, but she was one of those women who, like a fine wine, improved with age. Her mouth parted as though to say something, then closed as if she'd thought better of it. She took a breath. "Magnolia. You're back."

"And already in trouble," my mother said, crossing her arms.

Emily looked back over her shoulder. "You called me for Magnolia?" She didn't sound one bit happy about it.

"There was an incident earlier. Magnolia got into a disagreement with one of Luke Powell's guests. Then an hour later he turned up dead. The guest," she added as an afterthought. "Not Luke Powell."

I couldn't read Emily's expression when she turned back to me, but I assumed she wasn't drowning in sympathy. "And Magnolia's now a suspect."

"Yes," my mother answered.

"And you expect me to counsel her?" Her expression was no more transparent now than it had been minutes before, which was almost more unnerving than if she'd reacted with the outright hostility I'd expected.

"If you're willing."

The corner of Emily's mouth quirked into a slight grin, one I recognized all too well. "Then you should plead guilty, Magnolia."

61

My eyes narrowed. "I didn't do it, Emily, but then again, you never were a fan of the facts, were you?"

Emily's eyes became laser focused on mine. "I had all the facts I needed, Magnolia Steele."

"Magnolia!" my mother barked. "Emily's here to help you. The least you could do is be nice to her."

"Me?" I asked in dismay. "She's the one who—"

But before I could continue with my rant, Detective Holden opened the kitchen door. "Oh, there you are, Ms. Steele," he said when his gaze landed on me. "I was having trouble locating you. I thought perhaps you had left the premises."

Emily gave me a long, hard look, then turned to my mother and squeezed her shoulder. "If you advised my client to stay on the premises, then of course she did," she said, taking several steps toward the detective. "She's too intelligent to disregard a police directive."

I wondered how hard that had been for her to choke out. Kudos to her for making it sound convincing.

"Do you need to question Ms. Steele?" she asked, all business.

A sly grin spread across his face. "I've already taken her statement in regard to finding the body."

"That body was a person, Detective Holden," she said in a tight voice. "A person with a family and friends."

I almost corrected her. I was pretty certain Max Goodwin didn't have any friends, but it was fifty/fifty as to whether my observation would help my case.

"We're still holding *the victim's* name until his family has been notified."

"So will you need to question Ms. Steele further?"

His gaze drifted between the two of us before finally landing on me. "Not at the moment, but we'll need you to stick around town. I hope you weren't planning on heading back to New York for another stripper show." He gave me a lewd wink.

"What are you talking about?" my mother asked him, then turned to me. "What is he talking about, Magnolia?"

"Don't answer him, Magnolia," Emily said in an icy tone. "I could file sexual harassment charges against you, Detective."

His grin spread. "For what? Speaking the truth? It's out there in cyberspace for anyone to see." He waggled his eyebrows. "I had no idea I was interviewing a celebrity. I'm really looking forward to speaking with you again." Then he turned on his heels and left the room.

As soon as he was gone, Emily turned to me and said in an accusatory tone, "What did you tell him in your statement?"

"The truth." Mostly.

"I need the details." She looked around us. "But not here. Somewhere private."

"We can go to my house," Momma said.

Emily paused, biting her upper lip. "No. My office."

"I can't leave for another half hour or more."

Emily gave her a sympathetic look. "I'd like to speak with Magnolia alone, if you don't mind."

Momma looked surprised, but she quickly covered it. "Of course. But she doesn't have a car."

"I'll take her to the office and then to your house."

"She doesn't have a key," Momma said. "You'll have to let her in if I'm not home yet."

Emily nodded.

She had a key to my mother's house? Just how close were they? "Hey, y'all! I'm standing right here! Mind including me in this conversation?"

"This might take an hour or more," Emily said to my mother, ignoring my request.

"You better get going," Momma said, not looking at either one of us.

I wanted to protest, but it wasn't like I had a lot of options. My entire life was fresh out of options.

"Come on, Magnolia," Emily said. I started to follow her, but then a horrifying thought occurred to me. If the detective knew about my infamy, it was only a matter of time before *everyone* knew. Wouldn't it be better if the information came from me? I turned back to my mother.

"Let me see your phone."

"What on earth for?" she asked.

"Just give me your phone."

She pulled it out of her pocket, entered the password, and handed it over.

Magnolia Steele wasn't exactly a common name, and a quick search was all it took to find a slew of posts about my humiliation. I pulled up a *New York Post* story—it was one of the kinder reports—and handed the phone back to her without fully releasing my grip on it. "After what Detective Holden said . . . you need to see this. You need to be prepared." I let go and hurried out the door before she could watch it.

Emily led the way to a shiny black BMW. The car chirped and the headlights flashed as I walked around to the passenger door.

Neither of us spoke after we got in the car. Emily simply started driving, west and then south.

Luke lived in the rolling farmland north of the Harpeth River, still in Franklin. The area was full of trees and hundred-year-old low stonewalls. It was beautiful and ordinarily peaceful, but my nerves were on edge and my stomach was churning.

"It hasn't changed all that much since I left," I said, looking out the window. "Lots of trees and meadows."

"Plenty of places to hide bodies," Emily said dryly, her hands at two and ten on her black leather steering wheel.

"Planning on killing me and disposing of my body?" I asked.

"Please . . ." she drawled. "You wouldn't be worth the effort."

I pursed my lips together, too worried to come up with a retort. "Why did you take my case?"

She gave me a look of disgust. "I sure as hell didn't do it for you."

"That's comforting." I remember her earlier suggestion that I plead guilty. "How do I know you won't do a bad job of defending me just to make me pay?"

"So you're admitting guilt?"

"I didn't kill Max Goodwin."

"I know that." She shot me a snide look. "You're a lot of things, Magnolia Steele, but stupid's not one of them. If you argued with the asshole in public, you wouldn't have killed him an hour later."

"How do you know it wasn't an act of anger? Or passion?"

She smirked. "That would suggest you had a soul."

"Wow. Thanks . . . I guess."

"And I was talking about Tanner McKee."

"For God's sake, Emily. He asked me to homecoming twelve years ago. If you wanted him so badly, why didn't you go after him after I left?"

"He was too devastated to even think about another woman. *Everyone* was devastated after you left," she sneered. "Everyone but you. But then that was you, narcissistic Magnolia Steele who thought the sun rose and set on her."

"That is so not true," I spat out. "And you have no idea what I went through after I left."

She pulled up to a stop sign and turned her piercing gaze on me. "You're right, Magnolia. Why don't you fill me in?"

Oh. Shit. Stupid. Stupid. Stupid.

I should have never come back, but it was too late for that now. I was good and stuck here. Tears welled in my eyes, so I turned and looked out the window into the dark night.

"That's what I thought," she said, turning left. "It was always all about you. I see things haven't changed. Lila didn't tell me that you were coming back. I bet you just showed up on her doorstep, nearly giving her a heart attack."

I wanted to ask her why my mother would have confided in her, but the answer was obvious. My mother had replaced me with my archnemesis.

"So what are you doing back here? Hiding from the press?"

I still didn't answer, feeling dangerously close to getting sucked into a black hole of despair.

"You were never very good at staying in the background. I see that hasn't changed either."

We rode in silence after that, and I was surprised when she headed downtown—even more so when she pulled into the same parking lot my mother used for her business.

Emily started to get out of the car.

"I don't think this is going to work," I said, sounding more pathetic than I'd intended.

She stopped, staring at the dark building in front of us. "You want to hire another attorney?"

I knew that wasn't possible. Momma had hinted that she wasn't going to pay Emily. Only then did I remember that Momma had said she would barter for her services by catering for a party. Did her party have anything to do with the big solitaire adorning Emily's right ring finger? But shouldn't it be on the left if she was engaged?

"Magnolia?"

If she were getting married, who could it be? Was it someone I knew? Did he look like Tanner? I couldn't help wondering if I'd ever find someone who fit me. Despite how I'd felt years ago, when I was young and in love, it wasn't Tanner. But maybe Emily was right. Maybe I was a narcissist. Maybe I loved me too much to truly love anyone else.

"Magnolia." Emily's voice was softer now, almost gentle.

I turned to face her, trying to remember the last time she'd been nice to me.

"You're in shock. Everything's probably all setting in. Let's go into my office." She got out of the car. Moments later my door opened and her hand reached in and tugged on my arm.

"I didn't want to hurt her," I said, my voice breaking. "I couldn't help it."

"It's okay," she said in a soothing tone as she led me across the parking lot to one of the office blocks. She opened the door with a key, then pushed me into the stairwell behind it and locked the door behind us. "Up the stairs."

She stayed behind me, prodding me up the flight of stairs until I reached the top. A plaque on the door read, *Emily Johnson, Attorney at Law.*

She'd barely passed the bar, yet she had her own law firm? Her rich daddy must have set her up, but the world wouldn't care. All they'd see was a young woman who ran her own practice.

No wonder my mother loved Emily. She was everything I could never be. Everything she had hoped I would become. Respectable. Normal. Close to home. Her office was literally two doors down from my mother's business.

Emily opened the office door and turned on a lamp. She led me to a worn sofa, and as I sank into the leather, I realized my face and part of my shirt were wet with tears.

I was in a world of shit.

My sobs broke loose—years of built-up guilt, regret, and loneliness wanted out. The truth was, even when I'd lived in Franklin, I'd always felt alone. But that wasn't entirely true.

I'd never felt alone with my father.

But he'd left without a trace. No body. No note. No nothing. Rumors had swirled. His biggest client's wife had disappeared at the same time, taking some of her husband's money with her. The gossipers claimed Daddy had left us to be with her. Other people whispered that he'd pissed off the wrong people and met an untimely demise. My secret shame was that I'd always hoped it was the latter. It was the only explanation I could accept for his failure to contact me.

Emily sat in a chair by the sofa for a couple of minutes, then stood and handed me a box of tissues. "I'm going to get you some water."

I nodded. "Thanks."

She walked through a door, leaving me alone. The office was one long room that was divided into two parts by furniture. The sofa was in the front part of the office, along with a matching chair, but deeper into the room—in front of the windows over-looking Main Street—there was a desk and a few chairs. The place was nicely furnished but not ostentatious. Emily's father had set her up well.

I really didn't want her as my attorney, but I didn't have any choice in the matter unless I got a court-appointed one. But I'd seen that John Oliver report on TV about public defenders. As deep as I was, I needed someone who would spend more than seven minutes on my case.

I got up and moved to the windows, needing to think about something else. Anything else. I scanned the signs in the windows of the storefronts across the street, trying to figure out what was new and what had been here before. Then my phone vibrated in my pocket, and I pulled it out, figuring my mother was probably texting to make sure I hadn't bitten Emily's head off.

I wasn't prepared for what I found.

Welcome home, Magnolia. I've been waiting.

chapter
seven

When Emily came back into the room, I was still staring at the phone in my shaking hand.

She seemed surprised to see I'd moved from the sofa, and some of her harshness returned. "I need to talk to you about what happened tonight. Would you rather do it at my desk or the sofa?"

I was already on edge from the text. The number was blocked, so I had no idea who'd sent it. I told myself it was nothing, that some old acquaintance from Franklin had somehow gotten my number, but a cold sweat broke out on the back of my neck.

What if it was Blake? He was the last person I remembered seeing before my memories of graduation night cut off. Every time I tried to regain those two missing hours, I became nearly paralyzed with terror—which was why I'd finally stopped trying to remember years ago. But those images I'd seen while staring at Max's dead body . . . something told me they were from that night. I'd always suspected Blake was hiding what he knew. Was he responsible? What if I was in danger now?

I felt like a rat trapped in a maze.

Oh, God. Why had I come back?

"Magnolia, get your shit together."

Emily's earlier gentleness had caught me off guard, wearing down my protective wall. But this was the real Emily, the one I remembered, and I was back in self-preservation mode. "Your desk."

I slipped the phone back into my pocket and took a seat in one of the client chairs.

"Texting one of your Broadway friends?" she asked, handing me a bottle of water. "Sending a *you'll never guess what happened to me* message?"

"Something like that." I sat down and took a long drink of water. "How long will this take?"

"Got a hot date?" she asked in a derisive tone. "You sure didn't waste any time."

I shook my head in disgust. "Why did you take my case if you hate me so much?"

"I did it for your mother." She paused. "But if you're worried about it affecting your defense, keep in mind that I've successfully defended sleazier people than you, as difficult as that is to believe."

"That you were successful?" I asked in a mock sweet tone.

She sat back in her desk chair and pushed out a heavy sigh. "My reputation is on the line. I don't like to lose."

I'd learned that firsthand after Tanner asked me—and not Emily—to homecoming junior year. "Look. This all started back in high school, and neither of us ended up with the guy. Can we just let the past go?"

She lifted her eyebrows. "You're the one talking about it. My focus has been on your case."

CENTER STAGE

I rolled my eyes. "Whatever." I took another gulp of water. "What do you want to know?"

"Start from the beginning. Tell me about your encounter with the victim. Who was he?"

"Max Goodwin." She took notes on her laptop as I told her about the encounter. I went on to tell her about finding the body, but once again skipped the part about checking out my handiwork on his manhood. "I didn't tell the police about the argument. And I didn't tell them about meeting Max in New York two years ago."

"Tell *me* what happened in New York," she said, her fingers taking a break from their rapid clicking on her laptop keys. I hesitated long enough for her to look up at me. "I take it this isn't something that will work in your favor."

"No, I suspect the police frown on disfiguring penises."

"*What?*"

I recounted the sordid tale, telling her every last detail. She stopped typing at some point and stared at me in shock and a bit of horror.

When I finished, she gave herself a little shake. "And I take it he didn't press charges?"

"No. My friend Jody figured he didn't want women to think his pecker didn't work."

The corners of Emily's mouth twitched. "And did you see him again after that . . . encounter?"

"No. Not until tonight."

She typed for a few seconds and then stopped and gave me a long look. "Tell me why you're back in town."

The hair on my arms stood on end. "Why?"

"I suspect it will be part of your defense—should it come to that."

I didn't want to tell her anything, but I suspected she was right. "I had an incident."

"On stage, I hear."

71

I scowled. "If you already know, then why are you asking?"

"What I've heard is hearsay. I want the truth from the ass's mouth." She flashed a toothy grin. "I mean horse's mouth."

I was already humiliated. How much worse could it get? The truth was undignified, but it was all I had to offer. "You'll love this story, Emily. It's a classic. Girl meets director. Director tells girl she's his muse and casts her in a starring role in a new musical. Director tricks girl into giving him thousands of dollars to help finance said musical. Girl finds director screwing her understudy shortly before the musical starts. Said understudy mocks the girl on stage, and girl loses it. She goes home to find the director has tossed all her clothes into the hallway. She is penniless because she gave the director all her money. So now she is broke, homeless, and jobless. She charges a plane ticket, maxing out her credit card, and goes home to her mother." I gave her a hateful smile. "That about cover it for you?"

"Why haven't you come home before now?"

"Because I didn't feel like it."

"You left the day after we graduated. You had a scholarship to Southern University in Hillsdale, Tennessee. You and Tanner were supposed to go on a camping trip the week after graduation, although your mother thought you were going with Maddie. Then you disappeared in the middle of your own graduation party and showed up hours later, covered in mud and looking like a drowned rat. The very next afternoon you flew to New York City—which you had never, *ever* mentioned doing—and you never returned after that, not even for holidays, until you hit rock bottom." She gave me a long, cold stare. "What were you running from, Magnolia?"

If that wasn't the million-dollar question.

I felt like I was going to throw up on her wool rug. I was a fucking mess on the inside, but I had been trained to play any role on the drop of a dime. At the moment I was starring in the role of cold, heartless bitch. Fortunately for me, I'd played this role so many times I had it perfected to a T.

I crossed my legs and rested my hands on my knees. "I had no idea you were so fanciful, Emily. Back in high school you always seemed so dull and unimaginative."

A slow smile spread across her face, but her eyes were cold. "No," she said slowly, "I think you're confusing me with you."

"Don't try to tell me that you wanted the lead role in *Thoroughly Modern Millie* too. I didn't think you could carry a tune."

"Cut the shit, Magnolia. No one *ever* heard you say you wanted to act on Broadway. Not even your best friend Maddie."

"What did you do, Emily? Go around and interview everyone who knew me after I left?"

She rested her hand on her desk. "As a matter of fact, yes."

All my blood seemed to drain to the tips of my toes, leaving me lightheaded. What the actual fuck? "You always wanted everything I had, and it looks like you've done your damnedest to get it. You're like my mother's long-lost daughter. Let me guess—you're best friends with Maddie now, aren't you?"

The smug smile on her face told me all I needed to know.

I got to my feet. "I'm finding another lawyer."

"You just admitted that you don't have a penny to your name. You can't afford another lawyer. Why won't you tell me what happened that night?"

"I just told you everything that happened tonight. Do you have dementia in addition to your psychopathic tendencies?"

"Not tonight, Magnolia. The night of our graduation." She was as sneaky and stealthy as a cobra, but ten times as deadly. I was so, so stupid to have underestimated her.

"Stay out of my life, Emily Johnson. Leave the past where it belongs." I spun around, close to losing control, and made a straight shot for the door.

"Magnolia, come back," Emily called after me.

I unbolted the door and flung it open hard enough for it to

bang into the wall. I didn't bother closing it behind me before I dashed down the stairs.

"Magnolia. Where the hell do you think you're going?" she called from the doorway. "Your mother's house is three miles from here."

It didn't surprise me that she knew the distance. In fact it wouldn't even surprise me if she had it figured to a tenth of a mile. The sensible part of me knew I should let her take me home. Someone had killed Max Goodwin, and he or she was still roaming loose. But I was too pissed and upset to care. I'd rather take my chances with the boogeyman than deal with Emily.

I unlocked the door at the bottom of the stairs and ran out into the parking lot, unsure where to go. The only thing I knew for certain was that I didn't want to go anywhere with *her*.

This was one time I was thankful for sensible shoes. I didn't even think about where I was going until I realized I was walking over the pedestrian bridge to Pinkerton Park, away from downtown, glancing over my shoulder every couple of minutes to see if Emily were following me.

What in the hell was I supposed to do? Emily was right. I couldn't afford to hire anyone else, but Emily obviously had my mother wrapped around her little finger, which I found hard to believe. My mother wasn't the wrappable type.

There weren't any people around when I arrived at the park, and it was late enough that there wasn't much traffic downtown. My feet led me to the playground, and before I knew it, I was sitting in one of the swings. When I was a teenager, I would often come to Pinkerton Park after a fight with my mother. But the roots connecting me to this place ran even deeper. My father used to bring me here when I was a little girl, usually after his own fights with his strong-willed wife. It occurred to me that it was probably a stupid place for me to be. The whole park was essentially deserted—anyone could come up and finish me off without a single witness. But I couldn't bring myself to give a damn.

My phone buzzed in my pocket, alerting me to an incoming call. It was probably my mother. Maybe Emily had called and tattled on me. Maybe my mother had finally recovered from watching that video and was calling to tell me my belongings would be on the front porch when I got back.

I slowed down and pulled out my phone, my heart stopping when I didn't recognize the number. Was it my mystery texter? Was it the police telling me to come in for questioning? Or maybe my mother had given my number to Emily . . .

I answered with one hand on the swing's chain, bracing myself for the worst. "Hello?"

"Maggie Mae," a familiar male voice said, sounding worried. "Are you okay? Where are you?"

It took me a second to figure out who it was. "Colt?"

"Where'd you run off to?"

I pushed out a sigh, bending my head forward with relief. "I had a meeting with my attorney. And before you ask, it did *not* go well."

"That sucks."

"More than you know." I paused. "You remember how you made that offer to help me if I needed it? Is it too soon to cash that in?"

"What do you need?"

"A ride to my mother's."

"Where are you?"

"Pinkerton Park."

"Okay. I'll be there in ten minutes." Then he hung up. No questions about why I was hanging out at the park in the dead of night when the police could arrest me at any moment. Just "okay" and he was on his way. It was refreshing.

And true to his word, he was there in ten minutes. He parked his pickup and walked toward me with a brown bag in his hand. Giving me his wonder-boy smile, he waved to the empty swing next to mine. "Is this swing taken?"

I was in a terrible situation, but I found myself chuckling. Despite the fact that he so clearly knew he was charming, there was something about Colt that brought a grin to my face. "I think you're safe. All the five-year-olds are at home, tucked into bed."

"What about you?" he asked, pulling a can of beer out of his bag and handing it to me. "You want to be tucked into bed?"

I laughed as I popped open the top. "Not *your* bed."

"The ladies tell me it's a great place to be."

"And that's reason number one why *I* will never be there." I looked at the can and shook my head. "Coors Light? I pegged you as a Budweiser man."

"The Coors Light is for you." He pulled out a Budweiser, and I burst into laughter.

"You are so predictable."

He waggled his eyebrows. "Maybe not as predictable as you think." He balled up the bag and tossed it into a nearby trashcan. Then he wrapped his arms around the chain and gave a little push with his feet. "So you have an attorney, huh? That was fast."

"Yeah, well, my mother had her on speed dial. Emily Johnson."

"Ouch. I can't believe she called Emily."

"You know her?"

"Yeah, I know her," he said with a scowl, then took a drink.

There was obviously a story there, but it was just as obvious Colt wasn't spilling. As someone who had plenty of secrets that needed to stay that way, I could sympathize. "I need a new attorney, but I don't have any money."

"That's a problem." He took a sip of his beer.

"I might be stuck here in Franklin for a while. That's a problem too."

"How long were you planning on staying?"

"I didn't have a plan when I came here. That's *why* I came. But now I'm trapped, and there's no escape."

"No escape . . ." he said slowly. "That's a strange way to put it."

He was right. Of course, the situation with Max did make me feel trapped, but this went deeper. It had something to do with that well of anxiety I'd rediscovered tonight. Those images . . . I shivered. "I run the very real risk of getting arrested for a murder I didn't commit, Colt. Wouldn't you want to escape?"

He studied me for several seconds before asking quietly, "Do you *want* to escape, Maggie Mae?"

"That's like asking me if I want to win the lottery."

He dropped his gaze as he pushed off again, moving his swing in a low arc. "Not if you have the means to make it happen. The lottery is a pure gamble."

I snorted, but only half-heartedly. "You have the means to make it happen?"

"I know people." He shrugged. "Passports. Social Security cards. False identities that can get you credit cards . . ." His voice trailed off.

"Yeah, right."

"I do," he said more firmly. "Not long after I got to town, I took a job with some seedy people. I'm not involved with them anymore, but . . ."

I gave him a suspicious look.

"Hey, it was a job and I needed to make rent. I'm not proud of it, but the fact is that these guys have connections."

"That sort of thing costs money, which I've already pointed out I don't have."

"If you had it, would you do it?"

That was like asking if you'd use a time machine to go back and kill baby Hitler. But I had to wonder . . . would I?

Sure, I'd built a new life for myself in New York, but my

persona there was like a suit I put on every day, trying to convince everyone I wasn't Magnolia Mae Steele, the frightened eighteen-year-old girl who'd run away from Tennessee. And while I genuinely did love acting, I hated the politics and games that went with it all.

Wearing that other suit had become exhausting. And in the few hours I'd spent back home, I realized that I was tired of running. Tired of hiding. Tired of being alone.

To my surprise, I realized I was ready to come face to face with my past, ready to face the demons I'd left behind.

Even if it would put me at center stage.

chapter eight

We were silent for a couple of minutes, Colt letting me mull over his suggestion as we both slowly swung and drank our beers.

Finally, I planted my feet on the ground and stopped my swing. "I think I need to stick around for a while."

He didn't speak until I turned to look at him. "Are you sure?" he finally asked.

"If I disappear again—without a trace this time—it would kill my mother. I know she comes across as tough as shoe leather, but I hurt her when I left the first time. I'm not sure how she'd take it if I did it again."

"You think she'd prefer for you to go to jail for a crime you didn't commit?"

"I'm not going to let one more person abandon her."

A small grin lifted the corners of his mouth. "I'll respect your decision, Maggie Mae, but if you change your mind, let me know."

"Thanks." Narrowing my eyes, I smirked at him. "If you

think you can get in my pants now, you're going to be sorely disappointed."

He laughed. "A guy can hope."

"What I really need right now is a friend."

He reached over and covered my hand on the swing's chain. "I might be full of talk, but I can be a good friend if you'll let me."

"Thanks."

He stood and reached a hand toward me. "Come on, Cinderella. Let's get you to your mother's house before you turn into a pumpkin."

I took his hand and stood, suddenly feeling weighed down by the craziness of the last thirty-six hours. It would feel heavenly to sleep in my old bed.

Colt knew exactly where to go. When I asked him about it, he said, "I've been to your mother's house before, Magnolia."

My eyes widened.

"She hires me to do more than just bartend."

"Oh, my God," I said in horror. "Please tell me you aren't a part-time gigolo."

He burst out laughing, and when he finally settled down, he turned to look at me. "Trust me, darlin'," he said, wiping a tear from the corner of his eye. "Lila Steele doesn't need to pay money to get a man in her bed. She'd just order him there."

I shuddered. "I refuse to discuss my mother's sex life."

"Hey, you're the one who brought it up."

I cast a glance at Colt, trying to figure him out. If Momma had let him come to her house, that meant she trusted him. Once Momma trusted someone, they were in. But after my father's disappearance, it took a lot for someone to earn her trust. Especially if that someone was a man.

He pulled into my mother's driveway and slung his hand over the steering wheel.

"You know this truck is a total country music cliché, don't you?"

He laughed. "Is that supposed to be a bad thing? It makes the country songs I write authentic." He flashed his grin.

"You got a dog and an ex-wife to go along with it?"

He shook his head and chuckled. "But I'm working on one of 'em. Go inside, Maggie Mae. Get some sleep."

I considered asking which one he was working on, but I knew I was just stalling. My mother now knew all the sordid details about my Broadway debut, and there was no way in hell I was going to get away with not talking about it. I took it as a good sign that my luggage wasn't piled on the front porch.

"Thanks for the ride, Colt," I said as I climbed out and then walked up to the front door. It was the same trek I'd made less than six hours before, and I felt no less desperate this time.

The door opened as I reached the porch. My mother looked more worried than I'd ever seen her, but that worry quickly switched to irritation, as if someone had taken an eraser to her face.

I paused outside the threshold. "Am I still welcome?"

She waved her hand toward the entryway, her mouth puckering. "Don't be so dramatic, Magnolia. So you flashed your tits to the world. At least you're still young and they look good. Just imagine if I showed my drooping bowling balls. I could have started a world war. Or at least instigated a minor economic depression."

I walked inside, laughing, but my laughter quickly turned to tears. "Oh, Momma."

My mother shut the door behind me, then shocked the daylights out of me by pulling me into a hug.

"There, there, Magnolia. It's not the end of the world, I promise." She pulled back and cupped my cheeks, looking at me with teary eyes and a quivering smile. "This hasn't even broken off the seal to the beginning of the apocalypse."

"I'm so embarrassed."

"Why? Because you showed the world that your breasts are natural?" When I started to ask her how she knew, she dropped her hold and waved my almost question aside with her hand. "I know a thing or two about fake boobs."

That was a shocking statement, but I didn't have the energy to ask how she could tell.

Seeing my confusion, she winked and wrapped an arm around my shoulders, then walked me into the kitchen and toward a barstool. "You need a cup of tea."

This was the mother I remembered as a girl—not a pushover, but not so hardened around the edges. I realized I'd scared her enough to scrape the top layer off her armor. I didn't expect it to last for long, so I was going to bask in it while I could.

She grabbed the kettle off the stove and filled it with water. "How'd it go with Emily?"

Oh, dear. "Okay, I guess. I told her my side of the story."

"What did she say about your chances of getting out of any charges?"

"I don't remember her saying anything about that." No, she was too busy playing Nancy Drew with my past. "But I suspect she wouldn't have said much anyway. She wouldn't want to give me false hope or swing the other way and make me worry too much. Keeping it neutral would be the professional thing to do."

"Maybe." Then she looked back at me, her eyes narrowed. "Why did Colt bring you home?"

"I didn't want to bother Emily any more than I already had. Colt had asked for my number after I was questioned by the police. In case I needed help." I forced a grin. "Or bail money."

My mother shook her head as she turned off the water. "That boy doesn't have two nickels to rub together. I hope you wouldn't waste your phone call on him."

I wanted to ask her if I could call *her* if I ended up in jail, but I already had my answer. She'd called in a favor to get Emily's help, and besides, her reaction to the news of my public shame had been way better than I could have hoped. "How long's he been working for you? I'm surprised he's been to the house before."

"I still occasionally make things here in my own kitchen—where it all started. Sometimes I get nostalgic and like to remind myself what it was like in the beginning."

"It was hard. You damn well nearly worked yourself to death."

She looked back at me with fire in her eyes. "But I loved it. When you love what you do, it doesn't matter how hard you work. You love it too much to care. Or maybe you love it because you enjoy the fruit of working so hard." She gave herself a tiny shake. "I'm turning into a damn philosopher." But then her eyes met mine again, her gaze piercing. "Do you love what you do, Magnolia?"

"You mean acting?"

"I sure as hell didn't mean killin' people."

I cringed. The memory of Max's body would haunt my dreams. "I do. But after the other night . . . I think my acting days are over, like it or not."

"If you never acted again, would you miss it?"

"Yeah," I answered without hesitation. "I love becoming someone else. I love making the audience react. It's like making magic." I might have stumbled into it, but I'd found the thing that made my heart take flight.

"So you want to go back?"

Well, wasn't that a loaded question . . . I'd asked myself that very thing all day, and there was still no clear answer. I could only tell her what was in my heart. "All I know is that for now, I want to stay." I looked into her face. "I've missed you, Momma."

"I never left." The warmth in her eyes wavered. The wariness that replaced it broke my heart, but I had to admit it was warranted. Who was to say I wouldn't take off for another ten years? Maybe without leaving a forwarding address this time. I wasn't a safe bet.

I gave her a tiny smile. "I know." I hurried over to her and wrapped my arms around her back. She'd erected her wall again, not that I was surprised, but I squeezed her tight anyway. "I'm sorry I haven't been easy. And I'm sorry that I left you like I did. But it was never about you, Momma. I promise. I love you."

She nodded, her hair brushing my cheek, then pulled back and turned to face the kettle.

I yawned. "I'm exhausted, so I think I'll just go to bed. Can I get a rain check on the tea?"

"Yeah," she said, not looking back at me.

"Do you have any jobs for me tomorrow? Should I be up by a certain time?"

"I have to be at the office by nine. You can go with me and do some filing and office work."

"Okay." I headed for the stairs, but she called after me.

"Magnolia."

I stopped and looked back at her, not surprised she was still giving the kettle her undivided attention. "Yes, Momma?"

"I'm glad you're here to help."

I couldn't help but smile at the warmth those simple words spread through my chest. That was my mother's equivalent of *I'm so glad you came home. I missed you.* I'd take it. "Me too."

I decided to take a long shower, hoping it would relax me enough to sleep, but the hot water did nothing to clear my mind. The fuzzy images that had popped into my head earlier had faded, but the horror of them lingered in the back of my mind like white noise. Even though the dreams had faded long ago, I was certain those images I'd seen earlier had been plucked straight from them. Could they be memories from the night of my graduation party?

But if I'd seen something that terrifying, would I really have forgotten it? For a while I'd convinced myself there was only one plausible explanation—that I'd gotten drunk and blacked out in the woods. Except I only remembered having one drink. What if that wasn't what happened at all?

Hot water beat down on my knotted back muscles as I quieted my mind and tried to remember, ignoring the way my heartbeat spasmed from my anxiety. Just like it did every time I tried to think about that night.

I only remembered bits and pieces. Finding Blake in the woods with Ashley. Running in the woods as it began to rain. But there was more. Much more. I only had to make myself remember.

Start at the beginning.

My graduation party had started around eight, but the party wasn't in full swing until ten. I'd already had a drink—a wine cooler—to calm my nerves for what I knew was coming. I had the tiniest of buzzes when Tanner snagged my hand and took me up to my room, shut the door, and locked it.

But I moved past the memory of losing my virginity and all the awkward clumsiness that went along with it, including the disappointment that it wasn't all fireworks and magic like I'd expected.

Fifteen minutes later, we were back downstairs, and I was looking for Maddie. She'd anticipated my first time almost more than I had, so I wanted to let her know we'd *done the deed*. I was still trying to figure out how to tell her it hadn't been what she'd led me to believe. And that was when I saw Blake in the kitchen with Ashley Pincher draped across his chest. She winked up at him and slipped out the back door, the one leading to my backyard.

I continued to search for Maddie, but now I was watching Blake too. He kept shooting glances at the door. Then he looked around and followed Ashley outside.

He was about to cheat on my best friend.

I'd suspected for weeks, but this was my chance to prove it to Maddie, who had shut me down every time I'd tried to get her to listen. If I got proof, she'd be forced to believe me. I snagged my digital camera off the table Momma had set up for everyone to take photos of themselves for posterity and snuck out after him.

And that was where my mind started to erect a barrier, making my next memories hazy and painful. While I knew in my heart I'd seen Blake and Ashley together and then ran off, I couldn't clearly recall the images of them together. What if it wasn't true after all?

I had to force my way past it, which was easier said than done. My chest was so tight I felt like I was suffocating, and I started to shiver violently despite the hot water that was still steaming the tile walls. I was tired of wondering why I'd run away. Why I was so scared to come back. Why those nightmares had tormented me.

I took a deep breath and gave my mind a shove.

I slipped out the back door just as he disappeared into the woods. Feeling like a private investigator, I followed hot on his heels and walked past the tree line as quietly as possible. I heard them before I found them. The music from the party filled the night, drowning out their voices at the edge of the woods, but it soon became obvious what they were doing.

About fifteen feet in, I found them in a small clearing, his back pressed up against a tree and his pants around his ankles. Ashley was on her knees, her mouth wrapped around him as he fisted her hair and moaned her name.

While I'd suspected he was cheating, catching him in the act stole my breath away. Maddie would be devastated. It took me several seconds to remember the camera in my hand. Swallowing my nausea, I lifted it until they were perfectly centered in the scope. I needed to concentrate on getting proof.

Rain began to fall, the patter of the drops on the leaves getting louder as it began to pour. I considered giving up my quest, but I was already here. I owed it to Maddie.

My mother would kill me if the camera got wet and ruined, so I snapped several photos and then hid behind a tree to review the results. The photos would be worthless if I couldn't prove it was him, but the lighting was so bad I couldn't get his face in focus. So, my heart beating madly, I switched on the flash and snapped two or three shots in rapid succession, lighting up the ten-foot area as surely as if I'd shined a searchlight on them.

Releasing a roar of anger, Blake pushed Ashley away from him and snatched up his pants as I turned and started to run toward the house. But in my haste, I dropped the camera. I *needed* the proof, so I knelt down and fumbled around in the dark for it.

"Magnolia!" Blake shouted, his voice shaking in anger.

Terror washed through me as my fingers wrapped around the plastic case. I got to my feet, stumbling when I realized Blake was already blocking my path.

"Give me the camera, Magnolia." His voice was tight and menacing, but his words were slightly slurred. He was drunk. I'd seen a drunk Blake beat guys up for looking at him the wrong way. He sure as hell wasn't about to let me past him to go tell his girlfriend what I'd seen.

I tried to push my memories further, but my body resisted. I dropped to my knees and clung to the slick tiled shower wall. I was hyperventilating, and if I didn't get my breathing under control, I would pass out. Leaning my forearms on the shower wall, I took slow, steady breaths.

"You're okay, Magnolia," I whispered. "You're okay."

It was the mantra that had gotten me through those first two years in New York. I'd repeated it over and over and over—first out loud and then in my head—until I actually started to believe it.

Except I wasn't so sure that was true. Not now that I'd come back to Franklin. What if whatever had scared me away was still a threat?

A part of me had always known this—that I hadn't blacked out in the woods that night. Something so terrifying had happened to me that my mind had locked it away to protect me. But my last memories were of Blake, which convinced me even more that he had done something horrible. Why couldn't I remember?

A sob built up in my chest, bursting loose as I looked down at my leg and my finger traced the scar on my upper thigh. A backward C with a slash through it. It was from that night. I'd always told myself I'd simply cut my leg on the brush in the woods.

Now I wondered where it had really come from.

I took a deep breath and forced my sobs to subside. Crying wouldn't solve a damn thing. I needed to look at what I knew.

Something bad had happened to me the night of my graduation party, and Blake was to blame.

He'd sent me the anonymous text.

He knew I was back in town. What did he think I was going to do?

I hurried to finish my shower, then put on a long T-shirt and hurried down to the basement, my hair still wet and dripping down my back. Since the main floor was dark except for a dim lamp in the entryway, I figured Momma had gone to bed. Just as I'd hoped.

Sure enough, the padlocked box was tucked behind the green plastic Christmas tree. I breathed a sigh of relief, grateful that my mother was a creature of habit who hated change. The combination was still the same, and the squeaky lid suggested the box had not been opened in a while. I pulled out the familiar wadded brown hand towel and carefully unwrapped it from my dad's Glock. A quick examination showed me it wasn't loaded, but the package of cartridges at the bottom of the box would take care of that.

I rewrapped the gun and the ammo in the towel, then closed up the box. With any luck, I'd be able to return the gun before my mother ever missed it. In fact she'd probably forgotten it was there.

Once I reached the main floor, I went straight to the front door, making sure the deadbolt was in place. But what had I been thinking? My mother was a careful woman. She was the one who'd insisted on the steel-reinforced doors in the first place.

I placed my hand on the metal, letting the chill seep into my palm. I'd trusted this door with my life when I was a kid. I hoped I could trust it now.

I spun around to go upstairs, but my mother was at the top of the steps, watching me with her eagle eyes. I angled the hand with the towel behind my back, hoping the movement had been subtle enough to evade her.

"No one's gotten past that door in the thirty-two years I've lived here, Magnolia. That's not gonna change tonight."

I sucked in a breath, prepared to tiptoe around the questions I suspected were coming, but she simply returned to her room and shut the door behind her.

I hurried upstairs and slipped into my own room. After locking my door behind me, I plopped on the bed and loaded the gun, just like my father had taught me to do six months before his disappearance.

"I hope to God you'll never need this, Maggie Mae, but if you do . . ." His voice had broken then, but he'd forced a smile. "It's important you know how to use it."

He'd taken me to the gun range—without my mother's

knowledge—telling me it would be our special secret. I'd begged to go with him before, but Momma had always dug in her feet and said no, so he had no reason to worry. I didn't want to get into trouble any more than he did.

We had spent an hour shooting at outlined men on paper, only stopping when he was satisfied I could point the gun at someone and carry through with the threat, if need be, without killing myself or my little brother in the process.

When we went out to ice cream afterward, I asked him why he hadn't invited Roy to shoot with us. His mouth twisted as he considered my question, and he finally gave me a soft smile. "You and your brother are like night and day. You'll be the one to protect yourself and our family if it comes to that."

That made me laugh, and I insisted that Momma would never need protection.

"Don't be so sure," he said as he looked deep into my eyes. "I love you, Maggie Mae. No matter where I am, I'll always love you."

After Daddy disappeared, I told Momma I needed to get his gun. "Don't be ridiculous," she said in horror. "You'll shoot your foot off."

"Daddy told me I might need it."

Her horror turned to fear, and she grabbed my shoulders and gave me a little shake. "When did he say that?"

"Last winter."

"Did you tell anyone what he said?" she asked, lowering her voice.

"No, Momma."

"Not even Maddie?"

I shook my head. "Daddy told me it was our secret. I didn't tell anyone."

"Good. And it still is your secret. Don't tell a soul." When I started to protest, she added, "And no gun. No one's getting through the front door."

But tonight, as I held up the loaded gun and looked through the sight at my old poster of the Backstreet Boys, I wasn't so sure my mother was right.

While the steel of the front door had given me comfort as a child, the plastic and metal in my hand was my insurance now.

chapter
nine

I was running in the rain, my wet hair stuck to my face. Feet pounded the ground behind me.

   "Magnolia, you piece of shit, come back here!" Blake shouted.

The woods were dark and I struggled to see where I was going. I tripped on a branch and slid down a small embankment.

   "Magnolia!"

I'd lost my shoes and the bottom of my left foot throbbed after stepping on something sharp. I was totally out of shape, so it was no surprise I was out of breath from running. I wanted to stop and cry, but my mother's voice rang out in my head. "You're made of steel, Magnolia."

   I considered stopping and confronting him. What was the worst he could do? Would he really hurt me?

   "Magnolia," he called out, sounding breathless. "Come on. Can we just talk?" He paused. "I'm sorry, Maggie. Let's just go back."

   I stood behind a tree, my hand gripping the camera, right before I took a step.

   I jarred awake, my heart racing. Sitting up in bed, I turned on the lamp on my nightstand and grabbed my phone to check the time: 3:15. Pushing back the covers, I got out of bed and padded to the bathroom to fill a glass with water. I took a sip, then swiped the hair from my face with a shaky hand. This was the most I'd ever remembered at one time. Despite my earlier conviction, I wasn't sure I was ready to face the truth. What I'd remembered so far was fairly tame, but my instincts told me that I was just scratching the surface.

I was scared to go back to sleep, so I rummaged around my room and found one of my old romance novels before climbing back into bed. But I read the first page several times, unable to remember a single word. It was like that text from earlier was dancing in front of the words on the page.

I opened the bedside table drawer and pulled out the gun. Could I really shoot someone if it came down to it? I wasn't as sure of that now as I'd been at fourteen. But knowing I had it helped ease my fears. I put the gun back in the drawer and picked up the book. I read for several hours before I drifted off to sleep again.

This dream came in snatches.

A dark abandoned house. Blowing white curtains. A muffled scream.

A dark room and the smell of mold and dirt.

Blood. Lots of blood. And the cold vacant eyes of a lifeless woman.

I woke in a cold sweat, paralyzed with fear as sunlight filtered through the cracks in the blinds. The images were so achingly familiar, but how did I know what was real and what wasn't?

A sudden banging on the door made me jump, and I stifled a shriek.

"What are you doing in there, Magnolia?" my mother shouted. "You know the rule about locking doors in this house."

I stumbled out of bed, nearly falling on my face before I reached the door and then swung it open.

She was fully dressed in dark blue pants paired with a blue patterned blouse and low kitten heels. There was a long gold chain with beads around her neck. Putting her hands on her hips, she scowled. "I see you're still sleeping."

It took me a second to switch roles. There was no time to dwell on my fear. My mother expected me to be functional.

"And I see you're not. You're wearing *jewelry?*" I asked. I'd never seen her wear much more than her wedding rings, simple diamond studs, and sometimes a small chain around her neck.

Her mouth pursed in disapproval, but I wasn't the sole source of her disdain. "Tilly's doing. She thinks it makes me look more inviting to the clients." Her scowl deepened as she looked over my shoulder at the bed. "I told you that we needed to be at the office by nine."

"I know—"

"It's eight-thirty."

"Oh, shit."

"Magnolia."

"I could have sworn I set my alarm." I must have turned it off after waking up at three.

"We're leaving in fifteen minutes."

"I could stay here and work around the house. I saw a pile of laundry, and there was a dust bunny under the entryway table. I could have it all shiny by the time you get back home tonight."

"I've been too busy to give the house a good cleaning." She looked tempted, and on closer inspection, she also looked exhausted. She had to be exceptionally busy if her house had dust bunnies, but in the end she shook her head. "The house can wait. You're coming with me whether you like it or not. I'll take you in your pajamas if you're not ready, so get going."

After delivering this directive, she turned around and went back downstairs. I should have been pissed—seventeen-year-old Magnolia would have resented the hell out of receiving her marching orders, but twenty-eight-year-old Magnolia felt reassured by this sign that her mother cared. Momma didn't want to leave me alone. Whether it was because she worried I'd take off again or because she feared that I'd get arrested while she was at work, she wanted to keep me under her watchful eye.

Since I'd showered the night before, I only had to dress and do my hair and makeup. I had no idea what she wanted me to do besides file paperwork, so I chose a middle-of-the-road outfit with jeans, a lightweight cream sweater, and a pair of brown boots, topped off by my brown suede jacket. I pulled my hair into a ponytail and put on a little bit of makeup.

I opened the nightstand drawer and took a longing look at the gun. Part of me was tempted to bring it, but two things stopped me. One, in the light of day the boogeyman seemed a lot less scary, even after my dreams, and two, I didn't have a concealed carry permit. I sure as hell didn't need to be found with an illegal weapon if I were arrested for murder.

I made it downstairs with one minute to spare. Momma was already picking up a wicker basket full of Tupperware containers stuffed with different food.

"You have a kitchen at your fancy new store," I teased, taking the basket from her. "You could cook there."

She shot me a scowl. "I'm not senile. Tilly and the crew were busy in the kitchen yesterday. I used the kitchen at the house to prepare some sample dishes for the clients I'm meeting later today, which is why I was home when you got here yesterday."

She tried to take the basket from me, but I swung it out of the way.

"I'm perfectly capable of carrying that basket, Magnolia."

"I know, but I'm supposed to be earning my keep, remember?" I said, heading out onto the front porch. "How much is this worth? I'd say at least ten bucks. It's awful heavy."

I shot her a grin, and though she tried to hide her reaction, I saw her eyes light up with amusement.

"Why's your car out in the driveway? Why didn't you park in the garage? You wouldn't dream of leaving your car out before."

"Your brother's storing some things in there," she said as she unlocked the car with her key fob. "Put the basket in the backseat."

That surprised me. She hated junk piling up. Roy must have been desperate for her to agree.

I set the basket on the seat, but she kept giving it nervous little glances, so I pushed it into the middle and slid in beside it.

"How about I sit back here and make sure it doesn't fall off the seat?" I asked with a smile.

Surprise flickered in her eyes, but she nodded and slid into the driver's seat. A few minutes after she pulled out of the drive, she looked at me in the rearview mirror with a scowl. "You seem awfully chipper. You were always grumpy in the mornings."

Leave it to my mother to be cranky over me being in a good mood. "I still am, but it's an hour later here," I reasoned. "It's almost ten o'clock back home."

"I thought you said you didn't have a home."

"You know what I mean." I wasn't going to let her destroy my good mood, but she was right to question it. Why *was* I in a good mood? I was the lead suspect in a murder, and I was starting to remember the bad things from my past. Maybe it was a major case of denial. But then I realized the source of my content. It was my mother. I'd missed her more than I'd let myself admit, and I loved being back home with her. I would enjoy it for however long I got.

But Momma wasn't the only family I had here. "I was thinking about calling Roy."

She was quiet for so long I thought maybe she didn't hear me. "I don't think that's a good idea, Magnolia."

"Can he really hold a grudge for that long?"

"You Steeles are stubborn folk."

"You're a Steele too."

Momma shrugged. "I gained the name by marriage; the stubbornness is in y'all's blood."

"Well, Roy and I must have double-dipped because you're one of the most stubborn people I know. And I still want to call him."

Her mouth pursed. "I can't stop you."

"But you don't think he'll talk to me."

Her non-answer was answer enough.

My brother and I had never been close, but he'd become even more belligerent after our father's disappearance. The way I'd left town had only made things worse between us.

When we got to their headquarters, I carried the basket into the kitchen and set it down on a stainless steel table. Momma told me how to unpack it all, so I got to work and she headed upstairs to the office, telling me to join her there after I finished.

I put the containers away, making sure the heavy commercial refrigerator door was closed, and gave myself a quick tour. The kitchen had two forty-eight-inch ranges as well as several commercial ovens and dishwashers. Pride formed a lump in my throat. My mother and Tilly had come so far. I was sorry to have missed it all, especially since I'd been so integral to the beginning of their business.

I found the solid swinging door at the end of the room hard to resist, so I pushed through. To my surprise, there was a small sitting area on the other side. The walls were covered in photos of parties and catered events. The heavy fabric curtains, dark wood table and chairs, and white upholstered sofa gave the room a sophisticated look. Southern Belles Catering was painted on the windows in the same pretty script font I'd seen on the sides of their vans. There was a notice on the door that read, *By appointment only*, followed by a phone number.

I was impressed.

I wandered back through the kitchen, then headed out the back door and up a set of stairs similar to the ones leading to Emily's office. The space was similar to hers as well, only a little wider. Two desks were arranged on opposite ends, and there were papers and files everywhere. A television was mounted on the wall, tuned to a local news show. Tilly and Momma were both sitting behind their desks.

"The victim's name has just been released," a female news-caster said on the show. "Talent agent Max Goodwin was found dead during a party at the home of Luke Powell. Authorities are still investigating the events of the evening, and they say they have several persons of interest. There's no word yet on the cause of death, but authorities *are* calling it a homicide. We'll keep you updated with news as we hear it."

"That's good," Tilly said, her eyes glued to the screen. "They have several persons of interest, and they aren't naming anyone as a suspect."

Momma was looking down at the street, anywhere but at the screen, and she didn't answer.

"Well," I said, taking a couple of steps into the room, "I couldn't have been the only person who hated Max Goodwin. Hopefully they'll find out who actually killed him, and quick, so this isn't hanging over my head for long."

Tilly startled and clutched her chest as she spun to face me. "Oh, Mylanta, Magnolia Mae. You scared the daylights out of me."

"Sorry." I headed into the middle of the room, blocking Tilly's view of the television. "But what I said is true. I bet half the people at that party had a reason to kill Max Goodwin."

"Including your mother," Tilly said. "He insulted her cook-ing. It wouldn't surprise me one bit to learn she had something to do with it."

My mother scoffed. "If I was gonna kill him, I would have sharpened my carving knife first."

Tilly shot me an ornery grin. "How did he die, anyway?"

I shook my head. "I can't tell you."

"Oh, come on, Magnolia. It's not like I'm gonna tell anyone."

"You'll tell *everyone*. You're the world's biggest gossip. And seeing as how Luke Powell and I are the only ones who know, it will be traced right back to me. I'm already in a world of shit, so no. You'll just have to wait to hear it on the news."

"It couldn't have been a gun. You didn't have one."

Little did she know. "Tilly."

She grinned. "Well, you can't blame a girl for tryin'."

Momma released a huge sigh. "Magnolia's going to do some filing."

I picked up a file folder from one of the stacks and shook it at her. "I'm shocked you let this get so out of hand. You hate clutter."

Her mouth pursed as she looked at her computer screen. "We've been too busy."

"We just keep growing," Tilly said. "It's like we're exploding with business. We have to keep hiring kitchen help and wait staff. We can't keep up."

"I guess that's a good problem to have." I flipped the file open, revealing a mess of receipts and an invoice for a party. "You can digitize these, you know," I said. "You can set up spreadsheets and scan all of the receipts."

My mother looked up at me like I'd suggested she join a cult. "There's nothing wrong with the way we do things."

"If you enter them into a computer, they'll be easy to find, and if you save them in a cloud, you can access them anywhere."

The phone began to ring.

"A cloud?" Tilly said. "Now that's a good one. What would you do, shred them into tiny pieces and send them up into the air?"

"No, Tilly. A *digital* cloud."

Tilly picked up the receiver. "Southern Belles Catering."

"We're not using a digital cloud or a rain puddle or even a damn snow storm," Momma fumed. "There's absolutely nothing wrong with our system."

"Except the fact that you have documents lying around everywhere." I cast a glance at Tilly to gauge her reaction, but she was deep in a conversation about what services Southern Belles Catering offered.

Momma took off her reading glasses and arched her eyebrows. "Either start filing or find another job to pay your rent."

I gritted my teeth and faked a smile. "Where would you like me to file them?"

She set the glasses back onto her nose and returned her attention to her screen. "Good choice. We have cabinets in the basement. You can take the older ones in that cabinet—" she pointed to a tall black metal stack of drawers, "—and file them in the basement. Then file the new ones up here."

"This is going to take a while," I grumbled, my good mood quickly evaporating.

"Good thing you've got plenty of time," she said with some sass.

"I'm going to check out the basement first." I headed for the door, but Momma called after me.

"Don't forget the key," she said, pointing to a key hook. "The door's outside."

How had I not noticed that? I hesitated. "Can I get Roy's number so I can call him?"

My mother released a labored sigh. "Magnolia. If you really want to talk to him, then let me arrange it."

"Why can't I just call him?"

"Because you'll beat your head bloody trying to get through to him." But she grabbed a small piece of paper and scribbled on it, then handed it to me. "This is his cell number. Don't say I didn't warn you."

I snatched the paper from her, then snagged a lanyard from the hook and tromped down the stairs and out the back door. She hadn't told me which door led to the basement, but it wasn't hard to figure out.

But first I dug out my cell phone. I couldn't decide whether to call my brother or text him, but then settled on the element of surprise. Pressing my back against the building, I dialed his number. The phone rang multiple times before it went to voice mail, which was probably for the best.

"Hey, Roy. This is Magnolia. I just wanted to let you know I'm back in Franklin, although I'm not sure for how long. But I'd love to see you and maybe work things out, so call me back. I guess you have my number now . . . I'm sorry we don't talk, and I want to change that. Bye."

I hung up and tilted back my head, closing my eyes. Wow. That had sounded intelligent.

Time to get to work.

The door opened to a set of dark concrete stairs. I hesitated, frozen in terror.

I'd always struggled with small, dark places since I'd left home, but something about this felt too familiar.

I was going to do this. I *had* to do this. How could I explain to my mother and Tilly that I was afraid to go in their basement?

I would feel better as soon as I found the light switch. I propped the door open with a brick, which was probably kept there for that very purpose, then eased my way down, sucking in a breath to keep my anxiety at bay. Not that it helped. A cold sweat broke out on my neck and my hairline.

Finally, I spotted a string dangling from the ceiling several feet away. I tugged on it, turning on a single light bulb.

My anxiety only increased.

Part of my brain screamed for me to run up the stairs, but my body refused to cooperate. My chest was heaving, sucking in air and puffing it out so quickly my face was numb.

Calm down, Magnolia. It's a goddamned light bulb.

It took a good five minutes for me to calm down enough not to feel close to passing out and another five until I could actually focus on my environment. Sure enough, two filing cabinets hulked in the corner. I recognized one of them from home. It had been my father's business file cabinet.

I walked over and opened several empty drawers before finding one with a few files. The bulb made for a fairly dim light source though, and I had a hard time reading the tabs. Did they sort things by chronological or alphabetical order?

"What are you doing down here?" a man asked behind me.

I screamed and dropped the key onto the concrete floor, then spun around to see a dark figure in front of me, perfectly framed by the door behind him. I took a step back, bumping into the cabinet.

"Maggie Mae. It's me. Colt." He stepped to one side, moving into a pocket of light, and I could finally make out his features.

I bent over my knees, gasping for breath as I waited for my heart to slow down. *Don't pass out. Don't pass out.*

"What the hell are you doing sneaking up on me like that?" I finally huffed out.

"I wasn't sneaking up on you. I saw the open door and decided to check it out." He knelt and picked up my dropped key.

"What are you doing here?"

A smart-ass grin spread across his face. "I work here, remember?"

"I didn't think Momma and Tilly had an event today."

"They don't, but Tilly asked me to help her pick up supplies at Costco."

"Shouldn't you be singing or writing songs or something?"

He laughed as he handed me the lanyard. "Unfortunately neither one of those pays the bills right now. But I'm playing tonight if you want to come check me out."

"I already told you—"

"Yeah, I know. You don't want a boyfriend." He winked. "But I have several other friends coming, and none of them plan to sleep with me either."

"I don't know," I said, my voice trailing off. "I just got back. And I'm a suspect in a murder. I don't think I should be hanging out in bars."

"You're a person of interest." When I opened my mouth to ask him how he knew, he added, "I watched the news this morning." He grinned again. "Which I never do. Did you know that a church in Nashville has opened up part of their land for homeless people to live on? They've got these little bitty houses for them."

Since his question seemed rhetorical, I didn't answer.

He shrugged. "Turns out you learn all kinds of things watching the news. And you should come. You can't let the po-po keep you from living your life."

I lifted my eyebrows. "The po-po?"

He held out his hands. "I've been trying some gangsta words in my lyrics. Too much?"

"Um . . . yeah. I still think I'll stay home tonight—if nothing else, for my mother's sake. But thanks for the invite. Maybe another time."

He pointed his finger at me. "I'm going to hold you to that, Maggie Mae."

"Sure," I said, eager to drop the subject. Going out in public with a large crowd sounded like a dangerous proposition right now.

Colt followed me up the stairs to the office, and then he and Tilly left on their errand. I spent the next couple hours hauling files to the basement, and each time I descended the staircase, it took me a little less time to recover. After much debate with my mother, I convinced her to file them alphabetically.

"If they were digitized files, you could find them either way," I suggested on one of my trips upstairs. "They could be both alphabetical and chronological."

"Shut up, Magnolia," Momma grumbled.

My stomach let out a noise of protest, and it suddenly occurred to me I hadn't eaten in hours, probably since the previous afternoon. "Do you have anything to eat here?"

"No."

"But you have all those containers we brought."

My mother's eyes narrowed. "You touch those and you're dead."

"You have a massive kitchen and nothing to eat. There's something so wrong about that."

Momma grabbed her wallet out of her purse and pulled out some cash. "Go to the café across from the police station and get us some lunch."

"I'd rather stay as far away from the police station as possible."

She pushed out an exasperated groan. "Fine. There's a deli down the street. Toward the roundabout. You can pick up something there." She gave me her order, and moments later I was out the door.

Walking on the Main Street sidewalk brought back a rush of warm memories, all of them now tinged with regret. Maddie and I used to spend hours here, hanging out at the Starbucks at the opposite end of the street, going shopping, seeing a movie at the old theater. I was glad to see it was still open. There'd been rumors it was about to close, but now they had musical shows too.

I wondered what Maddie was doing now. It had been years since I'd tried to reach out to her. Would she talk to me if I called her? I was scared to try, but I needed to talk to her now more than ever as my memories were coming back. With my latest memories of Blake, I needed to know she was okay.

The deli was only a block away, but I had to wait in line once I got there. I spent my time Googling my name on my smart phone. Yesterday, the articles about my New York failure had embarrassed me and made me want to hide in a cave—or my childhood bedroom. Today, I was just happy there was nothing about me being implicated in a murder. Oh, what a difference a day made.

I finally made it to the counter and placed my order—giving them the name Maggie instead of Magnolia for a bit of anonymity, then stood aside and continued my search while I waited for them to call my name. I was reading Griff's apology to the theatre world on my behalf when a text popped up on the screen.

I'm going to kill you, Magnolia.

"Maggie," the server who had taken my order called out.

My heart slammed into my chest, and I took a deep breath, telling myself not to freak out as the text disappeared from the screen.

"Maggie!" The woman behind the counter said it more insistently this time, looking right at me. I rushed forward to grab the bag, but I bumped into someone and stumbled backward.

He grabbed my arm to hold me upright. "Are you okay?"

I nodded, staring into his warm brown eyes. He looked to be about my age, with dark brown hair and the kind of heavy stubble that's a precursor to a beard. I was still trying to calm down when my phone vibrated in my hand, alerting me to a new text. My head felt fuzzy. I should never have come back.

"You don't look okay," the man said, tugging me toward a table. "Why don't you sit down?"

Oh, God. The last thing I needed was to make a spectacle of myself. "I'm okay, really. I just got a little dizzy. I'll feel better as soon as I get some air."

"*Maggie!*" The woman behind the counter glared at me and hoisted up the bag.

The man grabbed the bag, holding it with his own order, then cupped my elbow with his free hand to lead me outside. But I was already starting to come to my senses, and the last thing I wanted was to be saddled with a stranger. I needed to see if the new text was another threat.

"I'm fine," I said, snatching the bag from him as he followed me out to the sidewalk. "Thank you for your help."

"Are you driving?" he asked, sounding concerned.

"No," I snapped. "Not that it's any of your business."

His back straightened. "It's my business if you aren't coherent enough to get behind the wheel of a car."

He was right, yet the way he announced it, as if he were King Solomon making a royal decree, got under my skin. Of course it didn't help that I was on edge. I was ready to go off on someone, and this poor man was it.

"I resent the insinuation," I sneered, putting a hand on my hip. "I would never knowingly endanger anyone."

"Why would you think I'm insinuating anything?" he asked in exasperation. "I don't even know you."

"That's right!" I poked my finger into his solid chest. If I weren't so angry, I would have stopped to appreciate it. "You don't know me, so what gives you the right to assume the worst of me?" I poked him again for good measure. "I'm a good person, dammit!"

People on the sidewalk were now openly gawking at us.

"Look," he said, grabbing my hand in his. "If you *had* driven, I was going to offer to either sit with you until you felt ready to drive or call someone to come get you. That's it."

Well, shit. I snatched my hand away and took a step backward. "I walked." I lifted my chin in an attempt to recover my fading indignation. "And I'm only walking a block, so there's little chance of me taking out a bunch of pedestrians with my takeout bag."

The corners of his mouth twitched a little, like he was fighting a grin. "Maggie, I'm sorry. I didn't mean to insult you."

I gasped. "How do you know my name?"

His amusement faded in an instant. "From your bag. And because the woman at the counter kept calling out Maggie and staring right at you."

"Oh," I mumbled, backing up against the brick wall.

"This isn't a normal reaction to a stranger knowing your name. Why are you so frightened?"

"Who made you an expert on people's reactions—"

I looked at the bag in his hand and added, "*Brady?*" What kind of name was Brady? He had to be another country music star wannabe. It fit his image—his solid chest, his ruffled hair, and that scruffy beard that looked downright sexy. And his voice . . . firm and authoritative. He could get on stage and command an audience to pay attention. I was surprised he hadn't signed with someone yet, but then again, maybe he had.

He studied me for several seconds, long enough for me to decide I needed to get the hell away from him. I knew people—I'd spent the past ten years studying them, first for survival and then for my acting—and I could tell this man was far too observant.

He started to speak, but I held up a hand and waved it in front of his face. "You know what? Strike the question. I don't want to know." Then I spun around and started down the street. "Thanks for your concern."

"Maggie."

He sounded so insistent that I found myself turning around to face him despite myself. Damn his voice. I put my hands on my hips and pressed my lips into a tight line.

"*What?*"

He looked confused, as if he couldn't figure out whether he

should run away or come after me, but ultimately he just ran his hand through his thick brown hair, making it look even more ruffled and sexy than before.

Damn it. Run, Magnolia.

He shook his head and gave me an ornery grin. "Don't mow anyone over with that bag of yours."

I rolled my eyes dramatically and then spun around again and headed toward Momma's shop. Once I'd made it to the corner, I snuggled up against the building and looked at my phone screen to read the second text.

Call me!!!!

It was from Jody, my friend and former roommate in New York. And so was the text that had arrived immediately before it —the one I'd taken to be a threat. I pressed my back against the wall, leaning my head back and closing my eyes, and reveled in the feeling of relief.

I pulled her number up on speed dial, then started walking again.

"What the hell is going on, Maggie?" Jody screamed into my ear as soon as she answered. "Why didn't you call me?"

"What were you going to do? You're in Philadelphia."

"Cincinnati, but who can tell?" Two months ago, Jody had gotten the part of Nessa in a traveling tour of *Wicked*. She was now touring the country, but she rarely stayed in one place for long enough to do much sight-seeing. "And that's beside the point, Magnolia Steele. This is huge. You should have called me!"

"I couldn't tell you, Jody. I was too embarrassed and horrified."

"I can't believe that asshole was cheating on you." She paused. "Wait a minute. I *do* believe it, but I can't believe he did the rest of it. And Sarah—*that bitch.* She'll never be as good in that role. *Fireflies at Dawn* is doomed to fail if she's the lead."

"That's not even my biggest problem at the moment," I said.

"You mean Griff kicking you out? Where are you staying? Don't tell me you went to Miranda's."

"I went home."

"Home? You got our apartment back?"

"No, *home* home."

"Oh, my God. You went back to Tennessee?"

"Yeah."

We were both silent for a moment before she said, "Wow." Jody had no idea why I'd left Franklin, but she did know I hadn't been back since.

I needed to tell her the rest. Well, selectively. "Do you remember Max Goodwin and our unfortunate meeting a couple of years ago?"

She giggled. "Are you kidding? I'll still remember that when I'm eighty-five and have forgotten all of my grandkids' names."

"Well, long story short, he and I were both at Luke Powell's party last night, and we had a very public disagreement."

"Oh, my God! You were invited to a party at Luke Powell's?"

"That's not the important part. About an hour or so after our disagreement, Max Goodwin was found dead. And I was the one who found him."

"Wait. *What?* Max Goodwin's dead?"

"Yes, and I'm a person of interest in his murder."

"Oh, my God, Magnolia!" She was silent for a moment. "What are you going to do?"

"My mother hired an attorney, but do you remember me telling you about my high school nemesis?"

"Yeah, Emma, right? And do people really have nemeses? Isn't that just for superheroes?"

"*Emily*, and call it whatever you like. She hated my guts for stealing Tanner, and she still holds a grudge. And now she's my attorney."

"That was like fifteen years ago."

"*Twelve*," I corrected. No sense adding to my age.

"Why would you use someone who hates you?"

"I'm completely broke after giving Griff all my money, and besides, my mom's the one who hired her. Jody, it's like Emily's pulled a *Single White Female* and tried to slip into my old life. She and my mom are thick as thieves, and she claims she's BFFs with Maddie, my old best friend."

"Is she with Tanner?"

"No, he's engaged to some super thin, tall, blonde bimbo. They were at the party too."

"So what are you going to do?"

"I don't know. I don't trust Emily Johnson to defend me, even if she did insist she hates to lose. While I can attest that's true, her hatred of me might trump that."

"I can't believe she would hold a stupid grudge over a boy . . . Oh wait. I've seen his photos online. Never mind. I do."

"What do you mean you've seen his photos online?"

She hesitated. "I may have Facebook stalked him."

"Oh, my God, Jody."

"I was curious. Sue me. He's a hottie. And Maddie is cute too."

I stopped walking so abruptly that someone ran into my back. Jody was proof that Emily wasn't the only person who'd been digging into my past. Would the police? Had Blake been following me through social media? That text message was an indication that someone was watching me now, whether it was him or someone else.

Why in God's name had I let Miranda, my second roommate who had taken me to the first audition for my first commercial, convince me that my name was too perfect, too memorable to change for a stage name?

I pressed a hand to my forehead, struggling to catch my breath. Then I noticed Brady was standing directly across the street from me, staring right at me.

The blood rushed from my head, and I felt like I was about

to faint. Why was he following me? What if he'd been in that deli because he was keeping tabs on me? Who was he with? The police or someone connected to my past?

"Jody. I've gotta go."

"Wait! What about—?"

But I'd already hung up my phone and stuffed it into my pocket. Brady was still standing there, staring at me just as blatantly as he had been moments before.

Lucky for me—or not, depending on the outcome—I had enough piss and vinegar flowing through my veins to confront this issue head on. Keeping my eyes on his, I started to walk across the street, not paying one bit of attention to the traffic. A car screeched to a halt inches away from me. Brady's eyes flew wide with fear, but anger trumped my regard for my personal safety. I continued to march the rest of the way across the road, ignoring the blaring horns.

I stopped in front of him and gave his solid chest a shove, but damn him, he didn't even budge. "Why are you following me?"

He blinked, looking like he was trying to figure out what was going on. "I'm *not* following you."

"That's bullshit and we both know it!" I tried to shove him again.

Good God. Were his pecs made of granite? *Focus*, Magnolia.

People were openly staring at us, watching our exchange— or more accurately, my assault on his chest.

"Maggie, I was walking this way," he said in a comforting tone. "I'm on my way to the outfitter store." He pointed down the street.

"Why were you staring at me?"

"Because you worried me outside the deli, and when I saw you stop in your tracks, I watched you to make sure you were okay. You didn't look okay, and I was trying to decide whether to come check on you." It all sounded so reasonable, and his voice was like warm honey, sinking through my skin and setting me at ease.

And that scared the shit out of me.

I dropped my hands and took two steps back, then turned to the small crowd that had gathered around us. "Nothing to see here. Go on about your business."

They started to disperse, giving us backward glances, and I was sure I heard one woman whisper to her friend, "Isn't that her?"

If Brady heard her, he didn't let on. But he might be storing the information, filing it away for a later analysis. He was the epitome of a strong, comforting man. Just the kind of persona a man would try to use to get close to a woman and dig up her secrets.

"Maggie, what's going on? What has you this scared?"

"Who said I was scared?"

"Both times you looked like you were about to pass out."

For once I had no witty retort. Damn his sexy voice. I was immune to men's wiles, so why was this one affecting me?

"Are you in trouble?" he asked, taking my silence as a good sign.

I released a sharp laugh and turned away from him. "You could say that."

"Do you have someone to talk to?" When I didn't respond, he said, "I have a friend at Bridges. I can call her and have her meet you somewhere to talk."

I turned to him in shock. "Bridges Domestic Violence Center?"

He thought I was a victim of domestic violence? It meant he wasn't a threat. He was a genuinely nice guy performing his duty to help a woman in distress. This probably wouldn't have happened on a New York City sidewalk.

To my shock, tears stung my eyes, but I blinked them back

and shook my head. "No, it's nothing like that. I'm fine. I promise."

He didn't look entirely convinced. He reached into his bag and pulled out a receipt, then grabbed a pen out of his jacket pocket and scribbled on the back of the slip. "You already know my name is Brady, and this is my cell number. If you ever need help—even if you just need someone to talk to—call me."

I shook my head in disbelief. "Why would you do that?"

A lopsided grin lifted his mouth. "Call me a sucker for a damsel in distress."

The title rankled. I'd spent the last ten years fending for myself. I didn't need some man to ride in on a white horse and save me.

But his voice . . . it was like a siren song that said *trust me*. And damned if I didn't . . . or at least as much as I was capable of trusting anyone. I took the paper and stuffed it into my pocket. "Thanks."

He nodded toward me. "Put it into your phone."

"What? I will later." Although I hadn't really planned to do it at all.

"You'll lose it. Put it in now."

I put my hand on my hip. "Are you always so bossy?"

His grin lit up his eyes. "My parents call it stubborn. My brother calls it pigheaded. And my sister calls it demanding, but you can call it bossy if you'd like. I just know you won't have time to dig a piece of paper out of the trash if you're in trouble. You need to have it handy."

"Who says I'll find myself in trouble?"

"Call it a hunch. So do it now, and I'll let you go on about your day."

Releasing an exaggerated sigh, I dug out my phone. As I programmed the number into my contacts, I told myself I could always delete it later. When I was finished, I showed him the screen. "Happy now?"

"Believe it or not, yes." Still he didn't make a move to leave. "Do you work down here? I haven't seen you before."

This told me two things. One, he either worked in this part of town or spent a lot of time here, and two, he paid attention to the people who came and went. My guard was back up.

"Thanks for your concern, Brady. I've got to take my mother her lunch. She's already going to be pissed her sandwich is cold."

I might as well have told him exactly who I was and where I "worked." I had no doubt whatsoever he was going to pay attention to where I went anyway, but there was no reason to make it easy for him. Without another word, I spun around. This time I was more careful about crossing the street. When I gave one last look behind me, Brady was standing at the corner watching me. But instead of looking guilty, he gave me a half wave.

And damned if a flush of heat didn't wash through me.

Crap on a cracker. I didn't have time for a man in my life.

Too bad my body didn't agree.

chapter ten

T he afternoon went quickly as I continued to work on the filing system, although it was easy to see that this job would only last me another day, tops. I couldn't imagine what else Momma had planned for me. I sure as hell hoped it didn't include sending me back out as wait staff, but I could think of a few alternative jobs that would be worse. When I was a teenager, she used to make me scrub tile grout with a toothbrush. If I were going to stick around, maybe I should start looking for a job.

Momma's appointment was at 2:00, so she went downstairs at 1:30 to start preparing the food. I sucked in a breath as I hauled yet another stack of files to the basement. Descending the basement stairs was easier when I realized Colt was already down there, hunched over a large rectangular box.

"What are you up to?" I asked as I set the files down, trying not to spill the contents.

"I convinced Tilly that you needed more light down here. Working in such dim conditions is bound to give you wrinkles from squinting."

My hand flew up to the corner of my eye.

He laughed. "I knew that would get you." I shot him a glare, but he only laughed harder. "Lucky for you, Maggie Mae, I got you a floor lamp you can move next to the cabinet." He lifted a light with three large bulbs out of the box, then looked around the dark cellar. "Now I just need to find an outlet."

I put my hands on my hips. "I'm not sleeping with you."

He glanced back at me, surprise on his face. "I know. You already told me that last night."

"Then why are you doing this?" I gestured to the floor lamp.

He slowly turned to face me, shaking his head. "New York must have really warped your mind. A guy can be nice to a woman without wanting to get her into bed."

"So you *don't* want to sleep with me?"

A slow grin spread across his face. "No reason to go that far." His eyes twinkled. "But let's say I'm content just being friends."

"For now."

"That's not in dispute, but I get the impression you think I mean to trick you into bed." He moved toward me until he was standing just inches away, then reached up to gently tuck a strand of hair behind my ear. "I'm not sure what you're used to up in the big city, Maggie Mae, but we're gentlemen here. When you go to bed with me, you'll be more than willing. No regrets."

Griff had been a charmer, but deep down I'd always known what he was. Colt's motives were less clear. Even if he were entirely pure of heart, I wasn't ready to start anything with anyone. But his easygoing nature and ridiculous good looks could wear down a saint or a nun, and I was neither.

I took a step back and gave him a haughty look. "While I love a guy with confidence, I'm not too fond of men who are cocky."

He burst out laughing. "If I weren't a gentleman, I would make a crude remark to that. Lucky for you, I am." He winked, then bent over and plugged in the cord. The bright light temporarily blinded me, but the area around the cabinet was still swathed in shadows.

I froze in place, terror washing over me as I stared at the sharp juncture of shadow and light, reminded of something I couldn't remember.

"I'll dig up an extension cord somewhere," he said, moving closer. "That should help. Hey, you're shaking like a leaf. Are you cold?"

He put his hand on my arm, and I jumped away from him, wrapping my arms across my chest.

He held up his hands in surrender, worry wrinkling his brow. "Easy now. I didn't mean to startle you."

"You didn't," I said a little too defensively.

Slowly lowering his hands, he gave me a grudging smile. "Yeah, I can see that."

I hugged myself tighter. "You were right. I am cold."

After studying me for a few seconds, he pointed over his shoulder toward the stairs. "How about I get your jacket when I go up?"

It was on my lips to tell him it wasn't necessary, but I offered him a smile instead. "No need. I'm about to head up and get more files anyway."

He nodded, then started for the stairs.

"Colt," I blurted out.

He stopped and glanced over his shoulder. "Yeah?"

"Thanks for the lamp. And . . . well . . . for everything, I guess. Thanks for being my friend. I don't have very many left."

"Give it time, Maggie Mae. The people from your past will be greeting you soon enough." He trudged up the stairs, his shoes clomping on the wooden steps, while my heartbeat kicked into overdrive.

What had he meant by that?

But then I admonished myself for being so suspicious. He was talking about my old friends, of course, but he had no idea how many bridges I'd burned. How many people I'd hurt. They wouldn't welcome me back with open arms.

When I headed back upstairs a few minutes later, my mother was in the kitchen talking to a young woman dressed in a pencil skirt and cardigan. With her Peter Pan collar, she looked straight out of an old movie. Her shoulder-length, strawberry-blonde bob and wide-eyed innocence only added to the effect.

Assuming she was my mother's appointment, I took a step toward the stairs leading to the office, but the woman's gaze landed on me, and my mother's soon followed.

The young woman gasped. "Magnolia?"

I froze in place and then forced myself to turn and face her. Once again I found myself at a disadvantage. I couldn't place her, but there was something in her eyes that looked familiar.

"Lila," the woman gushed, pressing her fingertips to her chest. "Why didn't you tell me she was here?"

My mother had the good sense to look embarrassed. "She just got home last night, and she's been filing down in the basement." Then she beckoned me forward. "Magnolia, come on over here."

After fighting my nerves for hours in the basement, I didn't feel up to sparring with someone from the past. It was best to just get the hell out of there.

"Oh," I looked down at my now-dusty clothes. "I'd hate to interrupt your meeting. I'll head upstairs."

Momma's eyebrows lifted. "This isn't my client. This is Roy's wife, Belinda."

The young woman gave me a warm smile. "Magnolia, I am so happy to finally meet you."

Now I recognized her—from the photo on the staircase wall, not to mention my Facebook stalking. I'd looked her up after my mother unceremoniously informed me my brother had gotten married. It had stung not to be invited to the wedding, but as my mother had so bluntly pointed out, I wouldn't have gone anyway.

That didn't mean I wouldn't have liked to have been asked.

But Belinda had drastically cut her hair since their wedding, making her look younger and more innocent.

I took several hesitant steps toward them. "Nice to meet you, Belinda. I'm sorry I only sent a gift card for a wedding gift. I called Roy to ask him what you wanted and offer my congratulations, but he didn't get back to me." Not that I'd expected him to—he'd refused to talk to me for years. But his marriage had seemed like the right time to reach out to him, especially since I couldn't remember the last time we'd spoken. I was pretty sure it was when Momma had dragged him to New York with her on her first visit eight years ago.

Belinda didn't seem concerned in the least. Her smile didn't even waver. "Roy's the worst with communication," she said, waving a hand in dismissal. "Why, just yesterday I found out his secretary had a baby *three months ago*. He'd never even told me that she was pregnant!" She laughed, a perky sound that I would have sworn was fake had she not looked so completely genuine. She circled around the stainless steel table and pulled me into a tight hug. "I'm so glad you're back." She leaned back and looked me in the eyes. "We're going to be the best of friends. I just know it."

My mother was giving me a warning look, but she didn't need to be concerned. I wasn't going to mock Belinda or whatever else she was imagining. While my new sister-in-law was coming on a little strong, I found myself intrigued. Could someone really be that nice? "I'm looking forward to getting to know you better."

"Really?" she asked, sounding shocked.

"Of course."

"Then come to Bunco with me tonight."

"Excuse me?" I asked, blinking. "Do what?"

"It's Bunco night. I think my friend Sylvia is hosting. I know she won't mind. Especially since you're a Broadway star."

I grimaced. "Oh . . . I'm not sure that's a good idea."

"It's a brilliant idea. Do you have plans?" She turned to Momma. "Does she have plans?"

I gave my mother a look that begged for mercy, but she grinned. "It just so happens she's free." Then she had the audacity to flash me a huge smile.

"Perfect!" Belinda gushed, clutching her hands together. "I'll pick you up at around 6:45. What kind of refreshments do they have at Bunco night in New York City?"

"I can honestly say I've never been to a Bunco night in either New York or anywhere else." I was pretty sure my mother's Bunco nights when I was a teen didn't count since I wasn't supposed to be there.

"They don't have Bunco in New York?" She sounded dismayed. "Imagine that." Then a grin brightened her face. "Not to worry. We'll have you up to speed in no time." Then she leaned closer. There was a conspiratorial gleam in her eyes as she said, "But some months we never even get around to playing."

"Like how they never read the book in some people's book clubs?" I asked.

Her eyes widened. "Oh, no. We *always* read the book at book club."

My mother rolled her eyes behind poor Belinda's back. "I think Momma might have something planned for me tonight." I looked at her, plastering on a huge fake smile that said *please, please, please.* "Weren't we going to scrapbook?"

My mother cringed milliseconds before Belinda squealed. "I love scrapbooking. Promise me you won't scrapbook until I can do it with you." Then she gave me the biggest exaggerated pout I'd ever seen, and I'd seen plenty to authoritatively judge.

"Uh . . ." I said. Hell, I didn't even know if Momma still scrapbooked. That had been my last-ditch effort for an out.

"But if you wait for me, that means you're free to come with me tonight after all." She wrapped her arm around my bicep and squeezed, pulling me tight. "I am so excited. I've always wanted a sister, and now I have one for real."

If she was so excited to be my new sister, I had to wonder why she hadn't reached out to me sooner herself. "Uh, thanks."

My mother must have taken pity after throwing me into the Bunco lion's den. "Magnolia. I really need you to take care of that file on my office chair." Her eyes widened as she nodded to get her point across.

"Okay."

Belinda gave me another pout. "Oh! I was hoping you'd be here for our meeting with the Morrisons."

Belinda was going to be there? Was she part of Momma's catering business? I couldn't imagine my mother dealing with my new sister-in-law for more than hourly chunks. She had never been a fan of perkiness.

"Magnolia smells of dust and mold," Momma said. "She should probably be more presentable before meeting one of your clients." When I lifted an eyebrow, Momma volunteered, "Belinda is a wedding planner. Her clients are using our catering services for their reception. In fact, she helped us get the party last night. Amy is Belinda's friend."

That made more sense, and Belinda seemed perfect for that profession. But from the way Belinda was currently behaving, it was obvious she hadn't heard about the disastrous end to the party.

I expected Belinda to ask how the evening went, but she moved past it, her mouth twisting. "You're probably right about Magnolia skipping the meeting, but now that she's here, I'm just so excited to show her off." She grabbed my shoulders and looked me up and down. "You are even prettier than you look in those pictures online."

I sucked in a breath, the blood rushing all the way down to my toes, before my mother said, "Your photos on that Broadway website. Belinda checks it regularly for updates."

"Oh," I murmured, trying to catch my breath. How many shocks could a person suffer without experiencing permanent heart damage?

I was starting for the stairs when I felt my phone ring in my pocket. I pulled it out and frowned when I saw the number. I didn't recognize it, but the 615 area code marked it as a local call. "Hello."

"Magnolia Steele?" a man asked in a brisk tone.

"Yes."

"This is Detective Holden with the Franklin Police Department. We met last night. We'd like you to come down to the station for questioning at your earliest convenience."

I suspected that last part was a flat-out lie, because no time would ever be convenient, yet I knew I had no choice. I took a breath to steady my nerves, but I still sounded shaky when I spoke. "I need to contact my attorney, Emily Johnson."

"I'll expect to see you *soon*." Then he hung up. So much for my earliest convenience.

The look on my face must have worried my mother, because she excused herself from Belinda and came over.

"Was that the police?" she whispered.

I nodded, the phone shaking in my hand. "They want me to come in for questioning."

She looked me over and then pulled out her phone and called Emily. The conversation was short and concise—my mother's usual way of handling things—and when she hung up, she put her hand on my arm. "Start walking. Emily will meet you outside her office."

"Is everything okay?" Belinda called out. "Are you and Emily going out to coffee? I would totally invite myself along if I weren't meeting my clients."

Based on her hyperactivity, I suspected Belinda had already mainlined several shots of espresso before showing up. Coffee was the last thing she needed . . . except for going to the police station with her sister-in-law.

"Maybe next time," I heard myself say.

My mother looked into my eyes. I could tell she was weighing the possibility of blowing off her appointment to go to the police station with me, but that was the very last place she needed to be.

I gave her a soft smile. "I'm fine. Really. I'm going to run up to grab my purse in case I need it. I'll call you as soon as I'm done." Then I added, "One way or the other."

If I was arrested, Momma was the only person I knew who would come bail me out.

A few minutes later, I was pacing the sidewalk in front of Emily's office. I kept glancing around to see if Brady was lurking somewhere, but the most threatening presence in the vicinity was an older man who looked like he needed some major dental work.

"You ready?" Emily asked from behind me.

I let out a little screech as I turned around to face her. "Don't sneak up on me like that!"

"I wasn't sneaking," she said, raising her palms toward me. "You're just extra jumpy."

"How calm would you be if you were going to the police station to give a statement to cops who assumed you were guilty?"

"I *am* going to the police station, and I'm a nervous wreck."

"That is not helping," I snapped. "You're supposed to be the professional. You're supposed to know what you're doing."

"Sorry," she said in a snotty tone. "I've never defended someone accused of murder before."

I stopped in my tracks. "*What?*"

"It's not like we have a ton of murders around here."

She kept walking, and I hurried to follow her. "Have you ever defended anyone for *anything* before?"

"Of course I have. Don't be daft."

"Well . . . ?"

"Well what?"

"What *have* you defended?"

She blushed. "A drunk and disorderly and a trespassing case."

I stopped again. "Are you kidding me?"

Emily spun around to face me. "I can do this, Magnolia."

I felt so lightheaded my vision started to fade and turn to black.

Emily dragged me toward a bench and forced me to sit.

"Oh, God. Oh, God," I chanted over and over, rocking back and forth. "I'm going to jail."

"You're not going to jail. Just take a deep breath, and we'll go answer Holden's questions. This mess will be over before you know it."

I stopped rocking and looked up at her. "Do you really think so?"

She sat down next to me and lowered her voice. "You didn't touch the letter opener, right?"

"Right."

"Based on what you've told me, it has to be the murder weapon. And if you didn't touch it, your fingerprints won't be on it."

I nodded. "Yeah."

"We can get Luke Powell to say he asked you to meet him in his office. We can get the bartender to state that you were talking to him at 9:40 and he saw Luke go down that hall minutes later."

I held my breath. "How do you know that Colt saw him? I never told you that. In fact, I have no idea if he saw him or not."

Her shoulders tensed. "It only makes sense, Magnolia. Do you want out of this or not?"

"Of course I do."

"Then let's go and tell your side of the story."

"But shouldn't we corroborate this with Colt first?"

"I don't see the point, but if it makes you feel better." But she didn't wait for me, and the clack of her heels grew fainter as she hustled down the sidewalk.

I started to send Colt a text, then changed my mind. I'd see what the police had to say first. Besides, his alibi would put me in that room minutes after the murder, not hours. It might not even help.

By the time we checked in with the police receptionist, I was already wondering if I'd made the right decision.

They led us to a room arranged with a table and four chairs, two on either side. My nerves were getting the better of me as I sat down.

"Calm down, Magnolia," Emily snarled. "You look guilty as hell."

"How am I supposed to calm down when they think I did it? I've seen all those TV shows. If they think I did it, they can make sure I go away for life."

"I'm sure the Franklin Police Department wants the real murderer put behind bars, don't you?"

"While I sure as hell hope so, I'm not counting on it."

She pursed her lips. "You always were a glass-half-empty person back in school."

"I was not!" I protested. "And now does *not* seem like the time to—" I cut myself off as the door creaked open and Detective Holden entered the room.

"Is there a problem, Ms. Steele?"

"No," I choked out. "My attorney and I were having a disagreement."

He looked back and forth between us, then sat down across

from me with a pad of paper and a pen. Then he took a breath so deep I was sure he was about to suck all the air out of the room. "Now, Ms. Steele. All we want is the facts. You already gave us a statement about finding Mr. Goodwin, but I have a few more questions."

I couldn't help wondering where his partner was. Probably on the other side of the mirrored wall taking notes.

"Okay," I said, clutching my hands in my lap.

"You said that you found Mr. Goodwin splayed out on the floor when you entered the room—is that correct?"

I nodded. "Yes."

"You said you then knelt by the body to check for his pulse, correct?"

"Yes."

"And then Mr. Powell walked in and found you with your hand on the victim's neck."

"Yes."

"And after that, Mr. Powell shut the door and left you in the room until his security guard showed up."

"Yes."

"Then how did your fingerprints end up on Mr. Powell's desk?"

I took a breath to steady my nerves. "When Luke locked me in the room, I freaked out. I'd never been next to a dead person before, let alone locked in a room with one by myself. I got lightheaded, so I sat on the edge of the desk."

"And how did you sit?"

I looked at Emily, wondering what difference it made, half-expecting her to protest. Instead she nodded.

"I backed up to the desk and sat with my butt against the edge. I think I grabbed the sides."

Detective Holden stood and reenacted my description. "Were your hands like this?" His fingers curled around the edges of the table.

"I think so."

"You think so?" His tone was challenging. "Wouldn't you know so?"

"I was freaked out. I don't remember all the details."

"Were you scared because you had just stabbed a man in the heart?"

"No!" I shouted. "I didn't do it."

"A young impressionable woman, already taken advantage of by Goodwin two years ago. And then you were embarrassed and humiliated on stage—you made national news, and your 'wardrobe malfunction—'" he used air quotes, "—is all over the Internet. Maybe you just snapped."

I pressed my mouth shut, glaring at my attorney. What the hell, Emily?

"Luke asked you to meet him for a romantic rendezvous, but you were shocked and horrified to find Max Goodwin waiting in his study instead. He told you that he would salvage your career if you cooperated, but you changed your mind the moment he dropped his pants to consummate the deal."

"What?" I screeched in disbelief.

"But Mr. Goodwin wasn't about to take no for an answer, and when you failed to dissuade him, you got desperate. You grabbed that letter opener off the desk, then stabbed him."

I was now openly staring at Emily, who was wide-eyed with fright and stammering like she'd suddenly acquired a speech impediment.

Well, fuck it all to hell in a goddamned hand basket.

I took another deep breath and told myself I was playing the part of a young defense attorney who had to face a heartless, misogynistic detective to save my poor defenseless client.

"And how exactly did you come up with this theory?" I asked, sounding cold and aloof.

My question and change of attitude stunned him. He

guffawed for a moment, then said, "It wasn't that hard to figure out."

"Really? Are you an author, Detective Holden? Are you like that guy on that TV show? What is it?" I snapped my fingers. "*Castle*! Do you write murder mysteries in your spare time?"

"What in the hell are you talking about?"

"I'm just trying to figure out how you made the leap from me finding his body to that very imaginative recitation you just finished."

"I already told you—"

"Yes, I heard you. You said it wasn't hard to figure out. But isn't the truth a much simpler solution?" I cocked my head. "He was dead when I walked into that room. You can be certain I wasn't the only person—male or female—Max propositioned or threatened that night. I suspect there were several others at the party. How many were there?"

"Excuse me?"

"Surely you've interviewed everyone who talked to him before I found his body. I bet I wasn't the only person who had a disagreement with him. Mine was only the most vocal."

His face turned red. "Are you trying to tell me how to do my job, Ms. Steele?"

"If you haven't interviewed everyone, then yes."

He banged the table with his fist, the jolt shaking Emily out of her stupor.

"Were my fingerprints on the letter opener?" I asked.

His glare was cold enough to freeze-dry coffee. "I'm not at liberty to say."

"Well, let's just save us both some time. You won't find them there."

"Because you wiped them off?"

"No, because I didn't do it." I shook my head. "We're dancing in circles."

"You'll be dancing all the way to the county jail," he sneered.

"Wow. That's original," I said, feeling extra pissy. "How long did it take you to think that one up?"

Emily sputtered some more.

"Are we done?" I asked. "Because I have an event to get ready for."

He looked like he was torn between strangling me or arranging for an involuntary psychiatric hold. I was wondering about the second myself.

"You are free to go, but you are still a person of interest." He pushed his chair back with a loud screech. "Don't leave town, *Ms. Steele.*"

Keeping my eyes locked on his, I stood and lifted my chin. "I wouldn't dream of it, *Detective Holden.*"

I stomped out, leaving Emily to trail behind me. As I passed the large, open room full of desks on the main floor of the department, a man caught the corner of my eye. He moved out of my line of vision too quickly for me to get a good read on him, but he was tall and dark-haired and dressed in a black wool coat—all things that matched my memory of Brady. But that description would probably fit twenty-five percent of Williamson County males. I was imagining things.

I didn't stop walking until I'd reached the sidewalk outside the station. Emily stumbled to a stop behind me.

"Magnolia!"

I stopped and turned around to face her, my hands on my hips. "What the hell happened in there, Emily?"

"I froze up."

"No shit!"

"Shhh!" She looked around. "You can't tell your mother."

I shook my head in disbelief. "What the hell are you talking about?"

"You can't tell Lila."

"You can't be my attorney, Emily! You completely freaked out in there!"

"I know. I know." She looked dangerously close to tears.

"What am I supposed to do? I need an attorney who knows what she's doing!"

"I'll figure it out." When she met my eyes, I saw something unexpected in her gaze. *Respect.* "You handled it really well. You threw him off."

"Why do I hear a *but* in there?"

"Because just like you, Holden's a hothead. He's bound to hold a grudge."

"Well, that's just fucking great." I sighed, resting my butt against a light pole. How was I going to get out of this one?

"In fact, he'll try harder than ever to pin it on you."

"Even better," I groaned. "Got any more good news, Mary Sunshine?"

chapter eleven

This was ridiculous. I was twenty-eight years old and my mother was running my life. But she had insisted that it was her house, her rules. There was no way I was getting out of Bunco night with my new sister-in-law.

"Don't you think this is a bad idea?" I asked. "I'm under suspicion for murder. What's it going to look like if I'm out there playing Bunco and drinking cosmos?"

Momma put her hands on her hips and gave me *the* look, the one that told me I didn't dare challenge her. "I know that if you stay inside all the time, sulking and hiding, you're gonna look guilty as hell." She narrowed her eyes. "Did you kill that man, Magnolia Steele?"

"Of course not."

She pursed her lips and gave a single bob of her head. "Well, that's settled then. You're going."

In all honesty I was beyond curious about Belinda. No one could be *that* nice. I had to wonder what she was hiding. But tonight was not the time to delve into her psyche. I had to focus on surviving.

So at 6:40 I was ready and waiting, wearing a maroon dress that looked conservative except for its plunging neckline. It only added to my list of worries, but in the scheme of things, when anyone could perform a simple Internet search and see the whole goods, wasn't a plunging neckline a moot point? I had to admit the color looked good with my skin tone, so if Detective Holden decided to pull the trigger and arrest me tonight, at least I'd look good in my mug shot. I wondered if TMZ would cover it on their website.

But I was still a basket case of nerves.

Not surprisingly, Belinda was punctual. She pulled up to Momma's house at promptly 6:45. She was wearing the same clothes she'd had on earlier—a pencil skirt and a cardigan—making me happy with my wardrobe choice.

Belinda walked in, took one look at me, and squealed in delight. "Oh, my word, Magnolia! You look just like a movie star."

I was ready for my mother's eye roll. She hated any kind of reference to my theatre life, even if Belinda had gotten the venue wrong.

"I'll have her back before midnight," Belinda said with a giggle, then grabbed my arm and dragged me out the door.

I wasn't surprised to see she drove a BMW, and a newer model at that. I climbed into the passenger side, then prepared myself to deal with the overly excited woman next to me. Belinda didn't disappoint.

"I can't believe you're actually back! I've been dying to meet you ever since I found out you were the real Magnolia Steele! I've looked at your profile on the Broadway website so many times, and I even saw you in the chorus in *Matilda*."

"Really? That was two years ago. How long have you and Roy been together?"

Belinda must have picked up on my hurt feelings, because she turned and gave me an apologetic smile. "I'm sorry we didn't invite you to the ceremony. It all happened so quickly, and Roy insisted you wouldn't be able to get away. He said you needed at least a month's notice to take time off, so there wasn't any point in inviting you and making you feel guilty for not coming."

She seemed genuinely upset, so I gave her a warm smile. "He's right. I usually need several weeks' notice."

"Besides," she said with a sigh of relief, "it was a small wedding. Nothing extravagant."

Belinda looked like a girl who would want a big fairytale wedding.

"Why?" I asked without thinking.

For the first time I saw her smile waver. "Roy didn't want one." The corners of her mouth quickly tipped back up. "Good thing for me, I have plenty of weddings to live vicariously through."

My stupid brother. He'd always been a self-centered twat, but I would have hoped he'd rein that in for his wife. "Belinda, I'm so sorry."

"Oh, don't be." She waved her hand as though to wave my sympathy away. "It was much more practical. We used the money we would have put into a wedding for a house."

While it seemed reasonable and logical, it was easy to figure out that Belinda had wanted the white dress and the flowers and the fancy reception.

"Well, I'd love to see the photos sometime. I saw one on Momma's photo wall in the stairway. You were a beautiful bride." No need for her to know about my Facebook stalking.

"You're so sweet to say so." Her smile twitched. I realized this conversation was making her uncomfortable.

The last thing I wanted to do was hurt her, so I changed the topic. "Tell me what to expect tonight." I had a good idea, but I hoped I was wrong.

Her shoulders relaxed. "You've really never played Bunco?"

"Yep. I'm a Bunco virgin."

The soft glow of the dashboard lights didn't hide her blush.

"Well, it's really very easy." Then she spent the next five minutes explaining something about dice and Yahtzee, but I'd tuned her out, my mind a jumbled mess from trying to figure out how to keep from getting arrested.

Before I knew it, Belinda had turned down a cul-de-sac lined with cars and a house with all the interior lights illuminated. A string of lights ran along the sidewalk to a southern-style front porch decked out with wicker chairs and cushions. The porch light completed the welcoming look.

Belinda parked across the street and turned to me with a sweet smile. "I can't wait to introduce you to everyone."

I only hoped they were as excited to meet me. My gut told me this would be a disaster, but Belinda got out of the car before I could beg her to go get mani-pedis or see a movie instead. She was waiting for me at the end of her car, her cute Kate Spade purse hanging from the crook of her arm.

I got out and hurried toward her, jumping a little when the horn gave a single loud honk.

"You can't be too safe," she said, shaking her key fob. She sounded very much like a mother in an infomercial for safety scissors.

It suddenly occurred to me that there were a lot of things she didn't know that her friends might—about my Broadway mishaps, for one, and my trouble with the law, for another. "Belinda, I'm not sure if it's a good idea for me to go in there."

"That is so cute that you're nervous." She gave me a patient smile and shook her head. "Don't worry, Magnolia. They'll love you. How could they not?"

I could give her a slew of reasons—the real question was where to start. "Belinda, you have to listen to me. There are several things you don't know."

"I know all about the videos," she said as she continued to

walk, her heels clicking on the concrete driveway. "You have nothing to be embarrassed about." She stopped and turned to me, grabbing my hand and holding it between her own. She gave me an earnest look. "You have a beautiful body, Magnolia Steele. Anyone who gives you grief over it is simply jealous."

I was fairly certain that wasn't true, and incredibly, that was much lower on my list of concerns than it had been the night before. "That's not it . . . or I mean all."

Belinda was already climbing the steps to the porch. She moved with alarming speed, probably hoping the host would open the door before I could run back to the car.

When she reached the middle of the porch, she spun around to face me. "Magnolia," she said in a mock stern voice. "You have nothing to worry about."

She rang the doorbell before I could stop her, then laughed at my look of shock when the tune to Rocky Top rang out in chimes. "I guess Blake went to the University of Tennessee. I hear he's kind of a fanatic."

The blood rushed to my feet. Oh, God. Had she said *Blake*? That had to be a coincidence.

The front door flung open and revealed a pretty blonde woman wearing a silky pink blouse and pearls paired with cream pants and ivory sling-back heels.

Oh, God. No. This was *her* house. But how? Belinda had said the party was at her friend Sylvia's house . . .

"Maddie!" Belinda said. "That was so sweet of you to fill in for Sylvia after her son came down with strep throat this morning. I hope it's okay that I brought a guest."

"Well, of course," she said in a bright voice, but all the color drained from her face when she saw me. Maddie looked as if she'd seen a ghost.

Belinda had turned to face me, so she missed her reaction. "Maddie, this is my sister-in-law, Magnolia."

I wanted to turn around and run, but my feet refused to move. Instead I stood my ground. "Hey, Maddie."

She still didn't speak, and Belinda was finally grasping that there was tension between us. "Do you two already know each other?"

Maddie crossed her arms as the color returned to her face, anger slowly creeping into her eyes. "I thought we did, but I was obviously wrong."

"I think I should go," I said quietly, wishing the ground would open and swallow me whole.

"That's right, Magnolia. Go on. You're good at taking off, aren't you?" she said. "The shocker is that you actually bothered to tell me this time."

"I'm sorry, Maddie. I'm so sorry," I said, my voice breaking. "I didn't know that you'd be here. If I'd known, I wouldn't have come."

"And you and I both know you do what *you* want," Maddie said, her tone as cold as a January wind in New York. She shrugged and glanced back inside before turning to face me again. "You can do whatever you want, Magnolia. It makes no difference to me one way or the other."

I watched her walk back inside with all the grace of an old movie star.

"Magnolia?" Belinda asked softly. "How do you know Maddie Green?"

Several years ago—before I'd stopped looking—I'd learned via Facebook that she'd married the lying, cheating bastard. I'd tried to reach out to her after leaving—if only to tell her that Blake was cheating on her—but she'd never answered my calls, emails, or texts. For all I knew, she'd deleted all my messages without checking them out.

The air in my chest froze and tears stung my eyes.

"Magnolia?"

"She was my best friend," I pushed out past the lump in my throat.

"Oh, gosh," Belinda said. "I had no idea."

"Didn't Momma tell you? Or Roy?"

She shook her head, dangerously close to tears herself. "No. I only know her because she's a neighbor, but we just bought our house six months ago. We're not really friends, just acquaintances. And Roy never spends any time with the neighbors. I don't think he knows she lives here. If he did, he sure didn't mention it." She paused, turning her attention to a car pulling up to the curb. "What do you want to do?"

"I don't know." I didn't want to go inside, but I didn't want Maddie to have further proof that I was a coward.

"You know what I think?" Belinda asked.

"What?" I whispered.

Her mouth turned up into a tight smile. "I think you should walk into that room and hold your head high. You're Magnolia Steele, Broadway star. Did you make mistakes before you left New York? Apparently, but I dare any of the people in there to lay claim to perfection."

"This isn't forgetting to send a birthday card, Belinda. I took off. Without a word. I broke Maddie's heart. And Momma's. And maybe even Roy's just a little bit. I tried to make it right with Maddie after I left, but she didn't want to hear it."

"No one takes off like that without a reason." She grabbed my hand again and squeezed it. "And maybe you'll trust me enough to tell me one day, but for now I just want to be your friend."

"Why?" I asked, wiping away a tear. "Because I'm Magnolia Steele, former Broadway star?"

"No," she said, leaning forward and squeezing. "Because you're Magnolia Steele, Roy Steele's sister and Lila Steele's daughter. That makes you my family, Magnolia, and family sticks together. I've got your back."

I shook my head. "You have no idea what you're doing, Belinda. You're so sweet you're probably friends with every woman in that room. If you walk in there with me, you may well ruin yourself forever."

She released a soft laugh. "Well, that's probably an exaggeration. I doubt I'll be ruined *forever*. And besides—" she gave me a sad look, "—my life could use a little shaking up." Then, keeping a tight hold of my hand, she walked through the still-open door.

As I crossed the threshold, I realized I was not only walking into Maddie's house, but Blake's as well.

Oh, God.

I felt like I was going to throw up, but Belinda kept her head held high and tugged me around several card tables decorated with tablecloths and mason jars full of fresh-cut flowers that couldn't have already grown and bloomed in middle Tennessee in March. A woman on a mission, she didn't stop until she reached two women. She flashed them her megawatt smile. "Trudy, Samantha, this is my sister-in-law, Magnolia. She's just come back to town."

The two women's eyes widened, and I couldn't help but wonder what part of my life shocked and offended them most. Maybe all of it. But Belinda, powered by her Energizer Bunny spirit, charged through the room, introducing me to at least half of the twenty or so women in the house, using her positive can-do attitude to challenge anyone who would dare to besmirch my name. Most of the faces were unfamiliar, but two of the women had gone to school with Maddie and me. They made sure to steer clear of us as Belinda made the rounds, not that I had a problem with that. It was no surprise to see where their loyalty lay.

As we wandered the first floor, my anxiety dropped several levels when it became apparent Blake was nowhere around. But there were plenty of other issues to keep the anxiety brewing.

Belinda led me into the kitchen, and I did a double take

when I saw Emily standing behind an island stacked with a multitude of food. She took one look at me and drained her wine glass. Her very next move was to refill it from a decanter.

"I heard you were here. You know, I was starting to think you'd changed. I never expected that you would stoop this low."

"I didn't know she'd be here." My whisper held a hard edge. "I didn't even want to come at all."

"It's my fault," Belinda assured her. "I had no idea there was history between Maddie and Magnolia. No one ever talks about Magnolia's past, and I only met Maddie a couple of months ago. She's never seen me with Roy, so we never made the connection."

Emily studied her for a moment before giving a slight nod. "It didn't occur to me to mention anything to you either." She gave us a halfhearted smile, then grabbed an empty glass and filled it.

"White wine sangria?" she asked as she held out the glass to me, giving me an anxious look. Was she worried her friends would find out Momma had roped her into representing me? Or maybe she was worried I'd tell everyone about how she'd frozen up in that interrogation room. She had nothing to worry about. I didn't plan to tell anyone any of it.

"Yes." The alcohol was masked by fruit juice and ginger ale, and I'd drained half of it before realizing what I was doing.

Emily offered Belinda an empty glass, but she shook her head with a sweet smile. "Oh, no thank you. I'm the designated driver, so I'll stick to sweet tea."

"Really, Magnolia—" the woman's voice was horribly familiar, and it came from behind me, "—I can't believe you had the nerve to show up after all these years and everything else."

Dammit. I didn't have the strength to do this. I spun around to face Ashley Pincher, the girl Blake had been cheating with on the night of our graduation. She'd hated my guts since middle school. She probably liked me even less now that I knew her little secret. "Talk about nerve, Ashley. I'm surprised you have time to play Bunco, what with all your extracurricular activities."

I took a sip of my drink, pretending like I didn't give a damn. Belinda and Emily gave me a curious look, but Ashley's eyes narrowed. She knew exactly what I was talking about.

"No one wants you here," Ashley said, enough venom in her voice to kill. "You should run off and leave like you did before."

"Maybe I should spill a few secrets first. Some Maddie might like to hear."

Her face paled, and the hatred in her eyes was overlaid with fear.

Belinda looped her arm through mine and said in her sweet, cheerful voice, "Leave? Why, that's the silliest thing I've ever heard." She turned to look at me and squeezed my arm, offering me a warm smile. "We're thrilled you're here." Something shifted in her eyes—ever so slightly—as she turned her gaze to Emily's, but I saw it and I know Emily did too.

Emily plastered on a half-smile. "Yes, of course. And so is Lila."

Maddie walked into the kitchen with a tray of appetizers. She stopped and her mouth dropped open at Emily's statement.

Oh. Shit.

But Maddie recovered faster than I probably would have given the situation. "Lila's like a second mother to me," she said to Belinda, ignoring me. "In fact, she gave me the recipe for these crab puffs. So if Lila's happy, then I'm happy for her."

She poured herself another glass of sangria. "If you'll excuse me, I need to check on my other guests." She shot me a glare, then cast one that read *traitor* to Emily and headed out of the kitchen.

I wanted to apologize to Emily, but I wasn't sure why. She'd held a grudge against me for years, and she'd basically taken over my old life. Was I supposed to apologize for coming back and disturbing her friendship with my ex-best friend?

But *I* had been the one to move on. *I* had been the one to make a fresh start, leaving everyone I cared about behind to pick up the pieces. Could I blame Maddie or Momma for the way they'd coped? Could I be upset that they had lives that no longer included me? Or that they resented my return?

"Let's get something to eat," Belinda said, handing me a blue Fiestaware plate.

Another look at Maddie's island told me that she'd drunk the Williamson County Kool-Aid. There was so much food displayed, it looked like she'd been preparing for days instead of since this morning. Multiple appetizers and dips, six desserts, the white wine sangria—which I recognized as another one of my mother's recipes—as well as sweet tea, margaritas, and cosmos. The food was staggered in varying heights so each dish could be displayed, and the pitchers of drinks were arrayed in a silver ice bucket.

I realized this would have been my life if I hadn't left. I would have come home after college, and then I would have gotten married and had kids. Two of them. Maddie and I had come up with almost identical life plans our senior year of high school. I remembered mine by heart: I would go to Southern University and major in education. Then I would come home, marry Tanner, and we'd start a family—a boy and a girl and a dog. Tanner and I would live in this very neighborhood, and we would have our happily ever after. But watching these women now, I had to wonder how happy they were throwing Bunco nights and cul-de-sac cookouts. Living in houses with literal white picket fences.

For the first time since I'd left, I wondered if I'd done myself a favor.

I put some food on my plate, but not much—my stomach was still churning with anxiety. It was like a bad case of stage fright, except the only way I was going to get applause from this group was if someone doused me with pig's blood at the end of the evening—which they'd only dare if they got me outside and next to the sewer drain, lest the blood leave a stain. But even that seemed unlikely. Thank God.

Instead I told myself I was playing the part of a young woman who had been deeply wronged, and had returned to her hometown only to be ostracized. Sure, it was remarkably similar to what was actually happening, but I'd learned it was easier to pretend to fill the role of someone else, even it was an imitation of my own life.

I handed my plate to Belinda and excused myself to the powder room, pausing first to finish off my drink and pour myself a new one. The door was locked, giving me time to study the photos in the hall. Maddie with Blake. Maddie holding a baby.

The photos of Blake made my nausea increase. Especially the ones where he was touching her in some way. I'd let Maddie marry a cheater at best . . . and at worst? What had happened that night ten years ago? What secrets had her husband kept?

But I knew her enough to recognize her fake smile, and there was evidence of it in half the photos. It looked just like her smile in the homecoming photos the year her mother made her go to the dance with Mike Pringle from down the street.

A lump filled my throat. If I'd been able to convince her that Blake was a cheater, would she have still married him? Would she be happier without him?

The bathroom door opened, and Maddie stepped out, dabbing her cheek with a tissue. Her eyes went wide when she saw me, and her mouth formed an O.

"You have a baby," I said, pointing to the photo.

She put a hand on her stomach, looking self-conscious. "Blake, Junior."

I tried not to think about her poor baby being saddled with his asshole father's name. "How old is he?"

"Six months." She shook her head and her voice broke. "Why are you here, Magnolia?"

I wanted to give her a laundry list of reasons for leaving, along with a string of apologies, but she didn't want to hear any of them, and I didn't blame her. "I wish you would have answered at least one of my calls or texts."

She sucked in her bottom lip, her chin quivering.

"I've missed you," I whispered.

That brought a fire to her eyes. "Don't," she spat out. "Just don't. You don't have a right to say that."

"Okay. You're right," I said, trying not to cry. "Are you happy?"

She released a bitter laugh. "You don't have the right to ask that either."

I expected her to storm off, but she remained rooted in place, while the voices of the other guests roared behind us. For a brief moment it was Maddie and me, caught in this four-foot-long hallway time warp.

"You're in my house, Magnolia. *My* home."

"I know, and I'm so sorry. I really had no idea it was your house, or I never would have shown up."

She wrapped her arms around herself. "You keep saying you're sorry, yet it doesn't change a thing."

"I'm sorry for that too." This was ridiculous. We were having a conversation that should have taken place somewhere private, not several feet away from some of Williamson County's most notorious busybodies. "Would you like me to leave?"

"You can't leave now!" she whispered in horror. "If you leave now, they'll think I couldn't handle it. And I most certainly *can*."

I had serious misgivings about that. She looked like she was about to fall to pieces, and it killed me to think I was hurting her all over again. "Tell me what to do, Maddie. Just tell me what to do to make it right."

She released a bitter laugh. "We're not kids anymore, Magnolia. Some things you just can't make right."

I'd already resigned myself to that, but her words still shot straight into my heart like an arrow. I nodded and swallowed. "I know. I'll try my best to lie low and keep to myself, and as soon as this thing is done, I'll leave."

She nodded and her gaze narrowed. "And then I never want to see you again." She pushed past me, her shoulder brushing mine.

I ducked into the powder room, fighting the urge to cry. I had no right to tears. Maddie was the wronged party here.

I got myself together by getting into my character, whom I'd revised to have a stoicism that kept her from getting hurt by barbs from her former best friend and a posse of snotty bitches who had no right to hate her.

Belinda looked relieved when I found her with a small group of her friends. They eyed me with some wariness, but it was easy to see they loved her. Two of the women had moved to Franklin a few years ago, so they had no knowledge of my sudden disappearance ten years ago, but they did know about my Broadway debut. They soon forgot about me and started talking about Lisa's husband, who managed the careers of two prominent Christian artists.

Lisa lowered her voice and looked around. "Did you hear about the sleazy talent agent who was murdered at Luke Powell's party last night?"

The piece of shrimp cocktail in my mouth suddenly tasted like chalk.

"I heard someone shot him in the head," the other woman said.

"Oh, my goodness!" Belinda gasped, nearly dropping her plate of appetizers. "I set Lila's catering company up with that party." She shot me a look of alarm before she turned back to her friend. "Do they know who did it?"

Lisa shook her head, but from the way she leaned in closer, it was clear that a lack of knowledge wouldn't stop her from speculating. "No, but there were plenty of people there who had motive. There was a country singer there who'd been hoodwinked by him, so you can imagine he was pissed. And then the vice president of Highway 24 Music was there . . . Max had screwed him over by chasing a big star away from the label. And then there were all the women he'd convinced to sleep with him in exchange for career help that never materialized. Narrowing the list down should take some time."

I felt a presence behind me, and I looked back and up at Emily, whose eyes were fixed on Lisa. She glanced down at me with knowing eyes, then walked away.

Belinda had said that some months they never got around to playing Bunco. I was hoping tonight would be one of those nights, but I should have known better. A few minutes later, Maddie rang a bell and announced it was time to play.

I had all of the bad luck in Franklin. Well . . . maybe slightly better luck than Max Goodwin.

I soon found myself in the most complicated game of musical chairs I'd ever played. Of course the five glasses of white wine sangria I'd downed weren't exactly helping me figure out the intricacies of the game. One thing I did register was that my partner and I would either switch tables or stay depending on how many points we'd gained in a round. Thank God Belinda was my partner. She was true to her word; she had my back.

Most of the woman were nice, but a few gave me dirty looks and made snide remarks about my photos online.

"Since your career on Broadway crashed and burned," one woman said with a smirk, "perhaps you can continue in the entertainment world at the gentleman's club in downtown Nashville. Just tell them your resume's on YouTube."

But as sweet as my new sister-in-law seemed to be, she was perfectly capable of turning into a momma lion. Keeping her attention on the dice in her hand, she said in the sweetest of tones, "I'm not so sure that's such a good idea, Sydney. Considering how often Lionel goes there, he'd be liable to get a lot of up close and personal time with Magnolia. He very well might want to leave you for her." She rolled the dice on the table and looked into the shocked woman's face. "Bless your heart."

"She did *not* just bless her heart," a woman behind me murmured.

"I think she did," someone else whispered in disbelief.

Sydney kept any other comments to herself, but judging from the deep shade of red tinting her cheeks, she was choking on them.

I breathed out a sigh of relief when another bell rang from the head table announcing that the game was over and the winners would be awarded their prizes in five to ten minutes. I couldn't stand one more minute of hostile scrutiny, let alone five to ten. I refilled my wine glass, grateful that Belinda was the designated driver, and slipped out of the kitchen and into the backyard.

The night had cooled off, but the alcohol had warmed my blood and dulled my senses. I leaned my head back and took in the stars in the night sky. A spectacular view I couldn't get in the city.

"Magnolia Steele. You are the *very* last person I expected to see in my backyard," a man's voice said.

For a moment I was certain I was hallucinating, but why was I so surprised? It was his house, after all.

I turned around to see Blake sitting in a lawn chair, his hands gripping the ends of the arms. He stood and took a couple of steps toward me. "I heard you were back, but I sure as hell never thought you'd have the nerve to show up here."

Fear coursed through my blood as I took a step backward. The memory of him shouting my name on that rainy night made me start to shake. "How'd you know I was back?"

"I have my ways."

But there was a logical explanation. One that wasn't too surprising. "Tanner called you."

He didn't respond.

Should I confront him with my fragmented memories? But he beat me to it.

"Are you here to tell Maddie?" He looked out at his impeccably landscaped backyard, then turned back to face me. "We were kids back then, Magnolia. We both did stupid things that night."

"Maddie has a right to know."

He closed the distance between us in milliseconds. Grabbing my upper arm hard enough to hurt, he tugged me closer. The liquid in my wine glass sloshed out onto my hand. "If you know what's good for you, you'll keep your mouth shut."

I steeled my jaw. I'd be damned if I'd let him know his intimidation was working. "I think Maddie would love to know about Ashley Pincher blowing you behind my house the night of our graduation."

He leaned even closer, his face inches from mine, and I could smell beer on his breath. "Don't mess with me, Magnolia. Things are different now. You don't belong here, so do yourself a favor and get the hell out of town before something happens that you'll regret."

"Are you threatening me, Blake?"

The hinges on the back door squeaked, and Blake immediately dropped his hold and took a step back.

"There you are, Magnolia," Belinda said, sounding relieved. "I've been looking for you everywhere." She started to walk toward us, but stopped in her tracks when she caught sight of Blake. "I'm sorry. I hope I didn't interrupt anything."

"No," Blake said good-naturedly. "Magnolia and I were just catching up." Sliding up to me, he wrapped an arm around my back and cupped my upper arm. "Me, Maddie, and Magnolia were all good friends in high school. I was one of the people who searched the woods for her the night she disappeared."

The light from the kitchen window cast dark shadows on Belinda's face, but the way her eyes widened with surprise made me wonder if she knew anything about that night.

Blake dropped his arm. "You ladies go on and wrap things up so I can go inside. Too much estrogen flowing in there right now."

I was torn between telling him off and running away—but my fear won out. I bolted for my sister-in-law, trying to ignore the shame burning in my gut for taking the chicken's way out.

I walked past Belinda, eager to get as far away from Blake as possible. She cast a glance over her shoulder back at him, then followed me inside.

Sydney was in the middle of announcing the winners when we walked in. ". . . and now the award for the most losses. Who had two?" Half of the ladies in the room lifted a hand. "Three? Four? Six?" She continued calling out numbers until she finally found a winner.

I drained the last of the sangria pitcher and gulped it down, ignoring the scrutiny of my sister-in-law. I flashed her a forced smile. "Who knew Bunco could make you so thirsty?"

I tried to drown out Sydney's voice as she went through several more categories, handing out candles and gift cards for the most wins, the fewest Buncos, then finally the most Buncos. The conversation swelled up again, but Sydney raised her voice over the murmurs.

"We have one more award to give out."

Several of the guests looked confused, but Sydney pressed

on. "And the prize for the person with the most nerve goes to Magnolia Steele for daring to show her face here tonight."

The murmuring stopped and all eyes turned to me.

I'd spent a couple of hours with these women, and while everyone knew about my bad luck on stage, most had no idea I'd skipped town a decade ago.

Maddie's mouth dropped open and her face went pale. It was obvious she had nothing to do with her friend's announcement.

"That's right," Sydney said, taking a step forward and wobbling to the side. "Magnolia Steele." She spat out my name like it was a mouthful of rotten fish. "Who destroyed so many lives, yet blows back into town like a spring wind." Her gaze landed on me, her gaze slightly unfocused. "Like a fucking tornado that rips lives apart."

Several of the women gasped.

Maddie's eyes glistened with tears as I looked on in horror. I should never have come—to Bunco, to Momma's, to Franklin.

Belinda bustled up to me and wrapped an arm around my shoulders. "I don't know about y'all, but I think Maddie's delicious white wine sangria must have snuck up on Sydney." Then she turned to Maddie. "Thank you for a wonderful evening, but Magnolia and I need to be leaving."

Belinda—ever prepared—had already grabbed her purse and jacket. Since I hadn't brought anything, she flashed her sweet smile at everyone and dragged me out the door and all the way to her car. But she didn't stop until she opened the passenger door and proceeded to push me in.

I took a step back. "Belinda, I'm perfectly capable of getting into a car by myself."

"You had more than a few glasses of sangria yourself, and since at least a dozen pairs of eyes are on you at the moment, I thought it best that you not fall on your keister."

"Keister?"

She ignored my comment. "You getting in?"

"Remind me not to get on your bad side."

She flashed an innocent smile that suddenly didn't look so innocent.

We were silent all the way home, until Belinda pulled into Momma's driveway. She put the car in park and turned to face me. "You don't have anything to be ashamed of, Magnolia."

I released a short laugh. "There are so many people who would disagree with that statement, my own mother included." I tipped my head toward the house.

"Just hang in there. Before you know it, people will stop talking and move on to something else. They always do."

Without another word, I climbed out and headed for the front door, grumbling to myself that I didn't have a house key. When I pulled out my phone to text my mother to let me in, I found a text waiting for me.

Secrets don't make friends.

A blocked number again. My head grew faint, and I almost fell over my knees, but I had to hold it together or Belinda would charge out of the car and pepper me with questions. The text could have been from half a handful of women at that party. Or Blake.

That one gave me pause. He'd admitted he knew I was back. He could have easily sent the first text.

Belinda was watching me like a mother hen, so I gave her a wave and blindly reached for the door handle, surprised and frightened to find the door unlocked. Had Momma left it that way, or had something more nefarious occurred? My heart pounding in my chest, I pushed the door open, but a folded piece of paper on the entryway table caught my eye before I could shout for Momma. It was a note from her, telling me she'd gone to bed early and left the door open for me.

Confusion followed my initial feeling of relief. Gone to bed early? It was barely past ten o'clock. Momma had always been a night owl.

Tossing the note down, I latched the deadbolt and pressed my hand against the steel, letting myself savor the solid feeling of it. This door gave me a false sense of security that would undoubtedly bite me in the ass.

I had so much bigger things to worry about besides women gossiping about my troubles. Or even the pain and betrayal in Maddie's eyes.

What did Blake know about ten years ago? Did I dare ask him?

There was no doubt that coming back to Franklin was a mistake, but I wasn't sure what to do about that now. I was good and stuck until my name was cleared.

When I reached my room, I opened the nightstand drawer and touched Daddy's gun. Once my name was cleared, I was leaving again.

And I was never coming back.

chapter twelve

M y sleep was fitful, my dreams a jumbled mess. Blake shouting my name. Running away from him in the rain. And the blood. But there was something new this time. A house in the woods, with peeling paint and broken windows, the inside empty and littered with trash. A basement, dark and dank. Fear so sharp it burned my entire body as it shot through my veins. A dripping sound.

Drop. Drop. Drop.

A puddle of blood.

I bolted upright in bed, my heart beating so fast I wondered if I was having a heart attack. I reached over and turned on the lamp to illuminate the pitch-black room.

While I'd returned home that night years ago with a splitting headache and a giant goose egg on the side of my head, the only injury that could have bled was the cut on my thigh, and there was no way it could have bled that much. So whose blood had it been?

It took me hours to get back to sleep, so I was none too thrilled when Momma flung my door open and strode into the room. Within minutes she was throwing open the curtains and letting sunlight flood into the room.

"Rise and shine, Magnolia. Time to get to work."

"What time is it?"

"Eight o'clock."

Releasing a groan, I rolled over and buried my face into my pillow. Mainlining sangria had seemed like a wonderful solution to my problems last night. This morning, not so much.

My covers were ripped off me next. "I swear, you haven't changed at all. Get up."

If only her statement were true. I *wished* I were the same girl.

"I'm twenty-eight years old, Momma. You don't need to wake me up in the morning."

"That's not true if you don't get out of bed in the morning on your own. Now get up and get ready. You have things to do."

I sat up, suddenly leery. "You're not making me waitress at your event tonight, are you?"

She snorted. "Good God, no. It's a small dinner—twenty people—so my experienced staff can handle it. Besides, after Luke Powell's party, there's no way I'd put you out in public."

"So what do you want me to do?"

"This morning? It may be a weekend, but you're cleaning. Then later you can work in the kitchen."

I groaned and flopped down on the bed. "Momma. I have a headache as big as Texas. Let me sleep another ten minutes."

"I'll see you *in the kitchen* in ten minutes," she said, stomping toward the door. "And I expect you to be dressed and ready to clean, or I'm going to tack fifty bucks on to your rent."

She hadn't yet told me how much I owed in rent or how much I was getting paid, but I knew her well enough to know she wasn't bluffing. Ten minutes later, I was dressed in a short-sleeved T-shirt and a pair of yoga pants, guzzling a half-empty cup of coffee in the kitchen. I'd already chased the first few sips with a couple of ibuprofens. Momma emerged from the laundry room with a plastic tote of cleaning supplies.

"This is a spring cleaning. Baseboards. Windows. The whole shebang. You can get started on this floor, and I'll work upstairs."

I spent the rest of the morning cleaning while I listened to the soundtrack from *Waitress* on my phone, occasionally dancing and singing along. I needed something to distract me from all the anxious thoughts running through my head on repeat. If Detective Holden was determined to put me behind bars, then I had to work twice as hard to stay out. Too bad I didn't know the first thing about getting out of murder charges.

I was mopping the dining room when someone tapped my shoulder. After my initial reaction of shock—jumping and screaming in place—I ripped my ear buds out and wielded the mop as a weapon.

Emily lifted her hands and took several steps backward, fear in her eyes. "Whoa. Don't whack me."

I lowered the mop and took a deep breath. "Sorry. You scared me."

"Obviously." She put a hand on her chest. "Who on earth did you think I was?"

"Nobody," I grumbled, hating that I'd made myself look suspicious. No wonder that asshole Blake had sent me another text. I might not remember what happened, but he didn't know that. I *had* entertained the idea that it might not have been him. I'd spent half the morning trying to figure out if someone at the party might have sent it. But too many drinks had made my memory fuzzy.

Brilliant, Magnolia. You're under suspicion for murder, not to mention in possible danger, and you're getting sauced on girly drinks. What an idiot.

I turned around, plopped the mop into the bucket, and then

wrung it out. I had hours of work to do. "Momma's upstairs cleaning her bathroom."

"Actually I'm here to see you."

There could only be one reason for that. I slowly turned back around. "They're about to arrest me."

"No. In fact, your fingerprints weren't found on the letter opener."

"I already knew that. That means they should leave me alone now, right?"

"Actually . . ." She looked over her shoulder, and I noticed my mother was standing at the bottom of the stairs, listening. The dark circles under her eyes made her look more exhausted than a few hours cleaning should have made her. "I'd like Lila to be part of this."

"Let's go into the kitchen," Momma said, already disappearing around the corner.

She started a fresh pot of coffee and cut each of us a slice of coffee cake, refusing to discuss anything until we were all sitting at the breakfast room table.

Emily picked up her fork and gave me a long hard look. "Like I said, your fingerprints aren't on the letter opener." When I started to say something, she held up the fork and cut me off. "But there's more." She broke off a piece of her cake and stuffed it into her mouth, releasing a satisfied moan that would be more appropriate to her bedroom than my mother's table.

Impatient, I finally asked, "What more could there be?"

"Your prints aren't on there, but no one else's were either."

I cocked my head. "What does that mean for me?"

Emily lifted her gaze to my mother's. "Nothing good." She picked up her coffee and blew on the surface. "It means that whoever killed him must have wiped off the prints. Which means you are still their number one suspect."

"So they're gonna arrest me?"

"Holden will try to build a stronger case first. But, yeah.

155

They're going to arrest you. It's a matter of *when* it's going to happen."

"So I'm just supposed to sit here and wait for it to happen?" I couldn't help but remember what Colt had told me about his friends. Escape was starting to sound like a pretty good option. Was Bora Bora a non-extraditing country? I'd worked out enough for my role in *Fireflies at Dawn* to look good in a bikini. At least I had *that* going for me.

"You have to fight it," Belinda said from behind me.

I spun around in surprise. From her mint green dress to her soft pink cardigan and matching flats, my sister-in-law looked like she had come straight from a sorority house. The ivory Coach purse hanging from her shoulder only added to the effect. Her strawberry blonde hair was pulled back into a pony-tail, making her look all of twenty-two.

"How long have you been standing there?" For some bizarre reason, I didn't want her to know I was a person of interest in the murder case. I liked the way I looked through her eyes, and I didn't want her to see me as everyone else did.

"Long enough to know you're in trouble." She walked over and sat in the empty seat next to me. She looked over at Emily and Momma with a no-nonsense face. "This is about that talent agent's murder, isn't it?"

Momma's eyes widened in surprise.

I'd been amazed that she hadn't quizzed me about it last night, after finding out about the murder, but there hadn't exactly been a lot of quiet moments at Bunco.

"It's not much of leap, Lila," Belinda said, shaking her head a little. "I know you and Tilly catered Luke Powell's party, and that talent agent was murdered there."

"But why would you jump to the conclusion that I was a suspect?" I asked.

She gave a half shrug. "That doesn't seem like the issue to me. The real issue is how you're going to fight it."

Emily gave me a look that suggested she wasn't going to say another word unless I wanted her to proceed.

"Why are you doing this, Belinda?" I asked. "How do you know I didn't do it?"

"Because you're a good person, Magnolia Steele."

I expected my mother or Emily to protest or smirk, but both of them remained surprisingly quiet.

"And besides, you're part of my family. And family sticks together."

I had to wonder what kind of family she'd been raised in to believe that. My brother sure wasn't here to support me. I hadn't even heard from him since I'd called him. Her support wasn't coming from him.

Belinda leaned over and settled her hand over mine. "But if I'm going to help, I need to know what's going on."

I glanced at Emily, but she looked uncertain.

Belinda had been more than helpful last night, which led me to the crazy idea that she might be able to help after all. So I took a deep breath and then told her everything—about Max Goodwin, the party, and even my interrogation at the police station the day before, though I left out the part about Emily freezing up. Emily's shoulders sank with relief when she realized I wasn't going to rat her out.

When I finished, Belinda turned her sharp gaze to Emily. "Are there any other suspects?"

"I don't know."

"Well, can't you find out?" She sounded like a prim and proper schoolmarm.

Emily's face hardened. "The police won't tell me anything, but I do plan on checking out a couple of suspects. Lisa Huddleston's husband is in the industry, although on the Christian side. Last night she mentioned a couple of people who had motive."

"You mean the country singer and the vice president of

Highway 24 Music?" I asked. "I wouldn't know the first thing about how to contact the vice president."

"Well, good thing for you I have an in," Emily said, looking smug. "Daddy knows Henry McNamara, the VP. They started out together back in the day."

Well, crap. Why hadn't I thought about that? Emily's father was an executive for a country label.

"See?" she said, holding my gaze. "I'm a good defense attorney."

My mother shot me a glare. "Were you insulting Emily's abilities?"

"No!" I gave Emily a look of disbelief, half-tempted to tell Momma the truth. It wasn't like I owed Emily a damn thing. But I couldn't do it. Standing in my own spotlight of humiliation, I felt no need to tug her under the glare.

But Emily didn't know that. "No. It was just a bad joke," she said, giving my mother a grim smile. "Magnolia's been a model client."

Momma didn't look so convinced, but let the subject drop.

"What about the singer? Paul Locke?" Belinda asked. "Can you contact him?"

Emily cringed. "That might prove to be more difficult. Daddy's my contact, and Paul Locke is under contract with another label. He can't reach out to him."

"I might have another way," Belinda said and gave me a grin. "Amy."

"Who?" Emily asked.

"Amy is Luke Powell's personal assistant," Momma said. "She and Belinda were roommates when they first moved to Nashville."

"Oh."

"Amy was in charge of the guest list," Belinda said, clasping her fingers together on the table. "She'll know how to contact him. She'll also know who else might have had a reason to kill him." She gave a tiny shudder.

Looking lost in thought, Emily turned toward Momma. "Did the police ask you for a guest list?"

"No," Momma said. "But I didn't have one. Just a head count, which wasn't accurate anyway, so there's a good chance Amy's list isn't complete."

"There's only one way to find out," Belinda said as she opened her purse and fished out her phone. She quickly pulled up a number and held the phone to her ear. "Hey, Amy, how are you? ... No. I heard all about the murder. I'm so sorry. How are you holding up? ... I know, but surely he can't hold you accountable."

Momma gave me a nod before she took a sip of her coffee.

Belinda was silent for a moment, her face scrunching up as she listened intently to the woman on the other line. "I'd love to see you. Maybe I can help. Can you meet for lunch this afternoon? I know it's short notice ... Great. How about that new restaurant on Cool Springs Boulevard—Austin's? Great. See you then."

She gave me an assessing look as she ended the call. "You need a shower," she announced.

"Excuse me?"

"We're going to lunch, and you need a shower. You're a beautiful girl, Magnolia, but that ponytail looks like a rat built a nest in it and is coming back to hibernate for six years."

My mouth dropped open in shock, but I quickly recovered and shook my head. "I suspect Luke Powell's assistant does *not* want to see me." Especially after our experience together after Max's murder. "Maybe you better go alone."

"Nope. You're coming." She returned the phone to her purse and stood. "I'll be back at 12:40 to pick you up. Make sure you're ready." Then she walked out the door, leaving the three of us speechless.

"I had no idea she had it in her," I said. "She seems so sweet and unassuming."

Momma shook her head with a look of pride. "And that's one reason she's so good at her job. Sure, she creates beautiful weddings, but it's how she handles things once they're in progress that gets her referrals. She's what you would get if Mary Poppins had a drill sergeant's baby. She keeps people in line without them even realizing they're being bossed around."

Emily stood. "So Belinda and Magnolia will talk to Luke Powell's assistant, and I'll have Daddy get me Henry McNamara's number."

"What am I supposed to do?" Momma asked.

I gave her a long look. She looked even more tired than she had earlier in the morning. I knew my predicament had to be hard on her, and I felt guilty all over again for coming back to town. But I knew my mother better than to point any of that out. "I think you should stay here and be home base. We'll all check back with you."

"I have to get to the kitchen by three."

I gave her a half-shrug. "Then we'll check in with you there."

Momma didn't look convinced.

"Don't worry. If we find some useful information, and if the police will follow the leads we give them, I might get out of this."

"That's a lot of ifs, Magnolia," my mother said, but then she motioned toward the stairs. "Go on and get ready. Belinda's right. You need to look respectable."

I left her and Emily at the table as I ran up the steps to get ready. After I shut the door behind me, I grabbed my phone. It was time to text Colt to see what he remembered.

I need to talk to you about Thursday night. Call me when you can. As an afterthought I added, *Tell me how your performance went. Wish I'd been there.*

The last part was only a partial truth, but if Colt was like most performers, he craved flattery and compliments. And I definitely needed to stay on his good side. Besides digging for other suspects, I needed to bolster the evidence of my own innocence. Emily was right; Colt's testimony would at least buy me some reasonable doubt. At this point, beggars couldn't be choosers.

But an hour later, I still hadn't heard from him. I debated whether to send another text, then decided to wait until after lunch. I suspected part of my appeal to him was my hard-to-get attitude. If I looked too eager, he might not text back at all.

At 12:30 I went back downstairs, ready to fill the role of the wrongly accused ingénue. My long brunette hair hung down my back in loose curls, and my makeup was minimal, giving me a youthful, innocent look. I wore a pale pink dress with a fitted bodice and a flared skirt. Anyone with any width would look hippy, but I'd lost ten pounds for the play. It fit perfectly. I might as well wear it before I started stress eating or found myself in an orange jumpsuit.

Taking a cue from my sister-in-law, I topped the outfit off with a cream-colored sweater and a pair of matching flats. It was fifty-fifty if the short strand of pearls at the base of my neck was too much. My mother zeroed in on it the moment my foot hit the bottom step.

Her mouth pursed. "You took my mother's pearls."

"I only borrowed them. There *is* a difference." I took a breath. "I'm nervous. What if we can't get what we need from her?" As soon as the words left my mouth, I regretted it. My mother did not tolerate weakness.

"You've been pretending your entire life, Magnolia. You can pretend to be brave."

I wasn't sure if that was a compliment or an insult.

"Belinda can weasel the secrets out of a silent monk, so you'll be a good team."

Compliment. I was surprised. "I take it Emily left?"

"She left to call that vice president and try to dig up some dirt on that dead agent."

I considered asking where she was digging and what kind of tool she was using, but decided to leave it a surprise. I had a little more faith in the scheming that Belinda and I were doing.

Five minutes later, I was standing at the window waiting for my sister-in-law.

"Don't think this gets you out of cleaning," Momma said, walking toward the stairs, the vacuum cleaner trailing behind her. "And I need you to come to the shop to help me in the kitchen as soon as you get back."

"Yes, ma'am," I murmured as my sister-in-law pulled up in her shiny black car. I ran out the front door, my stomach in knots. Either Belinda made good money in her wedding business or my brother was making serious bank. The latter seemed unlikely. Last I'd heard, Roy had forsaken his finance degree to become a sound engineer.

My entire life was a mess—and had been for some time—but for the first time in weeks, I felt like I was finally taking control.

chapter thirteen

We were a full ten minutes early, so I was surprised to see Amy already waiting in the restaurant lobby. I hung back as we entered, and Belinda greeted her first, pulling her into a tight hug. When they broke apart, Belinda still clung to her arms. "How are you doing, Amy? Really?"

Amy was about to answer when she looked over Belinda's shoulder. Her eyes widened in shock. "You . . ."

Breaking away from Amy, Belinda snagged my hand and tugged me closer. "This is my sister-in-law, Magnolia."

Amy looked shaken. "What is she doing here? She murdered Max Goodwin." But acting must not have been in her job description, because her delivery was anything but convincing.

"Why, that's the silliest thing I've ever heard," Belinda cooed. "Magnolia—a *murderer*?"

"But Luke found her next to the body."

Belinda tilted her head and gave her the kind of look a patient mother would give an irrational toddler. "That doesn't mean she killed him. She went up to meet Luke—just like he asked—and that's when she found Max's body."

A couple on their way to the hostess stand gave us a nervous look, having clearly overheard part of our conversation.

Belinda pulled Amy toward the opposite wall of the entryway. "Let's just get a table, and we can discuss it more privately."

But Amy kept her gaze on me, clearly not approving of this plan. "Why is she here?"

"I already told you that she's my sister-in-law. We want to talk to you about the party."

"No." Amy seemed a little too adamant for someone who had nothing to hide.

While I'd told Belinda about being holed up with Amy in that room in Luke's mansion, I hadn't mentioned Amy's bizarre behavior. At the time I'd assumed it was her way of dealing with the stress; now I was starting to wonder if it was something else. But what could that *something else* be?

Belinda's mouth opened as if on a hinge. "*Amy.*" She took a breath, then gave her a gentle smile. "Okay, how about this? We'll just have lunch and talk about everything *but* the party?"

Amy looked uncertain.

"You said you wanted to hear all about the Martin wedding. It turned out even crazier than we thought it would."

Amy's mouth twisted as she considered the offer.

"I can go if you want," I said. It was starting to seem like Belinda would get more information out of her if I weren't around.

"Don't be silly," Belinda said, placing her hand on my arm. "You can stay." She turned to Amy. "Tell her she can stay."

Amy paused, casting a glance to Belinda. "You can stay."

A few moments later, we were following the hostess to a table. I still wasn't sure staying was the best decision, but it seemed too late to back out now.

We sat down and Belinda and Amy made small talk about a

mutual friend until the waitress took our orders. Then Belinda launched into a story about a wedding she'd orchestrated for two people from very different backgrounds—the bride was from a stiff upper-crust Belle Meade family, and the groom hailed from a rambunctious family from a small Alabama town.

I downed my salad in record time, partly because I was starving and partly because I wasn't part of the conversation, not that I minded. Listening to Belinda's story meant I could momentarily forget the circus of my own life. But then she swung the conversation back to Amy.

"You've done a remarkable job handling the adverse publicity from the murder," Belinda said as she chased an olive on her plate with her fork. "I've heard no negative feedback whatsoever about Luke's party ending with a murder."

Amy shifted in her seat a little, and from the look on her face, it was like Belinda had caught her shoplifting. "I have to admit part of it came from Magnolia's idea." She gave me a grudging look of gratitude. "She helped me put a new spin on the party after the sales for Luke's latest album came in lower than expected. Your idea totally saved the day, by the way."

"Thanks."

Belinda gave me a warm smile.

"I tried to channel the same thought process you used to find a new spin on *this* situation." Amy raised an eyebrow. "I *might* have had a hand in the #GoodRiddanceGoodwin hashtag..."

Belinda seemed caught between horror and respect, settling on the latter with a nod. "Well, good for you." She finally stabbed the olive with a satisfying thunk and looked back up at her friend. "The way that hashtag has been catching fire, I suspect there must have been a lot of people at the party who had motive to kill Max Goodwin."

Amy looked uncomfortable.

"Why, I'll bet half a dozen or more of the guests held a grudge against Max Goodwin."

Amy's face hardened. "Belinda, I don't want to talk about it."

"Amy, what are you so afraid of?"

"Afraid of? What are you talking about?" But her hand gripped the fork a little more tightly than was warranted. "I'm just not supposed to talk about it."

"Who says you're not supposed to talk about it?" Belinda asked. "The police?"

Amy hesitated. "Luke."

"Because of the publicity?"

She didn't answer.

Belinda gave me a questioning glance, then trained her patient stare back on Amy. "Do you think you could give us a copy of the guest list?"

Amy looked down at her plate. "I can't."

"Come on, Amy. Surely Magnolia didn't have the strongest motive. I know for a fact that Henry McNamara was there. He hated Max, and so did Paul Locke after Max screwed him on his contract." When Amy stayed silent, Belinda leaned closer. "How about a hint on how to contact Paul?"

"I don't know . . ."

"Like Belinda said," I added softly, "there were a lot of people who wanted to get even with Max. You wouldn't be telling us anything we couldn't find out on our own. You'd just be helping us save time." I leaned forward and held her gaze. "Amy, I didn't kill him, but I'm pretty sure the police are about to arrest me."

Tears filled her eyes again. "I don't want to lose my job."

"Are you protecting someone in Luke's entourage?" I asked.

"No. Of course not!" But her response came out a little too fast and insistent.

"You know," Belinda said in a soothing tone. "Once Magnolia's name has been cleared, the police will go looking elsewhere. It's obvious you know of someone else who might have a motive but who, like Magnolia, obviously didn't do it . . . only maybe it won't be so obvious to the police."

Amy hesitated, gnawing on her bottom lip.

"While we're clearing Magnolia's name, we can look for evidence to prove he or she is innocent too. Maybe we'll find the real culprit and free them both." She paused. "But we have to know who you're protecting."

Amy glanced around to see if anyone was listening, then leaned close, whispering so low it was hard to hear her. "Luke. He could be a suspect."

That was the very last name I'd expected to hear from her.

"He didn't invite Max to the party—in fact, he forbade him from coming. Luke heard about your argument with him, and he was pissed that the security guards had let him in. I think that's part of the reason he had me go find you. To see who had dared to stand up to Max Goodwin in public. Everyone was afraid of that monster."

I shook my head. "You don't need to worry, Amy. It couldn't have been Luke. He was the one who walked in and found me next to Max's body."

She didn't look convinced.

"Couldn't the hallway guard just tell the police when he let Luke in?"

Amy shook her head. "No. Luke would have taken the back staircase."

That meant the real killer had probably used the back staircase too. Maybe Colt hadn't seen anything useful after all.

Belinda patted her hand. "You know, if you left your iPad unlocked and on the table, maybe even open to the guest list, you'd have no way of knowing if someone saw it."

"Belinda, I don't want to get into trouble. I shouldn't even have told you about Luke."

Belinda's hand squeezed tighter around Amy's. "You won't. No one will *ever* know."

Amy studied her for several seconds, then gave her a slight nod. She pulled her hand loose and took her iPad out of her bag.

After tapping on the screen for a few seconds, she said, "I need to go to the ladies' room." She gave Belinda a tight smile as she stood. "I suspect this might take about five minutes."

We watched her walk around the corner before Belinda grabbed the tablet and got to work.

"Why's she so nervous?" I asked, glancing back toward the hall.

"Luke is a pretty private guy. He doesn't tolerate people giving up his secrets."

"Yeah, but there seems to be more to it than that."

Belinda's face lifted and she held my gaze. "You of all people should understand celebrities' need for secrecy."

"But doesn't she trust you?"

She sighed as she tapped the screen. "Honestly, losing this job would be healthier for her. Luke doesn't appreciate her like he should, but Amy puts up with it." Her face lifted slightly to give me a sideways glance. "Amy is secretly in love with Luke, only it's not so secret to Luke and to a few of the people in his entourage." She paused and frowned. "He takes advantage of that."

Griff had taken advantage of my need for him, so I knew all too well what that felt like. "So she's terrified that he'll find out and she'll lose her job?"

She nodded.

"Why would she love someone like that?"

Belinda went still for a moment before she resumed typing. "We love who we love, Magnolia. Sometimes we're too damn blinded by it to take a step back."

I nearly gasped to hear Belinda curse, something I'd assumed would only happen on a cold day in hell, but the resignation in her voice gave me pause. Was she referring to Roy? I knew my brother, or at least I used to know him. It wasn't a stretch. He'd shown bullying tendencies when we were kids, and I wasn't so sure he'd outgrown them by the time I'd left.

My gaze lifted to the hall. "She's coming."

Belinda finished her tapping and then opened up Amy's photo folder. As Amy sat down, she pointed to an image of an ocean sunset. "This is gorgeous. Was that taken on the West Coast?"

"L.A."

This game seemed ridiculous, but that wasn't to say I didn't understand it. Plausible deniability. Amy knew we had looked at the file, but she hadn't seen us do it.

Setting the tablet down, Belinda waved to the waitress. "I'm sure you have a million things to do," she said to Amy. "But we need to get together under better circumstances."

Amy released a short laugh. "It's hard to believe we're still the same girls who moved to Nashville six years ago." Her mouth twisted into a sad smile. "Look at us now. Neither one of us are doing what we came here for. Do you ever wonder if you're on the right path?"

Belinda's smile wavered. "Of course. Everyone does."

Amy shook her head as she reached for her wallet. "Listen to me get all nostalgic. But you're right. I really do need to go. Luke's having another small party tonight. I need to get things ready for it."

"Industry people?" Belinda asked.

Amy's upper lip curled as she pulled out her credit card. "His hangers-on."

"You put your money away," Belinda said, patting her hand. "My treat."

Amy slipped her card back into the slot in her wallet, then stuffed it into her purse. She glanced up at Belinda with tears in her eyes. "I know you don't understand."

My sister-in-law was silent for several seconds. "I understand better than you think." She lowered her voice. "But someone killed Max Goodwin, justified or not. And it sure as heck wasn't Magnolia. I have to protect her."

"But you're choosing her over me, Belinda. We've been friends for years, and you barely even know her."

Belinda's jaw tightened. "These are two entirely different situations. I'm protecting her. You're just covering for your boss."

Tears flooded her eyes. "Don't be so sure about that." She stood to leave, but then turned and said, "Check out Tina Schmidt. I heard a rumor that she threatened Max at a club a month ago. Like *actually* threatened to kill him. She was at the party."

With that, she walked away, her heels clicking across the tile floor.

The waitress came to drop off the bill, but Belinda handed her a credit card without even reviewing it.

"Did you get the list?" I asked as she pulled out her phone. "You didn't write anything down."

"I emailed it to myself."

"What if Luke suspects she told us and checks her email?"

"It won't be there. I signed into my own email account, then uploaded the file and sent it to myself."

Belinda was turning out to be a whole lot savvier than I'd expected.

"But a quick search on social media tells me where Paul Locke and Tina Schmidt currently are."

"You're kidding."

She flashed me a sweet smile. "Feel like dropping in on a few people and saying hello?"

"Are you serious? You want to question people?"

Her eyes widened. "Sure, why not?"

"But you're so sweet. Going to people's homes and practically accusing them of murder seems so wrong."

She jutted her head back and frowned. "No one's accusing anyone of *anything*." She shook her head at my silliness. "All we're doin' is asking about the party. That's all."

"I think Momma is expecting me to come help her in the kitchen."

She pulled out her phone and started swiping. "I'll just send her a text to let her know we have some work to do. I'll drop you off when we're done."

"Maybe we should give the names to the police and let them look into it." But as soon as the words left my mouth, I wanted to reel them back in. I didn't trust Detective Holden to check into them. But even if it needed to be done, it didn't sit well. "So we're really doing this?"

Belinda's face lit up with a cheerful smile. "We're doin' it."

"Where do you want to start first?" I asked. She was the one with a car, a situation I needed to remedy soon. I'd had a car back in high school, but it was in Momma's name, so I was sure she'd sold it long ago. I hadn't needed or wanted one in New York.

"Let's start with Tina. She's easier to track down. She says on Facebook that she works at Macy's at the Belle Meade Shopping Center. And she used Instagram to post a photo of a tacky customer just an hour ago. What do you say we go have a chat?"

We were about to investigate Max Goodwin's murder, which had to be the craziest thing I had ever done, and after living in New York for ten years—and in the theatre world to boot—that was saying something.

I pushed out a deep breath. No one had ever claimed I took the safe route.

"Count me in."

chapter fourteen

We found Tina Schmidt in the housewares department, talking to a customer about thread counts on sheets. She looked like she was barely this side of jailbait. Max had used *her*? The thought made me sick to my stomach.

"How about I talk to her?" I suggested. "And you can stand close enough to listen."

Belinda nodded. "You put your acting skills to work."

The customer made her decision and headed to the register; Tina restacked the sheets she'd taken off the shelf.

Showtime.

"*Tina?*" I gushed. "Tina Schmidt?"

It was obvious from the look she gave me that she didn't recognize me one bit. "Yes?" She sounded wary.

I cocked my head. "I'm Delilah." A grin spread across my face. "You don't remember me, do you? I can't *believe* you don't remember." She looked confused, then horrified. *Bingo.* "From Luke's party." I looked down at my dress and laughed. "I was dressed a lot different from this. I just finished a modeling job. Gotta do what pays the bills, right? But last night I had on jeans and a sequined shirt." It was the most common combination I'd seen at the party.

"Right . . ." She narrowed her eyes. "Oh . . . yeah. I think I remember you now." She gave me a sheepish grin. "I confess that I don't remember much from the party."

Well, that would certainly explain why she didn't recognize me. It was obvious she was under twenty-one. Did Amy know underage children had been drinking at Luke's party?

Good God. When had I gotten so old?

Resisting the urge to shudder, I lifted an eyebrow in a conspiratorial look. "All that free booze . . . who can resist?"

She chuckled. "I know, right? But I remember a whole lot of what happened *after* I left." Tina wore the grin of a satisfied woman.

I grinned back and nodded, wondering what she meant. She seemed pretty pleased with herself, so maybe she'd be inclined to spill. "From the booze to that hot bartender on the upstairs landing, it was the perfect party." I sure as hell hoped Colt would never find out I'd said that. "That's why I couldn't believe it when I heard what happened to Max Goodwin. And right after you and I had just talked about how he'd screwed us both over. Like *literally*."

She blinked. "I can't believe I told you. I haven't talked about it in over a month. I've tried my best to move past it." She made a sweeping motion with her hand to prove her point.

"Oh, honey. Don't you worry. It was after Max yelled at that *really* cute and super sweet catering waitress. The way he treated her was just horrible."

"I kind of remember that . . ."

"In any case, you and I swapped stories about how Max promised to sign us if we'd sleep with him and then backed out of his end of the deal."

The frown on her face made her look more sad than angry. "Yeah."

This girl hadn't killed him. She was just trying to move past the pain and humiliation of being used. "Anyhow, I was walking through Macy's and saw you over here, so I decided I just *had* to warn you that the police are talking to people who were at the party. You'll need to get your story straight. You know . . . work out your alibi for where you were when he was killed."

She looked worried for a second, but then it faded. "That's not a problem. I hooked up with Lee Jackson."

I gave her a blank look. "The country singer?" Lee Jackson had a bunch of hits back in the 1990s—the type of songs that just wouldn't go away—and he was still living off the laurels and the residuals. His reputation was almost as bad as Max's. And he liked 'em young too. Stupid girls fell for his *let me show you a few tricks* scheme—only his tricks were all in the bedroom, not the recording studio.

She gave me a smug look. "One and the same. He told me he was looking for a backup singer and wanted me to audition. He took me home and I auditioned, if you know what I mean . . ." Then she winked.

I'd seen him milling around at the party. Years of living hard had not been kind to the man.

I swallowed the bile rising in my throat. "And it covers the time Max was killed? 9:30?"

"We were doing the nasty by nine." She winked. "Several times and ways. That man sure is creative."

"And the backup singer job?"

"Sugar, we both know there was no backup singer job."

I was relieved that I didn't have to recite the lecture I'd been preparing in my head. She'd walked away from the situation a happy woman. Who was I to judge?

"Thanks for the warning," Tina said, glancing at a customer by the towels. "Duty calls."

"No problem."

Belinda had been standing to the side, pretending to shop.

She fell in next to me as we left the store. "Learn anything helpful?"

"Other than that Lee Jackson is kinky as shit, no."

Belinda looked startled.

"That's Tina's alibi. She was *doin'* Lee Jackson."

"And you believe her?"

"She had the look of a very satisfied woman." A look I hadn't worn in ages myself. Griff had always been too selfish to make sure I would walk away satisfied, and I'd been so wrapped up in the excitement of *Fireflies at Dawn* that I hadn't dared complain. Asshole. "I believe her."

"So that leaves Paul," Belinda said, then cringed. "Your momma called while you were talking to Tina. One of her staff members called out of work, and she needs you to fill in."

I sure as hell hoped I'd be in the kitchen and not serving food.

"But you still have an hour, and I saw on Twitter that Paul Locke is at the Cool Springs Galleria Mall signing autographs. We have time to drop by and get his signature."

"I never would have expected such deviousness out of you, Belinda Steele."

She lifted her shoulder into a shrug. "It's not the least bit devious. We're just talking to people."

While she drove us to the other mall, I called Emily and put her on speaker phone. "Have you talked to Henry McNamara yet?"

"About an hour ago. According to him, he showed up late, but Luke wasn't mingling with the guests, so he and a group of guys left at nine to grab a late dinner."

"And he can prove it?"

"Yeah, I just talked to two of his friends, who independently confirmed his story and said they were there until after midnight. I might still stop by the restaurant to confirm the guys aren't just covering for him. How'd it go with Amy?"

I cast a glance at Belinda, then said, "Amy wasn't very forth-coming. In fact, she was trying to protect Luke."

"Luke? Luke *Powell?*"

When Belinda didn't jump in, I continued. "Yeah. She said he was pissed at Max. He'd expressly forbidden him from coming to the party, although she didn't tell us what motive he would have other than not wanting him to be there, so obviously we're missing part of the story."

"Anything else?"

"She told us about a country singer Max had tricked into sleeping with him. Apparently she threatened him in a bar about a month ago, but I just talked to her. She says she has an alibi, and I believe her."

"So that leaves Paul Locke."

"Belinda found out that he's signing autographs right now at the Galleria Mall. We're headed over there. I'll let you know what I find out."

"Sounds good."

Spring had sprung in Tennessee, and the mall parking lot was packed with people eager to spruce up their spring wardrobes.

Still, it wasn't hard to find him. All we had to do was follow the sound of squealing teen and tween girls to the food court. A thirty-foot line of girls separated us from a man in his early twenties. His light brown hair was styled, and there was light stubble on his cheeks. A dark T-shirt stretched across his well-defined chest as he bent over the table in front of him and signed glossy eight-by-ten photos of himself. Besides the gaggle of fans, there were two people standing behind him who obvi-ously worked for him—a man tapping on his smart phone and a young woman dressed in jeans, a white blouse, and a pastel pink blazer. Her dark hair was pulled back in a ponytail.

"Oh, my God," I groaned. "Do we have to wait in that line? I'm not sure my reputation will survive it, not to mention I doubt he's going to share much with a bunch of thirteen-year-olds listening."

Belinda studied the circus in front of us. "I might have a way to bypass it."

"You *do* realize that we risk getting jumped if we try that, don't you? Thirteen-year-old girls can be vicious."

"I think I know the woman next to him."

I turned to her in surprise. "Really?"

"You wait here."

"Okay." I had no idea why she wanted me to wait, but I had no desire to get close to the mayhem. One of Paul's fans walked around the table and squatted down next to him while her friend took a photo of the two of them with her phone. Paul turned at the last moment and kissed the girl on the cheek, which elicited another round of ear-piercing squeals. The man definitely knew his audience.

I pulled out my phone to check for more messages, and was shocked to see one from Griff. I debated whether to listen to it, then closed out my voice mail screen. Nothing good would come of any communication with him.

I looked up to see Belinda talking to the woman with the ponytail. The woman beamed at her and pulled her into a hug. They broke apart, chatting up a storm before Belinda motioned in my direction. The woman glanced at me before turning back to my sister-in-law and nodding.

Belinda was grinning as she walked back toward me.

"Unless you hug and chat with strangers, I take it you *do* know her," I said when she reached me. Actually, I wouldn't put it past her to do that very thing. We hadn't known each other long, but she had to be the nicest person I'd ever met.

But Belinda laughed. "That's Tandy. We knew each other when I first got to town. We were backup singers together on a short road tour for a band I'm sure you've never heard of."

"You were a backup singer?"

She laughed again, her pinks turning pink. "About six years ago. When I first moved to Nashville."

"You *sing?*" I wasn't sure why I was so surprised. I guess because she looked so prim and proper now.

"Ages ago, but that's beside the point. Tandy's going to let us walk Paul to his car when he's done. We can ask questions until he gets in the car."

"Wow. You're amazing."

She grinned. "But we have to go get coffee for him and Tandy and meet them back here in ten minutes. That's when this thing is over."

"Not a problem," I said a little too eagerly. "I could use some coffee myself." I suspected I might need a caffeine boost to get me through whatever Momma had planned for me. I'd hit the mid-afternoon slump, and my lack of sleep wasn't helping.

We were en route to Starbucks, across the food court from the signing, thank God, when Belinda's phone rang. She dug it out of her purse, and the smile fell off her face. "Magnolia, I have to get this. Could you get the coffees?"

Her reaction to the call worried me. "Of course. No problem."

"Tandy wants a venti caramel macchiato, and Paul wants a grande Americano."

"Okay," I said. "Anything for you?" I got it out as quickly as I could—I could tell she was getting more stressed the longer the phone kept ringing.

"A white mocha." Then she answered the call and hurried away with the phone pressed to her ear.

I couldn't help but watch Belinda as I stood in line. She was talking on her cell about thirty feet away, leaning against a post. Based on her body language, the person on the other line was being a jerk. Her shoulders were hunched, and she looked like she was folding in on herself, trying to make herself disappear.

"Can I take your order?" the woman behind the Starbucks counter asked.

"Yeah," I said, shaking myself out of my stupor to give her my order, adding my own drink as well. I spied on Belinda as I waited, getting angrier and angrier by the moment. Who in the hell was she talking to, and how dare he or she make her feel that way?

After a couple of minutes, Belinda returned her phone to her purse and joined me at the coffee counter just as the barista was handing me the first of the drinks. Belinda had a smile plastered on her face by the time she reached me. "I'm sorry about that. Clients . . ."

"What was it about?" I asked before I could stop myself. I valued privacy and rarely butted into other people's business, but I was genuinely worried and upset on her behalf.

Belinda gave me a reassuring smile. "It was nothing. Just a bridezilla who was upset because the cake decorator didn't have the type of icing she wanted. All fixed now."

We both grabbed a drink in each hand and headed back to the Paul Locke mob scene. "I couldn't do it," I said. "I couldn't deal with all those spoiled, demanding women."

"Oh . . ." she drawled, her accent deepening. "It's not so bad. Most of them just want the wedding of their dreams, and I do my best to make it happen. Sure, some go off the deep end during the planning process, but in the end, the beautiful wedding makes all the stress worth it."

It sounded like a nightmare job to me, but if anyone was patient enough to deal with the crazies, it was surely Belinda.

When Tandy saw us approaching, she whispered to several of the mall security guards and then announced, "Thank you all for coming, but Paul has another obligation he needs to get to."

Paul stood and waved to the crowd with both hands. "Thank you all for coming! Love you, Franklin!"

The girls started screaming, and security guards pushed

them back as Tandy and Paul made a beeline for us, followed closely by the guy who had stood behind Paul.

They snatched their drinks from us and marched toward the very close exit.

Shit, we didn't have much time.

Belinda shot a look at me, as if to say, *I've got this*, then turned her attention to Paul. "Mr. Locke, I heard that you were at Luke Powell's party on Thursday night."

He took such a long drag of his piping-hot Americano that I feared for his vocal cords. Then again, I'd heard his latest single. Maybe this was the secret to his scratchy voice.

"I was there," he said, sounding short. Paul Locke obviously had two personas—the one he showed the public and the one he forced on everyone else. "What of it?"

"Did you see Max Goodwin?"

Paul stopped in his tracks and turned to face Belinda. "You with the police?" he asked, looking her up and down. "I don't remember this being part of the uniform." He gestured to her dress.

Belinda wasn't about to be dissuaded. "Please, Mr. Locke, if you . . ."

He snorted. "Cut the Mr. Locke crap. And I ain't answering shit, Barbie. Now get the hell away from me."

And that was the limit for me. I'd already watched Belinda be berated over the phone. I wasn't about to let this dipstick wannabe treat her like crap in front of me.

I stepped in front of Belinda, getting in the pissant's face. "I am so sick of upstarts like you thinkin' you're all that, but guess what? Your shit isn't gold-plated. It stinks just like everyone else's."

"Excuse me?" He shook his head and blinked. "What the hell are you talking about?"

"You, you asshole," I said, poking his chest with my finger.

"You think you can be an asshole to anyone you want, but you're wrong. Now apologize to my sister-in-law."

Surprise flickered in his eyes. *"What?"*

"You were rude to my sister-in-law, so apologize."

Belinda leaned toward me, putting her hand on my shoulder. "Magnolia, you really don't have to—"

Judging from the disdain that had washed over Paul's face, he'd recovered from the shock of not being fawned over. "What the hell do you want?"

"We want to hear about Luke Powell's party," I said. "We know you were there."

He laughed, but it didn't sound good-natured. "You're Luke Powell groupies."

I groaned. I'd heard just about enough crap for one day. "We most certainly are *not*. I was at the party, asshole. I just want to know if you talked to Max Goodwin that night."

"What's it to you?" he demanded.

"In case you hadn't heard, he was murdered."

He curled his upper lip. "Couldn't have happened to a nicer person. There's a certain sense of justice to him getting stabbed through the heart, don't you think?" Then he turned and stomped toward the glass exit doors and the black SUV parked at the curb.

Tandy watched her boss stomp off and then turned to glance at Belinda. "Sorry."

"That's okay," Belinda said. "Do you know if he talked to Max that night?"

"No," she said, looking at the tile floor. "I wasn't there."

"Did he mention anything about the party?"

She let out a heavy breath and bit her bottom lip. "I really shouldn't talk about it."

"Maybe later?" Belinda asked.

Tandy looked torn, but she nodded a quick yes before she bolted out the door.

As we watched them go, Belinda wrapped a hand around my shoulders and said, "We really need to work on your interviewing skills."

I snorted. "Yeah, that went south pretty quick."

"Tandy warned me to start off slow."

"Well, that wasn't workin' out so great either."

"You didn't have to defend me," she said quietly.

"You defended me last night," I said, feeling awkward as I watched Paul Locke's SUV pull away from the curb. I wasn't used to letting people get close to me so quickly. It had taken Jody and me three months to get to this point. But Jody hadn't been helping me clear my name in a murder investigation.

"We better get you to your momma." Belinda looped her arm through mine. I would have shaken loose from almost any other person, but I decided to let myself revel in the feeling of letting someone else take care of me.

No, not just someone. Belinda. I only hoped I didn't regret it.

chapter fifteen

Belinda offered to stop at my mother's house so I could change before she dropped me off at the kitchen, but my mother called me twice while we were en route, so I told her to take me straight to the kitchen.

"I can do more digging while you're working," Belinda said. I marveled at how her hands hadn't strayed one bit out of their ten and two alignment on the steering wheel.

"You don't have to do that, Belinda," I said. "It's Saturday night. Don't you and Roy have plans?"

"We do, but not until later. We're meeting one of his clients for drinks."

"Sound engineers have clients?" I asked in surprise.

"Oh!" She gave me a quick glance before turning back to the road. "He hasn't been a sound engineer for a couple of years. He's a financial planner now. Working for your dad's company."

I sucked in a breath. "*What?*"

"I can't believe your mother didn't tell you."

"No. She never said a word." I had to wonder how my mother felt about his place of employment. I suspected she hadn't shared the information because she wasn't happy about it. Funny how she'd bragged about his work as a sound engineer every which way this side of the Mississippi River, but she hadn't breathed a word about his decision to follow in our father's footsteps.

"Your dad's partner offered him a job."

"But Bill *hated* Dad."

She shrugged, not looking too concerned. "I don't know anything about the past, but Bill and Roy get along great. And Roy is very happy there. Bill has turned over some of your dad's old accounts to him. In fact, we're meeting one of your dad's clients tonight. The Morrisseys."

My blood ran cold. "Does Momma know Roy is taking over the Morrissey account?" I'd always felt certain Bill James knew something about Daddy, but the police had assured my mother he was as clueless as everyone else. I hadn't believed it for a minute.

"No . . ." She sounded worried as she turned to me. "She knows Roy is working for Bill, but nothing specific."

"Then don't say anything to her. Mr. Morrissey's wife disappeared the same time Daddy did. I'm not sure what Roy's told you, but there were a lot of rumors about them having an affair and running off together. Especially since Mrs. Morrissey had pulled nearly a million dollars out of her joint accounts with her husband."

"*Oh, my.*" She pressed her lips together, worry furrowing her brow. "I had no idea."

"Belinda, don't you worry about it," I said, forcing myself to sound light and breezy even though I felt anything but. "It was all a long time ago, back when we were kids. Roy probably doesn't remember any of it. But I'd hate to upset Momma."

She nodded, still looking worried. "Yes, of course."

"Where are y'all going?" I asked.

"Uh . . ." she said as she tried to move past her shock. "There's a new place in Hillsboro Village, The Olive. It's a martini bar. We're meeting them at eight." She glanced down at her dress. "I'll have plenty of time to get ready."

"*Ready?*" I asked in surprise. "You look beautiful, and I don't hand out compliments that often."

She blushed and looked embarrassed. "Magnolia . . . that's so sweet of you."

"Thanks for helping me, Belinda. I mean it. I don't have a single friend in this town anymore. Hell, I don't know if Momma even wanted me to come back . . . She sure doesn't act like it most of the time."

"That's just how she is, Magnolia. You know that."

"I know . . ." Still, it would have been nice for her to tell me how she felt.

"You think of me as your friend?" she asked quietly, her face devoid of expression.

"Well, yeah."

"Because I'm your sister-in-law?"

God, I was an idiot. She was only helping me because she felt some odd, misplaced loyalty as a member of her new family. I was a hot mess with more enemies than I could count. I wasn't sure *I'd* want me for a friend. Especially since I knew how narcissistic I could be. "What you're doing for me is above and beyond what family does, Belinda. This is what *friends* do. But I understand if you'd rather keep this a family thing."

She shot me a look that said she thought I was crazy. "Are you kidding? I would love to be your friend, Magnolia. I'm honored." Tears filled her eyes, leaving us in an awkward silence as she pulled out of the parking lot.

"Tell me how you and Roy met," I said, both out of curiosity and to change the subject. Besides, if we were going to be friends, I needed to know this stuff.

She gave me a shy smile. "It's a boring story, really. I met him at a wedding."

"That doesn't sound boring to me. It sounds romantic."

She released a soft laugh. "He was a DJ at the reception I was working at. He asked me out, and the rest is history."

"How long ago was that?"

"Four years ago."

"And you've been married one year?" Getting information out of her was harder than I'd expected. "You had a small wedding?"

"Yeah." Her voice seemed strangely muted.

"What made you decide to be a wedding planner?"

She shrugged. "I just kind of fell into it. I wanted to be a country singer. That's why I originally came to town. I'm from Mississippi."

I nodded. "You said you were a backup singer, which I never would have guessed in a million years."

She was quiet for several minutes before turning to look at me. "I envy you, Magnolia—living your dream."

"News flash, Belinda. I'm not living my dream. I'm currently stuck in a nightmare."

She waved off my statement. "You'll be back in New York in no time. You should take your own advice and turn your negative publicity into something positive."

"I wouldn't even know where to start."

"Let's worry about restoring your reputation first, and then we'll worry about the rest."

She turned onto Main Street and pulled into a parking place behind the building. "I'd come inside, but Roy's probably fit to be tied. I need to get home."

"That's okay. Thanks again, Belinda."

THE KITCHEN WAS BUSTLING with activity when I walked in, which surprised me since the dinner was only for twenty people. I grabbed a hairband out of my purse and pulled my hair into a ponytail.

My mother looked up from the canapé she was filling and frowned. "About damn time, Magnolia."

Tilly was at the stove stirring a big pot with a long wooden spoon. "Give it a rest, Lila." She cast a quick glance in my direction. "Grab an apron to cover that pretty dress and get in here in the thick of things."

A couple of minutes later, Tilly had me pulling pans of food out of the oven alongside a woman no one bothered to introduce to me.

"What time is this dinner?" I asked Tilly as she lifted a pot off the stove.

"Seven."

"That's about two hours from now, and everything's almost ready. Why are you all freaking out?"

"Because Tilly got the address wrong," Momma grumped. "And the dinner's not in Brentwood like we thought."

"Where is it?"

Momma sent Tilly a glare.

"Hendersonville," Tilly admitted with a sheepish look.

Well, crap. Hendersonville was a good hour north of Franklin. Now I saw the problem. "Will the food stay hot that long?"

"That's not the problem, Maggie Mae," Colt said, walking through the door. "Lila and Tilly have warmers in the back of the van. The problem is they're doing construction on 65, and we're going to have to drive around it."

Momma handed Colt a tray. "This one's ready to load." Then she slid another pan across the stainless steel work surface toward me. "You take this one out."

I grabbed the pan and followed Colt out the back door to one of the vans. I waited for him to mention the text, but he didn't say a word. The back doors were open and Colt effortlessly slid his pan into a warmer and then grabbed the pan I was struggling to lift. He grinned as he put that one into the warmer too, then he hopped down beside me.

His gaze wandered up and down my body, ending at my face. "You look good in an apron, Maggie Mae. Nice legs."

"Are you one of those *I like my women in the kitchen* kind of men?"

His grin spread. "Hell, no. I prefer my women in my bed."

I shook my head in disgust and spun around to head back inside.

I fumed for the next ten minutes as we continued to load the van. Momma and Tilly were only catering a meal for twenty, but they must have prepared seven courses based on all the food we stuffed into the warmer and then onto the other racks.

Why was I letting Colt set me on edge? I attributed it to my nerves, but I had more immediate concerns. I couldn't let him get to me.

"That's all of it," Tilly said on our final trip.

Momma put her hands on her hips. "Colt, you head on up to the address Tilly texted you, and Tilly and I will be along shortly. Magnolia, you go with Colt."

"What?" I asked. "Why? Why can't I just stay here or go home? I'll see if Belinda can swing back and take me."

"Because you've pestered poor Belinda enough, and Tilly and I have some things to discuss." She shot Tilly a look that made me very glad I was not Tilly. My mother's friend just sighed and checked her cuticles.

I pushed out a long breath. "Then why don't I stay here and finish the filing in the basement?"

"No. You'll go with Colt."

She put so much emphasis into the statement that I couldn't help but narrow my eyes. "Why are you so insistent I go with Colt?"

Good Lord. I hoped she wasn't trying to match-make us. But that couldn't be it. She'd already told me he didn't have any money, and financial stability had always been important to her. One of the many reasons she'd bemoaned my career choice.

My mother let out a groan of frustration. "Because we've all agreed you shouldn't be alone."

That was even worse. "What do you mean *we've all agreed*? Did you have a meeting or something?"

She remained silent. *They had!* "Why?"

"You're in this predicament because you don't have an alibi. If you're with someone twenty-four/seven, you'll be covered."

I put my hands on my hips and shook my head in disbelief. "Just how many people do you think are going to be murdered around me?"

She gave me an exasperated look and flung out her hands. "I have no idea, Magnolia, but there's no sense in taking chances."

I gaped at her for a full three seconds before I walked over to her and kissed her cheek. "I love you too, Momma. Thank you."

Surprise filled her eyes and she stammered, "I didn't say a word."

"You didn't have to." This was my mother's way of saying *I love you. I'm worried about you.* My mother was a woman of action, and her message was coming through loud and clear.

I took off my apron and hung it up on a hook before heading to the parking lot. Colt checked the back of the van to make sure everything was secure, then climbed out and gave me a wink. "Just you and me, Maggie Mae."

"And dinner for twenty. Momma will tan your hide if it doesn't get there on time."

"There's always after . . ." His voice trailed off as he walked around to the driver's door.

I'd met plenty of men like Colt—full of a lot of talk and mostly harmless. The more he knew he didn't stand a chance, the more likely he'd go full-court press. I just needed to use that to my advantage without upsetting the apple cart.

Who was I kidding? I'd spent my entire life upsetting the apple cart.

"So you and me in this van for an hour," I mused, taking my hair down and letting it fall around my shoulders. "Plenty of time to chat."

His gaze stayed on me while he turned over the ignition and brought the engine to life. "I'm not much of a talker." Then he grinned, as if implying there were plenty of other things he *did* do, and pulled out of the parking lot.

"I guess you're not much of a texter either."

"Yeah, about that."

I waited for him to continue, and lifted my eyebrows after several seconds when he didn't.

He shrugged. "Tilly kept me busy."

I shrugged this time. I had at least fifty-five more minutes to get what I wanted out of him. I could be patient when I needed to be.

He turned on the radio. A Keith Urban song came on and he began to whistle, casting glances at me every few seconds.

"I bet you don't listen to much country music up in the Big Apple."

I gave him a condescending look. "*Fireflies at Dawn* was written by a country songwriter."

"What the hell is *Fireflies at Dawn*?"

I rolled my eyes and leaned back in my seat, resting my arm next to the window. "It's the hottest new musical in five years, thank you very much. And I had the lead role."

"That's the play that made you an Internet sensation."

"Well, there's that . . ."

"You *do* know that's impossible, right?" he asked.

"They did hire me to play the part. I think the proof is on Twitter and YouTube," I said, a little too defensively.

"No, the title. Fireflies come out at dusk. Not dawn."

I shook my head in confusion. "They come out at *night*." I

patted the back of my right hand with my open left palm. "And it's *night* until the sun comes up at *dawn*."

He shook his head, looking very much like a belligerent five-year-old. "I've never seen one."

"When have *you* ever been up at dawn?"

He gave me a mock gasp. "I'm offended by that question. I've seen plenty of dawns."

"Yeah, because you hadn't gone to bed yet."

A lazy grin spread across his face. "Guilty as charged. And I've never seen a lightning bug."

"Yeah, because you were too drunk or hungover to notice."

He shrugged. "Tell me, what was this *Fireflies at Dawn* about? Did you catch lightning bugs on stage?"

"No," I said in a huff, crossing my arms. "*Fireflies at Dawn* is a metaphor."

"So it's about extraterrestrials?"

"Not a meteorite. A *metaphor*." His grin was as big as a meteorite though, and I shook my head, not wanting to give him another reason to tease me. "Never mind . . ."

"Oh, come on." He gave my arm a shove. "Tell me what it's about."

"It's about a woman named Scarlett who falls in love with—"

He lifted his hand straight up. "Stop right there. Romance is all I need to know."

"You're a songwriter. Songwriters write about love."

"*I* don't write about love. I write about one-night stands, driving fast trucks, and drinking beer."

"Quality lyrics, I'm sure," I murmured sarcastically.

"You had your chance to listen to them last night."

"I had to go to Bunco night. I think I would have rather watched you." I swiveled in my seat to look at him. "And have you ever thought that maybe your cynicism is what's holding you back?"

A smirk. "Nope. Not once."

"So you've never been in love?"

"Nope. No way. You?"

What Tanner and I had once shared seemed like puppy love now, though at the time it had felt big and real and important. "I thought so once, but now I'm not so sure." I rolled my bottom lip between my teeth. "No. I guess not."

"How old are you? Twenty-five?"

I hesitated. "Yeah . . . about that. How old are you?"

He grinned. "Same as you." He was lying. "But we're both young. We've got plenty of time to fall for the big L. In the meantime, we'll just settle for the little L."

"Which is?"

"Lust."

I had to turn this conversation around to get the information I needed. "You sure had a lot of women lusting after you at Luke's party. How much money did you make from your tip jar?"

"A couple hundred."

"I bet you saw a lot of people coming and going up there."

His body tensed, not enough that most people would notice, but I was studying him, trying to read his cues. He was grinning again, but there was a new brittleness there. "Yeah, but most of the time I was focusing on the ladies."

"You saw me."

His grin widened. "In case you hadn't noticed, you're one of the ladies."

"Can you answer my question? Did you see anyone other than Max go down the hallway toward Luke's office before I did?"

He quirked his mouth to the side as he kept his eyes on the road. "Nope."

"Are you sure?"

He gave me an aggravated look. "Yeah."

I groaned in frustration. "Come on, Colt. You didn't see *anything?*"

His grin returned. "I told you I only had eyes for the ladies."

But I still sensed he was holding something back.

"So what is Bunco anyway?" he asked, resting his wrist on the steering wheel.

Yep. Definitely hiding something. But I knew better than to press him and scare him off. The better option was to wait and try again later. "I could tell you," I quipped, "but then I'd have to kill you."

"Ah, so it's a secret society?"

"Yeah. Just like the Illuminati."

He talked steadily for the rest of drive, telling me about coming to Nashville right out of high school and working more jobs than he could count—several of them unsavory, like the gig at the bar he'd told me about. But he'd started working for my mother and Tilly about three years ago.

"What about you?" he asked. "Did you land in New York and end up on stage right away?"

"Hardly," I snorted. "I worked two waitressing jobs for two years until my new roommate dragged me to a commercial audition and I got it."

"So you really are lucky."

"I wish. I didn't get another job for six months, and then it was another commercial."

"So when did you make it on Broadway?"

"Not until three years ago. And even then, it was mostly small parts."

"So the first two years were waitressing. The next year you had two commercials, and the last three you spent on Broadway. What happened in those missing four years?"

I gave him a pointed look.

He shrugged. "Hey, I can do simple math. What were you doing?"

"Off-Broadway plays."

"Why New York? Why not the movies? I would think it would pay more."

"I just like New York." It was my turn to dodge, but he didn't seem to notice. Or if he did, he was taking a page from my book. Waiting. Colt gave off the air of a laid-back guy, but I was beginning to wonder just how laid-back he actually was.

WE GOT LOST for a few minutes after reaching Hendersonville. Momma called my cell phone, yelling at me to hurry up and get there, but Colt didn't seem worried. Tilly and Momma were waiting in front of the house when we pulled up, Tilly looking nervous and Momma looking ticked off, although she surely couldn't be pissed at me. I hadn't even been driving.

We helped unload the pans from the van and into the kitchen while the wait staff bustled around inside. As soon as we finished, Tilly gave Colt a set of keys.

"You kids take my car and head back. You're off the clock. Lila and I've got this."

"Really?" Colt asked, surprised.

"I don't want her anywhere near the guests," Momma said as she removed foil from a pan. "But don't let her out of your sight."

"Yes, ma'am," Colt said, shooting me a secret grin.

"I don't need a babysitter," I groaned.

"Yes, you do," Momma and Tilly said at the same time.

I crossed my arms. "Fine."

Colt laughed all the way to the car, but I snatched the keys out of his hand. "I'm driving." I hadn't driven in ten years, and it was time to jump back on that horse.

He lifted his hands in surrender. "No argument from me."

194

I slid behind the wheel and pulled out my phone to check my messages, surprised to see some texts from Belinda.

"Do you plan on sitting here all night?" Colt asked.

"Just a minute," I said.

I shook my head in wonder. Belinda truly was a force of nature. She'd contacted another acquaintance who'd attended the party, and apparently he'd seen Paul Locke and Max arguing in the shadows on the pool deck.

"Sneaky devil," I said to myself. "You're definitely hiding something."

"Hiding what?" he said, sounding defensive. I gave him a long hard look, but a grin spread over his face. "You caught me, Maggie Mae. I'm trying to figure out the best way to win you over."

Doubtful. I suspected his defensiveness came from years of habit.

Snorting, I turned on the car. "Never mind."

I wanted to call Belinda, but I suspected she was getting ready for her night out with my brother. I still couldn't get over the fact that Roy was working for Bill James, my father's old partner. Especially since I was sure he knew more about Daddy's disappearance than he had let on. And Morrissey as his client? I couldn't believe Mr. Morrissey would want that reminder shoved in his face.

"So where do you want to go?"

Where indeed. I didn't want to just sit around all night, but I had no idea what to do to further my investigation with Belinda. I cast him a glance. I was certain Colt knew more than he was admitting. Maybe all he needed was a catalyst.

"Magnolia?" Colt asked.

I shot him a wicked grin as the wheels in my head kicked into gear. "Did I mention I haven't driven in ten years?"

His face lost all color. "What?"

I shrugged, giving him a playful grin. "How hard can it be?

Just like a bike, right?" Tilly had backed into the drive, so I purposely shifted into drive and let the car jerk forward.

His hand shot out to grip the dashboard. *"Magnolia."*

I pressed the pedal to the metal, squealing out of the driveway before slowing down once I hit the road.

I burst out laughing. "The look on your face right now . . ."

"Tilly's gonna kill you," he said, his voice tight. "This car is her baby."

"She gave the keys to you. She's going to think you did it."

That was mean, but I planned to take full responsibility for my actions if it came to that. But I wasn't going to tell him that. He'd let me stew all afternoon over my text. He could do a little stewing of his own. Besides, I was too busy dwelling on my brother.

I had an idea and Roy was going to hate it. All the more reason to go through with it. "How do you like martinis?"

"Can't stand them. Give me a beer or a tequila shot, but keep those metrosexual drinks away from me."

My grin spread wider. Even better.

chapter
sixteen

"Oh, hell no," Colt said as I pulled into the parking lot of The Olive. It was 7:30, which was good. It would look better if we were already here when they showed up.

"Momma said you had to babysit me, and this is where I'm goin', which means you have no choice in the matter."

"Just remember that payback's a bitch, Magnolia," he grumbled, reaching for the door handle.

"So I've heard."

The Olive was half-empty, so we didn't have any trouble getting a table in the back. Colt sat across from me and grabbed the small menu.

"I'm telling you right now that I only pay for a woman's tab if she's a sure thing." His eyes met mine. "Are you a sure thing, Maggie Mae?"

"I'm a sure thing, all right," I said, snatching the menu out of his hands. "I'm damn sure I'm not putting out for you tonight."

He chuckled as he eyed the menu.

We ordered burgers along with a beer for Colt and a Diet Coke for me. Colt gave me a strange look, probably because I'd dragged him into a martini bar and then proceeded not to order any alcohol, but I didn't bother making an excuse. I didn't owe him one.

We watched the band set up while we ate our food, and finally Colt narrowed his gaze and asked, "What gives? Why are we here?"

I shrugged. "Belinda told me about this place, so I thought I'd give it a try."

"This place is a dive, and you look like a brunette Elle Woods with your cardigan and pearls." He gave a backhanded wave toward me and then took a long drag from his beer bottle. "Hell, you're not even drinking. What's the real reason?"

The door swung open, and Belinda walked in with my brother. I hadn't seen him in eight years, but I would have known him anywhere. Tall, dark hair and dark eyes, strong jawline and Roman nose . . . he was the spitting image of our father, only a younger version.

He wore a shirt and tie, and Belinda had changed into a cocktail dress and put her hair up into a twist. He scanned the room, his eyes rolling right over me until they settled on an empty table on the opposite side of the room. Belinda looked different next to him—smaller, almost—and her eyes were downcast. Which meant she didn't see me either.

Colt's gaze followed mine and understanding lit up his eyes. "Ah, I get it."

I swung around to face him. "How could you get it?"

"Your brother, the asshole. You wanted to see him. You're curious."

"Why would I come here to see him when we live in the same town?"

"Because the prick doesn't want to see you."

My chest squeezed. His rejection sucked, no matter how much I had expected it. "How do you know that?"

"I know the guy, Maggie Mae."

"I think I need a drink after all."

He gave me a quick nod, then got up from the table and walked to the bar. When he returned, he set a glass of amber liquid in front of me and took his seat, holding another bottle of beer.

I lifted the glass to my nose and sniffed. Whiskey. "I'm still not putting out."

"This one's a freebie. You've had a rough few days, so we'll call it a gift from a friend."

I took a sip and felt the burn go down my throat and warm my stomach. "*Are* we friends, Colt Austin?"

"We swung together in the park. That's a solid foundation of friendship for five-year-olds, and since I've been accused of having a five-year-old mentality, I think that seals the bond."

I gave him a smile of gratitude as I took another sip. Now I had two friends, Colt and Belinda. The beginning of a collection.

"So what's the plan here?" Colt asked. "You just gonna spy on them?"

"I don't know yet." That was the stupid part of this whole thing. I really didn't have a plan.

They sat in a booth, both of them on one side, making it obvious they were waiting for guests. Belinda was pushed toward the wall, and my brother sat on the outside like a prison warden.

Where had that thought come from?

Colt gave me a wicked grin. "I think we should go over and say hi."

"You're kidding."

"You've spent time with me. It should come as no surprise that I like to stir up shit."

I took another sip, giving him a dubious glare. "So this is entertainment for you?"

"Come on, Maggie Mae. Don't tell me you don't want to tell off that prick."

"You don't understand, Colt. *I* was the one who left."

"And someday I hope you'll tell me why you did it. Believe it or not, I might be able to help you." He gave me a pointed look. "I'm not stupid, Maggie Mae. You didn't run off to New York to make it on Broadway. You didn't even audition for your first commercial until you'd been there for two years."

Me and my stupid mouth. I took another drink.

"But that doesn't give your brother a free pass to treat you like shit."

"How do you—"

"I told you. I know things." He shrugged in response to my piercing look. "Tilly likes to talk, and there's no love lost for your brother. Now are you gonna do it?"

"I don't want to hurt Belinda."

He gave me a long look, then said, "I think she'll be fine."

I finished off my drink, shuddering a little. "Let's do it."

I slid out of my seat. Colt started to lead the way, but I pushed him behind me. I had to handle this my way.

As I marched over to the table, my mind scrambled to pin down what role I'd be playing. The aggrieved sister? The snotty bitch? But that would mean I had some idea of how I wanted this to play out, and I didn't have a clue. I was going into this blind.

I decided to play me, as raw and exposed as that left me.

Belinda saw me first. Her eyes lit up, but then she cast a glance at her husband and her excitement fell as flat as a failed cake. He had finally caught sight of me, and there was nothing but anger in his eyes.

"Magnolia."

I gave him a tight smile. "Roy. You're a hard guy to reach."

"I'm a busy man." He held out his hands. "Some people have real jobs to occupy their time."

"Theatre is a real job, Roy."

"Then why aren't you there doing it right now?" he asked, his voice cold.

Belinda cringed, but she didn't say anything. In fact, she looked downright scared.

And that pissed me off.

I plopped down in the seat across from him and tilted my head. "I take it you know Colt."

Roy scowled. "We know each other."

Colt sat next to me. "We sure do."

There was obviously some history there, which explained Colt's eagerness to dive-bomb my brother's meeting. I'd have to dig into that later, though.

"You look good, Roy," I said, leaning my forearms on the table. "Look at you. All grown up."

"That happens as time passes, Magnolia. I know you didn't go to college, but it seems like a simple concept . . . Then again, you were never the brightest star in the sky." His eyebrows shot up. "Or should I say, the brightest star on the stage. I heard you got replaced."

His retort stung more than I'd expected. "I had no idea you kept up with the latest Broadway news, Roy."

"I don't. But my friends were all *very* eager to fill me in on things. I hear you're also under investigation for murder."

"And here I thought you didn't have any friends." I hadn't meant to let the insult slip. If I were looking for reconciliation, this was not the way to go about it. But now that I'd let the genie out of the bottle, there was no putting it back in, and some deep angry part of me wasn't sorry.

Roy sucked in a deep breath, his nostrils flaring as his chest expanded. "You're an embarrassment to this family, Magnolia, and this family has had more than its share of embarrassments. You need to go back to whatever hole you crawled out of and leave us the fuck alone."

Another zinger that struck deep, but I kept my face emotionless. I'd found my role. That of the unfeeling bitch. Nothing could touch me. Or at least I could pretend that was true as long as I was looking at Roy and not Belinda.

Colt started to say something, but I kicked his shin with the heel of my shoe. Any interference from him was unneeded and unwelcome. He clamped his mouth shut and shot me a glare.

Ignoring him, I narrowed my eyes at my brother. "Your clients don't like that your sister is a person of interest in a sleazeball's murder?"

His face remained expressionless for several seconds, as if he were considering his next move. "Go home, Magnolia," he finally said.

"This is my home too, Roy. Just as much as it is yours." I picked up the menu and pretended to scan the appetizers. It was a good thing I didn't intend to order anything else—the unshed tears in my eyes were blurring all the words. I blinked them away and steeled my back, reminding myself of what my mother had told me long ago. *You're made of steel, Magnolia. Don't you ever forget it. We do not bend to adversity. We stand up to it. We face it.*

"Are you here because you want money?" he asked, looking impatient. "I don't have my checkbook with me, but come by my office on Monday and I'm sure we can reach some kind of agreement."

Belinda stiffened next to him.

"What happened to you when we were little, Roy?" I whispered in horror, staring into the eyes of this stranger. "What made you turn out this way?"

"*You* happened to me, Magnolia. Did you ever once stop to think about anyone other than yourself when you took off? Have you ever once in your entire pathetic, fucking life stopped to think about anyone other than yourself?" But he didn't give me time to respond; he was just warming up. "Do you have any idea what it did to Mom? You ripped her heart out. I was fucking invisible in that house, living in the shadow of your absence. *And now you're fucking back?* You ruined too many lives to just flounce back into town like nothing happened." He cocked his head. "And since I seem to be the only one who knows you won't stay, let's just speed things along. I'm not sure why you're here, but I can sure as hell make it worth your while to leave. How much will it take?"

"Roy," Belinda whispered, her face pale.

"Stay out of this, Belinda. It doesn't concern you."

His dismissive tone shot through me, stoking my simmering rage. I pointed a finger in his face. "Don't you talk to her like that."

"What the fuck is it to you? Do you even know who she is?"

Belinda's eyes widened in fear.

She hadn't told him. He had no idea she'd spent time with me. One more stab to my already hemorrhaging heart. Time to dial up the bitchiness and extricate myself from this situation as quickly and gracefully as possible.

I gave him a tight smile that suggested I thought he was an idiot. "I know you got married and didn't invite me."

"I told Mom not to tell you."

"In case you've forgotten, Mom gives us the orders and *we* do as *she* says. And for what it's worth, I saw your wedding photo on the staircase wall in Mom's house."

"You've never obeyed anyone or anything a day in your whole pathetic life," he sneered.

I leaned forward and slowly grabbed his tie and tugged. "And look which one of us is the uptight prick."

He slapped my wrist with more force than necessary.

Belinda gasped and I jerked my hand back.

Colt released a low growl, his eyes darkening with rage. "Touch her again, Steele, and you're a fucking dead man."

Roy's hate-filled eyes narrowed in on Colt, and he released a short bark of laugher. "You already fucking my sister?"

Belinda's eyes flew open wide. "Roy!"

There was disgust on his face as he turned to look at his wife. "Everyone knows she's a slut."

Colt's face reddened, but I pushed his side with my elbow, trying to shove him out of the booth. I had to get out of here. I'd expected Roy to be angry with me, but I hadn't expected *this*. My protective armor was nowhere close to being strong enough to protect myself from this attack.

But Colt wasn't going anywhere. His hand curled into a fist as he rested his arm on the table. "I think we should take this outside, Steele."

Roy laughed, but it was devoid of humor. "You touch me and I'll have your ass in jail so fast you won't have a chance to grab your hair gel, you pussy."

Colt's body tensed even more, which I wouldn't have thought possible.

"Colt. Let's go. Now," I said, trying to keep my voice even. The wisecrack caught his attention, and he gave me a quick nod.

He slid out and grabbed my arm, helping me out as gracefully as possible. Part of me was screaming to do it myself, but I was so tired of doing everything myself. Just this once I wanted to let someone else help me. But as I got to my feet, I realized I'd already dropped my guard and let someone help me—Belinda. And now I'd lost her. The grief was overwhelming.

Roy gave me a look of triumph. "I expect our discussion to remain between us. I'm sure you appreciate using discretion."

"You mean you don't want me to tell Momma?"

His eyes narrowed. "I can assure you my account of this evening will be vastly different than yours. And which one of us do you think she'll believe?"

"What about Colt?" I shot back.

Roy's gaze lifted to Colt's face, turning hard. "Colt will

do what's in his best interest." Then Roy's face completely changed, as though a switch had been flipped. A warm smile filled his face as he slid out of the booth, already looking past me. "Steve. Good to see you. And Bill, *this* is a surprise."

I spun around to see a man in his late fifties with a woman half his age literally hanging on to his arm. Steve Morrissey and his latest wife. Bill James, Daddy's business partner, was standing next to him. His eyes widened when his gaze landed on me.

"Magnolia?"

I forced a smile. "Hello, Mr. James." It took everything in me to sound civil, but it came out convincing enough.

He reached out his hands and grabbed my upper arms, looking me over. "Look at you, all grown up." His gaze lingered on my chest before lifting to my face. "You're the spitting image of your mother, only ten times more beautiful."

I wasn't sure how to respond to that, but I could see he hadn't changed. Backhanded compliments had always been his style.

His eyes flicked to Colt, quickly assessing him, then narrowed in on me. "Will you be joining us tonight?"

"No." My brother's reply was terse, and it brooked no objections. "She was just leaving. Weren't you, Magnolia?"

He stood behind me. I felt a sharp pinch on my upper left arm that kept digging in.

I resisted the urge to jerk away. "Yes," I forced out past the pain. "We're leaving."

He gave one last vicious twist of my skin as a warning and then released his hold. "Don't let us keep you, Magnolia."

Then he gave me a tiny shove. Colt noticed my stumble and shot a dark look at Roy.

I had to get out of here *now*. "Colt, let's go."

Bill shook his head and licked his lips, a habit I remembered from when I was a kid. "Don't be a stranger, Magnolia. I'd love to catch up."

I gave him a tight smile and turned to Mr. Morrissey and Wife Number Three or Four. Wife Number Two was the one who'd disappeared when Daddy did. "It was lovely to meet you all, but if you'll excuse us . . ."

I felt Colt's hand on the small of my back, pushing me toward the door.

I looked up at him, trying to keep it together. "We have to pay the tab."

"Already taken care of." He wrapped an arm around my back and ushered me out of the bar. We didn't stop until we reached Tilly's car.

Don't lose it. Don't lose it, I thought as my mind went into panic mode. *Think about something else.*

"I know you paid for everything, but I'm still not putting out," I blurted out, but it lacked the attitude it needed. It sounded sad and pathetic instead.

He looked down at me with pity in his eyes. "Oh, Magnolia. We're friends. Friends stick up for each other." He moved closer to pull me into a hug, but I took two terrified steps back. If he touched me, I knew I'd lose all control. And self-preservation insisted I keep it all together—stuffed into the small box I'd stuffed everything into for years. I ignored the bulging seams that threatened to split it wide open.

I'd deal with that later.

"This is all my fault." His voice was tight and his eyes hard. "I pushed you to go over to him." He shook his head. "I swear, Magnolia, I never thought he'd treat you like that."

"It's not your fault. I came here to see him and I did. He's an asshole."

"But—"

"I don't want to talk about it anymore."

He took several deep breaths and paced the length of the car, locking his hands behind his head. Finally, he stopped and looked at me. "What do you want to do?"

"I want to go home." I was furious with myself when I heard my voice quaver. I lifted my head, willing myself to be strong. I'd been through too fucking much—a hell of a lot worse than this—to let that asshole who shared my DNA hurt me like this. I was tired. I just needed some sleep.

"Okay, we'll drop Tilly's car off at the office, and then I'll take you home."

I grabbed the keys from my purse and handed them to him. He made a move to open my door, but I held up a hand, warning him off. He gave me a short nod and got into the car.

We drove in silence until we got to the parking lot behind the office. Colt turned off the car and looked out the windshield, toward the back of the catering office.

"I know you don't want to talk about it, but that was messed up, Magnolia."

"Don't," I said. It came out harsher than I'd intended, but I was still too vulnerable to talk about it without totally losing it.

"Okay," he said softly, still not looking at me. "I'll leave Tilly's car keys in the office and then take you home."

"I still don't have keys." Maybe Momma didn't want me to stick around either. If she did, wouldn't she have made me a copy? Emily had a set.

"I have the keys to the office. Lila can get you a set next week."

"No. My house." I shook my head, a wave of grief rolling through me. "I guess it's not my house. It's my mother's house. Roy's right. I don't belong here."

He grabbed the steering wheel so tightly I was surprised it didn't snap in two. "That man is fucked in the head, Magnolia. Don't listen to a word he says."

I remained silent, staring out the windshield.

"Magnolia." I pushed out a sigh and turned to face him. "He's wrong. So wrong. Look at all the people who are happy you're here. Your mother. Tilly. Belinda, even if she has to hide it from Roy. And me too."

"You?"

He gave me a cocky grin. "I can't remember the last time I had this much fun sparring with a woman. You keep me on my toes, Maggie Mae. I need you to stick around."

I was desperately close to losing it, and I didn't want him to be around when it happened. "You don't have to worry about taking me home. I'll just stay here at the office."

He sat back, looking uncertain, then shot me a grin. "Okay . . . maybe we can have office chair races."

"*You're* going home."

He shook his head. "No can do. I'm under strict orders to keep you in sight at all times."

"Colt, please." My voice broke. "I just really need to be alone right now. Just lock me inside and I'll text you updates or something until my mother picks me up." I looked up at him with tear-filled eyes. "Please."

"Magnolia."

"*Please.*"

He got out of the car, mumbling something about women and tears.

As soon as I climbed out of my seat, he pulled me into his arms. I made a feeble effort to push him away, but then lowered my forehead to his chest and snuggled against him. The need to be close to someone was overwhelming, but as fun as Colt was and as helpful as he'd been, he was *not* someone I could count on in the long term. And I was too confused about what I needed to figure him out.

So I needed him to leave.

"I can't leave you like this, Maggie," he whispered in my ear. "You're too upset."

I looked up at him, his face blurry through the haze of my

tears. "If you really want to be my friend, then you'll understand that I need some time alone." I took a step back, breaking his hold.

Worry filled his eyes. "If I leave you here, what are you going to do?"

I gave him a weak smile. "I'm going to lock myself in the upstairs office and watch Tilly's TV, but only after I raid the fridge. I'm pretty sure I saw a cheesecake in there."

A wry grin twisted his lips. "Tilly will kill you."

"Good," I said without thinking. "She can do the world a favor."

His eyes widened, but I quickly shook my head. "Stop. It was just a very bad attempt at a joke. Now unlock the door."

He looked torn, but he did as I'd requested. I walked over the threshold, breathing a sigh of relief.

"Thank you for a wonderful evening, Mr. Austin," I drawled in a voice an octave above my own. "You may call me in the morning."

"Magnolia," he pleaded.

I grabbed Tilly's car keys and set them on the stainless steel island in the kitchen. "Your task has now been completed. You may go."

He let me push him out the door, but he stopped just outside. "Call me if you need anything, got it?"

"Yeah, thanks."

"We're friends, remember?" He leaned forward and his lips brushed my temple, lingering a little longer than would be appropriate for a "friend."

I felt a stir in my chest, but I knew from experience it was not desire. It was different, more desperate. This was *loneliness*. I'd lived alone for ten years, but after everything—the play, Griff, my uncertain welcome back to Franklin, the strange messages, and Max Goodwin's death—I needed to connect with someone on a deeper level than my usual superficial attachments. Maybe that was why Griff had cheated on me. Because I wouldn't let him in.

No, Griff was just an asshole looking for his next lay.

But so was Colt. I needed to remember that. If I was going to sleep with someone in this state, it had to be someone who didn't have a habit of fucking and running.

I gave him a soft push. "I'll text you tomorrow."

His grin wavered. "Not too early. I like to sleep in."

Liar. I had no doubt he liked to sleep late, but he'd come running if I needed him. At least I liked to think so.

A strange look crossed his face as he stood on the stoop. Something like guilt. "I probably shouldn't be telling you this . . ." His voice trailed off, indicating he might already be having second thoughts. "You didn't hear this from me, okay?"

I nodded.

"Powell's security guard left his post about fifteen minutes before you showed up. He wasn't gone long, but long enough for someone to sneak in and kill Max."

Then, just as I was about to ask why he wouldn't go to the police with that information, he turned around and bolted to his truck.

I shut the door and locked it. Somehow I managed to wait until I heard his truck start and pull away before I leaned the back of my head against the door and let the dam to my tears break loose.

chapter
seventeen

I cried for a good twenty minutes, sitting on my mother's kitchen floor with my back to the door, releasing years of pain and fear.

My limited memories of that night flooded back with a vengeance, tumbling one on top of the other until it was a jumbled mix of rain and mud, blood and terror. I hadn't remembered anything new, but I knew without a doubt that the house was key.

What had happened there?

When I'd calmed down enough to stop hyperventilating, I climbed to my feet, found a glass in one of the cabinets, and filled it with water. After I drained the entire cup, I filled it again. Then I dragged out the previously discovered cheesecake. I didn't even bother to put it on a separate plate. I just grabbed a fork and stabbed into it, not stopping until I'd devoured two full slices.

Good call on wearing this dress today. If I kept eating cheesecake and burgers, I wouldn't fit in it by the middle of the week.

My mind jumped back to the restaurant, and my eyes started

to tear up again at the thought of Belinda. Did Roy hurt her? I couldn't bear the thought, but I had no idea what to do about it. Besides, I wasn't sure she'd even speak to me again after tonight.

This was why I didn't let myself cry. Because once I started, I couldn't stop. Every little thing would set me off for hours. It was a lesson I'd learned the hard way in the first years after my panicked escape from Franklin.

What was I going to do? I took deep breaths, inhaling for a count of three and exhaling for a count of three, over and over until I felt calmer and ready to deal with the nightmare that had become my life. Or, more accurately, the nightmare that had steadily gotten worse.

The truth was that I was tired of it all. Of the running especially, since I didn't even know what I was running *from*.

I needed to remember.

At least that's what I told myself as I ran upstairs to the office and started digging around in my mother's desk. She'd left her purse in her drawer, which made it easy to find her car and house keys.

With everything else going on in my life, this seemed like the worst idea ever, but I *had* to know. I would never be able to find any happiness in my screwed-up life until I came to terms with whatever had happened that night. Once I accepted it, maybe I could fix everything else in my personal life.

As I drove to my mother's house, it occurred to me that it might be a more gainful use of my time to figure out what had happened to the security guard at Luke's party. Why had he left? How long had he been gone? Why was Colt making it such a big secret? But it was highly unlikely that Luke Powell would let me into his house to ask, and the police sure didn't seem disposed to help me.

Once I got home, I found a flashlight in the junk drawer in the kitchen, then started out the back door. But before I got very far, I stopped in my tracks, feeling an overwhelming need to protect myself.

I raced back up to my room and removed the gun from the nightstand drawer with shaking fingers. It was probably more likely to land me in trouble than to help me, but I still found myself stuffing it into a small messenger bag from the closet. I looped the strap over my head and raced down the stairs and out the back door before I could change my mind.

I'd barely left the backyard and entered the woods before I realized this had indeed been a terrible idea. I hadn't even changed out of my dress. But while I desperately wanted to go inside and change, I knew I might chicken out if I did that. It was time to face the truth, however ugly it might be.

I had no idea where I was going, but my feet chose my course. I shined the flashlight beam in front of me, trying to find something familiar to tell me I was on the right path. But that was laughable. I had rarely ventured out here when I was a kid, preferring to stay indoors and view nature out a window, but Roy had spent hours and hours in the woods. Especially during summer break. He and his friend Tyler had built a fort from discarded scraps of lumber.

After ten minutes of hiking, I was about ready to go back, relieved that I hadn't found anything. The Nashville metropolitan area wasn't known for its vast forest system, and the Steele family home was located on prime horse farmland. Despite all the hills that made this wooded area ill-equipped for horses, it stood to figure the woods couldn't be that deep. Besides, Roy had never mentioned seeing an abandoned house in the woods when we were kids.

I'd imagined it all.

But then I reached the top of one more hill, deciding it was time to turn back, and my heart slammed into my rib cage.

There—thirty feet in front of me—was the house. Just like I'd seen it in my dreams.

It was obvious it was abandoned. Almost all the windows were busted out, and the landscaping was either dead or overgrown.

Terror washed through me. I knew deep in my gut there was nothing to be afraid of tonight, but that night had been another story. Here. It had happened *here*. The memories tumbled back, clearer and deeper than ever before.

"MAGNOLIA, *you piece of shit, come back here!*"

I ran through the woods, the rain coming down in sheets, drenching me from head to toe. My dress clung to my body and my legs, the heavy fabric making it difficult to run. A tree branch snagged my hair, jerking me to a halt. I stopped and fumbled with the strands, ripping out a chunk and nearly dropping the camera in the process.

"*Magnolia. Come on. Can we just talk?*" *Blake paused.* "*I'm sorry, Maggie. Let's just go back.*"

I took off again, running until my bare feet slipped on a patch of mud. I fell face forward, landing on my hands and knees, but I quickly scrambled to my feet. Part of me wanted to find Tanner and tell him to beat the crap out of Blake. But Blake stood between me and home, and he was driving me deeper and deeper into the woods.

I wasn't sure he'd let me past him.

There were rumors that Delaney Farcus had stood up to him and regretted it. At least that was how some of the girls at school explained the bruises on her face.

Rape.

I hadn't believed the talk. Blake was a hothead, but would he really rape and beat a girl? No way. Despite my best efforts to shield Maddie, she'd heard the whispers too. She'd had doubts, but I'd assured her not to worry. Until I suspected him of cheating.

Now I wondered if it had all been true.

"Goddammit, Magnolia!" Blake shouted, sounding madder than before. He was closer too.

I started to run diagonally and then down a hill. My foot slid sideways, and I ended up tumbling down the embankment on my butt and landing in a stream.

If I stayed in the water, he couldn't follow my tracks, but the sharp stones that covered the creek bed would slow me down, not to mention shred my feet. The rain was coming down so hard and the woods were so dark that I could barely see where I was going. Could he really find my footprints?

I crawled up the hill, pushing on. Blake's voice had grown distant by the time I topped a hill and saw a dark building ahead. If someone was home, I could use their phone to call Tanner to come get me. Momma was out of the question. She'd lock me up for the rest of the summer.

As I came closer, I saw it was an old house. The overgrown weeds and broken windows suggested it hadn't been lived in for years. Maybe I could sit inside and rest, regroup, and figure out how to get home from here.

I knocked on the broken screen door, but it didn't surprise me when no one answered. The hinges squeaked when I pulled it open, making me wish for a flashlight. But a phone would have been more helpful. As my eyes adjusted to the light, I could see that I was in a mudroom— hooks and cubbies lined the right wall. A door stood ajar at the end of the small room, and I took a step toward it. The swooshing of blood from my increased pulse filled my ears.

TEN YEARS later I stood at the same door, hesitantly reaching for the handle. I'd finished the walk in a daze, but I knew one thing. I needed to go inside. I needed to remember it *all.*

I*T'S JUST AN ABANDONED HOUSE,* Magnolia. *What was I afraid of? Ghosts?*

I wasn't easily scared, but the house had an eerie vibe that was urging me to get out.

Lightning streaked outside the windows, lighting up a large empty room at the end of the hall, its tattered white curtains blowing madly in the gusting wind.

Thunder boomed outside, and I could have sworn I heard a faint scream, just low enough for me to question my sanity. At first I credited it to an overactive imagination, but then I heard it again, fainter and longer this time, blending with the roar of the wind. My hands shook as I sorted through the list of reasonable explanations, finally deciding it was probably a feral cat scared of the storm.

But I still needed to get the hell out of here.

I was about to turn around and run outside when another flash of lightning lit up the sky, quickly followed by a boom and the sound of a tree cracking. My already goose-bumped skin prickled as I realized it was too dangerous to leave until the storm calmed down.

I passed several empty bedrooms and a bathroom before I found myself in the living room, the kitchen to my right. The place was completely empty, and the open cabinet doors and drawers made it even creepier. That's when I heard it again.

The scream.

There was no denying it this time. It was a woman's scream, and it sounded like it was coming from the floor. I'd never believed ghost stories, but I was suddenly having second thoughts.

Lightning flashed again, lighting up the trees, and a dark SUV parked about ten feet from the house.

I dropped my camera as I clasped a hand over my mouth to hold back a scream.

Oh, my God. There was somebody in here with me.

Now, I stood in the same spot. Looking out the empty picture windows at the vacant drive. My breath came in ragged pants, and my cheeks were numb. I reached up to pat one, surprised to find it wet with tears.

Every part of me screamed to go back. Go home. But I had no idea where home was anymore. That night had stolen my entire life, and I refused to give it one more ounce of power over me.

I pulled the gun out of my bag and took off the safety. There'd be no need for it tonight, but if this was the security blanket I needed to face the truth, then so be it.

I RAN for the kitchen door, deciding I'd rather take my chances in the storm, but I tripped on an open drawer and fell against the counter, accidentally slamming a cabinet door shut.

Oh, God. Oh, God.

I righted myself and made it to the door. My hand was on the doorknob when an arm snaked around my waist, jerking me back into something hard.

I screamed, but a hand slapped over my mouth and nose, blocking my airway.

I couldn't breathe.

Panicked, I kicked my assailant's legs and dug my nails into his hand, trying to pry it off. But it clamped down like a vise. Terror flooded every cell in my body.

"If you don't stop, I will kill you now," a menacing voice

commanded in my ear.

But that was easier said than done. Every part of me screamed to fight, fight, fight. Fight to live. Fight to escape.

I sucked in a foul breath tasting of copper and dirt.

Tears streaming down my face, I tried to fight him again, but my head was growing fuzzy from the lack of oxygen.

This was how I was going to die.

My body sagged into his, and he began to drag me backward. But a new surge of energy shot through me, and I bit his hand and pushed his arm with all my strength.

The moment his hold faltered, I shot forward. I moved so fast I ended up almost face-planting on the floor, but my hands broke my fall and I scrambled to get to my feet. Make it to the door, Magnolia. Make it to the door.

But he captured me before I even got close to the doorknob, his fist smashing down on my back.

I cried out in pain as I fell, all the air knocked out of my lungs. He scooped me up around the waist and carried me like a rag doll, my body flopping over his arm as I fought to inflate my lungs.

Think, Magnolia. Think! *something deep inside me screamed.* Don't give up. Fight!

But I was powerless. As he started down a staircase, I did the only thing I could think to do—I reached for the doorjamb and wrapped my fingers around the trim. I only delayed him for a tiny fraction of a second. One hard jerk broke my grip free, and he carted me down a staircase, the thunk of his boots on the wooden steps filling me with more terror.

The basement was dimly lit, and I heard a muffled sound and the creaking of wood. As soon as we reached the bottom, he turned and I saw the source of the noise.

A woman was suspended from the rafters, her hands bound by rope and strung up on a pulley. She was naked except for her white bra and panties. Blood dripped from several cuts on her thighs and stomach.

Her eyes were wild with fear, and her mouth was stuffed with a rag. She pulled against the ropes when she saw me, standing on her tiptoes.

A new surge of terror rushed through me, and I kicked and screamed with all my might. It wasn't near enough. He threw me to the dirt floor, and the landing sent a shooting pain through my shoulder. He turned to the side and reached down to the floor, but I didn't waste time to see what he was doing. I got to my feet and ran.

I made it to the bottom step before he grabbed me again, dragging me backward as I screamed and screamed, my throat already raw and hoarse.

He slid a slip-knotted rope around my right wrist and pulled it tight as he dragged me over to a pole.

I kicked his leg hard enough for my bare toes to throb, but at least it had some effect on him, based on the grunt he forced out. He dropped me in a heap and knelt down beside me. Grabbing a handful of my hair, he shoved the right side of my head into the metal pole. Bright lights filled my vision, quickly replaced by blackness, leaving me only vaguely conscious as he tied my wrists to the pole. I tried to open my eyes, but they refused to cooperate.

He leaned in close, his warm breath on my cheek as he said, "Well, I'll be damned. It's Magnolia Steele. Too bad for you fate can be a fickle bitch."

He knew my name.

He knew who I was.

I knew I should care, that I should run, but my body refused to cooperate. The black fog of unconsciousness was already rolling in.

"Be a good girl, Magnolia, and I'll let you walk away from this." There was a smile in his voice.

I heard sobbing, but in my semi-conscious state, I couldn't be sure if it was mine or the woman's.

"I didn't do it," her voice pleaded.

"Wrong answer."

Her screams faded to whimpers, and I struggled to lift my weighted eyelids. I could see work boots and jeans. They paced back and forth. The exertion was too much, though, and my eyes fluttered shut. I started to drift off.

The woman's screams kept me awake even though my head felt blurry. I felt lost inside myself, like I was in the bottom of a long, long tunnel. But then I felt my dress being lifted to my lap.

He's going to rape me. *I told myself to fight, but I was too far inside myself to care.*

My head drooped forward. I didn't have the strength to lift it, but I could see him from the chest down. He left my panties where they were, but he hefted the knife toward my flesh.

This is how I die.

In a damp, dark torture chamber, with a bleeding woman's cries ringing in my ears.

The fog in my head was beginning to clear, and I wondered if my mother would ever know what happened to me. If I would become one more loved one who'd disappeared from her life.

When the knife tip touched my leg, my first instinct was to scream, but some inner strength rose up inside me. Don't give him the satisfaction. *I couldn't fight him off, but I wouldn't give him what he wanted.*

The blade made its first cut, and I gritted my teeth to keep from uttering a sound.

"Oh, Magnolia, what a brave girl you are," *he cooed as the knife glided a slow path across my skin.*

Tears slid down my cheeks, but I only allowed myself to whimper as hot pain dug into my leg.

When he finished, he grabbed my hair and jerked it toward my leg, sending a shooting pain through my head. "Look at it, Magnolia. This your reminder. Speak of this night, and I will kill your mother and your brother. I will make you watch. And then I will kill you."

The woman was sobbing across the room. She started crying harder as the man stood and walked toward her.

220

I stared down at the C with a line through it, watching the blood drip down my leg to the floor.

This isn't happening. This isn't happening.

The pain brought back the fog in my head, and I welcomed it, desperate for escape.

"I'm sorry," the woman cried.

"And so am I," he said. Her terrified screams ripped through the air, and then . . . nothing. In my semi-conscious state, I wondered if I'd passed out, but I realized I was still looking at my leg, the mark barely visible through the blood. I lifted my head only enough to see the puddle of blood on the floor under the woman's feet. My eyes slammed closed, but as my mind retreated, I registered the drip, drip, drip of her blood.

MY HANDS SHOOK SO VIOLENTLY that I considered putting the gun on the kitchen counter. Instead my grip tightened around the handle. I waited for tears, but they didn't come. Maybe I was cried out. I knew I was in shock.

I trained the flashlight beam on the door to the basement. Part of me wanted to go down there and completely confront my past, but I couldn't do it. Not in the dark. This was enough.

Heading for the kitchen door I had never gotten to open that night, I walked outside and breathed in the night air, equally relieved to know the truth and horrified by it.

That's when the tears fell, in a gush of anguish. Someone had been killed in that basement. I'd been there. Somehow I'd survived, but survive was the key word. I'd struggled to live after—without really understanding why.

After I turned the safety back on, I stowed the gun in my messenger bag. Then I practically ran home, unsure of what to do. Did I go to the police? I barely remembered any important details, and it had happened nearly ten years ago.

When I got close to the edge of the woods, new memories edged forward.

chapter eighteen

W hen I woke up, I was outside, beneath an awning of trees. Rain beat down on my face, and my leg screamed with pain.

My eyes flew open in horror—of what, I wasn't sure—and I struggled to get up. The sudden motion sent a sharp pain through my head, followed by a wave of vertigo. I rolled to my side and vomited.

I slowly climbed to my feet, feeling as if everything around me was very far away. I was ten feet into the woods behind my own house. How had I gotten here?

I trudged up the side yard to the front of my house, every part of me aching, but my head hurting the most. I stopped at the corner of my house, clinging to the side as I dry-heaved. When I finished, I righted myself and managed to put one foot in front of the other again. I had to make inside—if I could just get behind the front door, I would be safe.

Safe from what?

THE MEMORIES of waking up in the woods had always been hazy and indistinct, fully picking back up at my mother's front door.

When I had walked into the house that night, my mother had been in the living room, talking on the phone. Tilly sat on the sofa wringing her hands, while Tanner and Maddie and several of our friends were gathered in the kitchen. Tanner was shouting at the group to listen to him.

Suddenly everyone stopped; everyone stared. The room fell eerily quiet. All eyes were on me as I stood center stage in my own horror show.

"Never mind," Momma shouted into the phone. "She's here." She tossed the phone onto a chair, then rushed forward and pulled me into a hug.

"Oh, thank God," Tilly murmured from behind Momma.

Tanner was next to me in an instant, his eyes wide with concern. "What the hell happened, Magnolia?"

I looked at him, feeling very far away, and heard myself say, "I was in the woods."

"What in the Sam Hill were you doing in the woods?" Momma barked, anger beginning to chase away her fear.

Why was I in the woods? I wasn't sure. My gaze sought out Blake, who stood in the back, his eyes narrowed. He was the last thing I remembered.

"I don't know."

"You don't know?" Momma shouted. "What the hell kind of answer is 'you don't know?'"

"Lila!" Tilly admonished, pulling me into a hug. "Can't you see the girl is traumatized?"

Momma ignored her. "Why were you in the woods?"

Terror rose up, bringing me to the edge of hysteria. "I don't know."

"And you had to go to the woods to do it? You've been gone for two hours!"

"Maybe I got lost," I whispered.

I needed to be alone. I needed to get to bed. I needed something to make the hammer in my head stop pounding.

I pulled loose from Tilly and stared at my mother. "I'm sorry I left."

"That's it? You're sorry you left?"

Embers of frustration and anger ignited in my chest. Something bad had happened, even if I had no idea what, and my mother was shouting at me in front of all my friends while I was struggling to put coherent thoughts together.

"You've pulled some self-centered and selfish stunts before, Magnolia, but this one takes the cake."

My mouth dropped open, and tears welled in my eyes, but I just shook my head in disbelief.

Then her gaze dropped to my legs. "You have completely ruined that dress. Were you rolling around in the mud? And what is that?" She moved closer, bending forward.

I glanced down in confusion. What was the throbbing in my thigh?

I took several steps back. "I'll pay you back for the dress."

"You sure as hell will. You can forget that camping trip next weekend. You'll be helping me with the Fillmore wedding reception. You're grounded."

What was happening?

I took a step backward, my head pounding on the side and feeling close to throwing up again. Unable to take any more, I turned toward the stairs.

"Just where do you think you're going?" Momma demanded.

"To bed," I said, but my voice was small.

"We're not done talking about this!" she shouted after me.

But I ignored her—I ignored everyone—and slowly climbed the stairs, each step harder than the last. I passed Roy's partially open door on the way to my own room. He was lying on his back in bed, but he sat up, bracing himself on his elbows as he glared at me. "I know why you ran off."

I shook my head, setting off a fresh wave of pain. "What do you know?" Because I couldn't remember any of it.

"I saw Blake chasing you."

"Why didn't you tell Mom?"

His mouth tipped up into a grin, but it didn't reach his eyes. "We all have secrets, Magnolia. Even me." He plopped back down. "Now shut the door."

I did as he'd asked and stumbled into my room, not surprised to see Tanner coming up the stairs after me. If anything, I was surprised he hadn't come up sooner.

"I'm sorry about the camping trip," I murmured, my eyes on my bed. I just needed to make it that far.

"I don't give a fuck about the camping trip. I want to know if it's true."

I lay down, not even bothering to pull back the covers, and closed my eyes. "Is *what* true?"

"Were you screwing Jason Mooney in the woods tonight?"

I opened my eyes and looked up at him. Did he really believe that after giving my virginity to him hours ago I had slipped into the woods to fuck a guy I couldn't even stand?

I started to laugh.

"What the hell is so funny, Magnolia?" he demanded, standing next to the bed. "So you're admitting it?"

I laughed so hard I could hardly breathe, the middle of my back aching as if I'd slammed into something, my head pounding so hard it felt like it was about to explode. I just couldn't stop. "Why would you think that?"

"Blake."

I blinked, sure I'd heard him wrong. "What?"

"Blake said he followed you into the woods. He found you screwing Jason, but when he confronted you, you took off running."

Tanner actually believed his loser best friend's lies. It was obvious he had never really known me at all.

His eyes widened and he pointed to my leg. "What the hell is that?"

My laughter cut off abruptly, and I sat up and pulled my hem down in an overwhelming panic to hide it from him, although I didn't have a clue why. "None of your business. Now get out."

"Not until you tell me what that is!" But that wasn't concern in his voice; it was accusation.

What did he think he was looking at?

I got to my knees, seething with anger. "You're right, Tanner. I *did* have sex with Jason Mooney in the woods. I was gone for two hours because we were so busy fucking all over the goddamned place. And he was so good, I had a tattoo etched onto my leg to help me remember who was the better lay. Happy now?"

He stared at me, his face pale. "You're lying."

I climbed off the bed and got to my feet. "Which is it, Tanner? Either I'm lying or I'm not. You can't have it both ways, because both versions have me *fucking Jason Mooney!*" My voice was shrill and high-pitched, and it sounded every bit as hysterical as I felt. "The very fact that you would believe that tells me everything I need to know. You and I are *done. Now get the hell out.*"

I gave him a shove, but he didn't move an inch. "Magnolia, I'm sorry. Let's talk this over."

I started crying and pushed him harder, but he dug in his feet. When he didn't relent, I slapped at his chest over and over as I sobbed.

"Magnolia. Stop." He grabbed my wrists, but he brushed against mud-covered wounds that I didn't know I had.

I jerked away from him. "Get. Out."

My mother appeared in the doorway. "What the hell is going on here?"

Tanner gave me a pleading look.

"Nothing," I forced out past my tears. "Tanner was just leaving."

"Magnolia," he said, his face full of contrition. "I'm sorry."

"Go."

My mother marched into the room. "You heard her. Get out."

"Okay." He held up his hands in surrender. "I'm sorry. I'll call you tomorrow."

My mother waited until he left before she asked, "Did he hurt you?"

I shook my head. "No."

"You look like something the cat dragged in. Take a shower and go to bed. We'll talk about this in the morning." She headed for the door, then added, "When you're sober."

But I didn't make it to the shower. I locked my door behind her, overcome by the nearly suffocating fear that someone was coming to get me, and fell onto the bed.

My nightmares were full of pain and screams and blood.

The next morning, my mother burst into my room, the door banging against the wall. "What have I said about locking doors, Magnolia?"

I sat up, disoriented and dizzy. Nausea washed over me in a hot wave, and I jumped out of bed, stumbling a little from vertigo as I rushed to the toilet.

My mother followed and leaned against the doorjamb to watch me vomit.

"How much did you have to drink last night?"

I started to cry. I couldn't do this. I felt broken and battered and shredded to pieces, inside and out. I wasn't strong enough to do this, whatever *this* was. I looked up at her. "That's where your mind goes? You really want to think the worst of me?"

"What else am I supposed to think, Magnolia? I don't buy your story about going for a walk in the woods for a minute."

"So you automatically assume I did something wrong?"

"You're no angel, Magnolia."

She was right. Me being hungover wasn't outside the realm of possibility. It wouldn't have been the first time. But something bad had happened—my jumbled dreams had felt so real— and all I wanted was for my mother to hold me and tell me everything would be okay.

But she wouldn't. Because my gut told me I could never, ever tell her.

In that instant, I realized I couldn't stay home. Every minute I was here, I was putting all our lives at risk.

The one thing I knew with certainty was that I had to leave.

Where had that come from? I didn't know, but I knew I had to go. As far away as I could get. As soon as possible.

After she left for work, I packed two suitcases, gathered all four hundred sixty dollars of my graduation money, and used my mother's credit card to buy a one-way ticket to New York City for an early afternoon flight.

When the plane took off, I told myself I would never go home again.

But I had. And I'd reawakened a nightmare.

I'd always suspected Blake was the perpetrator that night. Now I knew that was false. But if he hadn't sent me the texts, who had?

chapter nineteen

I had to go to the police. I had to tell them what I'd found. But what had seemed like a good idea back home, after the fresh return of my new memories, I was having second thoughts about by the time I reparked my mother's car behind the catering business.

The murder took place ten years ago. Even if the cops could tie my memories to a case, what good would it do? I barely remembered anything important.

But what kind of person would I be if I didn't try?

I put Momma's car keys back in her purse. It was close to ten o'clock, so there was a good chance she'd get back before me.

Still, as I started down the stairs, new worries wormed their way into my mind. What if the police considered me an accessory to the woman's murder? As much as Detective Holden had it out for me, he might try to arrest me for obstruction of justice. Or think I was flat out crazy.

Maybe I really should take Colt up on his offer. I could just run—change my name, maybe even change my looks, and move to another country. Another continent. Maybe I could finally go to college somewhere and become a teacher in an American school in a European country. I'd already chosen my name—Miriam Daniels, just a boring girl from the Midwest who had lived a normal life. Or maybe I'd become British. I had the British accent down pat. This could be my way of achieving the happily ever after I'd always daydreamed of having.

And if Roy really meant what he'd said, I would have the money to fund my escape.

But if I did something like that, I could never come back. Ever.

And despite everything, I couldn't do that. I just couldn't. I had to clear my name. And then I could start over again as *me*.

I would go to the police with what little I knew about Max Goodwin's murder, including Paul Locke's name and the fact that the security guard stationed in the hall leading to Luke's office had been MIA for a period time, and they could sort it out. Anyone could have supplied those two pieces of information. They didn't have to know my sources. I saw no reason to include the people we'd marked off our list, including Luke of course.

I'd tell them about my restored memories too. The sooner, the better. They could sort out what to do about that too.

It felt good to have a plan, sketchy as it was. I went into the bathroom and looked at my reflection. I'd cried off my makeup —the only traces left were the mascara smudges on my cheeks. I washed my face and then patted it dry with a paper towel. I looked like crap, but the police wouldn't care. My distraught appearance might work in my favor.

I only hoped they would listen.

For a brief moment, I considered telling Emily my plan, then decided against it. While she might be great at investigating, she sucked in stressful attorney situations. I was better off handling this on my own.

My current quandary was how to lock up the kitchen, but then I remembered Tilly's keys on the island. I slid the business key off the ring and headed out the back door, tucking the key into a pocket in the side seam of my dress.

There was more activity before ten o'clock on a Saturday night than I'd expected. Several bars were open as well as the theater across the street and a coffee shop on the south corner. The police station was only a few blocks away, but my feet felt a little more like lead with each step.

It's a good plan. Just keep going.

The police station was hopping with activity too. There had been a bar fight in another part of town, and the waiting area was filled with families and friends of the arrested individuals.

The harried clerk turned her attention to me as I walked up to the reception window. "I need to speak to Detective Holden."

She shook her head. "Honey, he's off for the night. Give me your name and number, and I'll have him get in touch."

I lifted my chin. If I waited, there was a good chance I'd change my mind. All the dark things in my life—in my past—were weighing me down enough that I could barely breathe. "No. I need to speak to him now."

She released a put-upon sigh. "What's it about?"

"Max Goodwin's murder."

Her entire demeanor changed as she sat up straighter. This was a high-profile case. They wanted any information they could get to arrest their primary suspect: *me*.

That was a sobering thought. What if they turned the tables on me and used this visit to implicate me somehow?

But before I could question my half-baked plan, the clerk had already picked up the phone. She whispered something in a hushed tone and then hung up. "Someone will be out for you. Hang tight."

I swallowed. "Thank you."

The door to the back opened less than a minute later, revealing a uniformed officer. He scanned the room and stopped at me. "You're the one with information?"

I nodded, my mouth suddenly dry. "Yes," I croaked out.

"Follow me." He held the door open for me to enter the back, then led me down a hall and into a room full of desks. He motioned to a chair next to the side of a desk. "If you'll have a seat, Detective Bennett will be with you in a minute."

"Okay."

I didn't want to sit. My nerves were frazzled, and I had moved long past second thoughts and on to fourth and fifth. This visit was premature. I should have done more digging on Paul Locke before coming to the cops. What if Detective Holden didn't do anything with my information since he was so certain of my guilt? What if I was about to land myself in even deeper trouble?

I hadn't given the clerk my name, which meant that if I left now, there might be no consequences. My mind made up, I stood and spun around, prepared to head to the exit. Instead I ran right into a tall and very solid man.

He grabbed my upper arms to keep me from falling, and I gasped when I looked up into his face.

Recognition flickered in his eyes as well. This wasn't the first time we'd met this way.

"Brady?"

He looked different tonight. His beard was gone and his dark brown hair was a little neater, but I recognized the concerned look in his eyes from our first encounter. "*Maggie? Are you okay?*"

"I . . . uh . . ." I stammered, my heart pounding against my chest. What was it about this man that threw me off and made me feel like I was back in seventh grade? But more importantly, what was he doing here? "Thanks for keeping me upright. Again."

He had on jeans and a pale blue button-down shirt, which was rolled up to just below his elbows. He had solid forearms and a good grip—I knew because he was still holding my elbows.

I took a step back. He couldn't be a criminal. Had *he* been the victim of a crime? I had trouble seeing him as a victim in any capacity. "What are you doing here?"

"I work here." He gently guided me back to the chair. "You look like you've been through hell. Why don't you sit down?"

I obeyed him, shaking my head. "I don't understand. You work here?" He was too good-looking, too buff to be a janitor.

He knelt in front of me and gathered my hands in his, resting the bundle on my knees. "I'm a detective, Maggie. I can help you."

My lungs squeezed so tight I thought I was going to pass out. "*You're* Detective Bennett."

His smile warmed my insides and made my head feel amazingly light. "Yeah."

So many thoughts rushed through my head at once, and I struggled with which one to focus on first. "You really weren't stalking me?" *Brilliant, Magnolia.*

His mouth tipped up into a smile, and a dimple appeared on his right cheek. His brown eyes were soft and warm, and so inviting. Then the implications of what he'd said dawned on me, and I pulled my hands from his. "But you *were* following me."

He pushed out a sigh and rose. "I thought we'd already established I wasn't a stalker," he said, sitting in his desk chair and rolling it in front of me.

"Not as a stalker. You were watching me as a *police officer.*" I made it sound like the accusation it was.

He shook his head in confusion, the conversation obviously steering off the track he'd expected it to follow. "Why would I do that?"

I shot him a glare. "Why did you follow me?"

Instead of getting irritated with my line of questioning, he slowly leaned toward me, his eyes still soft and warm. "Maggie, it's just like I told you. You worried me. You looked terrified—just as you do now—and I wanted to make sure you were okay. But I swear I didn't follow you. I really *was* going to the outfitter store. But since we were going the same direction, I kept an eye on you."

"You were spying on me."

His shoulders tightened ever so slightly. "What reason would I have for spying on you?" When I didn't answer, he continued. "If I had been spying on you, I can guarantee you that you wouldn't have noticed me at all *and* I would have followed you around that building. Which I didn't. Instead I went and bought a pair of hiking boots."

Even in his defensiveness, he was calm and patient. Which made me distrust him all the more.

I jumped to my feet. "I have to go."

"Wait."

He blocked my escape, making my panic escalate. I fought to catch my breath, and he lifted his hands in surrender.

"I'm not going to hurt you, and I'm not going to make you stay if you really want to go. But why don't you wait a few minutes? If you still want to leave, I'll let you walk out, okay?"

I wasn't sure I could trust him, but I found myself nodding in agreement.

He took a long look at me, then glanced around the room before settling his gaze back on me. "On second thought, how about we get out of here?"

I sucked in a breath. "Why? Where would we go?"

"We can go for a walk. Or get coffee. Then you'll know you're free to go anytime you want." When I hesitated, he added, "*You* came to *me*, Maggie. I don't have any reason to hold you here." He took a step back and graced me with a smile. "It's a beautiful spring night in Franklin. Let's go for a walk. I won't be a police detective. I'll just be Brady, a guy you're taking a walk with. You call the shots."

"Okay." My voice was weak and small and I hated myself a little. Hated what the past few days had reduced me to.

He motioned to the front door and let me lead the way through the waiting room and outside to the sidewalk. I stopped short, fighting the sudden urge to take off running.

Brady moved a step closer to me, looking down at me with a gentle smile. "Where to?"

It was just a walk. I could do that. I took a breath as I tried to figure out where to go. Was he testing me? Would he judge me based on what I picked? I was being paranoid, but I told myself it was justified after everything I'd been through.

You're not building a nuclear bomb, Magnolia. Pick a direction to walk. "Main Street."

He smiled. "Main Street it is."

True to his word, he let me lead the way. I stayed on the opposite side of the street of my mother's business, not wanting to give away too much.

"Was I right?" he asked. "Do you live down here?"

I hadn't planned to answer, but his silence after the question unnerved me. "My mother has a business on Main Street."

"See? That wasn't so hard now, was it?" The smile he flashed me as a reward made me want to answer every question he had for me. I suspected he was very good at getting confessions from female suspects.

I gave him a suspicious look. "You're not going to ask me which one?"

"Nope." He flashed his smile again. "This isn't an interrogation, Maggie. I'm just curious. How about you ask me something? Maybe it will put you more at ease."

"You're suggesting I ask a police detective personal questions?"

"I already told you—we're just Maggie and Brady, two people getting to know each other as they take a stroll down Main Street. Ask away."

I couldn't help wondering if this was a trick—I was fairly certain Detective Brady Bennett was on the clock even when he wasn't—but I decided to try to use it to my advantage. At least that's what I wanted to believe. I didn't want to admit to myself that part of the reason I was here with him was that he made me feel like I *could* trust him. Because I knew better than to give in to that impulse. I couldn't trust anyone. "Why were you at the deli that day?"

"That one's easy. I was hungry for a ham sandwich on rye. With mustard. What did *you* order?"

"Um . . ." It seemed like a strange question. I put my shaky hand to my forehead as I tried to calm down and remember. "A turkey and avocado sandwich on wheat. No mayo."

"Avocado, huh? So you like guacamole?"

"Yeah."

His face lit up. "Good to know for future reference."

The hairs on the back of my neck prickled. What did that mean? Was he thinking about asking me out on a date to a Mexican restaurant, or was he making a mental list of what I'd eat in the county jail? I sucked in a deep breath.

Brady stopped and I stopped with him, certain this would be the part where he said *gotcha* and arrested me for Max's murder. I gave serious thought to running, but his legs were longer than mine and he'd catch me in seconds.

"Maggie." He smiled softly. "It's okay. Honest."

Run, Magnolia! It was the smart choice. Make some excuse and walk away from this man who was such a conundrum of danger and hope. But I didn't want to run. I wanted to stay still, even if it was just for one night, and pretend this man liked me for the woman he saw—Maggie, a nobody whose mother owned some random shop on Main Street—and not Magnolia Steele, humiliated Broadway star, and definitely not Magnolia Steele, suspect number one in Max Goodwin's murder.

"Now my turn. You already know I'm a detective, so tell me what you do."

Could I lie to him? It was obvious he still didn't know who I was, and I sure didn't want to tell him. Not yet. But if I didn't say anything, he'd get suspicious, and besides, I couldn't lie to a police detective. He'd find out the truth eventually.

"I'm a singer." Technically true.

He graced me with his beautiful smile. "Country or Christian?"

"Country." It wasn't a lie. The songs in *Fireflies at Dawn* were country.

"You any good?" he teased.

"That's three questions." I smiled softly. "And yes," I said, some of my confidence returning. "I'm damn good."

I had thought his previous smiles were gifts, but the one he gave me now was like manna from heaven. "Sing something for me."

I shook my head. "I can't do that."

"Why not?"

I stopped and looked around. "Here? On the *street*?"

"Like I said, why not?" A mischievous look filled his eyes. "Afraid?"

"Of course not." That was a lie. Singing would attract attention. Someone might recognize me, and that terrified the shit out of me.

"Then sing for me, Maggie."

Why did I feel this tug to please him? I'd spent most of my life putting my needs before everyone else's. Maybe it was time to stop. Even if it required me to do something as silly as singing a song in the middle of the street.

But I warned myself that Brady Bennett had the power to destroy me. The scariest thing of all was that part of me didn't care. The part of me that yearned to have someone look at me the way he was looking at me right now, like I was the only person in the world.

The part of me that needed to be loved.

Brady waited while my internal war waged, and the warm look in his eyes broke through the shield over my heart. Even if it was only a tiny crack.

"Okay."

A smile spread across his face, filling me with a feeling I didn't understand. One I craved like an alcoholic wanted booze.

Oh, yes. Brady Bennett was a very dangerous man.

But I was giving myself one night. One night to indulge myself in this luxury. I'd figure out the rest tomorrow.

I gave him a tiny smile, then put a hand on my stomach, hoping I would sound halfway decent despite not having warmed up.

I sang the chorus from "Chasing Fireflies," the main theme song from *Fireflies at Dawn*. It was a soft ballad I'd always loved, mostly because I felt the truth of the lyrics down to my bones. *"Shiny rainbows never hang around, four-leaf clovers are hard to find, shooting stars only last for a moment, but fireflies, they never let me down. Fireflies, they always come around. I'll forever be chasing fireflies."*

Several people had stopped to listen, watching me with rapt attention, but I only had eyes for Brady, who smiled at me the entire time. When I finished, they clapped and murmured their approval and then wandered off when they realized I was really done.

Brady clapped too, his grin so contagious I couldn't help smiling back.

"You *are* good, Maggie."

I lifted a shoulder and gave him a smug grin. "I told you so." I started walking again, but he easily caught up.

"Did you write that?"

I laughed. "No. I'm no songwriter. It's a Toby Keith song."

"Really? I'm a Toby Keith fan and I've never heard him sing that."

I could tell him it was from the musical, but I worried I'd give myself away, and I definitely wasn't ready to do that. Not tonight. "It's new. You'll hear it soon enough."

"So you have connections?"

"You could say that." I shot him a pointed look. "And I've lost track of how many questions you've asked. My turn."

"Okay. Ask away."

His eyes had a way of drawing me in, making me want to ask him a million and one things. But I reminded myself I needed to be careful. Brady worked on the same police force as Detective Holden, who had made it his mission to lock me away forever based on a groundless suspicion.

And that reminded me of the reason I'd walked into the police station in the first place.

Brady picked up on the change in my demeanor. "How about I help you out? I'll fill in a few details, and then you can jump in with questions whenever you like. I was born and raised here in Franklin. Never left."

"Not even for college?"

"Nope. I went to Belmont."

Belmont was a private college in Nashville that came with a hefty price tag. Which told me he hadn't always planned to be a cop. "What was your major?"

A satisfied grin lit up his eyes—I was playing his game. "Pre-law. But I prefer investigating to arguing. And I'm good at it. So I joined the police force and worked on becoming a detective."

"You like it?" I asked warily. "Being a detective?"

He stopped and turned to me. "Yeah. I do."

"Why?"

Something warred behind his eyes as he stared down at me, but he finally said, "So I can protect a pretty woman who sings like an angel when she finds herself in trouble. Why don't you tell me what's goin' on, Maggie?"

I broke eye contact, and when I glanced to the side, an open coffee shop caught my attention. If I were smart, I'd go back to the catering shop and wait for Momma. So why wasn't I doing that? My feelings were not to be trusted, but even though I knew that, I found myself cocking my head and looking up at him. "Didn't you say something about coffee?"

Relief washed over his face. "Yes, I did. Coffee sounds great."

I led the way across the street and into the shop, reveling in the rich aroma that filled my nose as soon as I walked through the doors. Brady followed me to the counter, where I ordered a caramel macchiato and he ordered his coffee black. He insisted on paying for our drinks, which was good since I belatedly realized I didn't have any money with me. We waited in silence until my drink was ready, then he motioned to an empty table in the back.

Moments later we were both seated, and I noticed my hands were shaking a little around my cup. This was a bad idea. *You're playing with fire, Magnolia.* But hadn't I been doing that for years?

"Did you grow up here?" he asked.

"Yeah." I looked down at the cup in my hands. "But I moved away for a long time."

"It couldn't have been that long unless you moved away in grade school," he said, his tone light and playful.

I closed my eyes and took a deep breath. Normal people talked about where they'd lived, so I'd just made myself even more suspicious. *Stupid move, Magnolia.* Maybe if I tried playing a role with him, I could get through this. The innocent woman and the good-looking detective. Or the ingénue with a secret.

But I didn't *want* to play a role with him. Brady Bennett made me want to be me. And wasn't that scary as hell . . .

I opened my eyes and stared into his, which had darkened. "This was a mistake."

He looked down at my left hand, then back up to my eyes. "Do you have a boyfriend? A husband?"

"No," I said softly, thrown off guard by his question. "Do you?"

A grin lit up his face, even though there was still a hint of worry there. "No, I don't have a boyfriend or a husband." He tipped his head to the side. "But if you're asking if I have a wife or a girlfriend, the answer is still no. And I confess it makes me happy that you asked." He reached up and tugged on his collar. "Although I can understand your confusion, given this shirt I'm wearing. My sister will be pleased to know her attempt to expand my wardrobe actually worked."

I laughed as he put his hands on the table. I couldn't help it. "You *do* realize there is nothing special about that shirt, right? It's a standard blue oxford, and you don't even have the collar buttoned."

He tried to look down, then lifted his hand to reach for the collar, but I laughed and grabbed his hand. "No, leave it. Buttoning it wouldn't look right on you." I paused before deciding to throw caution to the wind. "While you might be wearing a standard blue oxford shirt, there is nothing standard about you in it, Detective Brady Bennett." Then I gave him a saucy grin. "And I never suspected you were gay."

His eyes darkened again, and I suddenly realized my hand still covered his. I tried to pull it away, but he held on and lowered our clasped hands to the table.

My stomach tingled like I was racing downhill on a roller coaster. I couldn't remember the last time a man had made me feel this way. I licked my bottom lip and his gaze followed, sending a jolt much lower than my stomach. "I'm pretty sure you're not supposed to flirt with the citizens who walk into your police station, Detective Bennett."

His eyes held mine. "While that's true, I'm not here as Detective Bennett, remember? We're here as Brady and Maggie, two people who were out for a stroll and are now having coffee." He gave me a conspiratorial grin. "One could even call this a first date." His shoulder lifted in a lazy shrug, and his thumb followed suit, sending chills down my spine as it meandered over the back of my hand. "And this is what people do on first dates. They get to know each other."

"This is a date?" I asked, trying to ignore the thrill that word sent through me.

He ignored the question, giving me one of his own instead. "You said you went away. Where did you go?"

I tensed. We were back in minefield territory. "New York."

"What did you do there? If you're a country singer, wouldn't you want to stick around here?"

I gave him a helpless look. If I answered that truthfully, it would change our dynamic, and there'd be no getting this easy feeling back.

"Okay," he said, shifting his weight. "You don't want to answer that. That's okay. How about this—do you have a record deal? Have you made money as a singer?"

"I don't have a record deal, but I *have* done commercials."

"Oh, yeah?" His eyes lit up with excitement. "Any I'd know?"

"Probably not. One was a toothpaste commercial. I brushed my teeth in front of a mirror and then walked into a classroom and smiled at a boy. Pretty generic stuff." Which was why I felt safe telling him.

"And the others?"

"Shampoo. And a fast food commercial, but I was in the background." I may have been in the background, but it was a major chain and I still got residuals.

"So you're an actress too." His eyes filled with a dawning understanding, and I started to panic a little when he said, "You

243

were in New York. That's like the capital of the world for theatre, right? Were you in any plays?"

Realizing that Brady was *still* holding my hand, I slowly pulled it away. "A few."

He sat back, the patient look returning. "That's okay. Touchy subject. We'll talk about something else."

But my defenses had started to rebuild themselves. "You say we're here just as Brady and Maggie, but aren't you on duty?"

He shook his head. "Nope. I was about to leave when one of the guys told me there was a woman with some information and I needed to talk to her. So I did." He smiled. "But as soon as we left the station, I was off the clock. I'm really just here as me, Maggie."

"They didn't tell you what it was about?"

"No. Should they have? All they said was that there was a woman who'd insisted on talking to someone right away. When I realized you didn't feel safe talking, I decided you needed a friend more. So I suggested we leave."

"So why would you use your personal time to talk to me unofficially?"

He shook his head, his grin returning. "Isn't it obvious? I like you. I called this a first date."

I looked down. "I thought maybe it was just a line to get me to talk."

He was silent for several seconds, long enough for me to look up into his eyes. He seemed angry, but he swallowed and some of his irritation faded. "Maggie, listen to me, and this is important, okay?"

I nodded.

"I will never lie to you or try to trick you. Ever."

"It's your job," I said, wrapping my arms across my chest. "It's your job to trick people into confessing and telling you things."

A hood fell over his eyes, and for the first time since I'd met him, he looked guarded. "Do you have something to confess?"

"No!" I nearly shouted, scrunching my shoulders up to my ears when I realized I'd gotten the attention of the people around us. "I don't have anything to confess." But that was a lie that ate at my soul. I forced myself to look up at him. "I haven't done anything wrong."

But was that really true? I should be telling him about the house I'd found tonight, about the memories that had returned to me. Instead I was sitting here drinking coffee like it had never happened. But I had no idea if he would even believe me. Was it worth the risk? Those blocked texts could be from that man . . . which meant he might be watching me.

I shook my head and looked away, suddenly feeling hot. I scrambled to take my sweater off and then let it fall on the seat behind me.

Why was I still here? Why didn't I just leave? How could this man who was practically a stranger have such a hold on me?

Brady leaned forward and took both of my hands in his own again, his gaze lingering on my forearm. Horror filled my head when I noticed there was a bold purple bruise on my wrist from where Roy had smacked it away.

Had that really happened tonight? It felt like years ago.

Brady's eyes lifted to mine. "I need to make sure you know you can trust me. It's important."

"Why?" I asked with a hint of defiance.

"Because I meant it when I said we could call this a first date." When I started to protest, he squeezed my hands. "If you came in to report a crime, you didn't tell me anything. So I was never officially the detective on your case. Which means we can see each other again." He paused. "But if we want to explore this thing between us—and there's something between us, Maggie, I know you feel it too—then you have to be able to trust me. I can't let you go on thinking I would try to deceive you."

But I'm deceiving you. A lump filled my throat.

"Were you there to report a crime?"

I didn't say anything. I couldn't even look at him. My heart was breaking and I wasn't sure why. I barely knew this guy.

"Maggie." I looked up into his warm gaze. "If you want to tell me as a friend, then I'll go with you to the station *as a friend* and sit with you while you report it."

Tears filled my eyes. "You would do that?" I asked. "Why? So you can sleep with me?"

His eyes filled with sadness. "Someone must have hurt you pretty bad, huh? You think that's why I'm here? So I can sleep with you?"

"You're saying you don't want to?" I lifted my chin, my defiance returning.

"I most definitely want to sleep with you."

A flush washed over me at the thought of getting Brady Bennett naked, but it was followed fast by disappointment. He was just like every other guy after all.

Without shifting his gaze from me, he leaned over the table toward me. "Because I want more than a one-night stand, Maggie. I want the chance to see where this might lead."

"How do I know that's not some line you tell all the girls?"

"Because it's the truth." His mouth tipped up a little at the corner. "That's a fault of mine. Sometimes I'm honest when I should keep my mouth shut. Now your turn."

"My turn to what?"

"Tell me one of your faults."

I laughed, a derisive sound, and broke his gaze. "Where do I begin?"

"I can't believe there are that many."

I lifted my face with a jerk. "I'm a selfish, inconsiderate, self-centered bitch. Ask anyone who used to know me here. They'll tell you the ugly truths about Magnol—" I stopped, but I wasn't sure if I'd stopped in time. If one of Brady's faults was a predilection for honesty, another was being observant. Which meant he hadn't missed my slip. He just wasn't acknowledging it.

He smiled. "I don't believe you. Try again."

Should I just tell him the truth? He was going to find out anyway. But it would be better to guide him to it than to just blurt it out. It would help him see things from my perspective. "When you're investigating a crime, do you look at all the evidence?"

He studied me for a few seconds, probably trying to decide where I was going with this. "Yeah, of course. That's my job."

"A job you do out of love, right? You told me you love investigating."

"Maggie . . . I'm not sure what you're reading into this, but I swear I'm just trying to get to know you."

"Would you say you're thorough?"

Surprisingly, he didn't seem offended. "I'd like to think so, but I'm human, so that makes me fallible. Still, I try my best to be objective and get all the facts."

"But there are other detectives who are sloppy and don't do their jobs, right?"

"There are people like that in every job." Then he added, "And yes, some are more bullheaded and stubborn than others."

I hesitated. "I'm terrible about returning things," I said quietly, lifting a shoulder. "Library books. Netflix discs before they had streaming. Casserole dishes. My friends' clothes."

"So you're saying if I'm ever at your place and leave a shirt or something behind, you probably won't return it?" His eyes changed, a sexy look that twisted something deep inside me, making parts of me throb.

"Leave your shirt at your own risk," I said with a saucy grin, my pulse picking up.

"Good." His voice lowered into a seductive tone that brought my body to life. "Then I'll have a good reason to come back to see you. And I'm really looking forward to coming back for my shirt."

My face flushed. Actually flushed. Magnolia Steele was blushing. Jody would never believe it. I laughed.

"You have a pretty laugh, Maggie. I want to hear it more often."

No one had ever told me that. Ever.

His phone rang—a utilitarian ringtone—and his smile fell as he dug it out of his pocket.

"Bennett." It was his commanding voice, the one that had captured my attention the first time we met. His expression switched from turned-on to drop-dead serious in an instant, and he mumbled "shit" under his breath. Giving me an apologetic glance, he said, "I'll be right there."

"You have to go. *To work,*" I said as he hung up the call and set his phone on the table. He'd just gotten an official call. Which meant he really *was* on the clock. Did that mean he'd been using me for information after all? Had it all been some elaborate trick?

"I'm sorry, Maggie. I wish I didn't have to go."

"You lied to me," I said, my defenses returning. I got out of my seat and grabbed my sweater, my hands shaking so much it took me three attempts to swipe it. "You're still on duty." My voice shook with tears, and I was pissed at myself for letting him upset me.

He got to his feet, but his eyes never left mine. "I'm on call, Maggie. I didn't lie."

Before I knew it, he was on my side of the table, grabbing my upper arms. When I winced, he looked down at my arm and gasped.

"Who did this to you?" His voice was low and ominous.

I looked over my shoulder, gasping myself when I saw the giant dark purple three-inch welt on my arm. No wonder it hurt so much.

"Maggie. That's *two* bruises. I want to know who did this."

What was I going to do? Tell him my brother had done it? It was the truth, but I couldn't have him arrested for pinching me, regardless of how I felt about him right now. My mother and Belinda would never forgive me. "I ran into a door."

"That is the oldest fucking line in the book. Try again." He was speaking in his commanding voice, the one that made me want to get naked and spill my guts as pillow talk.

His phone rang again, and he groaned in frustration as he pulled it from his pocket. "I said I'm coming," he barked into the phone.

This was a side of him I hadn't seen yet, the angry Brady Bennett, and although his carefully controlled rage should have scared me, in truth it only turned me on more. Brady was a nice guy who was all alpha. The rarest of the breed.

"Get the damn crime scene tape up and keep the reporters out." He paused. "And call Holden if he's not on duty. Two murders in one house within days of each other? That can't be a coincidence."

My breath stuck in my chest. Two murders in one house? How many murders happened in Franklin? And how many murders had Detective Holden handled in the last few days? I suspected it was a very small number.

Brady shoved the phone into his pocket, and his rage faded as if it had never been. "You're as pale as a ghost." He took my hand and lowered his voice. "You can trust me, Maggie. I swear I don't want to hurt you. I only want to help."

"No one can help me," I whispered before my mind could catch up to my mouth. He had single-handedly trampled my protective coating of steel. I was so tired of running. So tired of hiding. I wanted to be freed of this burden, especially now that I understood it, and Brady was the first person who made me think it might be possible. If I saw him again, if I let him get close to me, I had no doubt I'd eventually tell him everything.

Every nitty-gritty detail of what had happened ten years ago. And if I did, what if he couldn't save me? Or Momma or Roy? I barely knew him, but I suspected he couldn't handle the guilt.

But Brady was waging a war of his own. He didn't want to leave me without getting the answers he wanted and needed, and yet he knew he had to go.

Do not cry, Magnolia Steele. Do. Not. Cry.

Deciding to make it easier for him, I grabbed my sweater and walked out the side door onto the sidewalk. Brady followed me and pulled me to a halt.

"Maggie. Wait a minute."

"Go, Brady. You have more important things to deal with."

He held my gaze. "*This* is important to me, Maggie. I don't want you to think it's not."

I smiled up at him, trying not sound so sad. "I don't."

"I want to see you again."

I laughed. "You've made that very clear."

"I don't play games, Maggie. I don't beat around the bush. I know what I want, and I'm very upfront about it." The corners of his mouth tipped up. "Some people would call that another fault."

If those were his faults, he definitely didn't want to be with me. "Sometimes I leave empty cereal boxes in the cabinet. *Definitely* a fault." I grinned even though I felt close to tears. There was no way I could see him again. I was surprised how much that hurt.

I took a step toward him and rested my hands on his chest. Just touching him made my heart race. "So we're officially calling this a date?"

"The shittiest date in all of history, but yeah."

I gave him a coy smile. "So do we get a first date kiss?"

"As skittish as you are, slow and steady seems to be the right course. I can wait for the second."

I lifted my hand to his cheek, fully aware that we were

standing on the sidewalk, even if it was dark. I wasn't usually someone who instigated public displays of affection, but I didn't care. This was probably going to be my only chance to kiss him. I'd deal with any embarrassment later. My thumb brushed his lower lip, and then I lifted up on my tiptoes, slowly closing the distance to cover his lips, pulling his bottom lip between mine, and then brushing it with my tongue.

He groaned and his arms tightened around me as he took over the kiss, showing me how much he really did want me.

He lifted his head and looked at me with eyes full of raw hunger. "You are a very difficult woman to walk away from."

I gave him a sad smile. "Good, then maybe you'll remember me." Although I wasn't sure that was a good idea.

"I can pretty much guarantee I won't forget you." He kissed me again, and when he stopped, I was breathless and unsure of whether my legs would hold me up.

His phone rang again, and he closed his eyes for a second. "Dammit."

I gave him a little push, and he dropped his hold and glanced down at his phone screen.

"You need to get to the Powell estate," I said. "It sounds like things are getting crazy. So go." As soon as the words were out of my mouth, I realized my mistake.

Oh, shit.

He frowned as if he knew something was off, but he answered the phone before he could say anything to me.

I took several steps backward as he gave his attention to whoever was on the other line, growling something about reporters and someone doing his job. I saw the moment when he registered my slip, watched as realization washed over his face, but I was already at the corner.

He covered his phone with his hand and called after me, "I never told you it was the Powell estate."

I grimaced and then turned and hurried across the street

until I was in the middle of the crowd emerging from the Franklin Theater. I ran under the overhang at the theater entrance and pushed my back against a shadowed wall, hoping I was hidden enough.

I watched as Brady jogged past me on the other side of the street, my sweater in his hand.

Shit. I must have dropped it when I kissed him.

He stopped and looked around, his free hand running through his hair.

My heart raced. What would he do if he found me? Was he too personally involved in the situation to arrest me?

He dropped his hand and swung it in a gesture of frustration before continuing toward the police station.

Nausea roiled through my gut when I thought about where he was going. Someone else had been murdered at the Powell estate. Who was it? Luke? Oh, God. What if it was Amy?

Bolting from the theater, I found a flowerpot around the corner and threw up into the purple and yellow pansies. Several people walked past me, making snide comments about me being drunk in public.

The good news was that I had a solid alibi from the time my mother woke me up in the morning until now, with the exception of about an hour this evening. Maybe it would be enough to clear my name.

The thought made me want to throw up again. If that was true, someone had paid the price of my freedom with their life tonight. I wasn't sure I could live with that.

chapter twenty

I'd missed six calls from my mother and one from Jody since I'd left for the police station. Jody wouldn't care if I took a while to call her back, but I knew my mother would be terrified. I had only thought to check my phone after getting back to the kitchen, and when I saw the notification, I called her back immediately.

"Magnolia Mae Steele!" she shouted in my ear. "You've aged me ten years!"

"I'm sorry, Momma. I fell asleep."

"You're not in bed with Colt Austin, are you? He's not answering his phone either."

"What? No! God, no. He dropped me off at the catering business and then left."

"I told that boy to stay with you."

"It's not his fault. I got a migraine, and the only thing that ever makes me feel better when I have a headache is a nap. So I made him drop me off here since I didn't have a house key. That's why I missed your calls." I hated myself for lying, but there was no way I was going to tell her about my trip to the police station. And I sure wasn't telling her about Brady either.

"Are you feeling better?" she asked, catching me by surprise. She wasn't usually known for offering sympathy.

"A little. I think a good night's sleep will help." Although that was unlikely to happen in the foreseeable future. I was too anxious to sleep.

"I was calling earlier to tell you we got tied up. But we're about five minutes out. See you soon."

I hurried to put Tilly's key back on her ring and then looked around the kitchen to make sure nothing looked amiss from my earlier meltdown.

But I mustn't have done a very good job. Tilly took one look at me when she walked in the door and shook her head. "Lila, get this girl home. I'll haul in all the pans."

"Do you know where Colt went?" my mother grumbled to me. "He was supposed to help us unload."

"No. He just told me to call if I needed him." I wanted to tell her about the new murder, but I didn't know how to do that without tipping her off to my unsanctioned outing with a policeman. I forced a smile. "I can help."

"You look like a cat that's been left out in the rain, then tossed under a hand dryer in a Quickie Mart restroom."

"Thanks." I sighed. "You always did know how to give a compliment."

"I'm just saying you look like you don't have any business working."

I grabbed my apron off the hook. "I need to work every chance I can get if I'm going to pay my rent."

"Rent?" Tilly asked. "You moving out of your momma's house?"

"No," I said, tying the apron strings. "Momma's rent. For staying in her house."

Tilly crossed her arms and tapped her foot. "Lila Steele, don't you dare tell me that you are charging that girl rent to stay in that house where you live all by yourself."

Momma flung up her hands. "Oh, for heaven's sake, I'm not really charging her."

"What?" I gasped.

Tilly didn't look one bit appeased. "Then why on earth does she think you are?"

A guilty look crossed over my mother's face. If only I'd had my phone out to take a photo. I could count on one hand how many times I'd seen that look before.

"I only told her that to see how serious she was about staying."

My mouth dropped open. "You made me work Luke Powell's party. You said I had to work to pay off my rent."

She flung out her hands in frustration. "I needed help, and I knew that was the only way you'd agree to go."

I wasn't so sure about that. While I hadn't wanted to do it, I liked to think I would have done it when push came to shove. But if I hadn't gone that night, I never would have been accused of Max's murder.

I pushed out a groan of frustration and shook my head. "It's water under the bridge now, but for the record, I'm going to help you cart those stupid pans inside whether you want me to or not. Only they better be a lot less heavy coming in than they were going out."

My mother looked suspicious. "Why are you helping us?"

"You want me to give you a list of reasons?" I asked, incredulous. "How about you're my mother, Tilly's damn near close to being a second one, and you both need my help?"

"Huh," Momma mumbled.

"Oh, my God. Do you really think I'm that much of a bitch?"

"Well, no . . ." She shrugged. "I don't know. You always complained about helping before you left."

"I was a teenager! It's like a requirement to complain!"

Tilly shook her head, still fuming. "I swear to God, Lila, I love you like a sister, but some days I want to wring your neck."

I was too damn tired and worn out to deal with this nonsense. "Momma, if you need help, just ask me for it. You're letting me stay with you, and believe it or not, I really do want to help you."

"Fine," she grumped. "I'll ask you. Now both of you get off my back and start carrying in pans."

It took us ten minutes to get everything unloaded and the truck cleaned out. Momma rinsed all the dishes and started the loads of pots and pans in the commercial-sized dishwashers. Once all of the preliminary cleanup was finished, she turned to me and said, "We'll clean up the rest tomorrow. Let's go home."

We drove home in silence, partly because my headache story was no longer a lie. My pulse pounded in my temples as I stared out the car window.

"You haven't heard from Emily, have you?" I asked, leaning my head against the seat.

"No. Not since this morning. Why?"

Would Emily even be aware of the other murder? How would I manage to get details without attracting the wrong sort of attention? "Just curious."

"I never asked how your meeting went with Amy."

"Great," I said absently, trying not to worry about her. It was Saturday night. She probably wasn't even there. "She was really helpful. She gave us a couple of leads to track down. I eliminated one as a suspect, and Emily eliminated the VP. Belinda and I talked to Paul Locke, the country artist, but he wasn't very forthcoming, so we'll need to figure out another way to talk to him. Belinda needed to get back so she could get ready to meet Roy for drinks."

I studied my mother's face as I mentioned my brother's name. She had to know what an asshole he'd become. My mother was a lot of things, but she'd never been blind to her children's idiocy.

It didn't surprise me one bit when she tensed. "I didn't know they were going out."

"I knew Roy didn't want to talk to me, but why didn't you tell me that he actually hates me?"

She swung her gaze to me, her eyes wide. "Did Belinda tell you that?"

"No, it was pretty obvious from the way he told me to leave Franklin and never come back."

Her mouth dropped open in confusion. "When . . . how did . . ."

"I saw them tonight. Colt and I went to a bar after we left Hendersonville, and Roy and Belinda showed up."

"Oh."

"You never told me Roy had changed careers. Or that he was working for Bill James."

"I didn't see the point."

"You didn't see the point in telling me my brother works for the one person who knows what happened to Daddy yet refuses to tell us?"

"Magnolia," my mother groaned. "We don't know any such thing."

This was a pointless discussion. My mother had never taken me seriously as a teenager, and it looked like that hadn't changed. At least where this was concerned. "Do you think Belinda's happy?"

My mother gave me a confused look. "Why do you ask that?"

"Roy seemed kind of mean to her."

"What are you talking about? He's never been anything but sweet to Belinda." She paused. "You must have misunderstood what you saw. You'll see for yourself how he treats her tomorrow."

"What are you talking about? Why do you assume I'm going to see them tomorrow?"

"We're goin' out to lunch with them after church."

"What?" I shook my head. "I really don't feel like going to church tomorrow." I didn't feel like seeing Roy either, so this would take care of two birds with one stone.

"A little church will be good for your soul. When was the last time you went?"

"Momma. I don't want to go. I can't face all those people."

"We don't hide from our problems, Magnolia. We take—"

"Take them head on. Yeah. I know," I said in defeat. "Look how well that turned out at Luke Powell's party."

"That was a fluke. This isn't New York. Murders don't happen every day in Franklin."

No. Just every other day or so. But I couldn't tell her that. "I don't feel up to it."

"Are you sick?"

I considered lying, but I couldn't even count the number of times she'd caught me lying about being sick when I was a kid. If I wanted to convince her I'd grown up, matured, that wasn't the way. "I still have a killer headache."

"Then I'll see you at the front door ready to go at 10:15."

Oddly enough, it was good to see some things hadn't changed.

I took a long shower after we got home. Then, against my better judgment, I texted Emily to see if she'd heard anything. I knew it was too late to be texting—it was close to midnight— but I was desperate to know what had happened.

I half expected to receive one of my mysterious texts—especially after my stroll down Main Street with *Detective* Brady Bennett—but it didn't happen. Emily didn't reply either.

I drifted off to sleep, thinking about Brady and wondering who had been murdered and how long it would take before he put two and two together. I suspected the next time I saw him would be fraught with a different kind of tension.

chapter twenty-one

My mother showed up in my doorway the next morning and banged on the wall. "Time to get up, Magnolia." She sounded annoyed as she moved closer to the bed. "How did you ever get anything done up in New York without me waking you up every morning?"

I pried my swollen eyes open to look at her, and her brows lifted with surprise.

"You really are sick."

"No," I said, my voice groggy. "I'm not. I just have an annoying headache." I'd spent half the night haunted by dreams of what I'd seen in the basement of that abandoned house.

Momma sat on the edge of the bed, leaning over and reaching for the back of my neck. She began to massage my stiff neck muscles, and I closed my eyes and moaned.

"I used to do this when you were a little girl," she murmured. "Remember? You'd wake up from a nightmare and have trouble going back to sleep, so I'd rub your neck and you'd drift off after a while."

"I wished it worked that way now," I said softly.

"I know I haven't told you this, but I'm glad you're back, Magnolia. I've missed you."

"I've missed you too."

She was silent, but her fingers continued to dig into my neck, coaxing the muscles to relax.

"When this is all settled, we need to talk." Her tone was so soft, more so than it had been since Daddy left.

Did she plan to press me for the real reason I'd left? What would I tell her? I gave a vague murmur that I hoped she took as agreement.

I drifted off as her fingers worked their magic, and I woke to her hand stroking back my hair.

"Why don't you skip church and sleep?" she asked. "I'll call you later, and we can meet for lunch."

"Okay. Thank you." She got up and I rolled over to look at her. "I love you, Momma."

Tears filled her eyes. "I love you too."

I AWOKE to the sound of rain beating against the window. My body froze, but I reassured myself I was safe. I was in my mother's house. I was in my own bed. I was behind my mother's magical door.

I reached for my phone, shocked to see it was almost eleven. I hadn't slept this late in years. But I also saw I had several missed calls. Three from Belinda, and two from Emily. One voice mail.

I decided to try calling them before listening to the message. Emily's phone went to voice mail after one ring. Seconds later, I saw a message pop up.

I'm in church. I'll call you when I get out. Then, seconds later: *I hope you're feeling better.*

How did she know I'd been feeling poorly?

I tried calling Belinda next, but when she didn't answer, I decided to check my own messages.

"Magnolia," Belinda's tearful voice said. "I don't know where to begin. I guess I'll start off by saying that I understand why you didn't answer. I'm so sorry." She choked up a little, and I closed my eyes. "We can talk about last night later, if you're still willing to talk to me. But we really need to talk to Amy . . ." Her voice broke again. "Promise me you'll be careful." Then the message cut off. Closing my eyes, I fought off a wave of vertigo.

At least that meant Amy was alive. Hopefully they had a suspect this time and my name would be cleared soon. But if they had a suspect, then why would we need to talk to Amy?

Unless Luke was the murder victim.

I dragged myself out of bed and into my bathroom. I sat on the toilet, leaning forward as I tried to wrest myself out of the haze that had descended on me. I still had vertigo and a throbbing head. I needed ibuprofen, which I found downstairs in the kitchen. Momma had made a pot of coffee, so I warmed up a cup and stood by the breakfast room window, nursing it as I waited for the drugs to take effect.

I grabbed my laptop and sat at the table, then Googled Luke Powell's name and the word murder. The page was full of news about Max's death, but at the top was an article about the murder last night. The only two helpful pieces of information it offered were that one, the murder victim was a man and his identity would be revealed after his family had been contacted. And two, Luke Powell was not available for comment. While he technically wouldn't have been available for comment if he were the victim, his name would have been released by now.

Belinda was right. We needed to talk to Amy.

My fingers hovered over the keys. Part of me wanted to Google my name and find out what everyone was saying, but the sane part of me closed the lid. My fragile psyche couldn't take any more criticism. I wasn't sure I could even handle it if my name had been officially linked to Max's murder.

In this particular instance, ignorance was bliss.

I still had to deal with my memories of *that* night. Maybe I should have told Brady like I'd intended, but any guilt I felt was outweighed by relief. He would have thought I was a crazy person. Who comes forward as a witness to a murder ten years after the fact—and while under investigation for a different murder?

But that didn't mean I couldn't do a little digging on my own.

I poured a fresh cup of coffee before opening my laptop again to start the search. The first words I tried were "murder Franklin, Tennessee May 2006," then expanded it to include Nashville.

But she'd been murdered at the end of May. What if they didn't find her body until June? I switched out June for May, but none of the results fit what happened to the woman in that basement.

Digging into the past was like poking a beehive with a giant stick. The bees were already swarming, so I might as well satisfy my other curiosities.

I opened Facebook and pulled up Maddie first. I'd looked her up dozens of times since leaving Franklin. While she'd unfriended me, surprisingly she hadn't blocked me. When I was feeling particularly nostalgic, I used to look at her photos from college and the sorority we'd both wanted to join. It was like looking at photos of the life I'd lost. I'd cry buckets of tears, then wake up with swollen, puffy eyes the next morning, looking like shit and feeling even worse on the inside. After a while, I grew wiser and stopped torturing myself, only giving in to my curiosity when I was drunk and feeling sorry for myself.

I hadn't looked her up in three years.

But there she was on my screen. Her and her baby. Her with

Blake. Now I was certain Blake wasn't the man in the basement, which meant he wasn't as bad as I'd spent the last ten years believing, not that I was about to give him a "Mr. Nice Guy" award. But at least I could sleep easier knowing Maddie wasn't living with a rapist. Or a murderer.

That I knew of, at least.

I looked up Emily next. She *was* single, and over half her photos were of her Maltese, whom she occasionally carried in her purse. She hadn't posted much, or at least not publicly. When she did post, it was usually to share some silly legal meme.

Enough indulgence.

I Googled Paul Locke, digging through a bunch of puff pieces about his rise to semi-fame. His core audience was teens and tweens—as evidenced by the crowd at the mall yesterday. But there were a few posts about Paul taking his agent—Max Goodwin—to court over a contract dispute involving agency fees. The fees had left him shockingly broke by the time his agent and his label got a share of the pie. Paul Locke had lost.

A month ago.

In my book, that made him a prime suspect in Max's murder, but it couldn't be a coincidence that two murders had happened in the same house within a few days. They were undoubtedly connected. I just needed to find out the identity of the newest victim, if Paul had been there that night, and if he'd held a grudge against this guy too.

Yeah, piece of cake.

When I was growing up, Momma used to get *The Tennessean* newspaper. On the off chance it would contain something helpful today, I unlocked the deadbolt to look for the paper in the driveway. Something else caught my eye instead.

A single magnolia blossom.

It sat on the front porch step in a small florist box without a lid.

My heart slammed so hard into my ribcage I struggled to take a breath. *Calm down, Magnolia. It could be from anyone.*

I walked down the two steps and picked up the box, holding it like it might be a ticking time bomb. My shaking legs protested holding me upright, so I sat on the step and put the soggy, rain-soaked box on my knees. The water on the concrete seeped through my pajama bottoms, but I was only vaguely aware as I lifted the flower from the box and found a card underneath, with a single typed line.

I'm still watching, Magnolia.

My pajamas were thin, and even though the rain was light, the fabric began to stick to my skin. Just like that night.

This flower could have been from anyone, yet my subconscious took over, reminding me of the details of all my worst nightmares.

My chest tightened, and I fought to catch my breath as a heat wave spread across my body. I began to sweat even as my body shivered from the forty-degree air temperature.

Other than in the basement two days before, I hadn't experienced a full-blown panic attack in years, and I refused to succumb to one now. Tears welled in my eyes, but I refused to let them fall. I was done with crying. It had never once done me a lick of good. Tears were for the weak and I was strong. I was a survivor.

When I finally got control and felt like I could stand again, I headed back into the house and placed the flower on the kitchen counter before heading upstairs. I soaked under a hot shower, letting the water sluice over my stiff neck and shoulders until it turned cold.

Forty-five minutes later, I had mostly pulled myself back together and restacked the wall that protected my heart. I was sorting through my suitcases, trying to decide whether or not to unpack my things, when my phone dinged with a text from Emily.

We need to talk.

My least favorite four words in the world. *I'm at Momma's.*

She called seconds later, sounding even more subdued than usual. "Have you heard about the second murder at the Powell estate?"

"Only bits and pieces. Who was murdered?"

"I'm not sure, but I heard he's an associate of Luke's."

"So this clears my name, right?" I asked. "I wasn't anywhere near Luke's estate last night."

"You haven't been cleared of anything. While the two murders took place in the same house, it doesn't mean they're connected. "

"Well, how was this guy killed?"

Emily hesitated. "He was stabbed . . . in the heart."

"Emily!"

"It's up to the police to say you're cleared—which they haven't done yet—so consider yourself under investigation. And don't be surprised if they show up wanting to know what you were doing last night."

"I have an alibi for last night." Mostly.

"Yeah, Lila told me already, although I'm worried about the time you spent alone in the shop. How long was that?"

I didn't dare tell her about my field trip into the woods or my stroll down Main Street with Brady. So I hedged. "I think Colt dropped me off around 8:30, and Momma showed up after ten."

"Well, crap," she grumbled. "The murder took place around nine. It sounds like he had another party."

I closed my eyes. Shit. My visit to see Brady might actually make me look even more guilty. Like I'd killed a man and then went to the police station to confess.

Which meant I needed to find out as much as I could about Paul Locke and any other leads I could find.

I cleared my throat. "Do you happen to know who was at the party last night?"

"No. I only know the facts my police source told me."

The way she said it made me think she knew about my trip to the police station last night. It occurred to me belatedly that there had to be cameras all over the place there. Even if I'd left without speaking to a detective, I still would have been captured on video.

But Emily divulged nothing, and I had to wonder if she wasn't using an interrogation method of her own on me.

"Okay," I said, ignoring the bait. "I'll see if I can talk to Amy and compare the guest lists. We can figure out who was at both parties. But I also want to do more digging into Paul Locke. He recently lost a legal case against Max involving a lot of money. He definitely had motive."

"Sounds good. I'll try to get more details about the murder."

Emily hung up and I was about to return to my suitcases when my phone rang again. My mother.

"Magnolia, how are you feeling?"

"Much better, and I'm ready for lunch. I'm starving." Which was true. I only hoped I could choke down my meal while sitting at the same table as my brother.

"Tilly's eating with us, so she's gonna pick you up and bring you to the restaurant."

"Okay. . . . but, Momma, I should probably tell you—"

"That there was another murder at Luke Powell's? Yeah, Emily told me this morning at church. I don't even know what this world is comin' to."

"I think it's gotta help my case, Momma. At least I wasn't there this time."

"Thank God for small mercies."

My second mother arrived fifteen minutes later. On a whim, I grabbed my laptop and stuffed it into my purse, hoping to do some investigating after lunch.

I greeted Tilly at the door. "You'll have to lock up," I told her. "Momma still hasn't given me a key." My tone carried more irritation than I'd intended, but this state of being constantly on edge had made me short-tempered.

"Give her time," she said, sounding more subdued than usual as she turned the deadbolt with her key. "She just needs to adjust is all. You know how much she hates change."

We got in the car, and Tilly was uncharacteristically quiet for the first few minutes of our drive to the restaurant.

"Spit it out, Tilly," I finally said. "Are you upset by what I said about the key?"

She licked her lips, a sure sign she was nervous. "Have you talked to your mother?"

"You'll have to be more specific than that. I talked to her on the phone a few minutes ago, and we also talked briefly this morning while she rubbed my neck. But I suspect you're not referring to either of those."

She cast me a grin. "You always were a spitfire, Maggie."

I chuckled. "I'm a burr under my mother's saddle. I'm sure she's eager to get rid of me."

"I wouldn't be so sure of that. You should stay."

I leaned back in my seat. "I wouldn't even know what to do here. As my brother pointed out, I don't have a college degree. Acting and waitressing are all I know, and I sure as hell don't want to be a waitress for the rest of my life."

"So if you don't stay here, where will you go and what will you do?"

"I don't know yet." But hopefully it wouldn't involve making license plates at the state pen.

Tilly cast a long glance at me, her face serious. "Before you go decidin' anything, talk to your momma first, okay?"

"Tilly . . ."

"Just promise."

"Fine," I sighed. "I promise."

Tilly pulled into the restaurant parking lot, saving me from further conversation, but my hands were shaking as we walked toward the restaurant.

I stopped outside the front door and grabbed Tilly's arm, pulling her aside. "Tilly, what do you think of Roy?"

She rolled her head and grumbled, "*That's* a loaded question if I ever heard one."

"I know I shouldn't put you on the spot like this. Just give me an overall impression."

She crossed her arms and pressed her lips together. "He's a weasel."

I pushed out a breath. "Oh, thank God you see it too."

"When did *you* see him?"

"Last night. Without Momma. It did *not* go well."

"Well, that momma's boy is with his momma today, so you'll see a whole different side to him. Let's go. I've got your back."

If Tilly thought I needed backup, then I was even more worried about what I was walking into.

chapter twenty-two

I followed her inside and forced a smile as I walked up to the table. Belinda gave me a worried look, then stood and gave me a perfunctory hug. "Magnolia, how are you feeling?"

"Much better, thanks." I tried to give her as little attention as possible, not wanting to upset her dipshit husband.

They were sitting at a six-person table—Roy and Belinda on one side and Momma on the other. I sat down next to Momma, directly opposite my brother. Tilly gave me a grimace as she sat next to Roy. I tried to hide a smirk of amusement.

"We barely got a chance to talk last night," Roy said in a breezy tone. If I didn't know better, I might have thought there was genuine warmth behind his smile, but I noticed he didn't go so far as to stand up and hug me. He probably valued his shins. "Tell me how life's been treating you, Sis."

"Just peachy, Bro," I said, in a tone that matched his. "Why just the other day, I got a *very* sweet offer."

His eyebrows rose, his discomfort obvious. "You don't say?" Then he lifted his water glass to his mouth to hide a scowl.

But Momma perked up. "An offer? What kind of offer?"

Roy lowered his glass, looking anxious.

I kicked up my smile by several hundred megawatts. "I'm pretty sure it was a high *five*-figure deal."

He choked on his water, spitting it out on the table.

"Oh, dear Roy." My voice dripped with sympathy. "Are you okay?"

Roy's mouth pinched into a tight line, and Momma shot him a look of confusion.

Tilly burst out laughing and said, "I'm eager to hear about this five-figure deal, Maggie."

The look on her face told me she suspected who'd made the offer.

"Oh, there's not much to tell really," I said coyly, grabbing a sugar packet from the middle of the table and twisting it in my hand. I kept my eyes locked with my brother's. "But I *can* tell you it involves relocation."

My mother stiffened next to me. "Are you going to take it?"

My eyes narrowed slightly, still fixed on my brother. "I'm keeping my options open. I'm waiting to see the official offer."

I couldn't help thinking this new murder *had* to help clear my name. And once that happened, I could get on a plane and fly away and never come back. I had no proof that the texts and the flower were from the murderer from ten years ago, but I couldn't let anything happen to Momma. Or Belinda. And much as I couldn't stand my brother, I couldn't let anything happen to him either. Maybe leaving was the best option.

But a sideways glance told me my statement bothered her. My mother had been our rock growing up. Most fathers carried the title, but ours had been a pushover. My mother had always worn the pants in our family, a true matriarch. But now she looked older and more worn than I'd ever seen her.

"Did you talk to Emily?" Momma asked. "I saw her at church and told her you were home sleepin' off a migraine."

"More like a hangover," my brother mumbled.

"Roy." Momma's tone was short and blunt. The voice she'd

used when we were kids. It had instantly gotten our attention then, and it was no less effective now, as evidenced by the look on my brother's face. "Your sister has been through an ordeal. You should show her a little sympathy."

His eyes narrowed, but he offered me a smile so obviously plastic I was surprised it didn't break from stress. "Of course, I'm so sorry to hear about your implication in a murder case."

I knew all too well *why* he was sorry to hear it.

I placed my hands on my chest, then said in a dramatic voice, "That was so heartfelt it brought tears to my eyes."

"If that's any indication of your acting ability, no wonder you lost your job," Roy drolled.

Tilly hid a grin behind her hand, and Momma released a groan. "Can you two please get along? This is the first time we've been together in eight years. Can you let me enjoy the moment?"

"Of course, Momma," I said, rubbing her arm. "I'm sorry."

Roy turned his smile on our mother. "I'm sorry I upset you."

She nodded and then looked down at her menu. I shot a questioning glance at Tilly. The momma I had grown up with never would have looked so resigned. Had age softened her *that* much?

Tilly held my eyes for several seconds before dropping her gaze.

Was this why Tilly was so insistent I talk to Momma before I made a decision to leave? Was Roy being abusive to Momma too? A new fire sputtered to life in my chest. I sure as hell wasn't about to put up with *that* nonsense. I wanted to confront him then and there, but Belinda interrupted my plan.

"Magnolia, what did Emily say?" she asked, her hands clasped together and resting on the table.

I took a second to calm down enough to answer. "She has a source at the police station—" which I still found surprising, "—who told her the victim was a man."

"And no suspects yet?" she asked.

"No."

Momma put down her menu. "Have the police contacted you today?"

"No. The only calls I've gotten today were from Emily and —" I stopped myself before I said Belinda's name "—and you."

"They'll want to know about your alibi," Belinda said, worry furrowing her brow. "Were you with Colt all night?"

Roy placed his hand over Belinda's, exerting a little more force than was necessary. "Belinda, darling. You need to stop that nonsense and let the police do their job."

"I know," she said, her jaw setting. "But your sister is a person of interest in another murder that occurred in the same house. It stands to reason that we need to make sure she's got an alibi during the time frame of the second murder."

His mouth gaped as he turned to her. "Didn't I just say to let it go?"

"But Roy—"

"Belinda, darling, you plan *weddings*. You do not have the mind of a police detective. Playing with wedding dresses is nowhere near as important as police work. Leave legalities to the professionals."

I could *not* believe what I was hearing.

"Are you *seriously* suggesting your wife is incapable of thinking for herself?" I demanded. Something deep inside told me to leave this alone, this was not my fight, but I needed to latch on to something I could win. And I had no doubt that I could outmaneuver Roy.

But the look of panic in Belinda's eyes warned me that I was messing with her life too.

"Stay out of this, Magnolia," Roy sneered.

"Roy." Momma's sharp outburst of his name made us all jump. "What has gotten into you?"

His face softened. "I'm sorry, Momma. I know I'm overreacting, but I love Belinda so much I can't bear to see her get hurt. You know what a kind heart she has." He looked back at her, taking her hand in his and squeezing. "People take advantage of that."

Something he knew firsthand. My brother was a bully. An abuser. I'd suspected it after last night, but now I had ample proof.

Did my mother see it too?

But she was looking down at her menu, and I realized his movement had been carefully planned.

Fucking bastard.

But Tilly's mouth pursed as her eyes drilled into my mother's bent head.

Our carefully worded conversation over the course of lunch could have been a sketch on a comedy show, but the dark circles under my mother's eyes suggested the farce was wearing her down. It made me realize she wasn't getting any younger, and my own troubles had added to her stress. I really needed to make sure my brother wasn't bullying her too.

Roy made a show of picking up the tab, and when we prepared to leave, he reached for me and pulled me into an awkward embrace.

I tensed and prepared to knee him in the balls if necessary, but he leaned into my ear and whispered, "It will take me a day to get the funds ready and make the transfer, so if you really want a five-figure offer, be at my office at two tomorrow. After you leave, I expect you to immediately skip town and never return. You don't show, and the offer is gone forever."

I pulled back and looked at him in disbelief.

"And just so we're clear, there will be a five in front of that." Then he winked.

Fifty thousand dollars? I'd been trying to bait him at the table. I'd never expected him to follow through. But fifty thousand dollars could get me anywhere I needed to go.

Could I leave Belinda with this monster? Could I leave Momma?

He turned to Belinda and kissed her cheek. "I'll go warm up the car, precious." Then he smiled at our mother. "Momma taught me how to treat my lady right."

He was out the door too quickly to hear Tilly's snort, but my mother had a worried smile as she watched him walk out. Did she see it too? Maybe she saw more than she wanted to—no mother wants to believe her son has become a bad man.

"I'm going to go to the restroom," she murmured, sounding tired.

Tilly moved in her direction. "I'll go with you."

They left Belinda and me in the restaurant foyer, along with several people waiting for their tables. Belinda kept her gaze on the window, wearing a goofy smile that made her look like she was on a parade float, and then she lifted her hand and gave a little wave.

My brother was outside the window watching her.

Taking her cue, I waved to him too. Trying to move my lips as little as possible, I said, "I need to talk to Amy. I need to see if she'll tell me who was at the house so I can compare both guest lists."

"I can't go with you."

"I know. Roy."

She swiped at the corner of her eye. "I know you don't understand—"

I pushed out a frustrated sigh. "Belinda, you don't owe me anything, let alone an explanation about your marriage."

"Thank you," she whispered.

"But I will say this. My brother is an asshole, and you deserve better. Leave him."

"It's not that easy." Her fake smile quavered.

"Nothing worth having ever is." Someone had told me that once, back when I was struggling to survive after landing in

New York. *Nothing worth having is easy.* I'd believed it back then, but now I had my doubts. Maybe life just wasn't easy, period. Whether you got what you wanted or not.

"I'll text you her number," Belinda said. "And send you the guest list from the release party."

The restaurant door opened, and Roy appeared in the opening. "Ready, precious?"

"Yeah," she said with a brittle smile. Then she turned to my mother, who had just returned from the restroom. "I'll call you later, Lila."

My mother gave her a lingering look before nodding. "You get some rest. You look tired."

Roy wrapped an arm around Belinda's back and led her to his Lexus, the white steam from the exhaust billowing in the gray mist.

"Momma, can I borrow your car?" I asked, still watching the parking lot.

"Why?" She sounded suspicious.

"I need to check on a few things."

"About this new murder? Does Emily know?"

I turned to her with a soft smile. "Yes to both. We think this will clear my name, but since my interrogation with Detective Holden went so poorly, we both feel the need to hedge my bets."

"What happened with the interrogation?"

"Nothing you need to worry about. We've got it covered."

Momma studied my face for a few seconds, a question on the tip of her tongue, but she handed me her keys. "Be careful, Magnolia. I didn't just get you home only to lose you again."

I leaned over and kissed her cheek. How many times had I done this as a teenager? "I will."

I walked to Momma's car, watching her and Tilly cross the parking lot. She seemed to be moving slower today than she had over the last couple of days, but I assured myself she just needed to rest. The stress was getting to her.

I got in Momma's car and turned the key, letting the engine heat up as I tried to come up with a plan. I needed Internet, and a coffee shop was the best place to find it for free.

The rain must have inspired half the town to get hot beverages. Starbucks was packed, but I was lucky enough to nab a two-person table while I waited for my nonfat cappuccino.

I decided to start off by doing a little more digging into Paul Locke. He wasn't famous enough for the tabloids to have gone digging into his personal life. But what little I could find hinted that he'd been raised by a single mother in a trailer park in Alabama. His first album had released two years ago, and his second was set to drop in a couple of weeks. An early release teaser single from the second album had shot to number two on the charts and hung there for several weeks before falling. A newspaper post from last week had suggested Paul was set to lose hundreds of thousands of dollars to Max—possibly millions—if his new album did as well as everyone expected.

I took a sip of my drink, and my phone dinged with a message from Belinda containing Amy's contact information. I wasn't sure how likely Amy was to answer a call from an unknown number, but it was a good place to start.

Surprisingly, she picked up on the first ring. "This is Amy."

"Hey, Amy, it's Magnolia. Belinda's sister-in-law." I left off *and person of interest in the murder at your boss's house.* No need for overkill.

"Magnolia . . . is Belinda with you?" Her voice was shaky, and she sounded close to tears.

"No." Did Amy know about her friend's issue-ridden marriage? "She's busy today, but I hope it's okay that she gave me your number. We heard about the new murder." She remained silent, so I pushed on. "I was happy to hear Luke's okay."

"Yeah . . ."

She sounded out of it. "Amy, are *you* okay?"

She hadn't handled the stress of finding Max's body well. Another murder might have pushed her over the edge.

"Yeah . . . no." She paused. "*I* was the one to find the body this time, Magnolia."

"Oh, my God. I'm so sorry. I know how shocking that is. Was it awful?"

"Yes." Her whisper was so quiet that it worried me.

"Amy, where are you? Do you have someone with you?"

"No." Then she cleared her throat, forcing strength into her voice. "I'm fine. I'm trying to control this publicity nightmare."

"Doesn't Luke have people for that?"

"They're dealing with it head on. I'm dealing with it in the background."

"Can you tell me who was killed and how? I heard a man was stabbed in the heart."

Amy sniffed. "It was Neil Fulton. Luke's attorney. I found him in the kitchen last night at around nine."

"Why was Luke's attorney there at nine o'clock on a Saturday night?"

"They say there's no such thing as bad publicity, but that's not true when murder is involved. Neil was probably coming over to give Luke an update."

"Why would Luke's attorney be in his kitchen?"

"He used to come over all the time, so he had the code to get in and out of the kitchen."

"Why would someone kill Luke's attorney?"

"I have no idea." But she didn't sound completely convincing.

"Did he have a connection to Max Goodwin?"

"Not that I know about."

"Were any of the people at Luke's party last night at his release party?"

"All twenty of them."

Well, that narrowed it down. "I hate to ask this, but did Luke and his attorney get along?"

Amy didn't respond.

"Amy, do you think Luke killed Max Goodwin and his attorney?"

"*No.*"

"Do you think the police might think he did?"

"I don't know."

"I want to help you, but I need a list of everyone who was there last night."

"I already risked my job by sharing that list with Belinda, and she's my friend." Her words had a bite to them. "I don't even know you, Magnolia Steele. Other than what I've seen of you on YouTube."

Ouch.

"Besides," she added. "You only want to clear your *own* name."

"Maybe so," I said, "but I'll be clearing Luke's too."

"No. No list."

Dammit. "Will you at least tell me if Paul Locke was there?"

She hesitated. "Yeah. He was there. Pissed at the world for having to hang out with a bunch of teenagers at the mall yesterday."

"Anyone else I should know about?"

"I think I've told you enough."

"Thank you for what you did tell me. I'll let you know if I find out something to help."

"I think I need a miracle," she said, sounding close to tears. Then she hung up.

Her last statement worried me. Did she really think Luke had killed Max Goodwin and Neil Fulton? Was he stupid enough to kill two people in his own house, days apart?

I pulled up Google and entered "Paul Locke + Neil Fulton," not surprised at the results.

Neil Fulton had represented Max Goodwin in the case against Paul Locke.

Hot damn. Maybe I'd just found my new career.

I needed to talk to Paul Locke again . . . or at least to the people who had been with him both nights. The problem was I had no idea how to find him. But Belinda might.

I texted her. *Luke's attorney, Neil Fulton, was the murder victim last night. I think Amy's worried Luke is guilty, but I found out Fulton represented Max Goodwin when Paul Locke sued him to break his contract. Paul lost . . . a month ago. I need to talk to him again. Can you give me Tandy's number?*

I sent the message, then had a mini panic attack that Roy might see it. Shit.

Instead of worrying about my sister-in-law, I decided to call Jody to give her an update, but she had one for me too.

"Have you seen Sarah's reviews for *Fireflies at Dawn?*"

"No," I scowled, picking up my cappuccino and taking a sip. "I've been a little busy with my bigger crisis." The last thing I wanted was to hear how much everybody had loved her.

"Hold on. I'm going to read a few to you."

"Jody . . ."

"Trust me. You want to hear this." She paused, then said in a stentorian tone, "'Chambers's performance has the nuance of a second grade production of *Cinderella* without the heart-warming feels.'"

"Ouch." I winced. But I couldn't help feeling elated. Served her right.

"Oh, that's one of the nicer ones. How about this—'A drowning cat would be preferable to Chambers's warbling high notes.'"

I sat up straighter and set my coffee on the table. "You're kidding."

"But this is my favorite—'One has to wonder if Steele's spat with Chambers was her attempt to save the world from the worst performance in Broadway history. While Steele portrayed innocence and childlike wonder in the role of Scarlett, Chambers has the countenance of a prostitute trying to pass as royalty.'"

"Wow," I said, floored. "That's amazing."

"I hear Griff is shitting his pants. Word is that he's prepared to offer you the part back."

That was the very last thing I'd expected her to say.

"What are you going to do?" she asked. "Could you work with him again after everything he did?"

"I don't know. He tried to call me yesterday, but I didn't answer, and I deleted his message. I figured he was calling to gloat."

"He wants you back. Definitely for the play, maybe back in his bed too."

"Well, that sure as hell isn't going to happen, but if I accept the job, I don't even know where I'd live. I was making barely above the minimum salary and rehearsals ran past the contract, which means I've made next to nothing for over a month. I have no money, Jody."

"Make it part of the contract. Get Jimmy to negotiate it for you."

I doubted I could get my agent to negotiate a deal at a swap meet. "Jimmy made it pretty clear we were done."

"Magnolia," she said in exasperation. "You're holed up in Hicksville, U.S.A., so you're not fully grasping what's going on in New York. This is big. Bigger than big. There hasn't been a controversy like this since *Spiderman*. You've gone from being a public laughingstock to being Broadway's biggest martyr. To bring you back would sell tickets, and you and I both know it's all about selling tickets."

I groaned. "First of all, Franklin is a suburb of Nashville, and there are so many music artists here that going to church is like getting a free concert. This is *far* from Hicksville. And second, I can't believe for one minute that anyone has called me a martyr."

"You go to church?"

"That is *beside* the point."

"*Magnolia*. Did you not hear that review I just read?"

"Jody . . ."

"All I'm saying is you're going to get a call, whether it's another one from Griff or from someone else who wants to attach your name to their show for the publicity. You need to be prepared."

"Thanks for the heads-up."

"Always. I've got your back, girl."

My phone beeped and I looked at the screen, not recognizing the 615 area code number. "Jody, I'm getting another call."

"When you get some offers—and notice I said *when*—let me know if you need someone to help you decide."

"Thanks." I hung up and answered the other call. "Hello?"

"Magnolia Steele?"

I recognized the man's voice, and my blood turned to ice water.

chapter
twenty-three

I steeled my voice. "Yes."

"This is Detective Bennett with the Franklin Police Department. I'd like you to come to the station so we can ask you a few follow-up questions after your interview with Detective Holden."

I could only choke out one word. "When?"

"The sooner, the better."

"I'll come now." I might as well get it over with.

He started to say something, but I'd already hung up before I realized it. Great. One more strike against me.

Packing up my laptop, I debated whether to call Emily. It was the smart thing to do, but she'd been so ineffective last time. Besides, it would be humiliating enough to see Brady. No need for me to bring Emily along to watch. I hadn't done anything wrong.

A different receptionist was at the counter, but she was waiting for me. "I'll let Detective Bennett know you're here."

My stomach twisted into knots as the door to the back opened, revealing Brady, who looked guarded. "Ms. Steele, thank you for coming in."

A barb sat on my tongue, ready to spring out, but I only nodded as the full truth hit me.

Detective Brady Bennett had used me.

My eyes stung, but I blinked back tears. It was time to play a role, something I hadn't thought I'd do with him. I was a wrongly accused woman facing the detective who had tried to play her for a fool. Well, he wasn't going to fool me this time.

"If you'll follow me."

I didn't answer. It was safer that way. I was still slipping into my part.

He took me to the same room where I'd met Detective Holden. Thankfully there was no sign of him. There was a woman at the table instead, and she stood as I entered the room. She wore black pants and a white blouse, and her black hair was cut in a short bob that brushed her jaw. Brady followed me in and shut the door behind us.

"Ms. Steele," the woman said, extending her hand. "I'm Detective Martinez. Thank you for coming in to answer more questions."

I shook her hand, impressed by her firm grip. My character had slipped into place. "Of course, Detective Martinez. I'm happy to be of help."

She gestured toward the chair next to me. "If you'd like to take a seat."

At your convenience. If you'd like to take a seat. All thinly veiled attempts to try and persuade people they had control. I hadn't had control for years. But they saw none of that; the woman I was portraying was the epitome of calm, cool, and collected.

I sat down and crossed my legs, wishing I were dressed in my sexy gray business dress and four-inch, black patent-leather heels. Instead my attitude would have to carry me.

"Ms. Steele, you came to the station last night at 9:53 asking to see Detective Holden."

So I was right about the cameras. "Yes, that's right." There was no point in denying it.

"Instead you spoke to Detective Bennett . . ." She looked down at a notepad in front of her and then back up at me. "Or should I say, you refused to tell Detective Bennett the reason for your visit."

I nodded. It wasn't a question, so there was no need to answer it. I wasn't about to give them any more information than necessary.

"What was the purpose for your visit?"

"I was worried," I said. "I know I'm a person of interest in Mr. Goodwin's murder, and it's very disconcerting to have that hanging over my head. I wanted to see if my name had been cleared." I sure as hell wasn't giving them what I knew about Paul Locke.

"Detective Bennett says you appeared distressed."

I'm sure Detective Bennett did. Asshole. I gave her a tight smile. "Detective Martinez, have you ever been called a person of interest in a murder investigation?"

She cast a glance at Brady, then at me. "No, I can't say I have."

"I assure you that it's a very stressful situation."

"Only if you have something to hide," she said as her gaze narrowed on my face.

"One only has to watch the news to realize that it's not all that uncommon for people to be arrested for crimes they didn't commit."

She cocked her head to the side. "Are you saying we're incompetent?"

I sat up straighter, resting my hands on my knees, and delivered my lines cold as an arctic wind. "I'm saying there are several detectives in this station who have yet to convince me they are looking for the true perpetrator of the crime and are not out to pin this on me."

"You have quite the imagination," she said.

I held her gaze.

"Where were you last night around nine o'clock?"

I'd known they would ask this question, and I'd considered how to answer it on the drive over. "I was at my mother's catering business."

"Doing what?"

"Napping."

Her expression told me she didn't buy it for a minute. "Why would you be napping at your mother's catering business? Does she have beds there?"

"Frankly, Detective Martinez," I said in a tight, controlled voice, "I don't like your tone. As far as I can tell, the layout of my mother's business has nothing to do with your investigation."

Her cheeks reddened with anger. "I can assure you it does, Ms. Steele, when I'm trying to determine the validity of your statement." She rested her forearm on the table and leaned closer. "Why would you take a nap at your mother's business on a Saturday night when you could have gone home?"

Something told me not to feel so smug that I was getting to her, but I couldn't help it. She was already aboard the *let's arrest Magnolia for a crime she didn't commit* train. I might have to enlist Colt's friend's help after all. "I was with my mother all morning. Then I spent the entire afternoon with my sister-in-law. She dropped me off at my mother's catering business, where I helped my mother, her business partner, and an employee load their van for a catering job in Hendersonville. The employee and I rode to the job together, and after the food was unloaded, he and I took my mother's business partner's car to Hillsboro Village, where we had dinner at a bar. My brother and his wife showed up. Afterward, I wasn't feeling well, so the employee dropped me off at my mother's business to wait for her to return."

"Why not just go to your mother's house?"

I lifted my chin. "Because I don't have a key."

She lifted her eyebrows. "You don't have a key to your own mother's house?"

"I moved away ten years ago. I left my key behind."

"So you took a nap at your mother's business? What? Did you lay on one of the prep tables?" she asked in a snotty tone.

For the first time, I cast a glance at Brady, but his gaze was glued to the table.

Fucking coward.

I met her cold stare with one of my own. "My mother and her partner have a sofa in their office. I slept there."

"What made you search out Detective Holden?"

"I already told you."

"Why would someone like you be taking a nap at nine on a Saturday night?" She held her hands out from her sides. "Why were you so upset?"

I took a breath, pushing myself to stay in control. "I haven't been home for ten years, Detective Martinez. Some people would rather I had stayed gone."

"Like Max Goodwin?" she asked.

"I have no idea what Mr. Goodwin's thoughts were on my return to Franklin."

"Then who?"

I shook my head slightly and made a show of rolling my eyes. "My brother. He made no secret of the fact that he was not happy to see me. I was upset after our reunion, so I asked Colt to bring me back to the catering business so I could be alone."

"Detective Bennett said you had a bruise on your right forearm and one on your left tricep."

I ignored the sharp stab of pain that penetrated the shield over my heart. "That would be correct."

"And where did you acquire those bruises?"

I wanted to reach across the table and slap Brady Bennett— who still couldn't look at me—but I suspected that wouldn't work in my favor. Instead I stayed in character. "That seems like a personal question."

"Ms. Steele, I'm sure you're aware there was another murder on the Powell estate last night."

"So I heard."

"Were you at the Powell estate last night?"

"No. After my nap, I walked to the police station and met Detective Bennett. I changed my mind about inquiring about my case and then proceeded to leave. Detective Bennett insisted on walking with me. He then tried to put me at ease by pretending to be my friend, but he was called away on a case. After that, I went back to my mother's office, and my mother arrived a short time later."

I could feel Brady's eyes on me, but if I looked at him, my persona would crack.

"Where did you get the bruises, Ms. Steele?"

We engaged in a staring contest while I wrestled with what to do—plead the fifth or tell them about my brother. I knew he wouldn't admit to it, but would Colt and Belinda corroborate?

I pushed out my breath. "My brother."

Brady shifted in his chair, sitting upright.

Detective Martinez ignored him. "I thought you saw your brother last night—which you called a reunion—and in a bar, no less. You're suggesting he beat you there?"

I shook my head, my persona cracking. "Why do you *care*? Contrary to Detective Bennett's insistence last night, none of you give a damn about my well-being, so don't try to pretend you're trying to protect me." I was proud my voice didn't crack. I was dangerously close to breaking character.

"Ms. Steele," she said, her tone as sharp as a razor's edge. "We have just cause to believe you killed again on the Powell estate last night. Only this time, there was a scuffle and you were bruised in the process."

"And why would I kill Luke's attorney?"

Oh. Shit.

An excited gleam filled her eye. "How do you know who was murdered? The name hasn't been released to the public yet."

I wasn't going to sell out Amy. "I have my sources."

"And how did you know Detective Bennett's calls last night pertained to a murder at the Powell estate?"

If she thought she was catching me off guard, she was going to be sorely disappointed. I knew the moment the words left my mouth the night before that they would bite me in the ass.

Would Brady get in trouble for talking about the case in front of me? I didn't give a shit. He'd sold me out to his partner. I wasn't about to protect him. "While on his phone, Detective Bennett mentioned the unlikelihood of two murders on the same estate. He also mentioned Detective Holden. I knew he was the lead detective on the Max Goodwin case."

"How did you know Neil Fulton?"

"I didn't."

"We'll figure it out, so you might as well save us all a bunch of time and trouble and just confess right now."

"If you were the least bit bright, you would be embarrassed with yourself right now, especially since it's so obvious I'm innocent."

Detective Martinez abruptly stood, her chair scooching across the floor. "Insulting a police detective investigating your involvement in two murders doesn't seem like the smartest move."

"Oh," I said in mock surprise. "You picked up on the insult? Then there might be hope for my case yet."

Martinez looked like she was about to lunge across the table for me, but Brady got to his feet and took a half-step in front of her. "Ms. Steele," he said in a professional voice. "Thank you for taking your time to come to the station. You're free to go."

I picked up my purse and headed for the door, which Brady had opened. He was standing beside it, looking down at me with a guilty look in his eyes, but I ignored him as I marched out of the office, not stopping until I was in the parking garage. My hands were shaking as I tried to dig the keys out of the bottom of my purse.

"Maggie," Brady called out, and my search became more frantic.

I found them underneath my laptop and pressed the unlock button, the chirp echoing throughout the garage.

"Maggie. *Wait*."

I had just opened the door when he reached me, but he gently pushed it closed.

"Will you please let me explain?"

You are cold as ice, Magnolia. You are untouchable. I almost believed it.

I lifted my gaze to meet his darkened brown eyes. "I really don't need a lesson on the sordid ways the police investigate suspects, *Detective* Bennett." My eyes narrowed. "How they prey on a young woman's distress to trick her into . . . what?" I gave a slight shake. "What were you hoping I'd confess to? Max Goodwin's murder?"

His eyes pleaded with me. "No. It wasn't like that. I swear."

"*Really?* I'm supposed to believe that? Last night you said you'd never lie to me or try to trick me, but look where I just came from—an interrogation in which your partner attacked me with information you gained after you told me you were simple Brady Bennett—" I held my hands out at my sides, "—just a guy wanting to get to know a girl. You pretended you had no idea who I was, but you knew all along."

"Maggie. I *didn't* know."

I poked my finger into his chest. "Don't you *dare* call me Maggie," I spat out through gritted teeth. "Don't you dare pretend to be my friend." My voice cracked.

"I'd been on vacation all week. Yesterday was my first day back—two days early because of the Goodwin murder. I had no idea who you were when I suggested we go for a walk." He released a groan of frustration. "Believe it or not, I only told Martinez so I could protect you. She's my partner, and she knows you came into the station and that I left with you. It would have looked worse for you if I *didn't* tell her what happened." He rubbed the back of his neck.

"So the two of you took what I'd told you and then figured out how to pin this new murder on me." I tried to open the door, but he stood in the way. My chest tightened. "Oh, my God. Are you *arresting* me?"

"No!" he shouted, then lowered his voice and said, "Did your brother really give you those bruises?"

"I'm giving you three seconds to get the hell away from my car and let me go, or I'm going back inside to file harassment charges against you."

"Maggie—"

I narrowed my eyes. "One."

He lifted his hands in the air, looking like someone had just run over his puppy. "Okay. I'll let you go. But if your brother—"

"Oh, my God!" I cried out, close to tears. "Don't even. Just leave me alone."

He moved to the front of the car, watching as I backed up and pulled out of the garage.

Tears filled my eyes, but I was damned if I was going to cry over him or any other man ever again.

One thing was certain: my fate was in my own hands. I had two—possibly three—detectives who were certain of my guilt. I needed to find out who the real killer was. And fast.

chapter twenty-four

B elinda had texted me while I was gone.

Paul Locke is shooting pool at O'Malley's tonight.

The time on my phone said it was four-thirty. I suspected Paul wouldn't show up at O'Malley's for a few hours, and it would be smart to give him another hour or two after that to get some drinks in him before I tried to finesse information from him. I wasn't sure what the exact protocol was to get someone to confess to murder. Maybe I should have asked Brady to give me some tips.

Since I had a few hours, I texted Momma to say I was heading home and offered to pick something up for dinner. She sent a short grocery list and said she'd make something for the two of us. I worried that she might be too tired, but I knew better than to argue with her.

I had just pulled into the grocery store parking lot when my phone rang again. I was shocked to see it was my agent.

"Magnolia, baby, how are you?"

I parked the car and turned off the engine. "Jimmy. I distinctly remember you saying you were deleting my number from your phone."

"Magnolia . . ." he crooned in his New Jersey accent. "We both said things we regret."

"Speak for yourself."

He laughed. "Okay, I can eat humble pie. Just throw on a heap of whipped cream and I'll eat it all damn week."

"What are you talking about?"

"Magnolia, baby—you are a sought-after commodity. There's noise that everyone wants you, and I mean *everyone*, including that asshole Griff."

"I thought you called Griff a theatrical genius."

"That was before he used my girl."

"You said *I* used *him*."

"That was before I found out that we're about to get an offer from *Fireflies at Dawn*. They want you back *bad*, precious."

I rested my hands on the steering wheel. "What role?"

"Scarlett, of course."

"What?"

"I'm in the process of negotiating with them, so don't get too comfortable there in Nashville. They'll need you here by the middle of the week."

"But I don't know if I can leave—"

He'd already hung up.

I went into the store, grabbed a cart, and headed toward the produce section, still lost in a daze when I pulled up my mother's text and scanned the list—a red onion, broccoli, garlic, and romaine lettuce. I was sorting through the onions when I saw Maddie pushing a cart with a baby carrier in the front. I froze as I watched her stop and lean over the baby inside. Touching his nose with her fingertip, she grinned and said, "Who's Momma's baby boy?"

He cooed and giggled, keeping eye contact with her as he kicked his chubby legs and waved his arms.

"That's right," she said, still beaming. "*You're* my boy." She straightened and her eyes locked with mine. Her smile fell.

I had two options: I could run or I could try again with her. Running would be easier, and since she'd told me she never wanted to see me again, I knew she would have preferred it, but I had to apologize at least one more time.

Leaving my cart in front of the onions, I walked toward her. My gaze landed on her baby.

"Oh, Maddie," I said in awe. His hair was dark brown, and his bright blue eyes latched on to mine. He looked exactly like the cherubs painted by Renaissance artists. "He's absolutely beautiful."

She started to say something, then stopped and gave me a tight grin. "Thank you."

"I bet your mother loves every minute with him," I said as he looked up at me, kicking his feet and grinning from ear to ear.

When she didn't answer me, I glanced up at her. The blank look on her face worried me, but then she said, "Mom died last year."

Oh, God. My chest was tight. "I had no idea."

That explained why I hadn't seen any photos of her mom with the baby on her Facebook profile.

Her guard was back up. "Of course you didn't. You weren't here."

I had no idea how to answer that. There was no denying it. "I'm sorry."

She shook her head. I wasn't sure what she wanted from this conversation, but at least she hadn't pushed her cart away.

"So you're a big Broadway star?" she asked.

"Not at the moment." My mouth lifted into a self-deprecating smile. "Although one could argue that I'm an Internet star." I laughed softly and she laughed with me.

"I always knew you were destined for greatness," she said with a soft smile.

My heart felt a few ounces lighter. I'd made her laugh, even if it was inadvertent. I had a million questions, but I had no right to ask any of them and no idea where to start.

"You said it wasn't my fault," she murmured, smoothing a wrinkle on her baby's shirt. "Whose fault was it?"

I could hardly tell her it was a vicious murderer's fault. Not when those text messages and the magnolia blossom indicated he might be far from gone. "Not yours."

"You broke my heart." Her eyes were amazingly clear. There were no tears in them, but no hatred either.

I held her gaze. "You have no idea how much I wish things had turned out differently."

"Are you staying?"

I shook my head. "I don't know, but I don't think so."

"Came home to lick your wounds, then going back?"

"Something like that."

"That's too bad," she said, breaking eye contact and looking down at her baby. "I was kind of hoping you were going to stick around." She glanced back up at me. "I'd like to hear about some of your adventures."

Not only was she talking to me, but she wanted to see me again. This was almost too good to be true. I smiled at her, my heart bursting. "I'd like to hear all about your life too."

She released a brittle laugh. "I suspect it would bore you to tears."

"I wouldn't be so sure about that."

The baby started to fuss and she released a heavy sigh. "I need to go."

"I know."

She started to push her cart away, but then she turned back and threw her arms around my shoulders, squeezing me tight. "I've missed you."

"I've missed you too." More than she probably realized.

Then, just as abruptly, she dropped her hold and stepped back, giving me a watery smile. "Have a good life, Magnolia."

"You too." My voice quavered.

She hurried away with her now squalling baby, but I was rooted to the ground next to the oranges, reconsidering everything.

chapter twenty-five

O'Malley's was a happening place for nine-thirty on a Sunday night. Momma had gone to bed early, so it had been easy to slip out of the house. She'd claimed she was coming down with something, but she seemed to be just plain exhausted, something I'd noticed a few times over the past few days. It was a reminder to think long and hard about the decision I had to make about where to go and what to do next.

O'Malley's hadn't existed when I lived in Franklin. It was in a refurbished strip mall on Highway 96, making it easy to find. Paul and his entourage—of twenty-something guys this time, not teen and tween girls—weren't hard to find either. They were hanging around four high-top tables in the back corner, laughing loud enough to broadcast to the room at large that they'd had a few.

I went up to the bar and ordered a beer, watching the group and trying to figure out how to approach Paul. This wasn't L.A. or New York. He wasn't surrounded by security. Nashvillians didn't ooh and ah over celebrities, one of the many reasons they liked living here. It wasn't uncommon to look up and see Wynonna Judd in the Target checkout lane buying toothpaste.

Still, that didn't mean I could walk up to him and start asking questions. Especially since he'd probably remember me from yesterday at the mall.

It didn't take long for the answer to present itself. One of the guys in Paul's entourage couldn't take his eyes off me.

I sent him flirty looks, so I wasn't surprised when he appeared at my side as I drained the last sip from my bottle.

"Corona, huh?" he asked. "I pegged a pretty little thing like you as a margarita girl."

I gave him a playful laugh as I set the bottle on the counter with a thud.

"I guess my momma was right about not judging a book by its cover."

I looked up at him through lowered eyelashes and purred, "And what's my cover saying?"

"Baby, you are all curves and sex appeal."

I gave him a coy smile. "Your momma teach you to pick up women like that?"

He laughed. "Hell no."

"What would she tell you?"

He laughed again and leaned his elbow on the bar, his face a foot from mine. "She told me to open car doors and shit."

I lifted my eyebrows. "And shit?"

His face reddened, and it was easy to see his bravado was alcohol-fueled. I could use this to my advantage.

I graced him with a *you might get lucky if you treat me right* smile. "How about you buy me another Corona, and I'll let you start over."

"I saw you watching Paul. You hoping to use me to get to him?"

My laughter was genuine. "Please. He's a baby. Let the thirteen-year-olds have him. I like real men." I batted my eyelashes and smiled up at him.

His smile was so genuine I felt guilty for using him. Then I remembered my all-too-recent police interrogation. If I wanted to play Scarlett—let alone stay out of jail—I needed to prove my innocence. He bought my beer and one for himself as he took the seat next to mine. I clicked my bottle with his, then took a drink.

Slow and careful, Magnolia. Don't blow this.

We spent the next few minutes making small talk. I told him my name was Maggie, and he introduced himself as Rusty. He lived in Nashville and was in Paul's crew. Unlike most of Paul's "friends," he wasn't an aspiring singer or songwriter. He just liked Paul and wanted to hang out with him.

Or so he said.

I was suspicious of people like him. They always wanted *something*, but then I guess I wanted something from him too.

"I heard Paul was at Luke Powell's release party," I said. "Were you there too? Did you get caught up in the excitement?'

He cringed. "Yeah, we were there."

"They're saying the police questioned everyone," I said, taking a sip. "Was it like in the movies? Did they take you to a room and shine a light on you?"

Shaking his head, he chuckled. "Someone's got an imagination."

"So they didn't question you like that?"

"They barely questioned us at all."

"Really? Even Paul?"

"Yeah."

He looked a little suspicious of my line of questioning, so I added, "It's like when Kennedy was shot or 9/11, don't you think? The whole 'what were you doing when Max Goodwin was shot?'"

He chuckled again. "You knew Max Goodwin?"

"I sure did," I said, then took another drink. "A little *too* well. I almost signed a contract with him." I shuddered.

"Be thankful you didn't. I'm sure you've seen Paul's case in the news."

I nodded. "I can only imagine how hard it was for him to be forced to be there with him."

"Yeah," he said, scratching his chin. "Paul took off for a while after he found out Max was there. Said he needed some air. Who could blame him? After the court's ruling, he knew he was stuck with that prick."

Paul was sounding fishier than a lobster boat on a hot summer day.

"Was Paul there last night too? Luke's house must be haunted or demon-possessed for there to have been two murders there in only a couple of days."

"It's not demon possession," he said. "It was revenge."

"I know a lot of people hated Max Goodwin. It would be easier to pick a date on *The Bachelorette* than figure out who hated him enough to kill him."

He leaned closer and whispered in my ear. "I have a theory about who killed both of those men."

I turned to look up at him, our faces only inches apart. "*Who?*"

"Luke's assistant."

"What?" I asked a little louder than intended, drawing the attention of the couple standing next to me. I lowered my voice. "Why would you think *she* did it?"

He gave me a conspiratorial grin. "Not everyone knows this, but she signed a contract with Max too. She gave up a career in music just to spite the bastard. That's why she's Luke's assistant."

My mouth gaped. Belinda hadn't told me that part. Did she know? "What about the other guy? I heard it was Luke's attorney."

"And his assistant just happened to find him." He winked.

The puzzle pieces tried to sort themselves out in my head.

Amy had acted really strange after Max's murder. And she *had* found Neil Fulton's body. But all the evidence was circumstantial, and I knew firsthand what it was like when people jumped to conclusions. Besides, it seemed to me that Paul had more motive than Amy. And according to Rusty, he didn't have an alibi.

"You really think she's guilty?" I asked in disbelief.

I felt someone wrap an arm around my back. "Who's guilty?" Colt asked from behind me, his breath tickling my hair.

Rusty's eyes narrowed.

I turned around and glared at Colt. "What are you doing here?"

"Not spying on you, if that's what you're thinking. I'm with a couple of friends, and I saw you over here . . . chatting." He waved to two guys sitting back by the pool tables, and they waved back, grinning like fools.

"Who are you?" Rusty asked, looking pissed.

Colt moved next to me, keeping his arm around my back, and grinned. "The name's Colt Austin. And I'm Maggie's boyfriend."

I tried to pull out of his hold, but his fingers dug in.

Rusty didn't look amused. "You never said you had a boyfriend."

I slapped Colt's hand off my waist. "That's because I don't."

"Come on, Maggie Mae," Colt teased. "I can't believe you're giving me the brush-off after everything we've been through. It was one tiny argument."

Rusty gave me a look of disgust and stomped back to his friends.

I spun around to face Colt, seething with anger. "What the hell was that?"

His grin fell. "I could ask you the same. What were you doing chatting up one of Paul Locke's henchmen?"

"Henchmen? He's a roadie."

"Roadie my ass." Colt laughed, but it was dry. "What were you doing?"

"What did it look like? He was trying to pick me up."

"And you were going to let him?"

I lifted my shoulder and gave him a haughty look. "I hadn't decided yet."

"You were asking him about the murders."

"What's it to you, Colt?" I asked.

"Because you're already in enough trouble with the police, Magnolia," he said, sounding pissed now. "If they find out you're asking questions, they can add interfering with an investigation to your charges."

I scowled. "Once again, what's it to you?"

Disappointment washed over his face. "For starters, I had this crazy idea we were *friends*."

I felt like a world-class bitch.

"And second, I promised your mother and Tilly I'd watch out for you, so like it or not, that's what I was doing."

"Colt," I groaned. "I'm sorry."

"Save it," he said, turning around and walking back toward his friends.

Guilt settled in, pressing on my shoulders. I'd had a lot of guilt over the last week. Over the last ten years.

I sorted through my options as I went out to Momma's car. I knew I should just go home, but I wanted to talk to Amy, if for no other reason than to warn her that people were tossing her name out as a suspect. Surely it wouldn't be long before the police caught wind. I considered calling her, but this seemed like an in-person conversation.

Lucky for me, Belinda had sent me her address in addition to her phone number.

Amy lived in an apartment complex in Brentwood. While it was nice, I would have expected something a lot nicer for someone working for a mega-country star. I felt a little guilty about knocking on her door a little after ten at night, but if the roles were reversed, I'd want to know.

She opened the door, her eyes wide with surprise. "Magnolia? What are you doing here?" She looked over my shoulder into the parking lot, then pulled me inside and slammed the door shut.

"I wanted to tell you what I've found out."

"You couldn't do it over the phone?" She walked over to her bedroom door and shut it, but not before I noticed the open suitcase on her bed.

"Uh . . ." Where was she going? But she worked for Luke, who flew all over the place. Maybe he wanted to get out of town to escape the negative publicity.

She crossed her arms, looking ticked. "Well, what is it? I have to be at Luke's early tomorrow."

"I think Paul Locke could be a suspect."

"We already knew that."

"Well, from what little digging I've done, he doesn't have an alibi." Then it struck me. "Why didn't you tell me that Neil Fulton worked with Max Goodwin on Paul's legal contracts? You said you didn't know how they were associated."

She lifted her chin and hugged herself tighter. "I didn't."

"That's not true. You were in the same situation as Paul. You tried to get out of a contract you had signed with Max, but Neil Fulton defended him against you and he won."

Her mouth dropped open. "How do you know that?" Terror filled her eyes. Why was she so scared?

"I only knew about the contract. The rest was a guess."

She pointed to the door. "Get out."

Oh, God. How could I have been so stupid? "You weren't trying to protect Luke. I haven't seen one indication that he had motive to go after Neil. You were trying to protect yourself."

She started sobbing and pushed my arm. "Get out."

"Amy, if you did it, we'll find you a good lawyer. We'll figure this out." I had no idea how, but Max Goodwin had been a terrible person. Surely that would sway a jury.

"I didn't do it! Get out!" she screamed in a high-pitched voice.

I let her push me to the door and then out onto the landing. "Amy, please let me help you. I know Belinda would want to help you too."

"It's too late for anyone to help me." Then she slammed the door in my face. I was even more confused than before, but now I was wondering if Amy was actually guilty.

I sat in Momma's car and sent Belinda a text. Right now I was more worried about Amy than I was about Roy checking my sister-in-law's phone.

I think Amy knows more about the murders than she's letting on. I stopped by her apartment to tell her Paul doesn't have an alibi, but she got hysterical and kicked me out.

Okay, so I was leaving part of it out, but that wasn't the kind of thing I wanted to put into writing.

I'm worried about her. You might want to check up on her.

I was surprised to see the little bubble alerting me that she was sending me a reply.

Thanks. I'll talk to you tomorrow. <3

There was nothing else to do tonight, so I went home and crawled into bed with my laptop. I sent Emily an email about everything I'd found out today, including my newest interrogation. She'd have a fit, but what was done was done. I told her about my suspicions about Amy too. After I hit send, I checked my nightstand drawer, making sure the gun was still there.

I might almost be free of one nightmare, but I was still stuck in another.

chapter
twenty-six

I woke up to sunshine in my face. I rolled onto my back with a groan and covered my eyes with my forearm. Another fitful night of sleep troubled by guilt and fear and nightmares. Maybe going back to New York would ease my troubled mind.

But my heart was heavy with the knowledge that I'd have to tell my mother I might be leaving again.

I found Momma at the breakfast table nursing a cup of coffee. A brown leather album lay on the table to one side. She was staring out the windows at the woods.

I poured my own cup of coffee and sat down next to her, both of us still silent.

"I keep thinking of that night," she said at last. "And the next morning. I've replayed it a million times in my head. What I could have done differently. What I shouldn't have said."

"You were scared, and when you get scared, you get pissed."

"It still doesn't make it right, Magnolia. I . . ."

I covered her hand. "It's over and done, Momma. I don't resent you."

"You must. You never came back."

"But I came back last week."

She took a sip, then lowered the cup to the table. "You're leaving again."

"I don't know yet. Maybe. My agent called yesterday and told me I can probably get my job back."

"When?"

"If I take the part, I need to be in New York by the middle of the week."

"But you're still under suspicion."

"I know. I'm hoping to be cleared today or tomorrow."

She flinched and was silent for several seconds before her eyes locked with mine. "And you'd take it? After what that man did to you?"

I pushed out a sigh. "I don't know. I don't want to work with him again, but this could be a defining moment in my career."

"Is that how you want your defining moment to be forever marked in history? Built on a scandal? You showing your tits on stage and knockin' over a set?"

I leaned back my head and groaned. "Momma."

"Magnolia, listen to me. You're good. I know you are. I read the reviews."

My eyes widened. "What?"

She nodded. "The theatre is important to you. Important enough to keep you from coming back. If it's important to you, then it's important to me. So I've paid attention." She slid the album toward me, her fingers gliding over the top.

I opened the cover and flipped the page, shocked to see a playbill from my first play, an off-Broadway production of *Sense and Sensibility*, stuffed inside a plastic envelope. I pulled it out, and sure enough, my name was listed in the cast.

"How did you get this?"

"eBay. Friends. Some I went to see myself."

"You came to see some of my plays and didn't tell me?"

She shrugged.

I returned the playbill to the envelope and continued flipping through the album. She had a playbill from every production I'd ever been in and reviews from the later ones in which I'd had more substantial parts.

A lump filled my throat. "Oh, Momma . . ."

"I know this is important to you. I know you need to go back, but there's something I have to tell you first." She looked into my eyes. "I have cancer."

The blood rushed from my head.

"Nobody knows but Tilly. And I only told her because we need to get the business sorted out."

My mouth felt like it had been stuffed full of cotton. "Why would you need to get your business sorted out?"

She gave me a wry grin. "You're a smart girl, Magnolia. You know."

Tears burned my eyes. "What kind?"

"It's in my blood."

I shook my head. "Can't they give you chemo or radiation?"

"They already have."

"How long have you known?" I asked in dismay.

"Two years." She sighed. "But it's not working anymore."

Panic swarmed around my head like a cloud of bees. "We'll get a second opinion. We'll go see a specialist. There's a great hospital in New York—Memorial Sloan Kettering. Jody's grandmother went there." I choked back my tears. "We'll find someone. We'll—"

Momma leaned over and pulled me into a hug. "Maggie. I've seen all the doctors. They all say the same thing. There's nothing left to do."

That was the first time she'd called me by my nickname in years. But I was too focused on her pronouncement to dwell on it. "How long?" My face was buried against her neck, so all my words sounded muffled.

"Maybe six months. Maybe three."

I leaned back to look into her face. "*Three?*"

"I didn't want to tell you, but Tilly insisted. Said she'd tell you herself if I didn't."

"Why wouldn't *you* tell me?"

"Just because I'm losing my life doesn't mean you can't live yours." She pushed out a sigh. "If I had my way, none of you would find out until the day I die. The last thing I want is everyone tiptoeing around me."

I stood and began to pace.

"I want you to go back to New York, Magnolia. I want you to live your life. But I want you to do it on your own terms, not some womanizer's, you hear?"

I nodded, tears streaming down my face.

She stood. "I need to get ready for work."

"I'll come with you."

"You don't have to do that, Magnolia."

"Shut up, Momma. I'm coming," I said.

That surprised us both, and my mother broke out into laughter. "Maybe you're more like me than I thought."

I worried that Momma would leave without me, but I took my time getting ready. I was meeting Roy at two, and damn it all, I wanted to look my best to meet my prick of a brother and address his offer.

Momma was waiting for me when I came downstairs. She gave me a smile as she looked me up and down, taking in my lightweight pink tunic sweater, white jeans, and the strappy pink heels that made me taller than her. She patted my cheek. "You're just as beautiful on the inside, Magnolia. Don't let anyone ever tell you different."

Tilly declared me too pretty to be filing in the dirty basement. Instead she stationed me in the front room beside the kitchen. She and Momma had clients coming in around eleven, and my job was to greet them and let Momma and Tilly know they were there. But they weren't coming for another half hour, so I could do as I pleased.

I opened the blinds and settled behind the desk, all the while trying to wrap my head around the fact that my mother was dying. I was studying the appointment book, thinking Momma and Tilly really needed to get into the twenty-first century and put their appointments on a computer, when the front door opened.

"Emily." I cringed when I looked up at her. "I know you're here to yell at me."

"No, actually . . . I have some news."

"Oh." I wasn't sure that was a good thing.

"I went by Luke's this morning to talk to Amy, but he was fit to be tied. She was supposed to show up at seven. I got there at eight and she still hadn't arrived."

"Last night, I saw her packing a suitcase. Do you think she took off?"

She took a breath, looking solemn. "Luke sent one of his bodyguards over to her apartment to check on her and make sure she was okay." She paused. "Magnolia, she's dead."

"What?" The blood rushed from my head, and I sat down on the sofa. "How?"

"It looks like suicide."

I shook my head. "No. I just saw her last night. I told you—she was packing a suitcase."

"And she bought a plane ticket to the Cayman Islands with Luke's credit card. Her flight left this morning, but it looks like she decided she couldn't leave."

"No!" I said, standing and beginning to pace. "How do you know she wasn't murdered? They just made it look like suicide."

"Magnolia, she left a note."

I shook my head. "Anyone could have forged that."

Emily moved in front of me and looked into my eyes. "Magnolia. The note was written to Luke. There were things in there that only the two of them would know."

"To *Luke*? Why?" Then I realized. "She loved him. She was

telling him goodbye." I just couldn't believe it. This felt so wrong. "Did she say why she killed herself?"

"She thought she was going to be arrested. They figure she didn't want to disgrace him with her arrest."

"But did she actually admit to killing either of them?"

"She didn't have to. Her fingerprints were all over the handle of the knife that was used to kill Neil Fulton."

I felt like I was going to be sick.

"Why are you taking this so hard?" Emily asked, looking genuinely puzzled. "You hardly knew her, and this clears your name."

I sucked in my bottom lip as guilt settled on my shoulders like a familiar yoke. "Because I knew she wasn't right last night. I sent Belinda a text and you an email—" I gasped. "Oh, my God. Belinda. I have to tell her."

"I already did."

"Is she mad at me?"

"Why would she be mad at *you*?" Emily shook her head. "I swear, you have to be one of the most narcissistic people I know." But the words didn't carry any heat.

"Last night I asked Amy if she'd killed them. I told her I knew about her contract with Max. I pushed her to this."

"That's bullshit. And more narcissism. You said she was packing when you showed up. She bought the plane ticket late yesterday afternoon. *You* did not do this. *She* did this."

I let that soak in for a few moments before I asked, "So what happens now?"

"The Brentwood police are working the scene, but I'm sure the Franklin police will notify me today that you are no longer a person of interest."

"And then I'm free to go?" I asked.

"You mean back to New York? Yeah, if that's what you want."

"I'm about to get offered my old part back. And a raise."

"Well, congratulations if that's what you want," she said, adjusting her purse strap.

"What's that supposed to mean?" I asked.

"Ten years ago you ran away from something, Magnolia," she said, holding my gaze. "Has it occurred to you that you need to face what you ran from before you can move on with your life?" Then she turned around and walked out the door.

Emily had no idea what she was asking. I'd thought so too until I'd discovered the truth. Now I wasn't sure what I should do.

She'd just walked past the window when my phone dinged with a text. I'd hoped to hear from Belinda, but it was from Jimmy.

Congrats, doll! You got your part back. Astronomical offer. Call me.

I should have been elated. Not only had I gotten back the part I loved, but I would be making a lot more money and Griff would have to kiss my ass. But after my mother's announcement, I wasn't sure I could leave.

My heart was divided between the stage and my mother. How was I going to choose? Then Jimmy sent me a follow-up text saying that if I took the offer, I had to be in New York by tomorrow, which only threw me into more confusion and uncertainty.

Momma's clients showed up at eleven. She and Tilly took them to the back, and I decided to expand Momma's spring cleaning to the obviously seldom-used front room.

At around 11:30, the bell on the door rang and I looked up to see Belinda standing in the doorway, her hand twisting a handful of her skirt. She offered me a hesitant smile as she asked, "Would you like to go to lunch?"

Despite Emily's insistence, I couldn't help worrying that Belinda blamed me for pushing her friend too far. "Yeah. Let me tell Momma." But she was busy with her client, so I sent her a text telling her that I was going to lunch with my sister-in-law but would be back soon.

We walked down to the deli where I'd met Brady. I felt a little twinge, but I told myself it meant nothing. Brady meant nothing. My life here in Franklin meant nothing. I had a life in New York I needed to get back to. But I wasn't really buying it.

We ordered our lunch and found a table. An awkward silence descended between us as we waited for our food, and finally I couldn't take any more. "Belinda, I'm so sorry about Amy."

Her eyes filled with tears. "I can't believe she's dead."

"Maybe I shouldn't have gone to see her last night."

Belinda searched my eyes. "I don't think it would have mattered, Magnolia. I find it so hard to believe that she killed those men. But she was under a lot of stress, and I guess she just snapped."

"But you knew her," I said. "Do you really think she was capable of *murder*?"

Her gaze locked on to a spot on the wall across the room. "I used to think people were incapable of all sorts of terrible things." Her voice lowered to almost a whisper. "But sometimes I think there's a monster in all of us."

I suppressed a gasp. Was Belinda talking about my brother or herself?

But she didn't give me time to dwell on it before she said, "I didn't know she was a cutter either."

I shook my head. "What are you talking about?"

She turned to face me. "The police asked me questions this morning. They wanted to know if I'd known if Amy was into cutting."

I released a tiny shudder. "Was she?"

"Not that I knew of, but they said she had several marks on her legs. Only more proof of her stress, I guess."

"Wow," I murmured.

The woman at the counter called our names, and Belinda jumped up, grabbed the bags, and brought them back to the table.

"I know the details of Roy's offer," Belinda said, keeping her eyes on the sandwich she was unwrapping. "I want to apologize."

I hesitated, unsure what to say before settling on, "It's not your fault."

Her eyes lifted to mine, her expression guarded. "Are you going to take it?"

I was sure Roy insisted that Belinda tell him everything. It was how men like him kept control. But he didn't know Belinda had spent the day with me on Saturday, which told me she didn't always carry out his orders. At the same time, I didn't want to put her on the spot by asking her to keep something from him—even if it was just for a few hours. "I'm going to see him."

"Oh," she said, sounding deflated. "So you're leaving." Her gaze lifted to me. "I know it's part of the deal."

"If I accept my part back, then I should probably leave tonight. I'd have to be at work by tomorrow afternoon."

"They're offering you back your part?"

"My agent says he has an offer."

"That's wonderful," she said, only she didn't sound like she meant it.

We ate in silence for several moments, then Belinda said, "I understand why you wouldn't want to be my friend, Magnolia. After Roy . . ." Her voice broke off, but she didn't look away from me. "But I want to thank you for indulging me with the sister-in-law thing this weekend."

"Indulging you?" I said in surprise. "Belinda, you're one of the reasons I'm finding it hard to leave."

Her eyes widened. "You don't want to go?"

The question was so complicated. This tug of war in my

heart and my head was confusing the hell out of me. "I don't know."

"Oh."

"But I have no job here. No life. Nowhere to live. My life is in New York. I've spent eight years getting to this point. I'd be crazy to throw it all away."

"Can I give you a piece of advice?" she asked.

"Of course."

"You know how people say follow your heart?" She paused, her face expressionless. "Well, be careful with that, Magnolia. Get your bearings before you leap—otherwise you may not recognize where you land."

I knew exactly what she was talking about, and it broke my heart to pieces. "Belinda . . ."

She offered me a smile, one that looked as fake as the ten-carat cubic zirconium ring Jody used to wear to theatre parties. "I have to get back to work, but I have loved every minute with you. Goodbye, Magnolia." There were tears in her eyes as she gathered up her food, stuffed it in her bag, and left.

I watched her go, my heart so heavy it felt weighted down by fifty-pound stones.

I didn't want to stay at the deli alone, so I packed up my own bag and ordered two sandwiches to take back to Momma and Tilly.

I stood to the side while I waited, continuing to wage my epic battle over what to do. When the woman at the counter called my name, I absently walked forward to grab the order, but someone else got to it first. I was about to protest, but I found myself looking up into Brady Bennett's contrite face.

Anger rushed through me like a wildfire. I was looking up at one very good reason to leave.

"We have to quit meeting like this," he said with a hesitant smile.

I snatched the bag out of his hand, spun around, and stormed out the door.

"Magnolia, wait."

It felt so odd to hear him call me Magnolia. I was used to Maggie coming from his lips. But then, everything about him—and us—had been a lie. I barely knew this man, so why did that hurt so much?

He chased after me, following me onto the sidewalk. "Magnolia. Please listen."

The wind had a cold bite, so I crossed my arms in front of my chest, tugging my sweater tighter. "You have thirty seconds."

"I'm sure you've heard that you're no longer a person of interest."

I gave my head a tiny shake. "No, actually. I hadn't yet."

He frowned. "Holden was supposed to call your attorney."

I shuffled the bags in my hands and pulled my phone out of my pocket. Sure enough, I had a missed call from Emily. I stuffed it back into my pocket and returned my attention to him.

"You have to believe me when I tell you I didn't know. I thought you might have come to the station to report a domestic violence situation. But there was just something about you, and I didn't want to take your report. I wanted to get to know you better." He searched my face. "Do you believe me?"

I shrugged. "Why does it matter, Brady? It's done."

"Because I want that second date."

Shaking my head, I laughed. Yes, here was a definite reason for leaving. Brady Bennett was far from safe. He would ask questions—questions about my past that I wasn't sure I should answer. "Well, the next time you're in New York, give me a call and maybe we can meet for drinks."

His face fell. "You're leaving?"

Was I? Was that my subconscious making my decision for me?

But this wasn't the time for soul-searching; I had to deal with him first. "You are fully aware of the reason I came slinking back here. *That* situation is about to be cleared up too. I'll probably be back on stage for the Wednesday matinee."

"I've been wanting to take a trip to New York," he said. "I'll come check out your performance."

I tightened my arms around my chest and shot him a glare. "You didn't get enough with all the videos on the Internet?"

"I didn't watch them, Maggie," he said, sounding resigned. "I respect you too much to do that to you."

That caught me by surprise. "But Detective Holden—"

"—is an ass."

My mouth tipped into a tiny grin. "Well, *there's* something we agree on."

The wind blew again, the chill seeping into my bones, and I shivered.

Brady started to shrug off his jacket. "Here, put this on."

I shook my head and took a step back. "Brady, you and I are a very bad idea."

He looked into my face, determination in his eyes. "I disagree."

"Then we are clearly at an impasse. Not that it matters." I started walking, but he caught up in a matter of steps.

"Maggie, I want to make this up to you. Saturday night I tried my best to earn your trust, telling you I would never lie to you, and then you thought it was all a ruse."

I stopped. "You want me to absolve you from your guilt? Fine. You're free of it. Call me stupid, but I believed you were sincere." Maybe he was sincere, but I still wasn't sure I could forgive him. I started walking again, but he was right there beside me, like a shadow I couldn't shake.

"Maggie."

I stopped and spun around to face him. "Brady, what do you *want* from me?"

He rubbed the back of his neck in frustration, then dropped his hand. "I don't know. I just know I'm not ready to let *us* go yet."

"There is no *us*, Brady, and there never will be. You go back to your life, and I'll go back to mine."

As I spun around and marched back to the catering shop, I knew I wouldn't be strong enough to resist him forever. I needed to get the hell out of here before I made one more regrettable mistake.

chapter
twenty-seven

I found Momma and Tilly in the office, and they beamed when I handed them their sandwiches.

"Emily called," Momma said as she unwrapped the paper. "The police have cleared your name."

"So I heard."

"Oh, girlie, you remembered my favorite!" Tilly said, opening the wrapping of her Reuben. "This job's working out pretty well for all of us."

"About that . . ." I looked at my mother.

She nodded her head, giving me a guarded smile. "You need to get back to what you love."

When she put it that way, I wasn't so sure it was the right choice after all. I did love acting, but I loved my mother too. "And if I decided to stay . . . would you give me a job?"

"Yes!" Tilly shouted.

But my mother shook her head. "Your life isn't here, Magnolia. But don't sell yourself short when you go back. Demand respect."

I nodded, my eyes burning. My mother didn't want me here. Then again, I had been gone for ten years. She was used to me being gone. What did I expect?

"When will you go?" she asked, her voice sounding rough.

"Tonight." My heart was breaking. The sooner I left, the better.

She nodded and looked out the window. "That's for the best." Then she pulled a check out of her desk drawer and held it out to me.

I took a half step back. "What's that?"

"Your paycheck. Now come take it. You need money to get settled." When I hesitated, she waved it. "You earned this, Magnolia. A deal's a deal."

I walked forward and took it from her, then shook my head when I saw the amount. Five thousand dollars. "This is too much."

Her eyes filled with a familiar ferocity when she looked up at me. "As you pointed out, we never settled on a salary. That's what you earned." Her expression changed to irritation. "Don't you have things to do if you're leaving tonight? The last time I checked, your clothes were spread all over your room."

"Yeah . . . I guess."

She stood and handed me her car keys. "Take my car and leave it at the airport with the keys under the mat. Text me the location, and I'll have Belinda take me to pick it up." When I started to protest, she held up her hand. "I have a spare set."

"That's not what I was going to say. I'll go pack my things, then come back and tell you goodbye."

"No, Magnolia. Let's do it here and now. Make a clean break."

How did I make a clean break from the woman who had given me life and would have given her life for me, especially when I didn't even know if I'd ever see her again? "*Momma.*"

She pulled me into a hug. "No tears, Magnolia. We Steele women are made to be strong." She released me and gave me a little push. "Now go back to New York and break a leg."

I turned around and walked out of her office, eager to get as far away as possible.

A T 2:00 SHARP, I walked into JS Investments, my father's office in downtown Nashville. When I told the receptionist I was there to see my brother, she led me down a long hallway, then pushed open a door before motioning for me to enter. My brother sat behind a massive desk that overlooked downtown Nashville. His eyes narrowed as the door closed behind me.

"Magnolia," he said in a slow drawl. "You are nothing if not predictable. Come join me."

"You made me an offer that needs further investigation." I took several steps deeper into the room, moving toward the desk. My heels sank into the thick carpet. A grandfather clock positioned against the wall to the left emitted a loud tick-tock noise that filled the large room.

He motioned to the chairs in front of his desk. "Please, take a seat. I have some paperwork that we need to address before I can give you the check."

"Paperwork?" I asked, lowering myself into one of the leather chairs. They were designed to suck you in, giving the person at the desk the advantage, so I perched my butt on the edge, keeping my eyes level with his.

Irritation flickered in his eyes. Momma had always declared that I had a penchant for drama, but somehow she'd failed to recognize the fact that it ran in the Steele blood. My brother loved it just as much, if not more so. While I was good at creating characters, Roy excelled at setting the stage—and he had carefully constructed this one. But I'd refused to sink back into the chair, which would give him the elevation to look down at me. I'd made myself his equal instead.

There was a small stack of papers in front of him, and he slid them across the desk toward me. "You sign this contract, agreeing to never return, and then I hand you the check. After that, you're gone."

I picked up the pages, scanning the text on the first page before flipping to the second.

"I have an airline ticket booked for a five o'clock flight," he said evenly, pressing his fingertips together in front of his face. "First class and with your name on it."

The corners of my mouth twitched as I flipped to the third page and looked up at him. I hadn't bought a plane ticket yet. Would it be so wrong if I used his? "Is it a one-way ticket to hell?" I asked in an amused voice. "Because it really should have your name on it instead."

He released an exaggerated sigh. "Clever, Magnolia. You always were such a clever girl. It's to New York." He slid an expensive fountain pen toward me. "Now sign."

I laid the papers on the desk and picked up the pen, turning it around and around in my hand. My gaze returned to his. "And here I thought you'd make me sign it in blood."

His jaw clamped tight, and his eyes narrowed to slits of anger. "If I thought your blood would be legally binding, I would insist on it."

My lungs squeezed shut when I realized he was serious. "What did I ever do to make you hate me so much?" I asked.

"You want a list?" he asked. "Breathing is at the top."

I lifted my brows. "You want me dead?"

"Let's just say if I could give our mother's death sentence to you, I would do it in a heartbeat."

That stung more than I cared to admit. While we'd never gotten along, I never would have guessed he hated me enough to want me dead. What had I ever done to warrant such hatred?

Coming back to Tennessee had disturbed my equilibrium, but I was still an expert at controlling my emotions. Or at least at hiding them from the world. I wouldn't give this asshole *anything*.

I stood, towering over him. "Why are you so willing to pay me fifty thousand dollars on the condition that I give up all claim to my inheritance and never return?" I smirked at his look of surprise. "I can read, you little boll weevil. I caught the bit about my inheritance buried in a clause on the second page."

"I will not tolerate name-calling, Magnolia."

I released a bitter laugh. "I see you've gotten very good at the art of deflecting issues you don't want to address. Bravo."

He slowly stood up, looking down on me even in my three-inch heels. "I learned from the master, Magnolia. Now sign the damned document and leave." In that moment, something shifted in his eyes. I saw it for a fraction of a second. He thought he was protecting someone.

I straightened my back as his previous statement hit me. "You know she's dying."

"Not that *she* told *me*."

"Then how do you know?"

He gave me a dry look. "I have my sources."

"How do you think sending me away will protect her?"

"How many times have you broken that woman's heart?"

I shook my head in disgust. "You would have to possess a heart to recognize that hers had been broken. And you, my dear brother, are not only heartless, but soulless."

Anger filled his eyes. "You are a cancer, Magnolia. A flesh-eating bacteria. You are toxic to everything that comes near you. I am simply saving our mother in the time she has left."

I shook my head with a short laugh. "Oh, no. You don't get to play the martyr card. I've seen you in action. You put your own best interests above all others. How does my leaving benefit you?" He continued to glare at me. "How much is Momma's estate worth?"

"Not as much as you hope, you conniving bitch," he spat out as he walked around his desk toward me.

"*Conniving?*" I was beyond furious, but I had to see this through. "How much?"

"She's mortgaged the house to the hilt to get that storefront on Main Street and the two vans. She let her life insurance policy lapse. Dad's 401K was decimated in that last economic downturn." He snorted. "She's worth negative two hundred thousand dollars, Magnolia, so in this instance the short-term bet is the smart one for you."

"Why are you paying me to leave?"

He ignored my question. "The only good thing that came out of her financial woes was my sudden desire to learn how investing worked. I vowed no one would ever take advantage of her again." His eyes bore into mine. "And that includes you."

This man—who would protect his mother at all costs—was so different from the abusive pig I had met the day before that I was struggling to wrap my head around it.

And then I suddenly understood. "This is a way for you to control an uncontrollable situation."

He burst out into bitter laughter. "I'm not some character for you to dissect. People are not so black and white." Then he looked at his expensive watch. "You need to sign and leave. I have another appointment in five minutes." He walked back around his desk, opened a drawer, and pulled out an envelope.

My gaze landed on his hand.

"Are you prepared to leave tonight?" he asked, all business.

"My bags are packed and in Momma's car, ready to go to the airport."

"Then here's a check for fifty thousand and the first class ticket. Just like I said. A one-time offer." He reached toward me and dangled it close enough to my face for me to see my name in large, bold script. "Now sign."

Anger burned in my gut as I picked up the pen. I flipped to the last page and scrawled quickly, then tossed the papers at him and snatched the envelope out of his hand.

The papers floated to his desk as I opened the envelope to see its contents. I was shocked to see he really had followed through. There was a check inside, written from his business account, and an airline ticket. I wasn't surprised to hear his low growl of anger.

"Fuck you, Magnolia."

I clenched my fists at my sides, now playing the role of a sister who didn't give a shit. It wasn't much of a stretch. "So you *can* read, although it said 'Fuck you, *Roy*,' not Magnolia." I took several steps backward toward the door.

He reached for the phone on his desk. "Don't even bother trying to cash that check. I'm having a stop payment put on it right now."

"Don't worry." I pulled out the lighter I'd put in my purse for this very purpose and flicked it on. "You can have it back." I held the flame to the edge of the envelope. It was slow to take, but the flames shot up the paper. I dropped the burning mess onto his wool carpet.

He started shouting after me as I calmly walked down the hall and out to the elevator.

I'd made a decision. I knew what my heart *needed*.

chapter twenty-eight

I stood on my mother's front porch, my stomach a swirling mass of nerves and anxiety. I knocked on the door and stood back, prepared for rejection.

But rejection was something I had become accustomed to facing. Most of my adult life had been based on it. I could handle this one too. Or at least that was what I told myself as the front door opened.

Momma stood in the opening, her eyes wide in shock. The skin on her face was paper-thin, and dark half-moons lay under her eyes. Her hair was thinner than before, and she'd lost weight. How had I missed the signs of her sickness? Maybe I saw it because I was looking for it now.

"Magnolia," she said in confusion. "You're supposed to be boarding a plane."

"I changed my mind. Can I come in?"

But she blocked the doorway. "I don't need your sympathy, Magnolia Mae Steele." Her eyes flashed with anger. "Nor do I need your pity."

"No worries, Momma. You should know by now that I'm incapable of feeling either of those two emotions." I jiggled my suitcase handles. "Now let me in."

Her eyes softened. "What about your part in the play?"

I sucked in a breath, still hoping I'd done the right thing. "I listened to your advice and decided if I go back, it will be with my head held high. I'm not going to try and ignore my disgrace like the emperor and his new clothes."

"So what's your plan?"

"I know you won't give me a job, so I'll find another one. And a place to live too. I don't expect a handout."

She frowned. "I live in a big house. You could stay here with me."

"We would be at each other's throats in a matter of days, and you know it. This is better." For now. I would probably have to move in to take care of her sooner rather than later. But I had to ease my way into it. We both did.

"Don't do this for me," she said, her voice tight with emotion. "Don't you go giving up on what you love for me."

"Momma, don't you get it? *You* are what I love. *You*. If I go away, I'm giving up you. And I refuse to do that anymore. No matter what."

A tear slipped down her cheek. "We might be able to arrange for you to have a job in the catering business after all." She winked. "Someone told me the files and the calendar need updating."

I knew it would require some serious compromises from both of us to make that work. We'd ease into that too. I gave her a coy smile. "We'll see."

"But the theatre . . ."

"A wise woman told me not to sell myself short. And if I go back right now, I'll be hiding in the shadows of my embarrassment. I'd rather let things die down and then start over." Starting over scared the shit out of me, but I'd deal with that later. "Can I come in now?"

She paused. "This won't be pretty, Magnolia. This is going to get ugly and messy, and you're gonna want to run from it. But if you stay, I need to know I can count on you."

"I'm not going anywhere." Then I ushered her back inside and closed the door behind us, making sure the deadbolt was tight.

Momma was right. Things were about to get ugly and messy, but not exactly how she expected.

Continue the story with Act Two!
Read the first chapter now on the next page.

act two
sneak peek

"What the hell are you doin', Magnolia?"

My hand froze in midair, holding the pastry bag suspended over the tray of hors d'oeuvres. I brushed a stray hair out of my eyes with my forearm. "I'm doing what you told me to do. I'm filling the shrimp puffs."

My mother put her hands on her hips and gave me her best *How did I give birth to someone so stupid?* look. I'd grown accustomed to it during my teenage years, but she'd dusted it off and used it more times than I could count over the last three days. "With *buttercream frosting?*"

I lifted up the bag and squirted some of the creamy filling onto my finger, then cringed after I tasted it. Definitely not cream cheese. "I must have grabbed the wrong bag."

"Just how many people at the art gallery show are gonna want to eat Cajun shrimp puffs filled with buttercream frosting?"

The answer was so obvious I saw no reason to respond.

She moved closer to the stainless steel table, taking in the trays lined with savory pastries. "And just how many have you done?"

Yesterday she'd berated me for dawdling, so in the moments before she'd shown up, I'd been giving myself a mental pat on the back for picking up the pace. I cringed. "Almost all of them."

Momma sucked in a breath and held it for three whole seconds, her face turning red, then flung her hand toward the front door. "Get!"

"What?"

"Get out of here! Go! *For three days* I've let you work in the kitchen. *For three days* you've screwed up everything you've touched! Now get out of here so I can make them all over again."

"Lila!" my mother's best friend barked, slapping down the spoon she'd been using to stir a pot on the stove, and turned around. "Maggie's tryin' her best." I'd never heard her use such a harsh tone with my mother, but then again, I could always count on Tilly to have my back.

"She's a failure in the kitchen, Tilly. *She's hopeless.*"

Tilly crossed her arms and gave my mother a disapproving glare. "Then we'll find somewhere else to put her."

"Where else are we gonna put 'er?" my mother asked. Her Alabamian accent was always stronger when she was exasperated—which, around me, was a lot. "Maybe we should dump all the folders she just organized in the file cabinets and let her file 'em again."

Anger burned in my chest as I jerked off my plastic gloves and threw them onto the stainless steel table. "You know I've never been good in the kitchen. I'm trying the best I can!"

"It's not good enough!" Momma shouted.

I tugged my apron strings loose, then ripped the apron over my head and flung it onto the table. "I never asked you for this job!"

"I'm leaving my half of this business to you!" my mother shouted. "You need to learn how to help Tilly run it!"

Before she died. She didn't say the words, but we were both thinking them. In that moment, though, my temper eclipsed my grief over my mother's death sentence. "Then maybe you should get my perfect brother to run it, because I quit!"

"Magnolia!" Tilly shouted in dismay.

But I was already making my exit stage left, stomping across the kitchen and through the swinging door to the reception area. I didn't stop until I was on the sidewalk in front of Southern Belles Catering. Only then did I realize it was raining.

Great.

Of course, it was April in Middle Tennessee; it would have been more remarkable if it hadn't been raining.

I ran toward the pizza restaurant at the end of the street, Mellow Mushroom, where I was supposed to meet my sister-in-law, Belinda, for lunch at noon. I was fifteen minutes early, but I was also newly unemployed. I might as well get a beer.

Moments later, I was sitting at the bar in the garishly decorated restaurant, staring at a mural of cartoonized famous musicians while I sipped a pint of Guinness. As I took the first sip, I lamented that my life had gone so drastically off course in one month.

Three short weeks ago, I had been poised to make my debut as the lead in *Fireflies at Dawn*, the hottest new musical to hit Broadway in a decade. But then I discovered that the director—whom I'd been living with—was screwing my understudy . . . and to say I didn't take it well would be an understatement. The understudy and I got into a brawl onstage on opening night, much of which was captured on video and posted on the internet. People especially loved the part where Woman on a Train #3—aka my boyfriend's new lover—ripped off the front of my dress and exposed my 34B breasts to the world.

After I lost my job (fired), lost my home (that asshole Griff kicked me out), and found myself destitute (said asshole had convinced me to sink most of my money into the musical), I had no choice but to max out my credit card on a plane ticket to Nashville, Tennessee, so I could show up on my mother's front doorstep in Franklin. My welcome home had been bumpy, to say the least, and not just because it was my first visit in a decade.

"Hey, Maggie Mae," a man said over my shoulder.

I turned around to find Colt Austin, fellow Southern Belles employee and womanizer—though not necessarily in that order—bestowing his sexy bad-boy grin on me. His short blond hair was styled, and he'd recently shaved the scruffy beard he'd been sporting. I thought he looked better clean-shaven, but I knew better than to tell him so. His ego was already a force to behold.

"Did Tilly send you to find me?"

"No," he said, sitting on the empty stool beside me and snatching the glass from my hand. "I was thirsty." He took a sip and grinned again, his blue eyes dancing.

"Get your own," I grumbled, snatching the glass back and taking a healthy gulp.

"Had a run-in with Lila, huh?" he said, waving his finger at the bartender. She came running with a bright smile plastered on her face. Colt had that effect on women—unfortunately, he knew it. "Hey, darlin'," he said, laying on the accent as thick as molasses. "What stouts do you have?"

The bartender batted her eyes and listed off his choices. Then they discussed which was her favorite and how long she had worked there, and by the time he'd finally settled on what to order, I'd nearly finished my drink.

Before she could walk off, I wrapped my hand around Colt's arm and laid my head on his shoulder. "I'll take another Guinness," I said, making my voice sound sweet and light. "Put it on my sweetie Colt's tab."

The bartender shot me a glare before stalking off to get the drinks.

"What was that for?" Colt asked, leaning away from me. "I was about to ask for her number."

I laughed and sat back up. "Just how many numbers do you have?"

He shot me a smug look. "I've got yours, so don't laugh too much."

"And we both know that's because you needed it for work." But that wasn't all. Despite the hard time I was giving him, I considered Colt a friend. I knew I could call him if I needed help. Now that I'd decided to stay in Franklin for the indeterminate future, I'd need all the help I could get.

He snaked an arm around my back and graced me with his sexy eyes. "We can change the reason I need it."

Things inside me began to stir, and it wasn't the beer sloshing around in my empty stomach. I may have decided not to become involved with Colt, but I wasn't dead. I was usually good at not letting guys affect me, but I'd let two men get under my skin since I'd come back to my hometown. Colt was not a safe bet. A good time, sure. But these weeks in Franklin hadn't gone easy on me. I'd become a murder suspect on my first night in town, and no sooner had I cleared my good name than I'd found out about my mother's terminal illness. Then there was the other thing . . . the one I still didn't like to think about. The memories I'd zapped from my mind before running away from Franklin ten years ago had finally come back to me, but I had no clue what to do about it.

I was, simply put, in no shape for a fling. My heart was too raw. I couldn't risk falling for Colt Austin, master charmer and —I was quite certain—lover extraordinaire.

I lifted an eyebrow. "And become lay number two thousand three hundred and sixty-seven?" I released a derisive laugh. "No, thanks. I have *some* self-esteem left."

He covered his chest with his hand. "You wound me, Maggie."

"I'm sure Mindy will help you through it."

"Who?"

Shaking my head, I pointed to the bartender. "The woman you're trying to lay. Perhaps you should have taken at least one glance at the name on her name tag instead of zeroing in on her cleavage."

He shuddered, but his eyes twinkled with mischief. "So crass, Magnolia Steele. And here I thought you were a lady."

I lifted my shoulder into a shrug. "Shows what you know."

Mindy came back with our beers and gave me an assessing glance.

"I don't want Colt," I said. "He's a free man."

She gave me a dubious glare.

"No, really. You're more than welcome to him. I've already used him up, and now I'm moving on to . . ." I spun on my seat, my finger extended as I scanned the quickly filling restaurant. My mouth fell open, and I found myself pointing at an older man with a pot belly and thinning hair. I recognized him from when I was a kid, but I hadn't seen him in fourteen years.

"Him?" Mindy asked in shock. "You're giving up this hottie for *him*? Why?"

"Because Colt has chlamydia," I said absently as I hopped off the stool. "He's a carrier."

Colt quickly—and loudly—protested my statement, but I was too busy trying to determine if I'd correctly identified the man sitting alone at a table for two.

I stopped next to his table and hesitated. What if I were right? What would I do?

I was still working on my approach when he looked up and gasped. "Magnolia?"

I wasn't surprised he knew who I was; the question was *how* he knew. The last time I'd seen him was when I was fourteen, and although I'd aged—barely!—I still looked a lot like I had as a teen. But the more likely reason he recognized me was that I'd made every gossip site and tabloid in the U.S., and Nashville had paid particular attention to the fact that I'd come back to Franklin to lick my wounds.

I could only imagine the attention I would have faced if my name had been released in connection with Max Goodwin's murder. Thank God it hadn't come to that.

"Mr. Frey?" I asked.

He rose from his chair and shook my hand. "Magnolia, I haven't seen you in years."

Precisely fourteen years and two months, in fact. The date he was referring to had been etched in my mind ever since.

It was the day my father had disappeared.

I'd had a dentist appointment that morning, and Daddy had taken me to his office for a little while. Something strange had happened right before he brought me back to school on his lunch break. Before we could board the elevator down to the lobby, a frantic Walter Frey, who had looked remarkably the same then as now, only with slightly more gray hair, had come barreling out of it. I remembered what happened next like it was yesterday.

Mr. Frey grabbed Daddy's arm and said, "Brian, I have to talk to you *now*."

Daddy glanced at me and stiffened. "I'm taking my daughter back to school, Walter. This will have to wait. I talked to Geraldo."

"It can't wait. *He knows.*"

Daddy's face paled, and he stared at Mr. Frey for a couple of seconds before he said, "Are you sure?"

"Yes."

Daddy nodded, taking a deep breath, then letting it out. "We can't talk now," he whispered. "Even if Magnolia weren't here. Meet me tonight at eight. You know the spot."

Walter nodded, bouncing like a bobble head.

Daddy pushed Walter back onto the elevator, but instead of following him in, he reached out an arm and held me back.

"We'll take another one."

"Why was that man so upset? Who was he talking about?" I asked.

Daddy looked into my eyes, and I didn't like what I saw in his gaze. Fear. "You forget what you heard, Magnolia. That was business."

"Why would he be so upset over business?"

"I'm a financial planner," he said. Another elevator dinged, and he led me into it. "People trust me with a lot of money. Sometimes it makes them anxious."

"Do you ever lose their money?" I asked.

"Sometimes, but I try really hard to make sure they lose as little as possible." He pressed the button for the lobby. "That's why Mr. Frey was upset . . ." I could see the wheels turning in his head as he talked. "He heard that a stock was doing poorly."

"But he said *he knows*," I said. "That didn't sound like a stock doing poorly."

"It's just business talk, Magnolia. You need to let it go."

And I had, mostly because I worshipped my father and making him angry at me was the last thing I wanted. But I knew it wasn't typical stockbroker stuff. Especially because he stopped by my room before he left that night to make sure I knew where his handgun was hidden. It was the last time I'd ever seen him.

The police had questioned Walter Frey based on my statement, but from what little I'd gathered, Mr. Frey had told the police the eight o'clock meeting had never happened, had never been discussed, in fact. The reason he'd come looking for Daddy that day was to discuss his Roth IRA account. The police had quickly dismissed Mr. Frey as a suspect or as a source of information.

His lies had infuriated me, but as Momma had so tactfully said, if given the choice, who would *I* believe? A flighty four-teen-year-old girl prone to drama or a respected real estate attorney?

Life had gone on after Daddy's disappearance, and I was told to accept that there would be no answers. Anytime I brought it up, my mother told me I was too young to worry myself over such things.

Well, I was all grown up now and Walter Frey had fallen into my path.

It was time to get my answers.

Read Act Two for Murder now!

Sign up for my Denise Grover Swank newsletter to hear about new releases, sales, and occasional bonus content.

about the author

Denise Grover Swank was born in Kansas City, Missouri and lived in the area until she was nineteen. Then she became a nomad, living in five cities, four states and ten houses over the course of ten years before she moved back to her roots. She speaks English and smattering of Spanish and Chinese which she learned through an intensive Nick Jr. immersion period. Her hobbies include witty Facebook comments (in own her mind) and dancing in her kitchen with her children. (Quite badly if you believe her offspring.) Hidden talents include the gift of justification and the ability to drink massive amounts of caffeine and still fall asleep within two minutes. Her lack of the sense of smell allows her to perform many unspeakable tasks. She has six children and hasn't lost her sanity. Or so she leads you to believe.

www.ingramcontent.com/pod-product-compliance
Lightning Source LLC
Chambersburg PA
CBHW030529190726
48283CB00006B/1828